Anne Baker trained as a nurse at Birkenhead General Hospital, but after her marriage went to live first in Libya and then in Nigeria. She eventually returned to her native Birkenhead where she worked as a Health Visitor for over ten years before taking up writing. She now lives with her husband in Merseyside. Anne Baker's other Merseyside sagas are all available from Headline and have been highly praised:

'Another nostalgic story oozing with atmosphere and charm' *Liverpool Echo*

'Truly compelling . . . rich in language and descriptive prose' *Newcastle Upon Tyne Evening Chronicle*

'A heartwarming saga' *Woman's Weekly*

'Anne Baker imbues her heartwarming Merseyside novels with rich local characters' *Nuneaton Evening Telegraph*

Also by Anne Baker

Paradise Parade
Legacy of Sins
Nobody's Child
Merseyside Girls
Moonlight on the Mersey
A Mersey Duet
Mersey Maids
A Liverpool Lullaby
With a Little Luck
The Price of Love
Liverpool Lies
Echoes Across the Mersey
A Glimpse of the Mersey
Goodbye Liverpool

Like Father, Like Daughter

Anne Baker

headline

First published in 1991
by HEADLINE BOOK PUBLISHING

This paperback edition published in 2002
by HEADLINE BOOK PUBLISHING

15

ISBN 978-0-7472-3766-2

Printed and bound in Great Britain by
Clays Ltd, St Ives plc

HEADLINE BOOK PUBLISHING
A division of Hodder Headline
338 Euston Road
London NW1 3BH

www.headline.co.uk
www.hodderheadline.com

To my husband

Book One – 1924

CHAPTER ONE

Elin Jones raced upstairs to her room, feeling like the farm dog newly released from its chain. It was Sunday, her afternoon off.

Snatching open her wardrobe door she saw the plain black frock and hat she'd had to buy in a hurry when her mother died. The black coat Bessie had given her drooped on its hanger. Elin hated the outfit, it made her feel drab.

It was a whole week since she'd been out, a sense of freedom was surging through her. On impulse she reached instead for her blue wool skirt and jacket, the last outfit her mother had made for her. Elin had bought one of the new cloche hats in exactly the same shade, a deep blue with a tinge of violet, the colour of wild geraniums. It had taken a whole month's wages, and she'd only been able to wear it once before she'd had to go into mourning.

She stood in front of her mirror, frowning with concentration as she fumbled her long golden hair into a bun on top of her head and pulled her hat over it. The severity of the style drew attention to her face. It gave her rounded rosy cheeks an aura of sophistication she didn't have. Her golden eyes were widely spaced and slightly slanting, riveting without the frame of hair. She turned quickly, twisting to see her back view. A smile flickered at her full mouth, lighting up her face to beauty. The outfit was smarter than she remembered. Her mother had been the village dressmaker and knew how to flatter with cut and colour.

Her smile faded quickly. Looking in a mirror – preening,

her father called it — always brought a rush of guilt. It was forbidden.

'Such vanity!' His lay preacher's voice seemed to vibrate round her room, as though he were watching her now. 'It's a sin.'

Elin had left home, and no longer expected to be tied down by her father's rigid rules. He had dominated her life for as long as she could remember. She told herself she had no further reason to be frightened of his temper, but the truth was, he still held her in thrall.

'We're starting out,' Bessie, her mistress, called, breaking the spell. 'Hurry up, Elin, or you'll be late.'

As she ran down the stairs of Tonteg, she felt more a princess than a girl in service on a sixty-acre hill farm. In the back kitchen, she grabbed the cake she was to take for her father's tea. When they'd baked yesterday, a small jam sponge had been made specially, put on an enamel plate and covered with a brown paper bag. Bessie was generous, always offering something.

Elin slammed the field gate. The sheep startled and raced away to collect in a distant corner. She had to run to catch up with the family.

'Bessie,' she panted as she drew level. Bessie didn't hear her, she was towing a small daughter along with each hand, her chest wheezing slightly. Exposure to winter winds had crazed her complexion with a mesh of fine lines, ageing her beyond her forty years.

Owen Roberts, Elin's employer and Bessie's husband, turned, but she couldn't ask him for such a favour. Bessie would be more understanding. Elin bounded to her other side.

'Please, Bessie, could I take my half day off in the week sometimes?' She had a half day every Sunday.

'You had a Saturday afternoon only last month.' Owen's voice was muffled by the hands of his two-year-old son who sat across his shoulder and held him round the chin.

'Yes, to sing with the choir in Porthmadog, but I'd love a half day to go shopping. If you don't mind.'

'It's not us that minds,' Owen said, turning his formidable

dark eyes towards her. 'Your father wants you to take your time off on Sundays. Only Sundays.'

'Why?' She felt the hot flush of resentment running up her cheeks.

'You know. Saw you coming out of the cinema with Bethan Morgan, he did. Too young, he thinks, to be out late in town.'

'We'd been to the matinée! It was six o'clock and hardly dark. And I'm sixteen.'

'It's the pictures your father doesn't like,' Bessie added in motherly tones.

'He's never been,' Elin said defiantly. 'He doesn't know what they're like. It was Rudolf Valentino. What's wrong with him?'

'Sixteen is still young.'

Old enough, Elin thought, to work fourteen hours a day. Too young to have any pleasure. 'There's not a lot I can do on Sunday, you see. There's still chapel.'

'Told you, I have,' there was a touch of irritation in Owen's voice now. She hated to see him angry. 'Sunday it has to be. Your father says there's less mischief you can get up to on Sundays. See she comes to chapel, he told me, then she's to come home to tea.'

'Elin's a good girl,' Bessie insisted softly.

'She'll need to be,' her husband retorted. 'She's the sort to bring the lads running.'

'She's too shy. Has nothing to say to them.'

'I'm surprised they aren't queuing at our back door now.'

Elin had paused to hustle the children along. She was choking on her anger. She'd wanted to go home when Mam was there, but not any more. She should have known her father was behind the arrangement.

'Little children should be seen and not heard,' had been one of his favourite sayings. When he had heard her, she'd been in trouble. Elin would have understood the punishments if she'd deserved them, but her father's anger had been easily roused. She'd been terrified of him. It had tainted her relationships with other men. She hardly spoke to Owen Roberts, and didn't like being left alone in a room with him. She knew he put it down to shyness, but it wasn't that. Women she could understand and like. Men she found difficult. She was unable to deal with the ugly memories of childhood.

'It's not too bad, Elin. We let you go to choir practice on Wednesday nights, if we're not busy,' Bessie said, screwing her face up against the watery sunshine, making her wrinkles more noticeable.

'It's generous you are, with my time off,' Elin agreed, but she continued to fume about her father for the rest of the way.

As they drew near, Elin could see her father's bowler hat, and the heavy black overcoat he always wore on Sundays. He was standing in front of the door of Llanddolfa Chapel, talking to a fellow deacon, looking dour. Elin held her sponge cake in a death grip. Resentment slowed her step as she followed Bessie up the path.

'Hello, Father.' She stretched up to put her duty kiss on his cheek. 'Are you well?'

'Yes, child.' His stern eyes were examining her clothes, his thin lips twisted with disapproval. 'You should be wearing black. It's quick you are to forget your mother.'

'I haven't forgotten her, I miss her very much.' Elin was fighting down the guilt he made her feel. She had to stand up to him. 'But it is six months, Father, and this is almost purple, a half mourning.'

'It is not! And the skirt is too short.'

'Skirts are being worn shorter now.'

'It's halfway up your calves. It's indecent for chapel. Indecent anywhere.'

'It's fashionable, Father.' She looked at what Bessie was wearing. Fashion hadn't reached her.

Her mother's laughing face came before her, holding up a garment she was sewing. 'I get the latest patterns. I can make almost anyone look smart, but everybody wants what they had last year and the year before that. Their skirts are still flapping two inches above their ankles.' But Mam had always dressed well, and encouraged her to do the same.

'Mam made it for me. She said it suited me.' Elin turned

hurriedly. Bessie seemed a safe haven, surrounded by fidgeting children; she was gossiping a few yards away with her friend Agnes Jones who kept the village shop. Elin joined them.

'Sorry for them at Nantgwyn, I am.' Agnes Jones had a streaming head cold.

Elin stiffened with interest. Nantgwyn was their nearest neighbour, only a quarter of a mile up the lane, and the biggest farm in the district.

'And more sorry for Bethan,' Bessie agreed.

Bethan was the youngest daughter of Nantgwyn. A month older than Elin, they'd been friends in school. Since she'd worked at Tonteg, Bethan had been in the habit of coming down to share a cup of tea in the kitchen and have a chat, but Elin had not seen her for over three weeks. Bethan hadn't come to choir practice, and she hadn't come to chapel. Bethan's mother didn't encourage Elin to visit Nantgwyn, even if she could find the time; she was the servant at Tonteg.

'What's happened?' Elin wanted to know.

'He's gone away. That Will Rhees.' Agnes Jones blew into her handkerchief, her large nose was red and sore underneath.

'Gone where?'

'Disappeared, he has.' Elin felt her heart turn over. 'Took his things and did a moonlight flit.'

'Oh!' Elin shivered, this was awful. Poor Bethan, she could see her face before her as it had been all those weeks ago, white and strained.

'What am I going to do?' she'd whispered. Elin remembered the surge of sympathy that made her hug Bethan, but she'd had no advice to offer. The prospect was too dreadful.

'He'll not be coming back?'

'Why should he?'

Elin's slanting eyes searched into Agnes's, willing her to tell what she knew.

'Bethan is her friend,' Bessie said, screwing her face into a mass of worry lines. 'She's upset.'

Elin fingered the card in her handbag. It invited her to Bethan's marriage on Saturday, 26 November 1924.

'Her banns were read for the third time in chapel this morning, but nobody came from Nantgwyn to hear them.' Agnes Jones mopped at her nose again. 'Plenty of talk there was afterwards. It's all over Llanddolfa that the wedding's off.'

Nobody from Nantgwyn had come to hear the banns read the first time. Elin remembered the feeling of surprise percolating through the congregation. Nobody even knew Bethan was courting. Nobody could place the intended groom, William Tudor Rhees of Llangurig.

Sitting on the unyielding pew, with an ache in the pit of her stomach, Elin remembered Bethan praising Will. How quick he was with a scythe. How good with horses. How handsome and such fun to be with. Elin had kept her mouth shut, but it was soon common knowledge he was the farm hand at Nantgwyn, only hired at hay harvest. Nothing was guaranteed to cause more gossip.

'Bessie, it's time we went in,' Owen Roberts said testily, taking two daughters with him. Elin rounded up the other children and followed Bessie. Her father sat with the other deacons in the pew under the pulpit. From behind, his ears shone red in the November sunshine streaming through the plain glass windows. The preacher mounted the rostrum and the service began.

Elin couldn't have said what the sermon was about, she couldn't concentrate. She felt edgy, worried about Bethan, conscious of the charged atmosphere.

Maldwyn Griffiths, a gangling youth in a too-tight suit, met her eyes across the pews and smiled. She'd walked to and from school with him until he left one year before her. Bethan referred to him as Elin's boy friend, but Elin didn't feel anything special for him. Until recently, he'd shown more interest in fishing and rabbiting than he had in her company.

Afterwards, they all surged outside to exchange news and offer invitations to tea. Her father never took part in this. He believed in keeping himself to himself, and was always the first to set off home.

Elin usually lingered with the younger members of the congregation, but today she could hear Bethan's name being bandied about. She set off down the road and found Maldwyn Griffiths beside her, complimenting her on her new outfit, his dark eyes trying to hold her gaze. Those of the congregation who lived down the valley trailed behind.

'Let's walk up the cwm,' he suggested as they drew near the gate. The cwm was a short cut they'd always taken to school. It was a steep narrow valley, filled with trees and thick vegetation. A stream bubbled its way down to the river, and a narrow path wound through.

'Father's gone round by the road.' Elin hesitated, knowing he'd not approve.

'So's my family. Keeps their shoes cleaner.'

'Is it muddy?'

'No, I came this way. We can sit and talk for a while.'

'Father will be cross if I'm a long time.'

They had to walk in single file but his hand felt supportive round hers as he towed her along. At the bridge that crossed the stream half a mile up, the ground levelled off. Soon they'd leave the shelter of the trees and have to follow the steep path up the field.

'Let's sit here and rest a moment,' he suggested.

'I don't want to spoil my best skirt.'

Maldwyn had carried his raincoat. Now he spread it out, lining side down, and threw himself on it. She sat as far away from him as the raincoat allowed.

'Did you know I've got a cow of my own? Birthday present from my grandma, it was.'

'A milking cow?'

'No, it's running with Dad's suckler herd. It's in calf, and I'm hoping for a good heifer. One day I'll have a herd of my own. I've got six good ewes, too. Well, three are a bit old, and have no teeth, but I'm hoping they'll all bring a lamb.'

'Twins if you're lucky.'

'Perhaps. Elin, can I see you back to Tonteg after chapel tonight?'

She hesitated. 'It's miles out of your way. Think of the walk home you'll have. In the dark, too.'

'I don't mind that.' He bent to kiss her cheek. His forehead touched her hat, pushing it up. Elin pulled it off.

'That's better,' he laughed, then his lips landed fully on hers. The intensity of his kiss unnerved her. She hadn't expected Maldwyn to be like this, it left her breathless.

'You must have lots of boy friends. You're the prettiest girl round here, even if your hair is falling down.'

Elin was not used to it in a bun. Usually she wore it tied back with a bit of ribbon. She took out the hair pins she'd borrowed from Bessie and it cascaded down her back.

'It's like molten gold,' he told her. 'Like the sun itself.'

She shook her head and the sun shimmered through it.

'Shall I ask my mother if you can come to tea next Sunday?'

She hesitated, wanting to agree. 'Father wouldn't like it. He wants me home when I'm off.'

'Ask him.'

'Perhaps.' He had spots on his chin; they made him seem vulnerable.

'But I can walk you home tonight?'

'No, Maldwyn, no.' The silence between them lengthened.

'I thought you liked me.' His voice was suddenly harsh.

'I do, but . . .' Maldwyn was growing taller and broader. Changing from a tree-climbing boy to a man, and she no longer felt at ease with him.

'But you don't want anything to do with me? You've got another boy friend?'

'No. No, I haven't.' It was her turn to sound anguished.

'Then what's the harm?'

She couldn't explain. She didn't really know. 'I'm sorry, I've offended you, I didn't mean to.' She felt terrible. Bethan had said she didn't know how to handle men. Maldwyn was staring down into the stream. She had to break the awful silence.

'What time is it?' Elin had no watch of her own.

'Ten past four.'

'Father will wonder where I am.' She leapt to her feet.

'He'll want his tea. Bessie lets me bring a cake.'

'Do you like working for her?' His manner was more distant now.

'She's kind, but the work's hard. I'd like a job in town, where there's a bit of life. I feel like a prisoner at Tonteg. It's miles from anywhere.'

'You should be used to that.'

She hurried up the two steep fields, matching her step to Maldwyn's longer one. As they drew nearer, she could see her father waiting at the cottage gate, his face like thunder.

'Good day to you, Mr Jones,' Maldwyn called, hurrying past.

Elin's step slowed. 'I'm a little late, Father, I'm sorry. I walked up the cwm with Maldwyn.'

'Such wicked wanton behaviour!' His bushy brows were drawn down tight in a scowl. 'What have you been up to?'

'I've not been up to anything.' She hurried him into the house, closing the door, not wanting Maldwyn to overhear. 'Not so loud, Father.'

'Don't tell me how to behave, you little hussy. Showing your legs and your hair swinging loose like that. You're temptation itself. You'll get yourself into trouble.'

Elin put her hat and the cake on the table, knowing exactly the trouble he referred to. She must not let herself be drawn into an argument.

'Throwing yourself at men. Encouraging them.'

'I walked to school with Maldwyn for years. He has to pass this door to get home.'

'It was different then. You were both children.'

'I'm not throwing myself . . .' Elin paused, she must talk of something else, he was working himself up. 'Did you know his grandmother gave him a cow, to start his own herd?'

'In broad daylight you let your hair down for everyone to see.'

'Mother liked it loose.'

'When you were a child. You're sixteen, a woman now. Anyway she spoilt you, pandering to your vanity. I told her so but she took no notice. It's wicked to linger with a man.'

'Maldwyn's only a lad, Father. He was telling me about his sheep.'

'He didn't tell you your hair was beautiful?' His voice was thick with suspicion.

She felt defiance spiral through her. 'Yes, he did. It is beautiful. I'm proud of it, and why shouldn't I be?'

'Vanity is a sin. You were always preening as a child. You're leading him on. Raising his expectations.'

Elin knew all men expected something of women. That too, made them difficult to cope with, and it had led to terrible trouble for Bethan.

He took a handful of her hair and pulled, bringing her face close to his. 'Oh, you're right, it is beautiful. It feels like silk.' Elin saw the sour lines round his mouth contort. She wanted to turn and run.

'Father, leave me be.'

'It's temptation all right, but I can help you there.'

Her mother's dressmaking scissors were still hanging on a hook on the dresser. He snatched them up. It was only when she felt the cold edge of steel against her neck that she realised his intention. The scissors crunched in her ear and eight inches of hair fell to the floor.

She screamed and tore herself from him, turning wildly to the mirror over the mantelpiece. In it, she could see ragged wisps where her hair had been cropped off half an inch below her left ear. She stared at her reflection, open mouthed with shock, then furious tears blurred the image. She screamed again, pushing him away. Too late, she saw the scissors flash in the mirror. He made another jagged cut, halfway round her head.

'No, Father, no!' She jerked away. It felt as though he was pulling her hair out at the roots. He was breathing heavily, his small eyes under their bushy brows stared down at her. She felt rage boiling through her. It gave her a wild strength to pull free of his stranglehold.

'My hair!' she wailed. 'Look what you've done! You've spoilt it.' She picked up her locks from the pegged rag mat on the hearth. 'It took years to grow. You've ruined it!'

'You're too beautiful. I told your mother many times she

was making a big mistake. Encouraging you. Making fancy clothes for you. Anyway, it's in your blood. You'll go the same way.'

'What do you mean, the same way?' she demanded.

'Nothing . . .' He was turning away.

Elin snatched at his arm. 'What's in my blood? What are you saying about my mother?'

'You might as well know now. Your mother had her fun and was abandoned when you were on your way. You'll end up the same, the way you're going on.'

'What?' What was he saying? That her mother had been caught in the same trouble as Bethan Morgan? That she had been the child . . . She found it hard to believe, and yet . . . 'No!'

'Oh yes. Her fancy man didn't stay long enough to marry her. She was glad enough to marry me.'

'Mam?' Elin felt the strength drain out of her. She didn't doubt it was the truth. His face swam before her eyes. 'You mean I'm . . . I'm illegitimate?'

'Oh no. I saved you from that disgrace. Saved you both from the workhouse, but few thanks I got from her. And precious few I'll get from you, I dare say.'

Elin froze, searching his face. 'Not my father?' Up till now she'd known her place. Knew where she owed allegiance. And now? She felt a surge of relief. 'I'm glad. Glad there's nothing of you in me.' He'd always had a hold over Mam, she'd sensed it. They'd both been wary of him.

'Who was my father?' Mam must have loved him, yet he'd left her when . . .

'I don't know. Your mother wouldn't speak of him. I doubt she knew.'

'She must have.' Poor Mam! 'What she must have gone through to accept you.'

His face twisted. 'She was glad enough of my name, I can tell you. She was ready to throw herself into the river.'

Elin felt sick. 'Nobody knew round here,' she said doubtfully.

'That's why we came.'

'Where from? I have to know.'

'No, you don't. You can't go round asking questions, blackening your mother's name. Would she want that?'

Elin released a long, shuddering breath.

'I'm afraid for you,' he hissed, his face ugly and contorted. 'I'm surprised it's Bethan Morgan, and not you.'

She shuddered. 'Did he come from these parts? My father?'

He stared down at her. 'How do I know?'

'She must have said something.'

'No.'

Elin shuddered. 'I wish she'd told me.'

'I warned her not to. It's best forgotten.'

She turned on him angrily, 'I thank God you aren't my father.'

'You ungrateful little hussy. I've done my duty by you, fed you, clothed you all these years.'

'You never showed me any love.'

He was silent for a moment. 'I did my best.'

What did that mean? She wasn't worth loving, didn't deserve it?

'I've looked after you. Found you a place when you left school.'

'Oh yes, you did that.' He'd arranged that half her wages should be paid to him. Well, she hadn't minded contributing to the house while Mam was alive, but not now. She had nobody she could call her own flesh and blood.

Oh Mam, she prayed silently. Why didn't you tell me? She had nobody to turn to either. Mam had loved her. She'd had a special way of hugging her, pulling her against her own body, especially when Evan Jones had been in a bad mood. She'd always known Mam wasn't happy.

'Men told her she was beautiful. She listened, instead of putting her trust in the Lord.'

'Mother?' Her mouth felt dry.

'Be warned, or you'll go the same way. You're too pretty for your own good.'

'You're mad. I can't help what I look like. Can you help being old and ugly?' She couldn't take her eyes from his. 'I'm glad you're not my father. If you were, I'd be ugly too.'

'Pride is sinful,' he hissed. 'It leads to self glorification. Self display.' He came towards her again, with the scissors ready to snatch another bite.

'No,' she backed away. 'No.'

'I'll have it off. It's safer. You're a wicked girl, you flaunt your beauty. Without it you'll be less likely to come to harm. You need someone to keep you on the rails.'

Elin was backing away, but she had to stand up to him. She took a deep breath. 'From now on it won't be you! I don't have to come here. I won't ever again. What's wrong with being pretty? What's wrong with enjoying life? You're always miserable, and you made my mother miserable too. She didn't love you, as she loved my father.' His fingers bit into her wrist as she tried to shake him off.

'Love? Hah! Your father didn't love her enough to marry her.' He came closer, scissors raised.

Elin watched him mesmerised, unable to breathe, as she remembered Bethan saying scornfully, 'Your father! Don't be such a mouse, Elin. I wouldn't be scared of him.' Suddenly she flew at him, bending his wrist back.

'You little cat.' His mouth twisted with the pressure she was applying, but he held onto the scissors. She pushed harder, almost crying with frustration.

'What a fury! The Devil has taken you.' She had to use all her strength to keep him still, but nobody could call her a mouse, not after this. She could feel him moving against her weight, and expected any moment to be thrown off. She must not lose this struggle.

Suddenly she bent her head and sank her teeth into his wrist. He shouted in pain and relaxed his grip on the scissors. Elin grabbed for them, and jabbed the points at the loose folds of skin on his neck. He staggered back, trying to regain his balance. The armchair caught him behind the knees, and he collapsed back into it. She caught his black tie and twisted. His celluloid collar flipped off the front stud. At last, the points of the scissors dug home into his quivering Adam's apple.

She could see real fear now in his eyes, and felt a moment of triumph. She'd dared to stand up to him. She'd broken free, and was no longer in his power. Two scratches on the loose skin of his throat oozed spots of blood. She was kneeling on his protruding abdomen creasing his best waistcoat. His hunter watch pressed painfully into her knee.

Years of concealed resentment foamed up and flowed over. 'I hate you, hate you.' She was grinding her teeth, digging the scissor points harder. The scratch deepened to a cut, blood trickled out.

Elin suddenly straightened up, appalled at what she was doing. She flung the scissors across the room and scrambled to her feet, gasping for breath, quivering with bitterness gone out of control. She couldn't believe what she'd done. She wasn't capable of violence. She was a shy little thing, a mouse, everybody said so. But underneath she had tiger's claws. She was sobbing with shock and rage.

What did it matter if he cut more off? She couldn't keep the right side eight inches longer than the ragged edges on the left. She'd been proud of her hair. Even on the mat it glowed with a light of its own, as though it still had life. She'd gloried in its beauty and worked to enhance it, brushing it with a hundred strokes every night, no matter how tired she felt. And she'd paid fourpence for soft soap to wash it instead of using Sunlight. Now it was ruined.

She moved on unsteady legs, made a sudden grab for her things on the table, and ran out of the house.

Back in the cwm, under the trees, she threw herself down on the grass, no longer worried about her best skirt. She flung her expensive hat down on top of the cake she'd picked up too. Not that she cared about the cake, she'd just snatched up the things she'd brought, with no thought for what they were.

She cried till her eyes were red and swollen and she could cry no more. The sun had long gone. With approaching nightfall, it grew cold, but she couldn't move. Couldn't go to chapel with her hair like this. She ate the sponge cake, breaking pieces off with her fingers.

She felt ashamed, horrified at what she'd done. She knew how easily she could have dug the scissors hard into his neck.

She'd wanted to. She'd gloried in the power that had been hers at that moment.

She'd go away. Leave the district. She'd have to, she couldn't see him every Sunday in chapel. She'd look for a place far away, in a big town. Away from father, away from Tonteg, and away from Maldwyn too.

The next week, Owen Roberts took some bullocks into Pwllheli market, and brought a newspaper back with him. In it, an agency advertised for domestic staff for jobs on Merseyside. Elin wrote to them, hoping to get away soon.

Gossip about Bethan increased. Some said she'd disappeared too, they were dragging the river for her. Others, that she'd gone to stay with her aunt in Liverpool. Someone else had seen her in the station, waiting for the London train, alone and with one suitcase, looking pale and ill, and at least six months pregnant. Everybody was certain disaster had overtaken her. She had been wild, they said, and the Morgans of Nantgwyn were not really Llanddolfa folk. They'd bought the farm only twenty years ago, and come from Aberystwyth.

One day, Elin saw Bethan's elder sister coming back from town with two large bags of groceries. Even though she was walking fast with her head turned away, Elin ran into the lane to stop her.

'I hear Bethan's in Liverpool staying with her aunt,' she said. 'I've got a job in Birkenhead. We might be able to meet if it's not too far. Nice for both of us being away from home.' The bags were eased down to the grassy verge for a moment's rest. 'Could you give me her address?'

'You heard wrong.' She was abrupt. Her dark eyes bristled with antagonism. 'Our aunt lives in Birmingham.'

The week before she was due to leave, the Minister of Llanddolfa Chapel, the Reverend William Wyn Evans, paid a visit to Tonteg. Bessie sat by the fire with him and talked, while Elin set out the best china and made tea.

From the back kitchen she could hear the cadence of his voice rising and falling as it did in chapel. Her father counted the Reverend William Evans a great support in trouble. She took in more logs to brighten the fire. His silver hair reflected the glow. As she handed him his cup, he said: 'You mustn't feel you're going a long way from home, Elin. I know Birkenhead well.'

Her golden eyes went to his face in fear; it was beaming with good will. She groped for Bessie's cup, feeling trapped.

'You may even see me from time to time, I preach on the circuit. I could give you the name of your nearest chapel. Make it easier for you.'

Elin felt suddenly cold. He was blocking her escape.

'Where are you going to live? You have the address?'

She had to tell him, though she didn't want to. Bessie was nodding her approval, urging her to find pencil and paper, the lines on her face accentuated by the fire's glow.

'I'll write to the Reverend Robert Roberts, and ask him to look out for you. You'll like him. It'll comfort us all to know you're in his good care. Especially your father.'

'Thank you, Mr Evans.' Elin took the address he gave her, twisting the slip of paper in her shaking fingers.

'We'll have news of you from time to time, and know how you're getting on. You need never feel alone or homesick. You'll be among friends. It's a Welsh chapel and a Welsh congregation. There's quite a big Welsh community in Birkenhead.'

'Yes, Mr Evans.' She swallowed hard, wishing she was going further afield. She'd never expected her father to be able to spy on her in Birkenhead. 'Thank you.'

His parting handshake was limp. 'Give my best regards to the Reverend Roberts,' he said, his gentle eyes full of the milk of human kindness. She must not be fooled, he'd report everything to her father. No, not her father, Evan Jones.

As soon as the door had closed behind him, she threw his slip of paper into the fire.

CHAPTER TWO

Elin smudged the window clear of condensation to see smoke streaming back from the engine as the train rounded a bend. Smuts were flying past, the taste of smoke was on her tongue.

On the other side of the carriage, a mother was peeling an orange for her child. The zest of it mingled with the smell of damp mackintoshes. Elin hadn't realised how far it was to Birkenhead. For the past hour she'd been wishing the journey was over.

Rows of small houses backed onto the line. Elin had a clear view into dirty back yards containing rusting mangles and tin baths. Through an uncurtained window, she glimpsed a squalid bedroom, with coats piled on the bed instead of blankets. The poverty shocked her, it was worse than any in Llanddolfa. The streets behind were grim and smoke-blackened.

The train was slowing and the lines multiplying. A ball of apprehension expanded in her stomach; they must be nearly there. Suddenly she felt reluctant to leave the security of the Pwllheli train.

She told herself impatiently she was lucky to get a job so quickly. She'd only got it because the agency could place any number of girls in domestic work just before Christmas and were willing to put her on their books unseen. She'd heard town girls preferred shop or factory work.

She'd worked for Bessie Roberts for two years, and she'd pleaded with her to stay. Elin felt she couldn't. In Llanddolfa there was no way she could avoid seeing her father. When they met, she could feel his evil eyes following every movement she made, menacing her. The whole village knew she no longer spoke to him. She was frightened by what she'd so nearly done. She'd had him at her mercy for a few moments and come very close to killing him. She couldn't look at herself in a mirror without being reminded of what had so nearly happened. Everybody she met asked why she'd cut off her lovely hair. She mustn't let anything like that happen ever again.

Away from him in Birkenhead, it couldn't, and there would be no hens to feed, or butter to be made. No hay harvest either, when everybody worked till they dropped. She'd only have indoor work; she'd be better off, it stood to reason. No more winter mornings when she'd have to carry buckets of water from the stream before she could make tea. Here water would come in taps, right into the kitchens. Even for a maid, life would be easier. She'd be able to go shopping on her day off, see a bit of life, have a bit of fun for a change.

The train slid into Woodside Station. She felt fear trickle down her back as she climbed down and walked past the metal advertisements – Beecham's Pills, keep you fit; Zam-Buk, rub it in. The air smelled different, smoke-laden and flat. Weighed down with her heavy suitcase and hat box, she followed the crowd out of the station. She found herself in a busy ferry, tram and bus terminus; roads and buildings stretched away into the distance. How was she ever to find her way to Birchgrove?

The woman who had shared her carriage walked past, the child whining and dragging his feet.

'Could you tell me where I get the bus to Oxton?' Elin wished she'd enquired sooner.

'You want the twopenny jogger, luv.'

'What?'

'Tram.' The woman pointed across the terminus.

'That's what you want, the electric tram.'

'Electric?' Elin stared in amazement, she'd never even heard of electric trams. There was no electricity in Llanddolfa. The trams were all two-storey. She decided at that moment she'd go on the top deck and see this great town. But which one should she take? There were five in the row, and even as she considered it, one pulled away. She didn't want to miss the next and have to wait in the drizzle. Already the afternoon was pulling in.

'You want the Oxton Circular,' the woman called after her. Elin relaxed a little, she could see one labelled Oxton Circular. Perhaps it wasn't going to be too difficult after all.

The conductor took her suitcase from her as she climbed on board and stowed it under the stairs. Elin hesitated; better not go on top after all. She mustn't lose sight of her case, anybody could take it from there. She slid into the nearest seat.

'I want to go to Bidston Road. Could you tell me when we get there? I don't know the town.' Bessie had told her to say that.

'We don't go to Bidston Road.' The conductor pushed his hat back and scratched his head. 'You'll have to get off in Shrewsbury Road and walk up.' She pulled out the letter she'd received, and showed him the address. 'I'll put you off on the corner of Beresford.'

The tram started smoothly, clicking over the points. She peered out of the window, eager to see the fine shops and theatres she'd heard about. The rain was driving against the glass, it was getting dark. The few shops she saw were no bigger than those in Pwllheli, but she'd never seen so many houses. As the tram progressed, the houses grew bigger.

'Your stop,' the conductor said, passing her and leaping for the stairs. Feeling numb, she dragged at her suitcase.

The rain was bouncing off the pavements when she got off. She set off briskly, passing large semi-detached Victorian villas standing back from the road. Her suitcase was heavy. She stopped to rest, and asked a woman coming towards her if she was going the right way.

The houses in Bidston Road were much grander, and were hidden behind high walls. At last she found what she was looking for; the sign on the gate read Birchgrove. Her stomach was churning, relief mingled with nervousness. It was a far, far bigger house than she'd expected. Elin looked up at its six stacks of twisting mock-Elizabethan chimneys and shivered. Its arched stone window frames were like those of a church. The front door was studded with nails and bigger than that of the chapel back home. It stood four storeys high and looked grim. Perhaps it was the tall trees huddling close, with rain dripping off them.

A gravel drive led to a massive porch. Bessie had warned her not to march up to the front door, but she could see no way round the back. On one side a glass conservatory joined the house to a six-foot wall.

She went in the opposite direction. Shrubs grew close against the dark windows. The wet lawn sucked at her heels; she was leaving holes. The grass stretched away into the night, close-cropped and desolate in the winter rain. She tiptoed back to the gravel and out to the pavement. Perhaps there was another gate somewhere.

She walked on, coming to another road, more houses. She'd never been in such a large town, with pavements stretching on and on, slippery in the rain. She turned back, afraid of getting lost. It was almost dark.

The gate clanged shut behind her, she could feel the gravel through the soles of her best shoes. She wished she hadn't worn them to travel in, the rain was spoiling them, and they pinched. It felt better under the porch out of the gusting rain, though there were butterflies in her stomach. She rang the bell, and heard it jangle somewhere inside.

Footsteps, and a man wearing a black jacket and waistcoat over striped trousers swung the heavy door open. Elin's stomach turned over. She was awed by his bow tie and white shirt, terrified she'd brought the master of the house to the doorstep.

'What do you want?' He was arrogant, his manner unfriendly.

'I'm Elin Jones, the new maid,' she began, her voice scarcely more than a whisper.

'What?' She was starting again, when his narrow lips tightened.

'Round the back,' he spat at her. 'Don't you know better than to come to the front door?'

It was like a slap in the face, she felt the scarlet tide rush up her cheeks. 'I'm sorry.' In the burst of panic she almost turned and ran, but the alien streets frightened her too. 'I . . . I can't find the back.'

'To the left. Fifty yards down the road, left then left again. You can't miss the back gate.' The door slammed shut in her face.

Elin swallowed back her horror. She felt tired, cold and unwanted, but there was nothing else for it but to follow his directions. She trudged with head bent into the wind, wishing she'd never come.

She found it, a great double door set into a six-foot wall, with a smaller door for pedestrians alongside. It was stiff; for a moment she thought it was locked, but it opened against her weight. She was in a yard with dustbins and a clothes line from which hung two flapping kitchen towels. The back door stood open to show a vestibule, empty apart from the door mat and a wire basket of sprouts. There was neither bell nor knocker on the inner door. She rapped with her knuckles. The noise she made seemed lost in the splatter of rain.

'Hello,' she called nervously.

'Come on in then.' The same man stood staring down at her, his dark hair stiffly Brylcreemed back across his head. She knew now he wasn't the master of the house, but to find he was a servant shocked her more. He was holding his chin at a haughty angle and looking down his Roman nose at her. 'We have to start as we mean to go on. The family don't like the servants using the front.'

Her head was spinning. She couldn't even think of a man doing housework, couldn't believe such a proud man in such grand clothes answered doorbells and waited on table. She'd never have accepted the job if she'd known. Men were unfathomable, frightening. She didn't like them.

Elin slid her bags to the floor, trying to stem the dislike she felt. She'd started off on the wrong foot with him. She must be careful not to make matters worse by showing how she felt. She was tired enough to drop. As she followed him into the kitchen, water was leaking under the collar of her blouse to trickle in icy runnels down her back.

'I don't know why Peck couldn't bring you quietly

through.' A woman with flushed cheeks turned from the gas stove. 'Instead of making you walk all the way round. Men! They're a pain.'

Elin warmed to her.

'I'm Bridie.' Harassed tendrils of dark straight hair were escaping from under her cap. 'Parlour maid is what I'm supposed to be, though you'd never know it.' Her figure had thickened, but her manner remained girlishly vivacious. 'It's Cook's half day, and Daisy's having one of her bilious attacks. I could do with a hand. Hang your coat up. There's a hook behind the door.'

Elin slid her arms carefully out of her coat. It was dripping moisture, leaving dark circles like pennies on the stone floor. She was cold, but after a moment's hesitation, she hung the jacket of her suit on a different peg. She mustn't get stains on it.

She saw Bridie's darting brown eyes fasten on her hair. 'Oh lor, I do like your bob. Bobbed hair's all the rage among the swells, isn't it? Lovely. Lovely golden colour too.' Her laugh bubbled up like effervescence.

Any remark about her hair reminded Elin of that terrible Sunday. Her hand went up to cover the ends before she could stop it. 'Is there an apron?'

'Borrow that one of Cook's.' Bridie indicated one hanging on the door.

Elin tied it round her waist; it was vast, reaching her ankles, with the bib jutting out loosely in front. She knotted six inches out of the loop to go round her neck. The man who had sent her on that unnecessary walk stood watching her.

'This is Peck,' Bridie told her.

'The butler,' he said.

'And valet to old Mr Oxley,' Bridie added. 'Mostly valet.'

He quelled her with one supercilious glance, and turned back to Elin. 'You'll be the tweeny here.'

'What's a tweeny?' Elin hoped she didn't sound too rude.

'You are a little innocent, aren't you?' His black button-like eyes wouldn't leave her.

'Innocent?' Elin shuddered, that was the last thing she

was! She'd lost her innocence that Sunday, and been haunted by what she'd done ever since.

'Haven't you been in service before?'

'Yes, but I did a bit of everything, looked after the children, even milked the cows sometimes. I was the only maid.'

'Oh, a farm!' He sniffed disdainfully, and patted his Roman nose with his handkerchief. 'You'll find standards much higher here.' One of a row of bells jangled overhead, making Elin jump.

'Drawing room,' Bridie said, carrying on with her work.

'You answer it,' Peck retorted.

'Can't you see I'm busy? It's Cook's half day.'

'She leaves everything ready for you. What's all the fuss?'

'I still have to cook it.'

'All you have to do is light the oven, girl.'

'I've done that. On your way back, bring the dishes down from the nursery. They'll have finished now.'

The same bell jangled again, more loudly. Slowly and with every show of reluctance, Peck got to his feet to answer it.

'Lazy thing,' Bridie said when he'd gone. 'It's no good being shy or turning those golden eyes on him. You'll have to stand up to him or he'll walk all over you. Look, a tweeny divides her time between the kitchen and the front. Mornings you light fires, clean up, make beds and dust in the front. Afternoons you help Cook in the kitchen.'

'Thank you. Tell me about the family. How many are there?'

'There's old Mr Oxley, his son Mr Laurence, his wife, and their little girl Mary. Oh and she's having another, but pretend you don't notice.' Bridie giggled again. 'Not that you would notice yet.' Another bell jangled. 'That's her! Almost as if she could hear us.' Bridie tucked her straggling black hair under her cap and took off her apron. 'I'll have to see what she wants. Come up with me, we'd better tell her you're here. Has she seen you?'

'No.'

'She didn't pick you out?' Bridie's dark eyes wouldn't leave her face.

'No.'
'I didn't think she had.'
'Why?' Elin asked anxiously. 'Don't you think I'll suit?'
'Course you will, but she'd have chosen a plain forty-year-old spinster. Someone more like me.'
'You're not forty?' Elin liked her big kindly face.
'Nearly, I'm thirty-eight.' Her giggle bubbled out again.
Bridie's figure was buxom, but her feet hardly seemed to touch the stairs as she bounded up. Elin had difficulty keeping pace with her. She had no time to look round, but got an impression of high ceilings and wide dark stairs.
Bridie halted abruptly and turned to whisper, 'This is her boudoir, and that's her bedroom. Wait here.'
Elin anxiously smoothed her hair with her hands, trying to imagine what a boudoir could be. The passage was hung with dark pictures, and had a strip of carpet up the middle.
Bridie came out and hissed: 'She wants to see you. Can you find your way down after?'
Elin nodded and then knocked nervously on the half-open door and went in. It was a small sitting room with comfortable settees and vases full of flowers. She'd been thinking of mirrors and dressing tables.
'Elin, is it?'
'Yes, Elin Jones.' She hadn't expected her new mistress to be so beautifully groomed. There wasn't a hair out of place on her blonde, shingled head, but she had a sour expression, her mouth drooped with discontent.
'When you answer, you address me as madam or ma'am.' There was no displeasure in her voice, but her manner emphasised the distance between them.
'Yes . . . ma'am.' She'd always known the women of Llanddolfa did not know what fashion was. Sybil Oxley was wearing a straight tube of beige silk, and her brown beads swung almost to the hem. Her shoes had high heels. Father would be shocked by her plucked eyebrows.
'Turn round.'
Elin felt bewildered. Had she heard right?
'Turn round slowly.'
Elin did so, feeling foolish. When she next looked at

Sybil Oxley, her lips had tightened to a pout of displeasure. 'Yes, well, I suppose you'll do.'

'I'll work hard, ma'am, and I'm clean in my ways. I gave satisfaction in my—'

'Your wage will be eight pounds a month, your uniform, and your keep. You'll have a half day off weekly, and a full day once a month.'

'Yes, ma'am, thank you.' Sybil Oxley couldn't have been more different from motherly Bessie Roberts in her floral pinafores.

'Mrs Dooley will explain your duties.'

'Yes, ma'am, thank you.' She knew she'd been dismissed. She turned and stumbled back to the stairs, creeping down two flights, trying to remember how many she'd raced up behind Bridie. The house was silent. Suddenly a door closed behind her and Peck, supporting a tray on one hand, came swaggering past like a lord. She followed.

The kitchen seemed vast and cheerless. The fire had gone out in the blackleaded grate, which had an oven each side. The big scrubbed table in the centre was covered with serving dishes. Peck was making room for those he'd brought down.

'Bridie, you'll love this,' he was saying. 'Two more for dinner. Mr Leonard and his family have arrived.'

Bridie gave a horrified gasp. 'They weren't supposed to get here till tomorrow! What about Master Robert?'

'He's here too. In the nursery, waiting for you to send up a tray with his supper. They made good time crossing France and caught an earlier boat.'

'Who is Mr Leonard?' Elin ventured.

'Brother to Mr Laurence, and something in the Diplomatic Service. He always comes for Christmas. I've reset the dining room table.'

'Then you'll have to reset it again,' Bridie told him grimly. 'Mrs Oxley doesn't feel like dinner. She'll just have soup in her room.'

'All the more for the visitors,' Peck retorted. 'Don't you know what's a help and what's a hindrance?'

'It would be more help if it was soup for starters instead of eggs mayonnaise.'

'Any leftovers?'

Bridie was already in the larder, pushing the bowls and dishes round. 'There's a cupful left, I'm in luck. Beef broth, she had it for lunch.'

'She must have liked it then. Just warm it up.'

'I will when I have a moment. We'll need another potato.'

'I'd make them do,' Peck said crossly.

'There's Elin, too, she'll want supper.'

'Can I peel some potatoes?' Elin was hungry and she needed something to do. Knowing nothing of the routine made her feel awkward. Bridie had been kind and she wanted to help. Moments later she was at the sink with potatoes and two handfuls of sprouts.

'Be quick,' Bridie urged. 'Cut them small. Dinner's ready, but they've got to eat the first courses. Damn! Cook put the cod mornay into scallop shells to make it easier, but she only made three.' She got another shell from the cupboard, and divided the fish pie returned from the nursery between that and a small plate, using her fingers to push the potato into a neat shape on top.

'Does it look all right? More cheese perhaps? Make sure old Mr Oxley gets this one, Peck.' She put them all into the oven to warm up.

'Now what? A tray for Master Robert. He'll be too tired to eat now, look at the time.' She rushed round, putting an apple and a fairy cake on a plate, filling a beaker with milk. 'Here Peck, get the plate of fish pie out and take this up to the nursery. Elin doesn't know where to go yet.'

As soon as the door closed behind him, Bridie bent forward and hissed: 'Peck indulged himself too much on Master's claret at lunch and feels a bit hungover. Always makes him nasty. He's all right when he's sober, except he's bone idle.' Bridie's hair had broken loose again and was damp with perspiration from her cheeks.

Eager to be helpful, Elin went closer to the stove. A joint was sizzling inside, filling the kitchen with an appetising scent. Her mouth watered, it was a long time since she'd eaten her sandwich on the train. Bridie was whisking round setting another tray, this time with more style. She poured the heated soup into a bowl.

Elin didn't know how it happened, but somehow her hip caught the corner of the tray where it overhung the table and sent it spinning to the floor with a crash. She jumped back in horror as the soup spread over the flagstones among the broken china.

'Damn,' screamed Bridie. 'Damn, damn damn! That's the soup gone.'

Elin felt the end of the world had come. 'I'm sorry.' Weary tears pricked her eyes as she bent to pick up the pieces. She liked Bridie. Though she was busy, she'd found time to give her a friendly welcome. Elin was grateful, but now she'd made more work for her. She felt clumsy, stupid, bewildered. Peck was back, looking down his nose at her.

In the act of whisking the tray to the sink to wipe it over, Bridie turned on him.

'The kettle's boiling. Nanny likes a pot of tea after her supper. Could you take it up?' She snatched a fresh tray cloth from one drawer, clean cutlery from another. Elin salvaged the hothouse carnation from the broken glass, and found a fresh specimen vase.

'She can come down and get her own tea,' Peck snarled. 'I'm not waiting on the likes of her!'

Elin picked up the silver cruet and wiped it. Bridie snatched it and slammed it on the tray before stepping over the mess to inspect what remained in the saucepan. 'I'll have to add water . . . Pity I drained the leeks.'

'Milk,' Elin suggested. 'Won't taste so thin.'

'Come and stir it for me.' Bridie turned the flames up under it, before starting to mash potatoes. Elin was stirring hard; on impulse she reached for a spoonful of mashed potato to add to the soup.

'You cook too?' Bridie's giggle fizzed up again as she dived under the table to pick up the bread roll. Wiping it against her apron, she added it to the tray and headed for the stairs.

As soon as Peck had taken the main course up to the dining room, Bridie was clearing space on the table for them to sit down. She'd roasted two breasts of lamb alongside the leg, with roast potatoes and gravy. Elin forked food into her mouth, and began to feel a little warmer.

'There's rice pudding left from nursery lunch, or syrup pudding from supper. Probably apple pie too, if we wait to see what they leave now.'

Elin shook her head, she'd had enough, her eyes were closing. 'What about the washing up?'

'We'll make a start. Daisy will have to finish off in the morning.'

For Elin, the novelty of endless hot water gushing from a tap helped, but the dishes seemed never-ending. The coffee cups were still upstairs when Bridie said: 'That'll do. Come on, I'll show you your room.'

Elin felt so weary she could hardly climb the steep back stairs with her bags. Bridie whisked up ahead with two cans of hot water.

'This is the lavatory we use.' She pushed the door open with her foot as she passed.

'A water closet?' Elin felt a ripple of interest. 'I've heard of them, of course. I just pull the chain? Marvellous not to have to go down the garden.' She heard Bridie's gurgle of delight.

If there was a water closet for the servants, the family would be similarly provided; that meant no slops to empty. Bridie touched a switch and the narrow room was flooded with brilliant light.

'It's like magic. Electric light!' So easy, no more lamps to fill with oil, no need to trim their wicks and polish their glasses. She'd been right to come. She'd get used to it.

'I'll knock you up at six. There'll be a lot to do, with it being Christmas. More guests expected tomorrow.'

Elin said goodnight. She hung her blue suit in the wardrobe. On the only chair were three neatly folded print dresses, three cotton caps and twelve white aprons with six coarse aprons. None of them were new, but they'd been washed and ironed. She fished the black stockings she'd been told to provide out of her suitcase, rinsed her hands and face in the warm water Bridie had left on her washstand, and got thankfully into bed.

It was narrow and hard. No feather bed here, but the sheets of stiff cotton still showed the folds of the iron. She was asleep in moments.

Bridie's voice was waking her unbelievably soon. Sleep-sodden but obedient, Elin swung her legs out of bed. It was still pitch dark outside. The cold was biting. An icy draught rattled the ill-fitting window frame. She washed her hands and face again, using the water she'd used last night. It was grey and icy. The lavatory flushed with enough noise to waken the whole house.

The print dress was stiff with starch and had to be prised open. The cap covered her hair completely, thank goodness; her new mistress had not seemed to like it. Perhaps it was outlandishly fashionable for a servant. But Father had been wrong about long hair.

Bridie was back before she was ready. 'Coarse apron on top, first thing. Come on.' Her voice wafted back over her shoulder as she hurried down the back stairs.

'You've got to clean out the grates and light the fires.' Bridie pushed a box of cleaning materials into one of Elin's hands and an ash can into the other.

Elin's first impression had been that it was a very fine house indeed, equipped with every modern convenience. Closer inspection this morning proved otherwise. The rooms were large and high, but very much in need of fresh paint and paper. The furnishings were not as she'd expected. Most dated from the turn of the century, carpets and curtains were shabby and worn. The ornaments made her shudder.

As she passed through the entrance hall, she saw a dozen crossed African spears decorating one wall, and a large tomtom which was used as a table. The drawing room had several carved native stools, and polished ebony heads, some life size, were everywhere. But it was old Mr Oxley's study that really appalled her. The walls were hung with ancient animal skins. One moth-eaten specimen she recognised as cow. When Bridie caught her gazing at another, she murmured: 'Monkey.' The monkey skins had revolting bare patches on what had been their backsides. A stuffed alligator stood in the window recess. On the chimney breast, grotesque wood faces, daubed with war paint, had holes for eye sockets. Their hair of dried grass was disintegrating with age. 'Masks,' Bridie added. 'To frighten their enemies.'

'They frighten me,' Elin shuddered. Neither did she like the collection of small drums and native musical instruments she could put no name to. All were dusty, some had woodworm.

'They make the house smell like a museum.' Bridie flicked at them with her duster, sending the Christmas cards on display fluttering to the carpet. 'Impossible to keep clean, look at this mess on the floor, they're crumbling back to dust.'

'They're so ugly. Do they really like them?'

'Old Mr Oxley does. He made his fortune in West Africa and brought these things home.'

Elin shivered. 'I'd burn the lot if I were him.'

'Hurry up, you've still got the nursery fire to light, and Mrs Oxley likes one in her room if she isn't getting up. Come on, I'll show you where the nursery is.' Elin scurried behind her up to the top floor, trying to memorise the direction.

'All still in bed,' Bridie said throwing open the door and starting to tidy up. 'I reckon nannies have it easy.'

Bridie didn't give her time to look round. Elin had to rush to clean up the ashes, light the fires, and sweep the hearths.

'Now, if you've got all the fires going, your next job is to refill the scuttles with coal.' Bridie was rushing downstairs again. Peck crossed the hall on his way to set the breakfast table.

The coal bunker was out in the yard. It was a cold morning with a damping of drizzle. Elin wondered if it would mark her starched cap. Someone else was already there shovelling at the coal.

'Hello. You must be the new tweeny.'

'Yes, I'm Elin.'

'I'm Daisy.' She straightened up on spindly legs ending in large boots. Her face was pale and painfully thin, she was little more than a child. Elin felt she could get along with her. 'I'm the kitchen maid.' She had a lopsided smile. 'See you at breakfast.'

As she shovelled, Elin hoped it would be soon. It was heavy work carting full scuttles upstairs. She was about to push the dining room door open when she heard voices.

'Do we congratulate you, Laurence?'

There was a gusty sigh. 'Naturally I'd like a son to follow me in the business, but . . .'

'I know, as a family we are cursed.' It was a woman's voice that answered. 'I was on tenterhooks all the time I carried Robert.'

Elin hesitated, not wanting to intrude on what seemed a private conversation, yet she couldn't leave the scuttle at the door, nor should she be standing here listening to what didn't concern her.

'Sybil is terrified. Once you have one handicapped child, another seems more than likely. I'll be glad when the waiting's over.'

Elin felt horror spiral through her. Her employer was talking about his own feelings, about his own family! She mustn't be found here listening. She screwed up her courage, knocked and marched in.

'Poor Sybil, no wonder she's on edge—'

Elin was conscious that the woman had stopped in mid-sentence, and two identical pairs of eyes twitched to her.

'Good morning, sir, madam.' She crashed the scuttle onto the tiled hearth, and turned to escape.

'Who are you?' one of the men asked. She supposed he must be her employer.

'Elin, sir, the new tweeny. I came last night.' She lifted her eyes to his face.

The men were like two copies of the same person, though one wore a Fair Isle pullover and the other a grey suit. Twins they must be, with their fair wavy hair, small fringe moustaches, and jutting chins. The men of Llanddolfa were never well groomed like this. They'd be about the same age as Peck, but neither was as arrogant.

There were differences all the same. The Fair Isle pullover relaxed in a chair, gazing calmly at her. His hair curved neatly to the shape of his head. The other man bounded about the room, his hair more wiry, with more curl to it. Energy seemed to crackle out of him. Intense blue eyes darted from her face to her feet, and back again. She felt he'd know she had bobbed hair, even though nothing of it showed. It was not a hostile examination. In fact, he looked at her in the way Maldwyn Griffiths had.

'Right. Just for the Christmas season?'

'Oh no, sir. Permanently.'

'Then I hope you settle in and enjoy your stay with us.'

'Thank you, sir.' He made it sound as though she was an invited guest.

'Tell Peck we're waiting for our eggs and bacon.'

'Yes, sir.'

Peck was crossing the hall with a loaded tray as she left.

'They're getting tired of waiting for you,' she hissed, and felt she was getting her own back.

CHAPTER THREE

After filling all the other scuttles, Elin went to the kitchen. It was calmer this morning, with Mrs Dooley the cook back in charge. Brighter, too, with a good fire drawing in the grate. Daisy had lit it and set the table for breakfast.

'We'd be hard pressed over Christmas without another pair of hands.' Mrs Dooley's podgy cheeks creased into a smile. Her eyes, dark and glossy as prunes, were lost in a pudding of a face. 'Been here ten years, I have, and though I say it myself, you won't do better anywhere else.'

Elin had known she would be big from the size of the apron she'd borrowed, but she couldn't believe anyone could have so many quivering rolls of fat. Mrs Dooley was enormous.

'Mind you, you'll have to work hard. I don't like shirkers. You can make the toast.' One huge arm lifted from the pan of sizzling bacon to point out the toasting fork and the pile of bread. Elin crouched near the fire, speared the first slice, and thought about her new mistress. How wrong she'd been believing Sybil Oxley had everything life could offer. A handicapped son was a terrible burden. She asked about him.

'Oh yes,' Mrs Dooley confirmed. 'James his name is. He's six now.'

'Seven,' Bridie corrected.

'All right, seven. He's in a home in Liverpool, though they call it a school. Supposed to be teaching him to look after himself, wash and dress and all that, but he never will. They don't want him here, it's a bit of a comedown for the likes of them.'

'She'll end up in a mental home herself, the way she's

going on,' Bridie volunteered. 'Worrying isn't going to help. It stands to reason, doesn't it? Either the baby will be normal or it won't.'

'She was just the same when she was expecting Mary, and that child's got all her marbles.'

'Too many marbles if you ask me.' Bridie sat down at the table. Already her cap had slid to the back of her head and dark hair hung in lank strands round her face. 'They spoil her rotten.'

Elin pulled a chair to the table, still thinking about her mistress's problems. She had compensations, she had a rich and attractive husband, lots of marvellous clothes, and a big house with servants. Daisy put a plate of eggs and bacon in front of her.

The kitchen door crashed back, Peck staggered towards the scullery with a tray piled high with dirty dishes.

'You can get upstairs to the dining room before you eat that,' he barked at Elin. 'The fire needs banking up.'

'Can't it wait a minute?' Bridie let the yolk of her egg flow onto a piece of toast.

Elin pushed her chair back with a sinking feeling in the pit of her stomach. It wasn't that she minded banking the fire. She'd failed to do her work properly; she felt embarrassed at walking in on the family. She tried to explain this.

'Knock and walk in,' Mrs Dooley advised, her chins shining with bacon fat. 'They probably won't even notice you. Say "Excuse me" if they do. They don't care what you hear.'

'You're just a pair of hands to do the work,' Bridie laughed. 'They aren't bothered about what you think.'

Elin ran upstairs. The dining room door was ajar, she could hear voices from halfway down the passage.

'I'm surprised Sybil let him hire a girl like that, especially after the problem with Ruby. Such incredible eyes.'

She'd knocked on the door before she realised they could be talking about her. She had to go straight in after that, though her face was burning. The twin in the Fair Isle pullover was with his wife, and the way they both started confirmed her suspicion.

'Come on, Catherine,' Mr Leonard said not in the least perturbed. 'If you've still got shopping to do, it's time you were on your way.'

Elin poked viciously at the glowing coals. The fire could have waited till she'd eaten her breakfast and the family was out of the way. Bother Peck, he was getting at her. She stamped back to the kitchen in a bad mood. But she mustn't show she minded, nor try to get even with him, it would make him needle her more. She understood that much about men.

'What happened to Ruby?' she asked, tucking into her breakfast though it had gone cold. In the sudden silence, she noticed Mrs Dooley's cautionary glance at Bridie. 'Mrs Leonard was talking about her upstairs.'

'She got too big for her boots,' Peck said, buttering toast. 'Too big in more ways than one. Came to a sticky end.'

'No, she didn't.' Bridie gave an embarrassed giggle. 'You've got her job.'

'Let's get this table cleared.' Mrs Dooley pushed her chair back and heaved her bulk up on her feet. 'I've got work to do, if you haven't.' The bell jangled for attendance in the drawing room. 'You go up and see what they want, Elin. If you need help, come back and ask.'

This, Elin decided as she ran upstairs, was very different from Tonteg, where she'd been treated like one of the family. The Oxleys reigned from a distance like royalty.

'Come in,' a voice called when she knocked. 'Ah, Elin.'

'Yes, ma'am.' She looked into Sybil Oxley's cold grey eyes.

'Did you light this fire?'

'Yes, ma'am.' Elin's eyes shot guiltily to the grey ash in the grate.

'It's gone out.' The coal she'd put on had burned away. The scuttle was full, but she hadn't thought to make it up, and neither had anybody else.

'Oh!' She knew she ought to be managing the fires better than this. 'I'll get some more firings, ma'am, and relight it.'

'In future, check they are banked up, Elin. The house goes cold very quickly at this time of the year.'

'Yes, ma'am, I'm sorry. I'll see to it.' As she went out, Mr Laurence and Mr Leonard came in. Again she was struck by how very much alike they were. Both five foot ten in height, their broad shoulders and medium build exactly matching. Mr Laurence smiled at her; she liked him better than his wife. For a man, and an employer, he was quite approachable.

The drawing room was L-shaped, the shorter leg being used as a library and writing room. When she came back with sticks and paper, she could hear them talking there.

'We could be in at the beginning with this.' Mr Laurence's voice was accompanied by his footfall, he couldn't sit still. 'The business is marking time. The war altered everything, but Father doesn't realise things have changed.'

Elin rattled the poker noisily against the grate to let them know she was within hearing. His voice continued unchanged. Mrs Dooley was right, they didn't care who heard them.

'With shipping lines making so many regular sailings, the number of people importing and exporting to West Africa has quadrupled since the war.'

'We're still making a profit.'

'Our share of the business is going down. The competition is stiffer. I tell you, we must look to new ways to earn a crust, Leonard.'

'You must. You forget I've got a career.'

'I know that, of course, but Father will leave half the business to you. I'll need your say-so if I'm to change anything.'

'You're jumping the gun. Father's still with us. You should talk to him, not me.'

Even their voices were similar, but Laurence spoke more quickly. There was a note of urgency in it now. 'He won't listen. He's past it. Still thinks he's living in 1890, and I'm a small boy.'

'It's his business.'

'It isn't making the money it used to. The world's changing, the business has to adapt to new conditions or we'll end up losing everything.'

'If you think you can do better, then by all means try.'

'But I need the capital! Don't you know the first thing about business? We could set up crushing mills in the Niger delta, right up in the palm oil belt. Everybody waits on the coast for the natives to bring the raw stuff down and then ships it home to process. We're all being cheated. Played off one against the other.'

Elin cleared her throat noisily. That too had no effect. She didn't want to be accused of listening to a private conversation. And it did seem terribly private. She couldn't understand why they weren't more careful.

'We'd be there on the spot, transport costs minimised. We could even start our own oil palm plantation. That's the way things will go in the future. Do you know all palm oil comes from trees growing wild in the forest? No wonder we can't get a regular supply. A plantation and a crushing mill on the spot would be an economical, reliable source, and industry in this country is screaming out for it. It would be a winner, but we've got to get in first.'

'You and your winners!'

'We can't lose, Len, but we can't afford to sit around and wait. The opportunity will be gone if somebody else corners the market. Look, we have Father's power of attorney from when he was ill last year. Let's use it and start the thing up.'

'Laurence!' Elin heard the horror in Leonard's voice. He'd lost his air of calm control. 'That's illegal.'

The match she tried to light rasped loudly. He must know she'd heard how he was trying to cheat his own father! The match went out. She had to strike another before the paper blazed up. She started to sweep the hearth.

'No, not illegal, he hasn't cancelled it.'

'Then morally wrong. You always want to use people for your own ends.'

'Oh, come on, Len.'

'I can't go along with that. You sail too close to the wind for me. You can buy me out when the time comes. I want to sleep easy in my bed.'

'Oh, for God's sake! You'll be sorry when I'm rich and you're still struggling on a salary.'

'How can you be so certain you're right? About the crushing mill and the plantation?'

'It stands to reason. I know what I'm doing.'

Elin slipped her brushes into her box and crept quietly away. She couldn't get over Mr Laurence wanting to do his own father down. He seemed fired with a terrible ambition. He'd get his business going, she was sure. He was clearly a man who always got his own way.

The days passed and Elin told herself she liked the place, that she'd bettered herself by coming. It was hard, of course, any new place was hard, and took a bit of getting used to. She really enjoyed her half day off.

Birkenhead was a revelation. She loved the mile-wide murky waters of the River Mersey with Liverpool crowding the opposite shore and freighters pounding busily up and down. The town hadn't existed before the industrial revolution. Then ferry boats were built with engines, and easy access allowed the rich merchants of Liverpool to build large comfortable villas on the Birkenhead side. Docks, shipbuilding and heavy industry followed, and soon terraces of little houses for the workers crowded as close to the docks as possible. Their red bricks were smoke-blackened now, but their blue slate roofs still shone in the rain.

Bridie told her she must see the park, even Mr Laurence had a high opinion of it and had said New York City had copied the design for its own Central Park. It stretched for more acres than the Tonteg holding. Elin couldn't believe the ponds, trees, walks and cricket pitches were all for the pleasure of the people.

There was more dirt and poverty here than where she'd come from, but she loved the vitality of the people. Peck said there were more Irish in Liverpool than there were in Dublin. Bridie's people had come over during one of the potato famines, and so had Mrs Dooley's. There were certainly more Welsh here than she'd expected. When she recognised their accents in the shops, she turned away half afraid she might come face to face with the Minister of Llanddolfa Chapel.

Mrs Dooley had said she could take time off for chapel, but she hadn't been. Bridie, Daisy and Mrs Dooley went to Mass very early on Sunday mornings. Peck took off at eleven supposedly for church, but Bridie said he walked in the park on fine days and went to the pub when it rained.

Elin walked down Grange Road and round the shops crowded with Christmas shoppers. Buskers played carols in the street on fiddles and banjos. She'd never seen so many desirable clothes. There were artificial silk stockings in the new nude shade for a shilling, and celanese camiknickers, almost like Sybil Oxley's, at affordable prices. She could buy a dress in the new tubular style in beige rayon. There were headbands and feathers and ribbons galore. She'd never dreamed such an array of affordable novelties was possible.

The huge market had even better bargains. The crowds were bigger, and there was more jostling and shouting. Elin loved the teeming life of Birkenhead. It was just a pity she had no money to spare yet. The train fare here had taken what she'd saved.

She'd found her way down to Woodside again. It no longer seemed formidable. An accordion band played 'God Rest Ye Merry Gentlemen', while a mongrel sat guarding the cap of coppers on the pavement.

She looked through the iron grille at the floating landing stage, and the river. The smell of the sea was tantalisingly close. Bridie told her it was well worth taking the ferry trip to Liverpool but it cost twopence each way, so that, too, would have to wait until she was paid.

For Elin the morning of Christmas Eve started like any other, except that she now had seven fires to light and tend instead of five, but she was managing them better. Two maiden aunts had come to swell the family, and a distant cousin.

She found the preparations in the kitchen unbelievable. A turkey, a goose, two ducks and a capon waited in the cold room. Two large iced and decorated Christmas cakes were ready in the pantry, with several plum puddings. A whole

York ham was baking in the slow oven now, and a tongue simmering on the stove. Yesterday, she'd worked with Mrs Dooley and Daisy to make five dozen mince pies, a raised ham pie, two trifles and a jelly. Today they were to make two chocolate Yule logs and a plain sponge, chestnut stuffing, sausage stuffing, sage and onion stuffing, as well as brandy butter and Cumberland sauce. Already, every meal was a feast.

Bridie had the flat irons in the fire and was pressing Mrs Oxley's personal linen.

'Isn't this lovely?' she asked frequently, holding a flimsy décolleté nightdress against her own ample chest for them to admire. Elin had never seen underclothes like them. Mrs Oxley even had the new Kestos brassieres; they all examined those closely. There were no corsets or petticoats like Bessie had worn, nor warm winter combinations.

Somewhere around mid-morning, the bell rang in the drawing room and since Peck was engaged with old Mr Oxley, and Bridie still had several gowns to press, Cook sent Elin up to see what they wanted.

She heard the laughter before she opened the door. When she did, she crossed the threshold and stopped. There were boxes all over the floor, and two small children were busy spreading their contents everywhere. Tinsel, candles, and coloured glass baubles for the tree covered every table and most chairs. Small toys mingled with branches of holly and mistletoe on the carpet.

Such an untidy mess, was her first thought, as her foot narrowly missed squashing a lead soldier. The children wouldn't be allowed to make it if their parents had to pick it up.

'We need help.' Mr Laurence's face was shining with Christmas spirit. His brother sat by the window, his legs outstretched, a glass in his hand. 'Can you put some of these things on the tree for us?'

'Yes, sir.' Only Nanny in her starched white uniform was working, tying coloured thread round small toys to hang them up. Mr Laurence pushed a box of glass baubles at Elin.

'Do you want them anywhere special, sir?'

'Just make the tree look nice. Something on every branch.' Elin picked up a red ball, but found most of the lower branches already had something tied to them.

'Do you think I've bought too large a tree, Elin?' he asked.

'Oh no, sir.'

'Of course you have, Laurence,' his wife said sourly. She was sitting near the fire, her legs neatly crossed on a footstool. Elin had heard Peck say the same very positively after he'd had to help offload the tree from the cart and erect it in the drawing room.

'It doesn't touch the ceiling, sir.'

'That's thirty feet high in here. Nanny is nervous of climbing the stepladder. How do you feel about it?'

She looked at him shyly. Decorate the tree! Surely they didn't consider that work? If they didn't want to do that, what would they enjoy? She'd never seen such gorgeous decorations, nor such a majestic tree. They'd always had a tree at Tonteg, dug up from the shelter belt Owen Roberts had planted to shield the house from the north wind. But a token tree compared with this.

'I'd like to, sir.'

'Right, go ahead.' He adjusted the stepladder. She went up quickly, feeling awkward because they were all watching her. Mr Laurence slid a box onto the top step, full of chocolates covered in silver paper.

'Is this for me, Daddy?' Mary, a chubby four-year-old with fine wispy hair so blonde it was almost white, had found a doll and was cradling it in her arms. 'Can I have it now?'

'Yes, cherub,' her father indulged. Elin studied the child. The pet name suited her, she really was cherubic. Her cousin Robert, five years older, had skin that was lightly tanned. His hair was several shades darker but still blond. Beautiful children, beautifully turned out. Mary wore a red velvet dress with a white lace collar.

'This is going to be a marvellous Christmas.' Robert was agog with excitement, setting out toy soldiers. High above on the stepladder, Elin agreed with him. Much better than at Tonteg, where Bessie made little parcels by covering empty matchboxes with coloured paper. Elin couldn't remember ever having a Christmas tree at home.

Mr Laurence stood beneath her, his eyes on a level with her feet, changing the box, so that there would be a good mix of decorations on the branches, standing ready to move the steps when she'd filled every branch she could reach.

She didn't know why she got the feeling he was looking up the voluminous skirt of her print dress, or what might be visible to attract him. Her sturdy black lace-up shoes showed an inch or so of black cotton stocking. Hardly worth investing 1/3d per pair, since the dress came to within four inches of the floor. She told herself she was being fanciful. Mr Laurence wouldn't be interested in her when his wife was so elegant, in sheer beige silk stockings and button-over high-heeled shoes. Bridie had said she was svelte, a word she'd picked up from the magazines discarded to the kitchen once they were finished with in the drawing room. Elin would swear she was wearing lipstick, too.

As she bent down to the box of baubles, Elin pushed against a branch. It scratched her face. She jerked away, and the branch snapped back, hooking her cap right off her head. She had to steady herself against the steps, then she smoothed her hair back. Mr Laurence laughed, and the children joined in.

'Look at her cap! Shall we leave it there over Christmas?' Mary clapped her hands.

'Not very Christmassy.' Nine-year-old Robert screwed up his Oxley nose. He, too, had the family characteristics.

Elin felt a flush run up her cheeks as she snatched it back and pulled it down hard to cover every single hair.

'Well, Elin, you are fashionable! I'd never have believed they'd heard of bobbed hair in the Welsh hills. Who cut it for you?'

She knew her cheeks must be scarlet. He was being so personal, and it was almost as though he knew what had happened. 'Mrs Roberts, sir, as I used to work for.'

He laughed. 'A hairdresser?'

'No, but she used to cut her children's hair, and her husband's.'

'Where did she learn to cut the bob then?'

'It's not a real bob, just short, sir.' It made her feel sick to talk about it even now. Bessie had levelled it off for her on that awful Sunday night.

'Well, don't expect help from your present mistress when you need it trimmed.'

Elin came slowly down the stepladder as Mrs Oxley said icily, 'Take your cap off again, Elin. Let's see this fashionable hairstyle.' Her own hair was golden blonde too, expertly shingled with not a hair out of place. She was groomed in a way Elin knew she could never achieve.

She hesitated, not knowing whether they were making fun of her or not. She felt in some way they were using her to needle each other. She snatched it off.

'Turn round,' Sybil Oxley commanded. Elin wanted to cover her face with her hands. She couldn't forget going through all this on the night she'd arrived.

'Would you go to Mrs Roberts yourself, Sybil, if she were nearer?' Laurence Oxley's fringe moustache was turning up in a smile.

'Oh no, ma'am,' Elin said, burning with embarrassment. 'Your style is much more . . . svelte.'

Sybil Oxley's eyebrows rose in weary scorn. 'I shall stay with Malcolm, thank you, Laurence.'

Elin wished there was some way she could escape. She picked up another box of glass baubles and headed back to the steps. She couldn't help but notice Nanny's starched disapproval, her prim lips set in a hard straight line.

Lunch had come and gone. The rich food had left Laurence Oxley feeling bloated. He glared at the unfamiliar bulk of the Christmas tree, letting the brandy roll over his tongue. Hell! It was supposed to be the season of good will.

'What else do you have to spend your money on, Sybil?' He was making a big effort to keep his temper. Lashing out at her would do no good.

'That's not the point. It's my money, not yours.' Her

steely eyes met his, he could almost see the sparks, but she was exercising restraint too.

'The car is for both of us.' He had to stay calm like Len. Damn Sybil, she was being difficult. He got to his feet. 'How about another brandy, coz?'

Too late, he remembered she hated to be called cousin now she was his wife. During their teens she'd liked it, said it made her feel part of the family.

'No.' Her grey eyes glittered with fury. 'You might at least have discussed it first.'

'I did.' Where was everybody? With a house so full of visitors, surely somebody could come in and save him from this?

'I don't remember.' She'd changed before lunch into an elegant grey dress that fell in soft folds, and was stretched out in a chair the other side of the fireplace, her feet on a footstool.

'You said we didn't need another car.'

'Well, we don't!'

'I explained why we did. The Ford's giving a lot of trouble. John doesn't seem to be able to fix it.'

'Why can't you pay for it then? Where's your own money?'

'You forget, Sybil, I haven't inherited a fortune as you have. My father is still alive.'

'Sometimes I think that's why you wanted to marry me.'

'Nonsense, love,' he said uneasily.

'But you have an adequate income. Your father pays all the household bills. Where's that gone? You're not gambling or anything?' Sybil was a year older than he was and had always had this big sister attitude.

'I'm very careful with money, I keep telling you. I've just set up a business, making tyres. At the moment things are a bit tight. Surely five hundred pounds isn't much to ask?'

'Well, yes, it is.' The family likeness was strong. Sybil had the same straight nose and blonde hair, but her chin was sharper, and her thin lips had a discontented droop. She had neither Laurence's energy nor Leonard's tranquillity. There was about her the look of a spoilt child who had been led to believe the world was her oyster and found instead it was a gritty irritation.

He heard the tap on the door, but Sybil was in full flood.

'I don't want a Bentley. I'd prefer a little Morris, something I could learn to drive myself.'

The door opened, he saw the new housemaid peep round. Her slanting golden eyes riveted his attention.

'Yes?' His voice was brusque.

'Please sir, John says there's a waggon in the yard delivering drums of something, and the man wants paying.'

'Drums?' Sybil asked sharply. 'What sort of drums?' She swung her legs to the floor. 'I suppose you expect me to pay him, too?'

'No dear. Father will pay, household account.'

'Please sir, John wants to know where you want them put.'

'I'll come.' He wanted to escape from Sybil, and it was an excuse to follow the girl. He hadn't been able to get her out of his mind since he'd watch her fasten the ornaments on the tree. There was a seductive grace about every movement she made, bending to the box and lifting her arms to the highest branches. Even her ugly print dress couldn't hide it. She was moving quickly ahead of him down the kitchen stairs. It didn't please him to hear Sybil's high heels tapping behind on the stone floor.

'What is it?' Sybil peered through the kitchen window, baulking at the cold damp air coming through the door. Laurence went out and saw a big bay carthorse backing a dray filled with forty-five gallon drums into the yard.

'Petrol, ma'am.' Mrs Dooley, her podgy hands floury, closed the door behind him. Almost immediately it flew open again, and Laurence was wiping his feet hard on the doormat.

'Do we need all that petrol? I hear it's quite dangerous,' Sybil said. 'Fires . . .'

'We always get a dozen drums, Sybil. Have to buy it this way, till there's more garages selling it. If we have a car, we need petrol.' He pushed his wiry fair hair back from his face and forced a smile. 'If you want me to invest some of your capital, I could build a whole network of garages. They could service vehicles too, sell spares and things. Even you can see the need. It's a marvellous opportunity to get in at the beginning.'

'Oh, for heavens' sake! Do you want us both to be penniless?'

In the awkward pause that followed, he paced to the table. 'Can I stir the puddings, Mrs Dooley? I hear it brings good luck.'

'We're going to need it,' Sybil muttered sourly. Bridie failed to stifle her giggle. It came fizzing out.

'The puddings were stirred in October, sir.' Cook's heavy jowls quivered with surprise. 'Sorry, sir, it's too late to stir.'

'Just boiling them up again, we are.' The new housemaid turned her slanting eyes on him again. He mustn't let Sybil see how charming he found her lilting voice. He mustn't let anyone see. He leapt for the stairs and the kitchen door slammed behind them.

'Don't get any ideas about that girl and her yellow cat's eyes.' Sybil was still at his heels. 'I hope you aren't lusting after her already.'

He put on a spurt, taking the stairs two at a time. Damn Sybil. He'd been dumbfounded that she'd hired such a good-looking girl. When she'd got rid of Ruby, he'd expected her replacement to be a replica of Mrs Dooley. But none of this would have happened if she hadn't put him out of her bed. Pregnancy was no excuse. How did other women manage? Sybil had made heavy weather of all her pregnancies. She'd been out of step with everything from day one. Totally unreasonable. Not that she was so obliging even when she wasn't pregnant.

Christmas Day dawned. Elin felt excitement building in the atmosphere as they hurried to get their chores done. Everybody was in high spirits.

At Tonteg, the treadmill of work had gone on throughout Christmas. The cows had to be milked and the sheep fed. They'd had presents, and roast goose for dinner, but it had seemed like a Sunday.

The Oxleys made much more of Christmas. Their lunch consisted of six other courses arranged round the turkey and Christmas pudding. It was mid-afternoon when they finished eating. Afterwards, Elin helped Bridie clear the table and set out a cold buffet on the sideboard. At supper time, the family would help themselves.

That done, the staff were free to celebrate their own Christmas. Elin rushed upstairs to change. She tossed her print dress over a chair and put on her blue suit. There was to be a special dinner in the kitchen. A feast with exotic foods Elin had never seen before.

'Left over from upstairs,' Daisy sniffed. 'I like the turkey best.'

'You should eat more,' Peck advised her in his lordly manner, looking up from his plate of pheasant. 'You're just skin and bone.'

'Nobody could say that about me.' Mrs Dooley's mounds of flesh shook with mirth. Bridie giggled.

Peck put down the wing he'd been nibbling. 'It's time you grew up, Bridie,' he said. 'You sound younger than Daisy.'

'Better than being miserable like you.' Bridie tossed her head back, bringing heavy tendrils of dark hair round her face.

When the meal was over, Peck brought down his gramophone and his record collection. He had all the latest from Gertrude Lawrence to selections from *Showboat*. They took turns to wind it up and choose the music. When Bridie put on a Henry Hall record, Peck came to claim a dance from Elin.

She didn't know what to make of him. Tonight he was laughing and enjoying himself, a different man. She'd never danced before with a man pulling her close like this. Father would explode if he could see her now. Peck was still twirling her round to 'Yes We Have No Bananas' when the family came down to see the fun.

The ladies stayed only fifteen minutes and handed out parcels. Elin sniffed with delight at the tin of bath powder she received; it smelled of money. She'd never had such a luxury before. Mr Laurence and Mr Leonard brought some bottles of wine with them and joined in the dancing.

'Come on, Elin, have a noggin.' Mr Laurence pressed a glass on her.

'What is it?' She knew she sounded suspicious, and laughed. All Llanddolfa was suspicious of alcohol, she'd grown up that way. Evan Jones would be proud of her.

'Punch. Just fruit juice and white wine. It won't do you any harm.'

She sipped cautiously.

'It's nice, isn't it?'

Elin smiled. She didn't like the taste. It was strong and bitter and she'd seen him lace the bowl with brandy. She left her full glass on the table. But she liked it very much when Laurence asked her to dance. She told herself it was silly to be nervous of men, she was doing well. Getting more used to them. Mrs Dooley said he was popular with everybody. Even though he was master and rich, there was no need to be scared of him. Elin had a natural grace that enabled her to follow his steps, though she'd no idea what she was dancing. She was enjoying herself.

At midnight, Mr Laurence went upstairs for more bottles. Another batch of punch was made. There was a buzz of chatter and laughter. Bridie's cheeks were on fire.

Elin felt her eyes closing. She'd been up since six that morning and had hardly stopped all day, but she didn't want to miss the fun. Mr Laurence came to dance with her twice more and somehow managed to steer her into the passage by the time the record came to an end. It was darker here, they had the place to themselves. He bent and kissed her lips.

'Oh!' Elin jerked back like a frightened kitten. In the distance she could hear Mrs Dooley saying it was time they all went to bed.

'An old English custom,' Mr Laurence murmured in her ear. 'A kiss under the mistletoe brings luck at Christmas.'

She looked up. There were a few sprigs tied to the pantry door. She couldn't remember seeing them there before. Then his lips were down on hers again, his tongue searching, demanding.

She tore herself from his grasp and ran upstairs to her

bedroom, slamming the door shut and leaning against it, fighting for breath. Was he following? She'd thought she heard footsteps on the stairs behind her. Why did he have to spoil everything, kissing her like that? There must be something about her that made men do it. She shivered. Evan Jones had been right.

He was going away, she heard his footsteps retreat to the floor below and a door bang far away. She could relax. Only then did she put on the light to see her way to bed. Of course, it was Christmas, Mr Laurence meant nothing.

CHAPTER FOUR

It was three days after Boxing Day and Peck's half day. He was ready to go out.

'Don't forget old Mr Oxley, Elin, he'll go to sleep and then complain if he doesn't get his tea.'

'I won't.'

At four o'clock, Elin removed her coarse apron in the kitchen and went to knock at the study door. There was no response, so she went in. A fetid wall of heat met her, smelling of illness and old age. Old Mr Oxley sprawled in his leather armchair, snoring loudly, with his mouth open. Only his false teeth prevented his mouth being a cavern; his cheeks were hollows. She'd not seen him this close before, and couldn't help but notice his clothes hung on him as though he'd shrunk. He looked, she thought, as though he wouldn't have much longer in this world. Peck had said he was ill.

The fire was dying back. She tiptoed over, poked it back to life, and tipped the contents of the brass scuttle on it.

'Bridie,' he croaked. When she turned, he was struggling to pull himself up the chair, his grey eyes glittering at her from deep sockets.

'I'm Elin, sir. I'm new here.' She put an arm through his and pulled him till he sat upright. He felt just skin and bone. She plumped up the cushion behind his head.

'Shall I bring your tea, Mr Oxley? It's four o'clock.'

'Yes, just tea.' He was struggling for breath. 'Nothing to eat.'

Five minutes later, when she returned with his tray, he was asleep again. Undecided, she put it on the table.

'Shall I pour it for you, sir?' She spoke loudly and his

'Shall I pour it for you, sir?' She spoke loudly and his eyes flickered open, stared at her blankly. 'Your tea, sir.'

'Thank you, Bridie.'

'Sugar and milk, sir?' He didn't answer so she put it in anyway, then pulled the low table forward and placed the Rockingham china cup and saucer beside him.

When she returned with the refilled coal scuttle, he woke again.

'Ah tea,' he murmured, reaching for the cup. His skin was tight and grey, except round his mouth where it was tinged with blue. It looked clammy. Elin turned on a lamp, closed the curtains against the fading afternoon and left.

It was well after six when she went once more to tend the fire. Again he was snoring hard and needed pulling up in his chair.

'Can I get you something else, sir?'

'Scotch.' His tongue and lips were coated, and his breath foul. His eyes went to the tantalus on the table.

Elin's heart fluttered as she made herself go over to it. Whisky! Father had been convinced that to have it in the house would sell his soul to the Devil. The congregation of Llanddolfa Chapel had been of like mind.

There were two decanters set into a silver cage which she couldn't open. Both contained a glistening tawny fluid, though one was darker than the other. She had no idea which was whisky. She picked up the tea tray and ran down to the kitchen to ask.

'Smell them to see,' Bridie advised. 'The other will be brandy.'

'I don't know . . . I mean that won't help. I don't know how either smells.'

'The Temperance Society would love you.' Bridie's giggle came fizzing out as she set a little tray with a jug filled with water, and a matching tumbler.

She accompanied Elin to the study. Taking a key from a little drawer in the side table, she pressed it into Elin's hand, jabbing her finger towards the lefthand decanter.

'How much?' Elin whispered.

'About an inch.' Bridie hurried back to the kitchen. Elin

fumbled with the lock of the tantalus and finally got the decanter out. It was heavier than she'd expected. She looked across at the old man but he was dozing again. Luckily, time meant nothing to him, he wouldn't realise how long she was taking. She put a stiff measure in the tumbler.

'How much water, Mr Oxley?' He didn't stir. She went closer. 'How much water do you want, Mr Oxley?'

This time he snorted and opened his eyes. 'Little.'

An ounce flopped in and splashed over onto her hand. On the way back to the kitchen, she put her tongue on it. It didn't taste of anything.

At seven o'clock, Bridie said: 'Where's he want his dinner then? I've set his place in the dining room.'

'I don't know, he hasn't moved from his chair all afternoon.' Elin frowned. 'He looks really poorly.'

'Go and ask him.'

She went into his room and turned on another light. The old man grunted and opened his eyes. 'Get me another Scotch, will you?'

Elin refilled his glass and asked him about dinner.

'What is it?'

'Poached turbot and chicken casserole.'

'Just the fish. I'll have it here.'

In the kitchen, she set a tray. When Cook dished up the turbot, she placed the silver cover on top, and took it up. The old man had slipped down the chair again, his mouth wide open. She put the tray down and went to help him sit up.

Immediately she sensed the change. The whisky glass was on its side, its contents darkening the red carpet. He wasn't breathing! Elin jerked backwards, her hand flying to her mouth. She had to force herself to look at him again. His face was white and slack. His chest still.

'Jesus!' Her first thought was that the whisky had killed him, just as everybody in Llanddolfa would have predicted. She backed to the door in horror. 'Oh Jesus!' The room was spinning. She felt dizzy.

She turned and ran to the dining room where the family was at dinner. Bridie was handing the turbot round the table. Everybody looked up as Elin crashed the door back.

'Old Mr Oxley's dead,' she gasped. 'Dead, I'm certain.' She looked round the table as five pairs of eyes stared back at her, frozen. Then Sybil Oxley dropped her fork onto her plate with a crash. Laurence Oxley leapt to his feet first, but both men came. Elin ran ahead, back to the study.

'Do something,' she urged. 'The doctor . . .'

Laurence was feeling for the old man's pulse.

'He's dead, I know it.' Tears were blurring Elin's sight.

'Yes, I think you're right.' Leonard was standing over him.

Hysteria rose in her throat, she'd never seen a corpse before. 'I killed him! The whisky!' she ended on a strangled scream.

'Nonsense.' Laurence took a tumbler from a cupboard, half filled it, and pushed it into her hand. 'It's brandy. Go on, you've had a shock.'

'No, I daren't . . .'

'Go on, get it down you, you'll feel better.' He pushed the glass to her lips. Obediently she gulped. It burned like fire, making her cough.

'Drink,' he insisted. 'It's medicinal, we all need a drink now.' He poured another two fingers into the glass she held.

'I'd better phone for Harris,' Leonard said. 'We'll need a death certificate. You found him like this?'

'Yes, sir,' she coughed. 'Only minutes since he asked for whisky. Did I give him too much?'

'No, it's nothing you've done. Don't be silly.' Laurence paused. 'Yes, Len, get Harris, and tell the ladies.'

'And he wanted his dinner. Asked what it was.'

'It's all right, Elin. It's the best thing for him.' Shocked, she stared up into resolute blue eyes. Hadn't she heard him say how much he wanted his father's business? He wasn't sorry! 'He was old and frail.'

'He died alone. Nobody with him.' Her teeth chattered. She was beginning to feel light-headed. 'He would have wanted you with him. Stands to reason. Nobody wants to die alone.'

'I don't think it would have bothered him.'

'He needed you.'

'For God's sake pull yourself together. It's happened, and nothing can undo it.'

'I should have known. Should have been able to let you know.'

'For God's sake!' He poured more brandy into her glass and pushed it to her lips. 'Go to bed, you'll feel better in the morning.'

Elin sank down on a chair, her head in her hands. She thought perhaps she should. The room was spinning round her. She felt sick. 'Mrs Dooley . . .'

'I'll tell her I sent you to bed. Go on.' Leonard was holding the door open for her.

'Just you and me now, Len,' Laurence was saying, the triumph in his voice unmistakable. 'What about the crushing mill? No need to wait.'

'The cards certainly fall your way.'

'I'm one of the world's winners, Len. Can't go wrong.'

Elin didn't know how she pulled herself up the steep stairs. She fell onto her bed, only just able to struggle out of her clothes. She closed her eyes, and the bed was spinning too. Better to keep them open. She'd forgotten to put the light out, but she couldn't get up. She tried to focus on the text on the wall. She knew it said: 'Blessed are the pure in heart, for theirs is the Kingdom of Heaven.' It was floating about, the writing distorted. At last she fell into a restless doze. It was hours later when she heard her bedroom door open.

'I wondered how you were, Elin.' His voice sounded a long way off.

She still felt fuzzy and sleep-sodden. Was she dreaming? It was hard to open her eyes, but when she did, Laurence Oxley was standing by her bed, unbuttoning his shirt. The room was turning slowly. She closed her eyes, trying to still the movement, but it made it worse.

When she opened them again, his torso was bare, attractive wide shoulders with a downing of bronze hair on his chest. He was undoing his trousers. She sat up in horror, realising his intention.

'No,' she gasped. She felt the thin blankets being pulled off her, and though the flock mattress was very firm, she felt it move as he got in beside her. His fingers came across her mouth as though to soothe her.

'Shhh.' They smelled of cigars. He was cold, but his arm came round her, pulling her close. It seemed he'd put the light out.

'Are you feeling better?' His breath was warm against her cheek. His moustache tickled. Elin felt terrible. Her head throbbed. She put it down on his shoulder. His flesh had a masculine fragrance. She knew he was taking off her nightdress. His fingers were soothing her bare back.

With one deft movement, he tossed her back across the pillows. She caught sight of his chin above her, and panicked.

'No! Oh no!' This was what she must avoid at all costs. She felt nausea rising in her throat, the drink had made her feel out of control. She had no strength left.

'It's all right, Elin.' His voice was a soothing whisper. 'Safe as houses.'

'No. You'll give me a baby,' she protested, panic rising in her.

'No, I won't. Modern science and Marie Stopes can take care of that. No, you'll be all right.' His mouth was on hers, silencing her, pressing and more passionate. Elin tried to think what she'd done to get Mr Laurence into her bed. She couldn't understand how this had come about. Father must be right. It was something inherent in her.

'You're beautiful,' he whispered. 'You know that? Beautiful.'

She didn't know when he left her. She woke up feeling sick, and knew immediately she was alone in her bed. She pulled herself up against the pillow feeling sore and bruised. It had been real enough, not a dream. She felt stunned, sickened. It must be her. There must be some signal that went out to men that she was different. That she had bad blood. How else would Mr Laurence know? Father was right about that, as he'd been about the whisky.

She let out a long shuddering breath. How would she ever look Mr Laurence in the face again? Or Mrs Oxley? She certainly couldn't go near Father, he'd know immediately it had happened.

The room swam as she got to her feet to put on the light. She had a raging thirst. There was clean water on her washstand and she poured some into her tooth mug. She drank it back, refilled the mug and drank again.

She felt dirty and sticky. She washed herself down with her face flannel and cold water. Then she shook on some of the bath powder Mrs Oxley had given her for Christmas. It smelled fresh and flowery but she still felt unclean.

Why, oh why had it happened to her? She felt tears start to her eyes, but she mustn't cry, because her eyes would be red and sore in the morning. It would draw attention to her. Everybody would know she'd wept, and would know what she'd done. Perhaps it would show anyway; she felt quite a different person. Mr Laurence had been rough. He'd pinned her hands beneath her, and not allowed her to push against him. She'd thought gentlemen were always gentle, but perhaps that was her fault too, she'd made him like a wild animal.

A tear washed down her face though she tried to hold it back. Perhaps they would think she cried for old Mr Oxley and not herself, but she must not cry. Far below she heard the grandfather clock begin to strike. She counted five. There was no sign of dawn in the sky, she'd go back to bed. The streaks of blood on the sheet shocked her. Proof for everybody to see. She sponged at them with her flannel till they smudged away. Then she ripped the sheet off, turned it over, and made the bed up freshly. It felt cold and damp when she got in, and still not clean. She tried to remember exactly what had happened. She was still confused as to why. What had she done to bring this on herself?

When the time came to get up, she found the house in semi-darkness. Mrs Dooley instructed all blinds were to be kept half down and all curtains half-drawn as a sign of respect. Peck put the light on in the dining room as he spread the cloth.

'One setting less this morning,' he said cheerfully, lifting one eyebrow at Elin as she brought in the coals. She found it hard to believe Mr Oxley had sat there to eat his breakfast yesterday. So many terrible things had happened since. Order had gone.

Later, when she went to the kitchen, Peck was sitting in the armchair in front of the fire. Bridie was busy cutting bread for breakfast, thin slices, both white and brown, and then thicker for toast. Elin put a tray on the table and loaded it with four kinds of marmalade, two kinds of honey and Mrs Oxley's strawberry preserve.

'It's all right for some.' Mrs Dooley was busy at the gas stove. 'Got nothing to do, Peck?'

'They'll all be late for breakfast this morning,' he sniffed.

'Why? Mr Laurence is an early riser. He always wants his breakfast by half seven.'

'Up half the night, wasn't he?' Peck sniffed superciliously.

Elin dropped the butter dish onto the tray. Did Peck know?

'Sat up late drinking they did. Almost two bottles of whisky between them. Can't see they'll be up early after that.'

'I expect you helped.' Mrs Dooley's triple chins quivered as she spoke. 'Bet half a bottle went down your throat.'

'No,' he denied quickly.

'Then it's waiting in your room till you feel more like it,' she retorted.

Elin's heart fluttered in her chest like a nervous bird. He'd not been to bed then before coming to her room. She crashed the sugar bowls together, brown for the porridge, white for the fruit and for tea.

Mrs Dooley turned on her. 'My, you're jumpy this morning. You mustn't let it upset you. It's a good way to go. Quickly like that. He was an old man.'

'I'd be jumpy if I'd found him,' Bridie sympathised.

Elin snatched up the laden tray and made for the dining room. Dread spiralled through her when she saw Mr Laurence go in before her.

'Good morning, sir.' She busied herself setting out the milk and sugar.

'Good morning, Elin.' His voice was full of good will as

he swept back the curtains to let in the grey morning light. 'We've got to be able to see what we eat.' His eyes came round to her face and he smiled. 'All right, this morning?'

She backed to the door. 'Ye-es.'

'Good girl. Tell Peck we're ready.' He rang the bell to reinforce the message. She turned and ran downstairs, her face scarlet with embarrassment.

When breakfast was over and the beds made, Elin was sent to turn out the study and remove all traces of old Mr Oxley. She had to steel herself to go in. The worst thing was the sickly smell of the old man, as putrid as ever, clinging to everything. She went to open the window. Some of the sashes were stiff, one cord broke, so that the window slid lower on one side than the other, but the garden was full of damp mist. It billowed in fresh and cold.

She hated the monkeyskin rugs as she shook them through the window. The dust of ages had settled into the indented hide of the stuffed crocodile, and no amount of flicking at it with a duster would remove it. She washed the hearth, brushed the carpet, and polished the tables. Peck came to carry out the leather armchair he'd died in.

'It's to go up to the attic, Mrs Oxley doesn't want it here. Nice chair though, do you want it in your room?'

'No,' she almost screamed. She didn't even like the idea of having it on the same floor as her bedroom.

Preparations for lunch were well in hand.

'I'm going up to pay my last respects to old Mr Oxley.' Mrs Dooley's bracelets of flesh shook as she took off her enormous apron. 'He's laid out now in his bedroom.'

Elin shuddered, her golden eyes wide with trepidation.

'Bridie's been. It's the thing to do. He'll expect it.'

Elin wanted to ask who would expect it. The Lord on high? Mr Laurence? Surely not old Mr Oxley?

'Do you want to come with me?'

In case it was the Lord, she decided she'd better. Her mouth was dry, and when she got to his room, she hardly dared look at the corpse.

'He can't hurt you.' Mrs Dooley's bulk shifted. 'Wouldn't

have hurt you when he was alive, why should he now?'

Elin breathed again, she needn't have worried. He looked better than he'd done alive. His mouth and eyes were closed. He lay on his bed, wearing his black worsted Sunday suit, and polished Oxfords. He might have been dozing after his dinner, except he'd have taken off his shoes. Banks of hothouse chrysanthemums filled the room with a bitter-sweet scent. Mrs Dooley was the only person Elin saw shed a tear for him, though Mr Leonard went round with a serious face, and both the Mrs Oxleys dabbed at their eyes with lace handkerchiefs.

It was three nights later, and the night of the funeral, when she heard her bedroom door open again. She pulled herself up on her pillows to see Mr Laurence move like a shadow to her side. It hadn't occurred to her he might come again. What had happened had been brought on by the stress of old Mr Oxley's death, by the whisky, by something she'd done.

'I need a bit of comfort, Elin,' he whispered, and her hand flew to her mouth.

'No,' she shouted. 'No.'

'Ssssh, not so loud.' His fingers were gentle against her lips. Her heart was thudding. Why hadn't she complained, made a fuss last time? He obviously thought she condoned it.

The weeks were passing, Laurence continued to come to her room on three or four nights each week. There were nights when Elin wanted him to come, and felt exhilarated by his lovemaking. But when he wasn't with her, nothing took away the awful nagging anxiety that he'd father a child on her. She felt cold every time she thought about it. It had happened to Bethan, and it had happened to her mother. Her father had predicted it would happen to her. When she was due, she was sick with dread for two days, followed by blessed relief when proof appeared that all was well. She made up her mind it would have to stop.

On her next day off, she bought herself a small bolt, some screws and a screw driver. Laurence would surely go away when he found he couldn't get in. She found it hard to fix, but managed it eventually and went to bed the next night feeling more secure. He didn't come, or the following night either. On the next, she was roused from a deep sleep.

'Open this door! Elin, do you hear me? Open this door.' He was rattling it against the bolt.

She was wide awake in an instant, fear pulling at her stomach. She wasn't going to let him in, not after paying a shilling for the bolt and ninepence for the screwdriver and screws.

'Go away,' she hissed, pulling the bedclothes over her head, but there was no way she could go back to sleep while he was out there.

'Elin, open it up. Come on. I don't want to break your door down.' She shut her eyes tight until she heard his footsteps going away. She was rigid with tension at standing up to him, but flushed too with success that she'd managed to keep him out. She was too agitated to sleep although her new alarm clock showed half an hour after midnight.

Then a new sound made her head jerk up from the pillow. A rasp of metal against metal. Surely not!

She got out of bed and switched on the electric light. Through the ill-fitting door, a file was working against the bolt.

'I'm going to get in, Elin. You might as well let me in now. It might take me an hour to file through this. Do you want to wait while I do it?'

Elin took a long shuddering breath, trying to make up her mind. The night was short enough as it was. The rasping started again, the head of the file darting in and out. A thin grey dust fell to the linoleum. She didn't doubt he'd get in eventually. Slowly she drew back the bolt.

'Mr Laurence, I don't want—'

'Oh yes you do, you enjoy it as much as I do.' He stood before her, smiling. His hands went to her hips. She retreated to the bed. 'That was naughty. Do you know that? A tease.'

'It was no tease, I meant it.'

'Nonsense, you let me in, didn't you?'

'Why don't you do it with your wife? That's what you're supposed to do.'

'She's having another baby. She's not up to it now.'

'But why me?' she wailed. 'Why pick on me?'

His face was close to hers. She could see the fixity of purpose in his blue eyes, the ruthless gleam. How could she have doubted he'd get his way?

'Because I like you. Because you're beautiful, and because you like me a little. You do like me, don't you, Elin?'

She turned her face into the pillow and refused to answer. The truth was he fascinated her. But she was playing with fire, he could only bring trouble.

'Look then, I'll make it worth your while.' He lifted the trousers he'd just shed, felt in a pocket and slid a coin onto her dressing-table. 'Now then, is that enough?'

Elin froze, it was not what she'd meant. Take money for this? She felt worse, cheapened and dirty.

'All right.' She heard the clatter of sovereigns. 'For all the other nights.' The tears ran down Elin's cheeks, but he didn't even notice.

'Look, I've brought you a present,' he said. 'I wouldn't have if I'd known you were going to lock me out. Don't ever do that again, Elin, I don't like it. Not in my own house. I'm good to you, aren't I? Thinking of you, and finding presents for you.' He was feeling in his jacket pocket, drawing out a bundle of black lace. He tossed it to her.

She gulped. 'Camiknickers! Are they hers? I mean Mrs Oxley's?'

He laughed again. 'Does it matter? Try them on. I want to see you in them.'

'Of course it matters,' she flared. 'She'll think I've stolen them. I could be blamed. Lose my character.'

'She'll never miss them,' he said with a bitter twist to his mouth. 'It's true I bought them for Sybil, but she won't wear them, she'll never miss them. You put them on. Don't be shy.'

'No. No, I . . .'

'Come on, now. I won't take no from you.'

For a moment Elin was tempted to scream, but what good

would that do? He was master here. The house was solidly built. She was the only person on this floor. His fingers were unfastening the buttons on her nightdress again, cold against her shoulder as he pulled it off. 'Don't just clutch them against you. Put them on.'

She ought to hang her head in shame, but his eyes were following every movement she made with appreciation.

'Come on, put your leg through here.' He was holding the garment open in front of her. 'Such a lovely body.' He fondled her rump as she tried to cover it. 'You should hold your shoulders back. Jut your breasts out. See how young and pointed they are, how firm. You've got something to be proud of there. You're wasted doing cleaning. You'll spoil your lovely hands.'

The garment felt cool and silky against her skin. It made her legs seem longer and more slender in the spotted mirror on her wardrobe. But it was wicked. Just to think of her father seeing her like this made her feel faint with terror.

'Turn round slowly.' His voice was thick. His hands slid up and down the thin silk, feeling her through it. Making her want it.

His face came closer to hers. He was already in another world. Like a child looking at chocolate. He frightened her. Had it been like this for her mother?

'Mr Laurence . . . I mean Laurence.' She made one last hopeless plea. 'Look, for me this is dangerous. It would be awful if I had a baby. Please leave me alone.'

He was already unhooking the straps of the black camiknickers from her shoulders. The garment slid down. For a second it rested on her hips, and then fell to the floor.

'Oh, you're lovely.' He pulled her to the bed, burying his face in her breasts. 'Safe as houses, Elin, I promise you. Haven't I shown you the Marie Stopes protection?'

'Are you sure it works?' She felt desperate. He was nuzzling her, his pencil moustache tickled her cheek.

'Of course it does.'

'But you didn't have it at the beginning.'

'Yes, I did. I got it for Sybil.'

'Fat lot of good it did her!'

He laughed, and she had to laugh with him. Next moment she was lying across the bed again. Laurence was making love so fiercely that she gasped and moaned, crying out with a full bodied lusty roar. She thought Bridie would hear and come rushing up to see if she was being murdered, but still the scream kept coming, swelling, spilling, she couldn't stop it. When it was all over, his smile was triumphant.

'You can't tell me you don't enjoy it,' he whispered.

Later he said, 'Look, you aren't pleased with me. I can see that but, Elin, you and I get on well.'

'We don't. I only see you here in my bed. You'd be ashamed of being seen with me.'

'No, I wouldn't. You're beautiful, Elin, such glorious, slanting golden eyes. I'd love to take you out. Everybody would envy me. We could have fun. Come on, say yes.'

'Yes, sir, I suppose.'

'Yes, Laurence, don't keep calling me sir. We could go away. What do you say to that?'

Her lips fell open. 'Go away?' She'd heard gossip some years ago about a Pwllheli schoolmaster who had gone away with the Baptist minister's wife. He'd found himself another school and a new life. She saw a new life for herself, being mistaken for Mr Laurence's wife. A life of gentle idleness and riches. She'd be a lady.

'Think about it,' he said. 'I'll work something out.'

For a week she thought and dreamed of nothing else. She was euphoric, quite sure he was planning how it could be done.

'Come on, Elin, jump to it.' Mrs Dooley's bracelets of flesh were shaking with irritation. 'What's the matter with you? I've asked you twice to take that tea tray up.'

'Sorry.' She jerked out of her dream world.

'You're half asleep. Better get to bed early tonight.'

She had to ask him the next time he came to her room, she couldn't wait any longer to hear about his plan.

'Did you mean it? About taking me away?'

He was resting, staring up at the ceiling. As he turned towards her she saw him smile in the half light. 'Yes, I need a break.'

She was suddenly rigid with disappointment. She couldn't believe that was all he'd intended, and yet . . . She tried to think exactly what he had said. Nothing about going away for good. It had all been wishful thinking on her part. What a fool she was!

'I could manage a couple of days away from the office next week.' She had to squeeze her eyes shut to stop the tears coming. 'A little holiday would do us both good.'

How could she have been so wrong? What good was a holiday if she then had to come back to this?

'I thought of Wales.'

Elin paled. 'Not Wales,' she almost screamed. What if she was seen and recognised by someone she knew?

'All right. The Lake District if you prefer. Or the Cotswolds. We could have some fun. Motor down, stay in a local inn. You'd like that, wouldn't you?'

'No.' For Elin, a holiday fell far short of what she'd been expecting. How could she have been so blind? Of course he wouldn't move away from his business, his home, his wife and family. 'No, it would be living in sin.'

He laughed. 'What difference does it make where you are?'

Elin gulped and got up quickly. She was living in as much sin here, and working hard as well. He was another woman's husband, wasn't he?

'I don't want you worn out carrying coals. I'd like you to have energy for other things.'

Her hairbrush snatched at her blonde hair, faster and faster. Other things! Why couldn't he say it outright? Lovemaking and sex. That's all he wanted from her.

'You fall asleep on me.' He was lying back on her bed, his arms behind his head. His chest and its brown fuzz seemed to grow in size.

'I've been up since six this morning, and I'll have to get up at six again.' Her eyes went to the clock. It was two already.

'That's what I mean, a rest would do you good.'

She saw herself sitting beside him in his car, like a real lady. Seeing the country, staying in hotels and being waited on. She was tempted, even if it was only for a few days.

'Tell Mrs Dooley your mother's ill and you want time off to go and see her.'

'My mother's dead. She knows that, I've made no secret of it.'

'Well, your father then.'

'Hum,' she sniffed.

'Mrs Dooley will ask my wife, and she'll agree. You pack your bag, and pretend you're going back to . . . wherever it is.'

'Llanddolfa.'

'And I'll pick you up at the tram stop. What could be easier? We'd have a good time, Elin.'

'Why don't you take your wife?'

'She doesn't want to come now. Doesn't feel up to travelling. The baby, you know. Not good for her.'

'Not good for me either,' Elin said tartly.

'Nonsense, you'd love it.'

She shook her head numbly.

'Then what do you want?'

'To be left in peace.'

'Nonsense, Elin. You must have some ambition.'

'I just want a good place to work, and not be bothered by men. Unless they want to marry me. Please God, I don't get caught.'

'Get caught? Who's going to catch us? Sybil?'

'Get caught with a baby, I mean.'

'You won't, don't worry.'

'I can't help it. It's as though I'm asking for it.'

'Modern science has the answer. Birth control.'

She closed her eyes, feeling poised on the top of a cliff with the ground beneath her feet crumbling. 'I wish you wouldn't come, all the same. I'm frightened.'

'It won't happen, Elin. Even if it does, I'd look after you, honestly. Come on now, give me another kiss. You're always expecting the worst.'

Elin sighed. He couldn't see how different things were for her. 'I suppose you have grand plans.'

'Well, I plan to be rich.'

'You are rich.'

'I'm not. My father made money, but he wasn't really rich. He grew too old. Too old-fashioned in his methods to make much, but he wouldn't let me take over, wouldn't listen to me. It was absolutely awful waiting in the wings for him to die.'

Elin felt as though he'd poured icy water down her back. With all the advantages he'd been given, he'd liked his father no better than she had hers.

'You don't have to wait any longer.' She pushed away from him. Picked up her hairbrush again.

'Between my father and my wife, I was much tied about. Did you know that, Elin?'

'Then there'll be no holding you now.'

He threw back his head and laughed, his pencil moustache quivering.

Elin shivered, she still missed her mother. Money was not everything.

CHAPTER FIVE

One night, Elin was having supper with Bridie and Peck when Nanny came into the kitchen. Her uniform crackled with starch as she bent to turn the gas up under the kettle.

'Mary's got chickenpox. She's quite poorly, and covered with spots.' She turned round, her prim lips sagging with exhaustion.

'On her face? They won't leave marks, will they?' Bridie swept the hair from her fiery cheeks; she always looked harassed when Mrs Dooley was off.

'They might.'

Elin remembered the Roberts children having chickenpox and felt a prickle of sympathy.

'She won't stop scratching, though I've told her it'll mark her for life.'

'Such a shame.' Elin thought of Mary's cherubic face and blue eyes. 'Wouldn't want to spoil her skin.'

'Such a pretty little thing,' Bridie said. 'With her ash-blonde feathery hair.'

'Angel's hair,' Elin said. 'Is she sick?'

'Fractious.'

'A good tanning on her backside is what she needs.' Peck got up to fetch the burgundy bottle from the draining board and poured what remained into a glass.

'She's hard work when she's ill.' Nanny pulled the knitted cosy over the aluminium teapot used in the nursery. 'I haven't had a minute to myself all day.'

'Trained you to get your own tea at last?' Peck lifted one supercilious eyebrow. She ignored him.

'I know it's Cook's half day, but could you make Mary

some lemon and barley water? The doctor says she must drink. I daren't leave her for long.'

'How do you make it?' Bridie munched on the boiled ham.

'I know,' Elin said. 'I'll do it.'

A week or so later, Nanny took to her bed with a bad bout of shingles.

'It's the adult version of chickenpox.' Mrs Dooley's bulk shivered. 'Hope we don't all catch it. You'll have to look after Mary for a bit.' Elin was pleased. She was going to get a rest from lighting fires after all.

'Rather you than me,' Peck smiled. 'She's a little Turk, that one.'

'I like children,' Elin retorted.

Nanny was moved out of the night nursery and Elin made the bed up with clean sheets for herself, glorying in the thought of being able to go to bed when Mary did. She'd lie there till the child woke. Mr Laurence wouldn't be disturbing her, not with Mary sleeping in the same room. It would be a real rest cure.

She wasn't prepared for the way Mary precipitated a head-on clash. The first morning, Elin opened Mary's wardrobe and took out a long-sleeved checked dress with smocking on the bodice and a woolly cardigan to go over it.

'Not that frock,' Mary said, standing in her liberty bodice and knickers. She was feeling better, though she still had a few spots.

'Which one then?' Elin asked, pushing the check dress back.

'This one,' Mary pulled at a floor-length skirt of blue satin. 'My bridesmaid dress.'

Elin hid her smile. 'You can't wear that. Nobody's getting married today.' The next moment she was shocked to see Mary tossing with rage on her bed, making the springs groan and creak.

'Let's choose something else,' she said as calmly as she could. 'What about this kilt?'

'Want bridesmaid dress,' Mary shouted as Elin heard the day nursery door open. Full of guilt, she went to see who had come. Bridie was bringing the ash can and sticks for the nursery fire. Elin, breathing with relief, snatched them from her.

'I'll see to it. Fires are easy compared with . . .' She nodded towards the night nursery. A defiant Mary appeared in the doorway, with the blue satin dress on. She'd been unable to fasten the back.

'You'll spoil it,' Bridie said sharply.

'If you get it dirty you won't be a bridesmaid at all.' Elin's golden eyes glittered.

'You'll be sorry on Easter Saturday, and your Daddy will be cross with you,' Bridie added.

'Let's take it off.' Elin whipped the dress over her head, slid the hanger inside, and had it locked in Nanny's wardrobe within seconds. She took the check dress out again.

'No,' screamed Mary. 'Not that.' Eventually she put on her dressing gown and slippers and came to the door to watch Elin light the fire. Elin managed to get her engrossed in rolling newspapers to help, but it didn't lift her bad mood.

When Elin went down to the kitchen to collect the nursery breakfast tray, Mary trailed down behind her. She watched with gimlet blue eyes as Elin set the food on the nursery table and sat her in front of her bowl of porridge.

The child stirred it round. 'Don't want porridge.'

'An egg then?' Two boiled eggs stood ready.

'Cake,' Mary said. 'I want sponge cake. With jam and cream.'

'We have cake at tea time, not breakfast.'

'Cake,' Mary demanded. 'Cake now.'

Elin started on her own porridge, somewhat taken aback. The Roberts children were glad to eat anything. Mary threw herself down on the hearth rug and screamed for cake.

Elin was on edge. The noise was surely enough to bring her mother running? And what a fool she'd look, unable to handle a four-year-old.

She did what Bessie had advised for a temper tantrum, ignored it, though now the child was drumming her heels as well, and Elin expected the nursery door to burst open any minute. It must sound as though Mary was being murdered. Surely Bessie had said temper tantrums were over by four years?

'There is no cake,' she said, but wondered if she should go and get some to shut her up. She'd been looking forward to a leisurely breakfast, but there was no pleasure with Mary's screams reaching crescendo.

She finished her own porridge. It was nicer than usual. On impulse, she reached for Mary's plate and started to eat hers instead of the egg. The heels stopped drumming, the screaming died down. Mary got to her feet, her angry blue eyes level with the table.

'That's mine,' she said.

'I thought you didn't want it.'

Mary didn't answer. Elin took another mouthful then pushed the bowl back across the table. Mary climbed into her chair and began to eat. Elin poured herself a second cup of tea and closed her eyes with relief.

The Roberts children had never been difficult like this. They'd played in the water when she did washing. Rolled out pastry when she baked. Carried water in tins when she carried buckets. They'd had square sturdy limbs and cheeks like rosy apples. Mary was dainty and looked angelic, but it seemed to Elin her one aim in life was to pit her will against authority.

Bessie's children had one pair of boots laced up with leather thongs, the soles tipped and studded with steel nails. Their Sunday shoes were handed down from one to the other. Mary had nine pairs of shoes, of different styles and colours. Elin didn't mind which pair she wore, but Mary sensed this and refused to wear any. Elin tried to ignore her bare feet.

Mary also had shelves of children's books, and it surprised Elin to find she could read them already. Her idea of play was for Elin to set her sums. She would clutch her pencil with total concentration and work them out correctly. Lizzie Roberts was a year older, had just started at Llanddolfa school and hardly knew her alphabet.

It happened that Birkenhead was enjoying the first warm

spell of the year. The sun shone from a pale blue sky. Elin took Mary out into the garden, pushed her on her swing, and played ball with her.

Sybil Oxley came out with her shingled yellow hair freshly set by her hairdresser. She took Mary round the garden, teaching her the names of the flowers, and told Elin it was a shame Mary couldn't go to her nursery classes and dancing lessons for another week. Afterwards Mary surprised her by identifying the flowers and shrubs again.

Elin found life in the nursery a constant battle. All the Roberts children had had their faces wiped with a damp flannel before they snuggled down in their beds. Mary had a bath. It took ages to persuade her in and even longer to get her out. Then her teeth had to be cleaned, hair brushed, and prayers said. When Elin pushed her between the sheets, Mary was never ready for sleep. She would want a bedtime story, and then another. And a drink of water. Her mother always came to kiss her goodnight, and often they had to wait.

Elin would tiptoe back to the day nursery feeling limp, waiting for Mary to go to sleep. One night she had just got herself undressed and into bed when Laurence came. Mary woke up, and he retreated with indecent haste. Elin didn't know whether to be glad or sorry. It took her another half hour to get Mary off again. It was rare for her not to wake in the night; frequently it happened more than once.

'I've timed it right tonight,' he whispered as he made love to her in front of the dying nursery fire the following night. But Elin spent the time listening nervously for approaching footsteps on one side and Mary's creaking bed springs on the other.

She felt no more rested when a week later Nanny was deemed well enough to return to her duties, and she moved back to her attic.

Now when her work was over for the day, Elin would run upstairs full of anticipation. She would wash carefully before putting on one of the new nightdresses she'd bought in the market. She'd asked Laurence if he liked the slim tubes of art silk with thin straps over her shoulders, and he'd said yes. They were low in front, revealing her breasts.

She knew Sybil Oxley had similar ones. Bridie held them up for all to admire when she had them to wash. Mrs Dooley could hardly bring herself to look.

'No warmth at all in them,' she always said. 'What good are they?'

Elin chose Bridie's day off to wash her own, and hoped Mrs Dooley would think they were Mrs Oxley's too. She did wonder if they were worth all the trouble because Laurence would have them off inside five minutes. Mostly she'd be asleep when he came sliding into her bed, but his touch against the art silk was electric in its effect.

'Sweetheart, be kind to me,' he'd whisper against her ear. Within moments she would flame to his touch, wanting him as much as he wanted her.

He was coming more often, hardly a night passed now when he didn't. She loved the nights they fell asleep with their arms round each other. It was comforting to be held close against this firm body. All day she was a skivvy, but at night he made her feel wonderful. He was always in a good humour when it was over. He would laugh and say: 'I look forward all day to creeping into your bed. You're my golden girl, a real sparkler. We make a good pair, you and me.'

For Elin it made the line between fantasy and reality blur. She liked to believe he wanted her by day as well as by night. She saw him in every hearth she cleaned, the straight classic lines of his face burning with ambition, intense blue eyes showing single-minded pursuit of his own needs. She saw perseverance in his strong jaw, knew what the sense of privilege did for his vigorous body. Laurence could get whatever he wanted.

Elin saw herself riding in his car again. She dreamed of the clothes she would have, the life she would lead. Imagined herself mistress of this house.

She believed him when he whispered across her pillow, 'You're lovely. You know how to give a man a good time. You know I'll always look after you, Elin.'

She was falling in love with him, could no longer have enough of him. It was easy to see herself in Sybil's place.

She always raced to answer the bell pull if he was home. She made more journeys to bank up fires than were necessary, was always ready to set or clear tables, and take up tea trays. She hung around listening to what he had to say to everyone else. Sometimes, when they were in bed, she recounted what she had heard and they both laughed.

'You quarrelled with Sybil today.'

'Not really, Sybil hates being pregnant.' Sybil was becoming more irritable as her pregnancy progressed. It was not hard to believe he'd prefer someone else.

'Why does she get that way then? Surely she doesn't have to with the Marie Stopes thing?'

'Well, she loves the babies once they're here. We both want a family. I specially want a son.'

'You have one, haven't you?' It was only when the words were out she remembered no one ever mentioned James.

'I want someone to follow me in the business. A son carrying the Oxley curse won't do.'

She thought about him all day as she went about her work, resenting the time he spent with Sybil, resenting the time she couldn't spend with him. Despite the lack of sleep, she could see stars in her slanting eyes when she looked into her mirror. Her hair cast a sheen of gold on her skin. She felt exhilarated.

He said he loved being with her, but never that he loved her. Surely it was just another small step? He talked of how much she meant to him. Elin pushed the niggle to the back of her mind, and gave herself up to enjoying him.

All that came to an end when his brother Leonard came to stay again.

'A business matter to straighten out,' Laurence told her. He didn't talk much about his business, but she knew he was pleased with the success he was having.

She helped Peck serve them dinner. They were late starting. Mr Leonard and his family had only just arrived. Elin thought the atmosphere less friendly than it had been at Christmas. A little strained. It was ten o'clock when Sybil and Catherine went to the drawing room for coffee. The brothers sat on over the port.

Elin hovered, clearing the sideboard. She heard the ladies close the drawing room door on their way to bed. She took the coffee things down to the kitchen. Daisy finished the washing up, and Mrs Dooley sent her to bed too.

'Time we all went,' Peck said, pouring himself more wine from a half-finished bottle he'd brought down from the dining room.

'Go and see if the fire needs attention,' he suggested. 'They've had long enough now. Poke it hard, make a noise. Maybe you'll move them. I want to go to bed.' Purposely, she'd left the dining room door ajar. She approached quietly and heard Leonard's voice.

'You're using me, Laurence, just as you used Father. I won't have it.'

'Don't be silly. It's the best way. I want to run the business, you don't.'

'You end up with all the advantages.'

'I'm going to work for them, not you.'

'You use us all. You use Sybil. You only married her to get your hands on her share.'

'I love Sybil,' he retorted.

Elin knew she let out a gasp. She pressed herself back against the wall, unable to believe her own ears.

'She's not happy.'

'She's not happy because she's pregnant. It's always like this for her, she's worried in case it's another – like James.'

'I think it's more than that. She's changed.'

'We all change.'

'Father was against you two marrying, wasn't he? Didn't think Sybil was right for you.'

'Water under the bridge now.' She heard the clink as the decanter touched the rim of his glass. 'I don't believe there's one woman in the world that's special for any one man. It's a hormone drive, Len. The truth is, a man can be happy with any woman. A change now and then works wonders.'

'If you believe that, I'm sorry for you. Sorry for Sybil

too.' Elin strained her ears to catch every word. She felt a little sick.

'You needn't be. I happened to marry Sybil, it could have been any one of a number.'

'You have to believe the woman you marry is the only one in the world for you,' Leonard said. 'That's love, and that's how you find happiness.' Elin heard a step behind her coming up from the kitchen. She was tempted to take to her heels. Instead, she took a firm grip on herself, knocked on the door and went in. She could feel the bile rising in her throat.

'Are we keeping you up, Elin?' Laurence half smiled at her before tossing down the contents of his glass. 'Do you want coffee, Len?'

'Yes.'

'We'll have coffee here. Tell Peck to lock up, and then you can all go to bed.'

'Yes, sir, thank you.' She felt numb, she'd been a fool to trust him. Half-blinded by tears, she ran straight into Mrs Dooley's fat arms.

'Eh, love! What's the matter?'

'Sleep-walking,' she made herself joke, before repeating Laurence's instructions.

'See to the coffee, Elin. I'm on my way up.'

Elin felt terrible. 'Good in bed,' Laurence had whispered across her pillow. 'Better than Sybil.' She'd thought that praise. She was no better than a common harlot.

Peck had dozed off in the chair with his mouth open. She kicked his foot and told him to go to bed.

The coffee pot was three-quarters full but stone cold. She turned the gas up high under it.

'No consideration,' Peck mumbled, tipping the last of the wine into his glass and taking it with him. 'It's nearly midnight.'

'Don't forget to lock up,' she called.

Laurence didn't love her. He was using her as he used everyone else. It had cut her to shreds to hear him say it, but deep down she had known. He only wanted her while his wife was having a baby. He was not worth loving. She kept telling herself that. He was not worth loving.

* * *

'Seventeen on Saturday.' Mrs Dooley bit into a slice of her fruit cake. 'Wish I was seventeen again.'

'Don't we all,' Bridie agreed.

'I'll make you a birthday cake, and we'll have something special for lunch,' Cook promised. 'You'd better take your half day then.' They'd had finnan haddock for supper and the kitchen was still filled with its scent.

'Thank you,' Elin said pleased at their interest. She felt more at ease with them now. 'Seventeen is grown up, quite old really.'

Peck lifted world-weary brows. 'Seventeen is extreme youth. We all regret its passing. Fancy a night out? I'll treat you to the Argyle, if you like.'

'The music hall? I'd love it.' She was even getting used to Peck, but he wasn't usually this friendly.

'I often go on Saturday night.'

'Be a treat for you to have a good-looking girl on your arm,' Bridie giggled.

'You're all very kind,' Elin faltered. She was grateful. She was looking forward to her birthday, though she couldn't say she was happy. Not while Laurence was playing with her like a cat plays with a mouse. Just to think of him brought a flush to her cheeks. As long as she didn't let herself think of falling for a baby. As long as she didn't expect anything from him.

Later, when she and Bridie carried the dishes through to the scullery to wash up, Bridie was laughing. 'Everybody seems to be doing something for your birthday, except me.'

Elin turned the hot water tap on full. Under cover of the swishing torrent, she said, 'There is something, Bridie, I've been meaning to ask you. It's about Mr Laurence . . .'

'Listen,' said Bridie. 'You be careful of him. I've seen him looking at you. He's got a way with girls – you know.'

'Only too well.' Elin couldn't look at her, but she had to tell someone. 'He's been coming to my room. In the night, almost every night.'

'What? I did wonder. I thought I heard someone on the

stairs . . .' Her dark eyes were wide. 'Not doing . . .? Really doing?'

Elin busied herself at the sink, staring at the taps. 'Yes, won't take no for an answer.'

'Oh, my God!' Bridie's mouth hung open in horror. Strands of lank hair hung down her face. 'I know he's like that. Always after someone. Got to have a girl on the side.'

'I can't stand it. I'm thinking of going to Mrs Oxley.'

'No! Don't tell her!' Bridie's mouth opened wider. 'He was chasing Ruby. Just chasing, she said, not succeeding. She went to Mrs Oxley and she put her out before her feet could touch the floor. Pack your things and go, she told her, just like that. Paid her up, but she got no notice and no reference. Said it must be her own fault. Or she was mistaken about his intentions.'

'Oh, Bridie!'

'You'd better come to my room to sleep. He won't come there.'

'Thank you,' she choked. 'What happened to Ruby?'

'She couldn't find anywhere to sleep that night, it was almost six when she was put out. She had to creep back up to my room, there was nowhere else. She tried for another job, but it took her three weeks, and all the time she was creeping back here at night. We kept her things in the attic. I was terrified we'd be found out and I'd get my marching orders too. Much better if you find yourself another place first.'

'Oh Bridie, thank you. I'll look for another place. It's the only way.'

'He's a bastard. Uses everybody for his own ends.'

That night she got undressed in her own room and crept down to Bridie's bed, which was three-quarter size so there was just room. She felt safe lying with her arm round Bridie's ample waist, listening to her breathing. In the morning she ran upstairs to her own attic to wash and dress, confident she'd found the answer.

On Friday morning she did the same, only to find her own bed occupied. Laurence was stretched out against her pillow waiting for her.

'Where do you think you've been?' She backed away, but he was out of bed, and grabbing for her wrist. 'This won't do, Elin, I've had to wait all night. I don't like waiting.'

'Not now, I can't. I've got to start work. Mrs Dooley will be after me if I'm not down.' His intention was in his eyes, clear as daylight. 'No, Mr Laurence.'

'It won't take long.' He was tugging at her nightdress, one of her old ones with long sleeves and a high neck, pulling her towards the bed at the same time.

He was not gentle with her. She loathed herself for finding pleasure even then. He got up quickly, put on his trousers, and tossed some coins onto her mantelpiece.

'I pay you well, Elin. Be here for me. If you're not, I'll come and get you. I know where you've been. You've been with Bridie, but she won't stop me.'

Her bedroom door slammed behind him. Bridie and Mrs Dooley would be up and about on the corridor below, but he didn't seem to care who saw him. Elin went to her washstand, angry with him and also with herself. She ought to be able to stand up to him. Stop him doing this. The problem was that one half of her didn't want to stop. Her slanting eyes looked back at her from the mirror. They were filled with defeat. Her hair no longer lifted into shining golden curves. She had to hurry, Mrs Dooley would think she'd overslept. She reached for her cap, covering her hair, pulling it down hard.

She was overdue. The first day, she told herself, it needn't mean anything. She mustn't think about it. The second day, the same. The third day was Saturday, her birthday, the day she'd been looking forward to. She woke up a little before her alarm went off. The mornings were lighter now. Her first feeling was of nausea rising in her throat. She lay tensed against the cool sheet, telling herself she was all right. But she wasn't, she felt sick.

She'd known all along it would happen. Like a fool she'd gone along with him, wanting to believe him when he said it was safe. Now the gnawing doubt was a certainty. She was stiff with horror.

The alarm clanged. She'd have to get up. As soon as her feet touched the floor, she knew she was going to be sick. She ran to the lavatory, tasting the hot bitter fluid rising in her throat. Thank God, it was empty. She bolted the door, and barely had time to turn round. She mustn't make a noise here, other people were close. But the noise was beyond her power to control. She flushed the pan to cover it, and then had to sit there sweating while she waited for the cistern to refill, so that she could do it again.

'Happy birthday, Elin. Happy birthday.' Everybody had a smile for her. She felt dreadful. It was going to be the worst birthday she'd ever had. She grabbed for her box of brushes, dusters and morning sticks. She had to put this catastrophe out of her mind. She wouldn't survive if she let herself dwell on it. She'd think about it when she was alone.

Somehow she got through the morning, even managed to eat some porridge at breakfast. By lunch time she felt better, and was trying to convince herself she'd imagined she was pregnant. It was something preying on her mind rather than a real problem.

In the kitchen everybody expected her to be in high spirits. She pretended she was, though there was a hard ball of horror in her stomach. It was an effort to eat the roast pork and birthday cake, but she had to pretend she was enjoying it.

They were singing for her, the candles were lit on her cake. She had to laugh and blow them out. One breath wasn't enough.

'Bad luck, not to get them in one,' Bridie giggled.

Bad luck! Bridie didn't know how dreadful her luck was.

She was free at last to go out. Hurrying down Beresford Road, she gulped huge lungfuls of cool fresh air, and caught the twopenny jogger down to the market. She went to the labour exchange, just as she'd planned to. She looked at the jobs available to her, but now everything had changed. What was she going to do? She hadn't the first idea, and she felt desperate.

Peck met her as arranged and took her to the Cosy Café for high tea. He pushed ham on her and she enjoyed it, feeling hungry again. The show at the Argyle took her out of herself. It was another world of glamorous costumes, bouncy, catchy tunes, and innuendo.

In the semi-darkness of the theatre, her eyes went across to Peck. He looked very respectable, with his hair Brylcreemed back from his forehead and wearing an expensive suit which he admitted had been a hand-me-down of Mr Laurence's. He was quite old, of course, and he had his moods, but even he was more friendly now. He was laughing at some stage joke, and turned to see if she was too.

Afterwards, he insisted on taking her for a drink. It was her first visit to a public house; everyone in Llanddolfa believed them to be places of sin. She felt fearful, and didn't enjoy the smoky atmosphere. Even the lemonade she drank seemed tainted by the place.

As she got ready for bed, she hoped Laurence wouldn't come. Tonight, she just couldn't. She closed her eyes, aching all over. She had to think, had to have some sort of a plan. She certainly couldn't stay at Birchgrove.

Elin supposed most girls in her position went home, but she couldn't. To face her father was out of the question, she daren't suggest keeping the baby in his house. He'd crucify her. The whole village would gossip, and anyway, she doubted her father would have her back.

Bessie Roberts had been good to her, but there were already too many babies at Tonteg. Bessie would never let her bring another. She'd have another girl by now anyway.

That meant staying in Birkenhead, the overspill from Liverpool, a town based on heavy industry with a grimy smoke-laden atmosphere. She liked what she'd seen of the place, even though it was noisy and sometimes squalid. There was anonymity in the crowded streets.

She had enough money to rent a room for a few months, but how could she work with a baby? It would mean the workhouse when her money ran out. She'd heard in Pwllheli they kept fallen women for fourteen years till the baby could support itself. Did they have workhouses in Birkenhead too? She'd heard there were Relieving Officers, who assessed the needs of those who threw themselves on charity. She shuddered; she might come to that.

If she had to take the baby to Llanddolfa when it was born, she could pretend she was married and her husband had been killed. Not that anyone would believe her. In prison perhaps? That had a hint of shame about it, not something you confessed to unless it was true. Yes, prison was more believable.

For the moment she'd stay where she was. She had a job, she could survive here for a few more months, stay as long as possible. Her best chance was to conserve what money she had, and do her best to collect more.

She got out of bed, put on the light, and took out the bundle of coins she'd tied into a handkerchief and hidden at the back of a drawer. Eighteen pounds, twelve shillings. Riches indeed, but how long would it last?

She recognised his footfall on the stairs coming up to her attic. She knew she was cringing as the footsteps came closer, but what did it matter now? The damage was done.

She must tell him. He'd promised to look after her. She took a long shuddering breath as the door opened.

'Hello, Elin.' His smile stretched his pencil moustache so that it turned up at the edges. There was something of the tease in his manner. 'Not in bed yet?'

She pushed the money back in her drawer and rammed it shut. Suddenly she was afraid to tell him. Afraid he'd not keep his promise about looking after her.

Hadn't he promised this would never happen? How she'd wanted to believe that. It was time she learned sense. Laurence was not the sort of person anybody could rely on. He was all for number one.

His fingers were gentle against her throat as he undid the buttons on her nightdress. His eyes were smiling too. He had lovely eyes, they could make her believe almost anything. He was a real gentleman.

CHAPTER SIX

'You're beautiful, Elin.' Laurence's voice was soft with admiration. 'The most beautiful girl I know.'

Her eyes searched through the half-dark into his. They smiled back at her, deeply blue and pleasure-filled. His bronze hair crinkled round his relaxed face. He looked satisfied, even satiated. She found it hard to believe he couldn't feel the knife edge cutting into her.

The words burned her mind. 'I'm pregnant. Please help me.' She had to tell him. He had to know, but the words still wouldn't come. They dried on her tongue. She'd put it off for months.

She was frightened he wouldn't help. What if he threw her out? It was too late now to hope for another place, her pregnancy was beginning to show. Not too bad in the full-skirted print dress, but her blue suit showed a bulge.

She had told Bridie that Laurence was leaving her alone. Bridie had giggled and said he must have someone else, but of course he continued to come. He didn't bother to count up the days, or ask if she was overdue. All he asked was that she should be available. How could he be so blind?

Many mornings she felt dreadful when she got up. Bending double over the fires didn't help the sickness. She caught a glimpse of her face as she passed a mirror in the corridor. Did it have a greyish tinge? There was nobody about, and she stepped back to look again. There were mauve shadows beneath her slanting eyes. She looked haggard, even ill.

She felt terror hanging about her in clouds, thick enough to touch. She expected Bridie to guess. It surely must be plain enough for all to see? She was a nervous ghost of herself.

After breakfast, if she could eat something, she usually felt better. The smell of frying bacon upset her more than anything. She learned to stick to porridge and tea. She was losing weight. Surely that couldn't be right? Perhaps, after all . . .? But that was wishful thinking and she knew it.

If, when sweeping the carpets or dusting the furniture, the coming baby was on her mind, she forced herself to think of something else. Something nice. She had decided what she would do, as far as she was able. The only way she could survive was not to dwell on it. To do so terrified her.

The night came when Laurence was lying on top of her, passion making him press painfully on her tender breasts. Her breath sucked in painfully. He stopped.

'Elin?' His fingers came again, feeling now each breast in turn, assessing their new size and shape. She thought he'd found naught amiss, his kisses were passionate again. Later, when it was all over, and he'd rested, he got out of her bed, put on the light and pulled the bedclothes from her shivering body.

'You're pregnant! For God's sake, you're pregnant!' He stood over her, his blue eyes burning with shock. 'Why didn't you tell me?' His fingers hurt her chin as he turned it out of the pillow. She had to look at him. 'Why?'

Panic was washing through her. Her strength ebbing away. Her eyes would tell him she hadn't dared. 'I was afraid.'

'Afraid?'

'Afraid you'd turn me out. I've nowhere else to go. What's going to happen to me?'

He pulled her close and hugged her. Poured gentle kisses on her forehead. 'Elin, my poor sweet Elin. I'll look after you, I told you. How far on are you?'

'About five months.'

He drew back, his face aghast. 'Oh God! It's too late.'

'What do you mean, too late?'

'Too late to have it taken away. You little silly. I could have fixed it for you.' Elin turned cold inside. 'Didn't you want that?'

'I didn't know it could be done. I've never heard of it.'

To have it taken away would have suited Laurence down to the ground. She wanted to die at that moment. She would have agreed, if she'd known such a thing was possible. It seemed such an easy way out.

'You are a little innocent.' He sighed heavily.

She was holding her breath. Was that all the help he was going to offer?

'Well, it's too late, too dangerous now, you'll have to have the baby.'

Elin stared up at him, feeling sick. She'd faced that months ago.

'But I don't like the idea.'

'Neither do I,' she found the strength to say, hating him at that moment.

'Why did you have to keep it to yourself till now? What a naive little fool you are.'

She felt the sting of tears. He didn't even like her. He thought she was a fool.

'You will help me?' she whispered. 'You promised.'

'Yes, yes, of course.' His hand was on her abdomen, pressing so hard it hurt. 'Oh God! I know a doctor who'd take it away. It wouldn't have been a trouble to us.'

'To you,' she wanted to say, but couldn't quite. She mustn't upset him, or perhaps he wouldn't help after all. He was sitting still, his lips in a hard straight line below his pencil moustache, his expression far away, thinking hard.

'What do you think? What's the best thing for you? The best way to solve this problem?'

'To get married,' Elin said. He stared back at her in silence. Surely that was the obvious answer?

'Have you got a boy friend?' he asked at last.

'No, of course not. Only you.'

'I'm already married. You must count me out.'

'I already have,' she said bitterly.

'Don't worry. I'll think of something. I'll see you're all right.' He sighed again. 'Oh Elin, Elin, why did you have to do this? And now, too, just when I'm so busy with other things.'

'You did it, Mr Laurence,' she said stonily. 'There was no stopping you.'

For the first time, she saw him without his aura of confidence. 'I'll see you're all right,' he told her.

Elin was still shivering as she went about her chores the next morning. It was a weight off her mind that he knew. She'd kept it to herself for five months, and there had been times when she'd been sick with worry. Now at least it was a problem shared, and he had promised to help.

It was the way he'd promised that bothered her. He'd made her feel it was all her fault. If only she'd spoken up sooner, it could have been easily solved. It would have meant killing the baby, but it would have been all over by now. To think of that made her feel worse.

It wasn't over. She wouldn't stop worrying until she knew exactly what Laurence intended. She was so afraid he would do nothing.

At breakfast she was deep in her own problems when John the gardener came in, waving his arms around, his face flushed with excitement. She missed what he said, but the others had stopped eating and were staring at him.

'What was that?' she asked.

'There's a notice just gone on the gate. For sale.' John had brought mud into the kitchen on his boots; under normal circumstances Mrs Dooley would have been infuriated.

'This house is up for sale?' Bridie's brown eyes were glazed with shock.

'Where are we going?' Elin took another mouthful of porridge. It was news, but it paled into insignificance compared with her troubles. Anyway, unless it was sold quickly it would make no difference to her.

'No idea.'

Mrs Dooley's fat jowls quivered with indignation. 'He might have told us, instead of letting us find out like this.'

'We don't know as we're going anywhere,' Bridie said. 'My, you're cool, Elin.'

'Stands to reason,' Elin explained. 'They'll still need staff.

I mean, can Mrs Oxley cook? Bet she couldn't boil an egg.'

'But all of us?' Mrs Dooley sat frowning over her bacon.

'It's unsettling, not knowing,' Bridie complained.

'Perhaps they won't have a garden.' John couldn't stand still, a circle of muddy footprints showed on the floor Daisy had just washed.

'Bet they'll have a bigger garden and a bigger house,' Elin comforted. If only her problem was so simple. 'You know what Mr Laurence is like.' She could ask him of course, though she'd be unable to divulge any secrets. It wouldn't do to let them know she had Mr Laurence's ear.

'I shall be thinking about it all day,' Mrs Dooley said. 'Worrying, until we know.'

'I won't,' Elin shrugged. 'My half day's come round again. I'm going to forget my worries. All of them.'

Peck, at the head of the table, smoothed back his oily hair with both hands. 'Do you fancy a trip to New Brighton this afternoon?'

Elin had often commiserated with Bridie that they could not be off together. She wanted company when she went out. Peck had taken her to the music hall for a birthday treat, and she knew he took Mrs Dooley sometimes, but for him to suggest an outing was unexpected.

'I mean, it's a fine day, and Saturday, there'll be a bit of life there. My treat.'

Elin could see they were all hanging on her reply. Bridie knew she hadn't forgiven him for slamming the front door in her face the first night.

'Peck's all right, when he's out,' Bridie had told her. 'Acts like a real gent. He's moody here, specially when he's got a hangover. What you've got to watch with him is that you don't do his work as well as your own.'

'Here's your chance, lass,' Mrs Dooley laughed. Her mouth opened like a cavern in her pudding face. 'I'd take it while you can.'

'Have you arranged to do something else?' He seemed less arrogant, ready to accept her as an equal.

'No, I'd like to come. Thank you, Peck.' It would be better than being on her own. She'd already been round pricing the cost of a room, and the necessities for the baby. She felt she couldn't spend anything on enjoying herself.

'Two o'clock then,' he said. 'We'll have a good time.'

'Of course,' Bridie pointed out, 'you can take more time off now, Peck. Life's a lot easier for you.'

'Could be too easy.' Mrs Dooley poured herself another cup of tea. 'Did you already know he was selling this house?'

'No,' Peck said coldly. They all stared at him. Elin saw disbelief on every face.

Later that morning she went round banking up the fires. She thought it wasteful to keep so many burning in the present spell of fine June weather. Laurence and his wife were in the drawing room, poring over plans laid out across a coffee table.

'A staff bungalow in the grounds would be better, Laurence,' Sybil was saying. They hardly looked up as she entered, but she knew Laurence was aware of her. She had that effect on him. 'Much more privacy for all of us.'

Elin crashed the poker against the coal.

'More convenient to have a couple of extra bedrooms in the house.'

Elin wondered if Sybil knew what was going on. It sounded as though she did, and was planning that in future he'd have farther to go for his pleasures.

'No,' Sybil insisted. 'I would prefer two separate buildings.'

'It would cost more.'

'It doesn't matter what things cost if you want them,' she flared, rushing to the door. 'Only if I do.' It slammed, the draught fluttering at the plans. One drifted to the floor. Elin swept up the hearth, rehung the brush on the companion set, and stifled a smile.

'Would you like to see how my new house will look, Elin?' Laurence asked, retrieving the plan.

Holding the empty scuttle she paused by the table to study it. 'I'm sure it will be very nice,' she said. 'Put the cat amongst the pigeons, Mr Laurence, it did, when the staff saw the notice on the gate.'

He laughed. 'Keep them guessing. On their toes.'

'But why move? Nobody can understand why you want to.'

'This was my father's house. Now he's gone, I want a change.'

Elin frowned. In Llanddolfa, farms and property stayed in the same family for generations.

'It's not my kind of house. It's old-fashioned and too big.'

'Too big?'

'Much too big, and it's falling down. Well, almost. Father never wanted anything changed. Sybil wants to move to a better locality. Farther out of town. Oxton isn't what it was.'

'So you're having a new one built?'

'Yes. This time it'll be exactly what I want. I've got a fine site in Caldy. Lovely views over the River Dee. Plenty of fresh air for the children. It'll have every modern convenience, central heating to save all this stoking of fires.'

'No fires?' Elin marvelled, she spent half of every day tending fires.

'One fire in the drawing room and a boiler in the kitchen, that's all. Hot water always in the taps, hot water in the radiators, the whole house cosy. No fuss, and much more privacy for us.'

'So you'll have no need of me?'

'Haven't I said you're wasting your talents? It'll be a more convenient house all round.'

'But I won't be coming?'

'No, Elin, you won't. I'm working on something for you.'

'What?'

'You'll have to be patient. You'll be all right.'

'All the others will go with you?'

'Except for Peck.'

'He'll not like that.'

'I don't care what he likes. He was my father's valet, and he drinks too much of my claret. Don't say anything yet.'

'Of course not. What would he think, me knowing that?'

'The family can't move for servants here. We have to pay for servants to look after servants. Goodness knows what Peck does to fill his day, but I'll see he's all right. See you're all right too, Elin.'

Poor Peck, she thought, he doesn't know he's about to get the sack. Or does he? He'd been very quiet when the others had been sounding off about the sale at breakfast. She'd swear he knew more than the others. 'He knows,' she guessed. 'You've told him.'

Laurence Oxley laughed.

It seemed strange walking out beside Peck. Strange to be sitting next to him on the tram to Woodside.

It was a bright, blowy day, warm enough for her to wear her pink cotton dress. It had a wide skirt that hid her altered shape. The sunshine cheered her. As soon as they got off the tram she could smell the river.

'I've been promising myself a ride on the ferry for ages,' she told him.

'We could do it today if you like,' he said obligingly.

'To Liverpool?'

'Ferry to Liverpool and then another to New Brighton. Need never leave the landing stage. Come on, it's a lovely day for a sail.'

The wind buffeted her face and threatened to lift her straw hat as they stood against the rail, looking down at the brown swirling water. Liverpool was laid out before her on the opposite bank. One day she'd come and look at the shops. Now it was enough to look up at the fine buildings at the Pier Head, and see the famous Liver birds.

She drew her cardigan round her shoulders, sniffing at the scents of tar, rope, and engine oil. Beneath her feet the engine settled into a steady thrum. It was all so new to her, so different from anything she'd seen before, that she forgot her troubles.

The water was choppy with white crests on the waves, the sun sparkled and the seagulls screamed. Even Peck looked as though he was enjoying it as he hung onto his straw boater.

She couldn't stop looking at him from under her lashes. He looked smarter and more a man about town than Mr Laurence, though of course he wasn't. Grey flannels with a knife-like crease, a navy flannel blazer and a red and white striped tie. Surely they couldn't all be Laurence Oxley's hand-me-downs?

New Brighton, at the mouth of the Mersey, was a delight to Elin. Approaching on the ferry, she could look up at the buildings clinging round the tower, the fun fair huddling beneath it. In the other direction were the golden sands, the old fort, and out beyond the rolling breakers, the Irish Sea.

The pier reached out into the river and the ferry slid alongside. Elin held onto Peck's arm as they strolled up the promenade, mingling with the fashionably dressed crowd enjoying the afternoon sun. There was such a vigour to life here, and so much to see. Ice cream was being sold at the pavement edge, cockles too, and donkey rides along the golden sands.

They came to the fun fair. Though Elin didn't fancy the roundabouts now, she enjoyed seeing other people swirling round. Peck fancied his chances at a shooting gallery. She watched him squinting along the barrel of a rifle, trying to look as though he used one as often as he answered the front door at Birchgrove. She saw other women looking at him. He cut a fine figure, though his shooting failed to win a prize.

'Hear what the future holds.' A gypsy woman, whose heavy gold earrings stretched her lobes to long thin strips of flesh, stood outside a mock Romany caravan.

'Have your fortune told,' Peck pressed her. 'Go on, see what she says.'

Elin hung back, knowing too well what the future held for her.

'Just sixpence,' said the gypsy.

Peck put his hand in his pocket. 'You tell the young lady what's in store for her. I'll have another go at the shooting range, Elin.'

Once she realised he didn't intend to listen, Elin was happy to follow the gypsy into the caravan, her heart beating a little faster. The curtains were drawn, inside it was dim and stuffy, and just a little eerie, with one tiny light over the table at which they sat.

While the gypsy studied her palm, Elin studied three large

whiskers twitching on her chin, and wondered if she'd know. If she said anything about a baby, she'd believe everything else. If she didn't know about that, then she wouldn't know anything.

'I see you'll get your wish. Your dearest wish.' Elin almost jerked her palm back. 'You'll be married soon to your young man.' Elin had to smile at that. The gypsy had seen Peck and jumped to the wrong conclusion. Her smile widened. Young man! She couldn't think of Peck as young.

'I see you with a home of your own. It's what you want.' The gypsy's voice was flat and nasal. 'But still, life for you will not be easy. Always, you'll want something more. You'll be blessed with a baby.' Elin felt an icy trickle run down her spine. 'A daughter, she'll be a great comfort to you. You'll have hard times. You'll know poverty, but I see wealth coming your way eventually. Be patient. I see work, hard work. You'll not have good health . . .' She stopped, released Elin's hand. 'You haven't got much to worry about there, have you?'

Elin sighed. That was a matter of opinion. 'I will be married?'

'Yes, it's there in your palm.'

'When?'

The woman took her palm again. 'Your young man is keen to get it settled. Very soon. He's waiting to ask you now.'

Elin almost giggled as she stood up. She had a vision of Peck proposing to her on his knees. He wouldn't, of course. A husband that soon was wishful thinking.

He was waiting for her outside, clutching a green furry animal. 'I won this for you.'

'Lovely!' How could she not be pleased? She turned it over. It was meant to be a dog. The sun was chasing away her mood of depression, it had hung over her too long.

'What did she say?'

'Who?' Elin felt the colour run up her cheeks.

'The fortune-teller, of course.'

'She said you were about to propose!' Elin laughed out loud. She'd better make a joke of it. 'That we'd have a house of our own, and a baby daughter. Come on now, own up, has she spoiled your surprise?'

'Yes, as a matter of fact, she has.'

'What?' The green dog slid through her fingers. She couldn't get her breath.

'Well, why not?' There was a self-conscious grin on his face. 'It's time I settled down. I understand it's what you want.'

Suddenly she couldn't look at him. She bent to pick up the ball of green fluff to hide her scarlet cheeks.

'Who told you that?' Her voice was a whisper.

'Mr Laurence. Is he right?'

She felt she was choking. Perspiration broke out on her nose. He might have told her!

'Well, is it or isn't it?'

'Yes, that's right. Did he tell you . . .?' What kind of a fool must she sound? How else would he know? Laurence might have warned her this would happen.

'Yes, and that the daughter is his.'

'Oh God.' The hurdy-gurdy music was making her head spin. She turned it as far away from him as she could. 'It might be a son.'

'I thought the gypsy said daughter?'

'How does she know!' Elin flared irritably.

'Whatever,' he shrugged.

'And you're happy to do this for me?' She found that hard to believe.

'Well, as I said, it's time I settled down. Ought to get myself a wife and family.'

'Thank you, Peck.'

'You'd better call me Percy.'

'Yes, Percy.'

'We should get to know each other. Go out together when you can get off.'

'When will we be married? She laughed again. 'I can't believe this is happening. When?'

'Say in a month. It'll take a little time to set up. I must find another job, and then there's the house. Come on, let's have a cup of tea to celebrate.'

Elin paused at a refreshment stall, expecting to be handed a thick cup with even thicker tea.

Peck shook his head.

'I'd rather sit down to it today.'

They strolled along the front, passing several cafés, mostly well attended. At last he led her up the steps of the Grand Hotel. Elin felt her feet sinking into carpet and heard the tinkle of cups and saucers from the lounge. A waitress showed them to a table set with fine china cups that even Sybil Oxley would have been pleased to drink from. The starched cloth brushed stiffly against Elin's legs as she sat down.

Peck's hair shone stiffly under its dressing of oil, the marks of the comb still in it. He wasn't that old, she thought, though his jowls were thickening. At least he knew how to do things properly. She felt almost a lady.

Her problem, if not over, was much eased. If she could be Mrs Peck, she'd stay respectable. The baby would have a name and neither of them would starve. The ogre of the workhouse receded. Percy would do well enough. She warmed to him. He must like her a lot to do this. Laurence hadn't let her down after all; he'd arranged it. She felt exultant, relieved, she'd be able to manage. The cakes were sugary and more highly decorated than Mrs Dooley's. She had somebody to plan with, somebody to help her, Peck. She really must get used to calling him Percy.

It was only after they'd returned to Birchgrove that Peck kissed her chastely on the cheek. She went up to her attic room and considered him as a husband. She was lucky Percy liked her well enough to offer marriage. As Bridie had said, he wasn't a bad sort.

She got into bed, her mood of exultation fading, but she was far too excited to sleep. She heard the stairs creak. Try as he might to be quiet, they always betrayed Laurence's approach. She heard her door open and click back on the lock.

'Elin?'

'Hello.' She raised herself up on one elbow, watching him undress in the shaft of light coming between the curtains she hadn't quite closed. The silver light accentuated the rippling muscles in his back. As a husband, she would have much preferred Laurence to anyone else. He turned and came towards the bed.

'I'm not sure you should be coming here like this.' Her tone was teasing. 'I think I'm engaged to be married to someone else.'

He laughed. 'Give me a bit of room, move over.' His feet felt cold. 'So Peck has proposed. Will that suit you?'

'Peck will do well enough.'

'Peck's a lucky fellow. He doesn't realise what a good turn I've done him.' His fingers were rippling up her back under her nightdress. She giggled.

'I wish you'd told me what to expect. I was quite overcome when he asked.'

'Couldn't. I didn't know how he'd do it.' His fingers were tugging at her nightie. She was always afraid he'd tear it.

'But what did you do? How did you manage to persuade him?'

'I offered him money, of course.'

Elin stiffened, then broke free from his arms and pulled herself up the bed.

'You paid him! How much?'

'I had to pay him. He's doing you a favour, isn't he? Doing us both a favour. Marriage is a lot to ask, and it's none of your business how much.'

'I've got to know,' she said stubbornly. She'd been a fool again, imagining Peck did it because he liked her.

'Three hundred pounds. On the proviso you both leave the district.'

Elin pulled herself farther up the bed. 'Why leave the district?'

'We don't want any talk. It's safer for both of us. Can't you see that?'

'I see it's safer for you. With me married to Peck, it would be hard to claim the child was yours.'

'Quite,' he said. 'There has to be something in it for all of us. You get a husband with enough money to buy a house.'

'You get rid of Peck.'

'It was always my intention. I don't need him.'

'And you get rid of me.'

'Now, Elin, you know that's not entirely fair. I've always been very fond of you.'

'Until you made me pregnant.' Suddenly she was struggling with fury. That Peck had to be paid to marry her altered everything. What sort of a husband was he going to be?

CHAPTER SEVEN

Elin drummed her fingers on the kitchen table, wishing Peck would hurry so they could start their afternoon off. She felt hot in her blue suit, but dared not remove the jacket because her waist had expanded too much to fasten the skirt. She'd had to anchor it with a large safety pin.

'It's all a bit sudden, isn't it?' Bridie asked.

Elin tried to smile, telling herself there was nothing suspicious in Bridie's tone. 'Swept off my feet.' She'd promised Laurence not to say anything about the baby, not to mention it to anybody connected with Birchgrove. He'd been very insistent about that.

'You don't look as though you've been swept off your feet,' Bridie went on. 'Are you sure about Peck? He's a bit of an upstart, you know. Likes to give the impression he's a gentleman when he's really out of the gutter. He's not the smoothy he seems, it's all an act.'

Elin nodded, trying to look as though she knew. Where was he?

'You don't look well.' Bridie's darting brown eyes were peering too closely, but Elin had half expected that comment. Her eyes had stared back from her mirror this morning, no longer sparkling like gold, more a washed-out yellow. Too big in her colourless face.

She almost said, 'I'm all right,' but bit it back; it wouldn't sound as though she was in love. 'I've got a bit of toothache,' she managed by way of explanation. The job was heavy for her now.

'I'll get you my oil of cloves.' Bridie was full of sympathy. It made Elin feel worse. 'Is it bad?'

'No, Bridie, thank you. I've taken aspirin.'

'Have I kept you waiting, my dear?' Peck swept in with a wave of masculine scent, his sallow face shining, hair freshly slicked back.

'My, you've done yourself up,' Bridie giggled. 'Did that suit belong to old Mr Oxley?'

'Nobody would know, would they? I've had it altered to fit.' He turned to Elin. 'Ready now.'

'Where are you going?' Bridie asked. 'All dressed up like a dog's dinner.'

'Nosey old bag! Now, Elin, my arm.'

Elin stood up, glad to get out, conscious of the perspiration on her forehead. As he escorted her to the back door, Bridie's voice followed them: 'You're not getting married today, are you? You've done yourself up as though you are.'

Elin winced, and let go of his arm. She was putting on an act, trying to show an attachment to Peck she didn't feel. Looking at him now as he strode to the tram stop, he seemed a total stranger.

Was she making a mistake? There were moments when she knew she was. Panic washed over her as she thought of the future. In three months she'd have a baby. Impossible to hide the fact much longer, and then she wouldn't be able to work. Impossible to cope alone with no money and no home. Surely any husband was better than none? Peck was a Godsend, and she mustn't forget it.

'Where are we going, Peck?' She must make more effort to call him Percy.

'I might have a job. I couldn't tell Bridie.'

'Why not? They know Mr Laurence doesn't want either of us in his new house.'

'They don't know he wants us to go to London.'

'What? He didn't say that to me. Why London?'

'He wants me to take you away. Not necessarily London. Scotland would suit him fine too.'

'But . . .'

'But I was born and bred in Birkenhead, and I want to stay. Go to London indeed, how can I manage that? Anyway, you want to stay here, don't you?'

'Yes, but he might not give you the money if you don't do as he wants.'

'So you know about the money?'

'He told me. It's to buy us a house. Just think of us being house owners.'

'That's why you mustn't tell him about the job. Don't tell anybody at Birchgrove.'

'No,' Elin said. 'It's getting to be a house of secrets. What sort of a job?'

'Head waiter at the Woodside Hotel. I've got an interview this afternoon with the manager.'

'Head waiter? That sounds splendid.' On the day she'd arrived, she'd seen the charabancs unloading their passengers outside the hotel at the train terminus. 'Do they pay well?'

'More than I'm getting now, but I won't be getting my keep. Just meals on duty.'

As they got off the tram, Elin looked up at the big building. 'It looks a fine place.'

'Best hotel in Birkenhead. I'll be proud to say I work here.'

'You haven't got the job yet.'

'I will, you'll see.' Percy straightened his shoulders confidently and marched through the front door. The reception desk was deserted.

Elin lingered on the steps. 'I'll wait here.'

'Come into the lounge to wait. You need a seat.' He threw open a door for her as though he was already on the staff and she an honoured customer. Inside, the sharp smell of beer sat heavily on tobacco smoke. Elin recoiled. Llanddolfa had ingrained into her the belief that a public house was the Devil's recruiting ground. It didn't help to tell herself this was a hotel.

Percy was heading towards the dining room where they could hear a rattling of cutlery. The last lunch customer had finished eating and a waitress was resetting the tables for dinner. Elin felt overpowered by the smell of steak and kidney pie overlaid with cabbage.

'Is the manager, Mr Croft about? He's expecting me,' Percy asked in lordly tones.

'I'll wait outside,' she said hastily and retreated to the front steps. She could see right over the floating landing stage to the river, with Liverpool looking hazy in the afternoon sunshine. The seagulls wheeled and called on the creosote-laden breeze.

She knew, the moment she saw him coming towards her, that the job was his. He had a triumphant smirk on his face and was holding his Roman nose higher than usual. 'I start on Monday,' he exulted.

'So soon? Won't Mr Laurence mind?'

'No, of course not. Start at eleven thirty. No breakfast work, just lunches and dinner.' He laughed. 'Everything's going our way, Elin.'

'But today's Wednesday, you'll have to find somewhere to live. Mr Laurence won't want you sleeping at Birchgrove if you're working here.'

'Let's see if we can find a house then.' He took her arm and guided her across the wide terminus of Woodside in what Elin thought was a gentlemanly manner.

'If we skirt the railway station, we'll soon come to houses,' Elin said. 'We don't want to go far. You'll be coming home late at night.'

Percy hesitated. 'I don't feel like walking. Here's a tram going up Derby Road, let's go a few stops.' Elin felt the first stirring of satisfaction as they sank on the nearest empty seat. It might all come right for her. A few minutes later, they were strolling up a street of terraced houses.

'Here's one.' Percy's step quickened at the sight of a 'To Let' notice above a privet hedge. 'Bigger than average.'

Elin put her face close to the bay window, shielding her eyes from the sun. 'It's not very clean.' She could see a broken mirror over a grate of cracked tiles, and a threadbare armchair inside.

'You'll soon change that. We'll probably have to paint and paper wherever we go. We want it nice.'

'I thought we were going to buy?'

'No time now. We'll have to rent.'

'But we'd have the security . . .'

'Everybody rents, Elin.'

'Where I come from, farms are handed down from father to son. Everybody wants to own. My family only rented.'

'A farm? Your family farmed?'

'My father worked on a farm. We rented a smallholding. Four acres. It makes it harder. Every week, the rent to find.'

'Why tie up all our capital? It'll give us comfort and security to have it behind us.'

'I don't like this house.'

'Well, there'll be others. People are moving house all the time. Come on.' They walked on along street after street of Victorian terraced houses. The larger ones had bay windows, the smaller sash widows. Some had a two-foot wall enclosing a privet hedge in front of the bay, the grander ones a few feet of hard-packed earth as well. All were of brick, darkened by decades in a soot-filled atmosphere. They reached the crest of the ridge.

'There's a view of the river from here, I like that.'

'There's two more to rent,' Percy said.

'Rent or buy, the sign says,' Elin pointed out.

'Then they'll please both of us. We can rent to start with, and if we like it we'll buy. What could be fairer than that?'

'Only two hundred and ten pounds,' Elin marvelled. 'We'd still have money behind us.'

'We'll need furniture.'

'Mr Laurence said I can take what's in my bedroom. He doesn't want to move it to his new house.'

'He told me the same. We're going to do all right out of this. I've got a new bed, I said the other made my back ache.'

Elin peered through a window. 'This is a friendlier house.' The front door opened straight from the pavement to the parlour.

'No room to swing a cat,' Percy grunted behind her. 'Tiny, and we've come rather far.'

'We need to see inside.'

'Let's go round the back. I wonder how much the rent is.' There was a back jigger, with high gates leading into back yards.

'Nothing to see. If I could climb over into the yard, I could probably get in.'

'You'd break in to look?' Elin asked.

'Why not? They aren't furnished, there's nothing in any of them worth taking.'

'You'll spoil your best suit,' Elin reminded him. 'Anyway there are two houses to see. Let's go to the agent.'

'I'll know better than to wear my glad rags if we come house-hunting again. Such a waste of time.'

'We might be able to get a tram down to Market Street,' she said as he copied the agent's address from the sign. 'Lucky they're both with the same one.'

'Do you want to stay here? I'll be as quick as I can. Better for you than rushing around, and it'll save the tram fare. Look up the next street or two, there might be another you like better.'

The road fell steeply away. As Elin walked on she could hear the ring of hammers on metal. Below was Camel Laird's. She could see a ship being built on stocks in the yard. There were other houses to rent. She took their particulars on the back of an envelope she found in her handbag, but she preferred what she'd already seen higher up on the crest of the ridge. She went back.

A middle-aged woman wearing down-at-heel slippers came out of the house between the two offered for rent and lifted a bottle of milk from the step. She smiled at Elin.

'We're looking for a house,' Elin said. 'Could you tell me what these are like inside?'

'Why didn't you say, luv?' The woman wiped her hands on her dirty pinny. She had curlers in her greasy grey hair. 'I saw you looking with your husband. Where's he gone?'

'To the agent, to get the keys.'

'I've got keys. I can show you around if you want.'

'Could you? I'd like that,' Elin was pleased. 'Thank you Mrs . . .?'

'Higgs. Beattie Higgs.'

'We never thought to ask. Percy will be furious, he's gone all that way.'

Beattie Higgs fetched the keys. The lock was stiff, she had to put her shoulder to the front door. Elin followed her into the parlour. Dust motes danced where the sun streamed in through the sash window.

'Cosy,' Elin said, feeling the first spiral of satisfaction; she could live here.

'Not in winter. They're hellish draughty.'

'I like it.' Excitement was growing in her. Relief. There was a living room behind, with stairs going up to the bedrooms and down to the cellar. Beyond was a lean-to scullery with a brown stone sink under the window. Water on tap! This was luxury in Llanddolfa.

'There is electric. Landlord had it put in all along the street.' Mrs Higgs flicked the switch, nothing happened. 'Well, it's off now, but it works grand.'

Elin felt joy blossoming within her as she ran upstairs. There were two bedrooms, one overlooking the street, the other the yard. She laughed and ran downstairs again.

'You like it?'

'Yes, I think we'll take it.' She stopped at the back door. 'Do you know how much the rent is?'

'Seven shillings a week for this one. The other is six and sixpence.'

'What's the difference?'

'Needs decorating.'

'I'd better look at the other too.' First she went out in the yard, enclosed by a six-foot wall. At the far end was a brick outbuilding; half was a store large enough for a pram, the other half was a water closet. Elin reached across, ignoring the spider's webs, to pull the chain. The flush worked. She relaxed happily against the door. She'd soon clean the pan. Her own water closet! Everything was going to be all right. She could be happy here. It would make a good home for the baby.

She went back to the bright little parlour and thought about the furniture they'd need. For the first time for months she wanted to laugh out loud. Her depression was banished. She could see her way into the future.

'I think we could end up being neighbours,' she told Beattie Higgs, a slow smile lighting up her face, touching it with gold once more.

'Come into my place, luv, and wait in comfort for that man of yours to come back. You'll have a cup of tea?'

Elin followed her in and Beattie removed a pile of clothes from an easy chair so she could sit down. While the kettle was being filled in the back kitchen, Elin looked round. It was a replica of the house next door, untidy and not too clean.

Beattie's gossipy voice told her where she would find the best shops in the neighbourhood, and the cheapest coal. Elin drank the cup of strong sweet tea she put into her hand, and heard about the milkman, and best removal van to bring her furniture. Beattie had a curler working loose that drew her attention, it took an effort to look into her friendly dark eyes instead.

Percy returned at last with the agent's office boy, looking hot and irritable. Elin knew it did nothing for his temper to find she'd already seen over both houses.

'Too small, too poky, and not a cupboard in the place,' he complained. The agent's office boy showed him the cupboard under the stairs and the walk-in pantry. 'Too far from Woodside.' Elin pointed out the tram stop at the end of the road. It was expensive, why pay an extra sixpence a week when she'd want the place painted anyway? Nothing would do but they go over the other house again in minute detail. There, redecoration was essential, and Elin assured him she'd be satisfied with the first house as it was. At last he agreed, but began haggling over when he should start paying rent.

'Rent day is Monday.' The office boy stood with his cap on the back of his head, his feet apart. 'You have to pay a week in advance. Today is Wednesday. If you want the house, you have to pay fourteen shillings now, and seven shillings again on Monday. That's how the boss works it.'

'We'll pay fourteen shillings on Monday,' Percy told him. 'We won't be living in the place till then.'

'In that case, if someone else wants it, they'll get it,' the lad said firmly. 'That's the boss's rule.'

'I'll pay,' Elin said opening her bag. After all, Laurence had left her ten shillings again last night. 'We don't want to lose it. We don't have much time, Percy, if you are starting at the Woodside on Monday.'

Grudgingly he agreed. The office boy produced a rent book, marked the sum in it, and gave Elin the key, before riding off on his bike. Percy was not in a good mood; it spoiled Elin's pleasure in finding the house. She tried to find excuses for him.

'I'm exhausted,' he complained. 'Rushing round, while you've been sitting back drinking tea. I need a drink. They'll be open again by now. Shall we go back into town or look for our local?'

She'd told him she didn't like public houses, but she didn't dare object now, with his patience wearing thin. A tram was coming along the road. They jumped on and went back into town. Only when they were seated side by side in the lounge of the Grange Hotel did Percy say: 'No pillow talk now. You'll have to watch it. Don't tell Mr Laurence I've got a job at the Woodside. Nor that we've taken a house in Tranmere. He wants you further away.'

'But we'll have to tell him we've got a house to get the furniture he's promised. We can't just have a removal van turn up at the door.'

'Right, tell him I've got a job, but it's in Liverpool.' He took a sip of his whisky. 'No, Liverpool isn't far enough to suit him, he's got an office there. Southport, say I've got a job at the Prince of Wales Hotel in Southport. We've taken a house there. That's it. We want our bedroom furniture and anything else we can get. Fortunately it won't take much to furnish such a poky place, but we'll need pots and pans, and a hundred and one other things.'

'Do we have to tell all those lies?' Elin sipped reluctantly at the port and lemon he'd bought her; it made her pull a face. Last week he'd bought her sherry and she'd hated it. He'd bought her cider, and she'd not liked that either. Why couldn't he do as she asked and get lemonade?

'Yes, of course we do. Haven't I just explained? Mr Laurence might not pay up if he thinks we're this close.' He took a long drink from his glass and rolled it round his tongue. 'I'll try and get a removal van for tomorrow. We can move straight in. It doesn't matter what happens once we've got his money and the furniture. Bet he'll be glad to see the last of us anyway.'

Elin felt the blood ebb from her face. 'What about getting married? We can't move in till that's done.'

'What difference does marriage make?' He looked down his nose at her.

'But that was the arrangement! You did ask me.'

'Who's to know the difference?'

Elin felt suddenly cold. He was trying to cheat her, too. She banged her glass down on the table untouched. 'I'll know the difference.'

'Oh, come on now. We can get married any time. There's no desperate urgency. I've got the job and the house, we'll go from there.'

'Percy Peck, you're a rotten cheat. You're doing Mr Laurence down, taking his money and ignoring his conditions.' Anger was rising in her throat, suddenly she was hot again. 'You're doing me out of owning my own home. Mr Laurence meant the money to be spent on that.'

'Why tie up all that capital? It doesn't make sense. It's the same house even if we pay rent.'

'Now you're trying to get out of marrying me. Well, I won't let you get away with that.' She had to be married! They put girls in her condition in the poor house. She was only just getting the arrangements made in time. Angry tears were pricking her eyes. She'd thought it was all going to be managed quite gracefully. Now this. She had to have the security of marriage lines, of a wedding band on her finger. For the baby's sake she had to have it.

'What difference does a ceremony make? You can call yourself Mrs Peck if you want.'

'I want to be Mrs Peck,' she said through clenched teeth. She knew how she'd manage it. She knew who had the power to force it through.

'But there isn't time.'

'Either we go straight to the Registry Office and arrange it, or I'll tell Mr Laurence everything. He'll be interested in your plans to cheat him. I'll get him to give me the three hundred pounds instead. I'll buy the house, and you can go to . . . to hell.' It took a lot to make Elin swear.

'Registry Office will be closed now, it's half six.'

'Tomorrow then.' She met his gaze, held it till he dropped his eyes to his glass.

'Do be reasonable,' he grunted.

Elin was pushing the table away and standing up. 'You're only doing it for the money, aren't you? You'd have to leave the Oxleys anyway.'

'I need somebody to keep house too.'

'Oh, of course. Somebody to do the work. Goodbye.'

'Don't go, Elin.' He tossed down his whisky and followed. 'I've never pretended it was love, have I?'

She strode towards the tram stop, raging against Percy, angry with herself for wanting to marry him. Angry with Laurence for putting her in this position.

'Aren't we going to the pictures then? I thought you wanted to see—'

'Don't you want to get out of that too?' Dislike for him was rising in her throat. He was a lying trickster. What did she want to tie herself to him for? He'd make a rotten husband. 'I want to go home.' A tram swayed round the corner. She got on without looking at him again. It was a surprise to find him edging along the seat beside her.

'If you want to get married that bad, Elin, we'll get married.'

She pursed her lips in silence. Where was her pride, pleading with this old man to marry her?

'Tomorrow morning we'll go to the Registry Office and fix it up as soon as we can. Just don't say anything to Laurence Oxley, or you'll blow the whole thing.'

He wanted the three hundred pounds, of course. He was being paid to marry her. He had no other way of getting so much money, and he was getting himself a housekeeper. Elin kept her mouth shut.

'Please, Elin, don't do anything you'll regret.' The conductor came. Although she had the coins ready for her fare, he insisted on paying. When the time came, she got off without another word, and walked fast enough to stay ahead of him.

'Look, we had a good thing going,' he puffed. 'Do be careful what you say to Laurence Oxley, or we'll both lose out.'

'Good night,' she said, as she sailed up the back stairs at Birchgrove.

'Elin, wait . . .'

She knew she ought to think this out carefully, but she was too upset to think at all. She couldn't forget Percy's look of assumed innocence as he'd tried to back out of marrying her. She was in turmoil. All her plans had gone awry.

It was still early, she'd had nothing to eat since lunch, but she wasn't hungry. She got undressed and into bed. She hadn't expected it to be so easy to fall asleep.

Laurence Oxley woke her. She felt refreshed. Her mind was clear, and miraculously made up. If she could get the three hundred pounds for herself, then she'd be better off without Peck.

She knew Laurence wouldn't listen till he'd had what he'd come for. He used her. Despite that, she liked him better than Percy.

'A good one, Elin?' He liked to think he gave her pleasure, but it hadn't been good. She wasn't so easily roused to passion now.

She told him Peck had a job, but Peck had already spoken to him.

'You'll like Southport. I considered moving there myself. It's a pleasant town.' He'd also heard about the house.

'I'm having second thoughts. About marrying Peck, I mean.' She ran her fingers through his wiry bronze hair, the way he liked her to. 'He's very devious. He's trying to cheat me by renting this house. He wants to keep the money for himself. He says everybody rents.'

'Most do. Property is quite expensive in Southport. He said you could rent for a while, and think of buying later if you like it. That seems sensible. Besides, it takes time to buy.'

Elin took a deep shuddering breath. Peck had got his story in first.

'He isn't keen to marry me. He's trying to get out of it.'

'He told me he would.' The intense blue eyes looked into hers, the pencil moustache turned up in a smile. He didn't believe Peck would cheat.

'He's inclined to tell people what they want to hear, and then alter things to suit himself. Why can't you give me the money? I'd promise never to bother you again. I think I might manage better on my own after all.'

'Nonsense, Elin.' He gave her a hug. 'He'll look after you if you're married. He said so, this evening. It's pre-marriage nerves, lots of girls have them. I think you'd be better off married. Much better for the baby.'

'Much better for you too,' she said.

He didn't answer.

'You've already told me. As Peck's bride, I can hardly claim the child is yours. Nobody would believe me.'

'As I said, there's something in it for all of us.'

She wanted to cry. There was precious little in it for her.

'I'm sorry, Elin, that it had to turn out like this.'

'And Peck gets the three hundred pounds?'

'Yes. That's what I arranged. You agreed.'

'Don't give it to him till I've got the wedding band on my finger. I don't trust him.'

'I'm sure you're wrong, Elin. He seems very fond of you.'

'You don't know Peck as well as I do, Mr Laurence. He'd murder his own mother if there was something in it for him.'

When he'd gone, Elin tried to think, but her mind was going round in circles. She had no alternative but to marry Percy Peck. History was repeating itself. She was going to do what Mam had done, marry a man she didn't love. It had turned out badly for Mam.

Elin tried to banish from her mind the picture of Father saying prayers over them before breakfast. Using phrases like 'Help the miserable sinners amongst us to see your light', calling down the wrath of God on those who might sin again. Poor Mam had never been allowed to forget.

But Peck wasn't like that, he was more of a sinner than

she was. For her, things would be very different. She hoped they'd be better.

Elin put another dab of polish on the table to make the room smell fresh and wholesome, and rubbed hard to bring up the patina. She counted herself lucky to have her own furniture, and the house looked better than she'd dared hope.

Laurence Oxley had offered them furniture from the attic at Birchgrove. The choice had been limited, because most of it was too big, but they'd found a cupboard for food, and a table and three dining chairs to put in the kitchen. She was specially pleased with the little tub chair upholstered in grey tapestry.

They'd had to buy their own linoleum from the market, but she'd been able to choose pale grey to complement her chair. Percy had made her pay for it, though he had helped lay it.

They had curtains at every window, though they were too full and too long, and matching ones to hang behind the front and back doors, to exclude draughts. She had also bought a secondhand Singer sewing machine, and would soon have them fitting better. In the meantime they were up, and made the place look lived in.

She wanted it to look its best today because Bridie was coming to see it. Bridie kept suggesting it, and she'd thought it wiser to settle an early date, before she became too obviously pregnant.

She wiped down the kitchen mantelpiece where dust collected so readily. Peck had insisted on placing four shell cases from the Great War there as ornaments. 'My mementoes,' he called them, though she didn't believe he'd served in the war at all. She'd polished up the solid brass till they shone. Two had been made into vases, the other two still had their black nose cones on top. They were eighteen inches high and very heavy, dwarfing everything else. She didn't like them, they looked dangerous. Percy had laughed at her.

It hadn't occurred to her she'd miss Bridie and the rest

of the staff from Birchgrove, but she did. Her own house seemed lonely. Most of all she missed Laurence Oxley. She couldn't get him out of her mind. She found herself comparing him with Percy, hungering for his touch. She was missing his company, and his lovemaking.

Elin had asked Beattie Higgs in for a cup of tea, and chatted to her several times, glad of her company. Percy had come home one day to find them talking on the front steps. He'd pushed Elin inside and slammed the door, but not before he'd said loudly, meaning Beattie to hear: 'I don't want you getting too friendly with that slut next door. Not our sort at all.'

She'd turned on him in fury. 'What did you do that for? She's a goodhearted soul. You'll offend her.'

'I meant to, you don't need people like that. She's not clean. Why waste your time gossiping with her?'

'I have to have somebody to talk to. She's friendly.'

'She's dirty. Look at her torn pinafore.'

'Does her pinafore matter? Anyway, she's hard up.'

'I thought you were more fastidious,' Percy sniffed, his Roman nose held at its most supercilious angle.

She went round to apologise to Beattie, but though she continued to talk to Elin when she was alone, her friendliness cooled.

Percy didn't get home from work until late at night, and tended to stay in bed until mid-morning. He had only a cup of tea before setting out for the Woodside again, and took all his meals there.

'No point in eating at home,' he said. 'We have to pay for it here.' In fact, he was able to bring food home for her sometimes. 'Surplus to requirements,' he would say bringing a couple of joints of cold chicken for her dinner or some cold pork and sausages. Before his day off he even brought some choice steaks and a bottle of claret.

Elin hadn't made up her mind about her new way of life. With her marriage lines and the gold band on her finger, she felt no different. Father wouldn't consider her married anyway, not in a Registry Office. She had found it an anticlimax, and didn't write to tell anyone in Llanddolfa.

They would talk about her, and know it was too sudden. Yet to Elin, it gave her status. To have a home of her own added further status. But closer contact with Percy made her like him less.

They had both brought their bedroom furniture from Birchgrove. Percy wouldn't listen when she'd told him he was bringing too much. A wardrobe, washstand, tallboy and two chests would not all fit into either bedroom. He brought it anyway, and had managed to sell the chests, though they had been in the back yard for three days.

It hadn't occurred to Elin they would not have a bedroom each. The front bedroom was the bigger of the two, and the only one with privacy, for the stairs opened into the back room, and to reach the front it was necessary to walk through it. Peck had his possessions carried up to the front room and her bed put in the back.

On the day they moved in, she was exhausted with the carrying and unpacking. By nine o'clock she could hardly pull herself up the steep narrow stairs. Percy stayed below, finishing off half a bottle of whisky he'd managed to bring with him. She was drifting off to sleep when she heard him shouting. She was too drowsy to answer.

'For God's sake, Elin, where are you?' The bare electric light bulb over her head burst into life. She pulled the bedclothes over her head, only to have him snatch them away. 'What are you doing here? There's no sense in us both balancing on a single mattress.'

'What?' Elin was blinking back to wakefulness.

'That thin flock mattress wasn't worth bringing. It would hurt my back, even if it was bigger. Come to the other room.'

'Oh!' Elin pulled herself up the bed in dismay. She'd not expected a disturbed night. Only once had Percy ever shown her any physical affection, when he'd put his lips against her cheek after their trip to New Brighton. Mostly he treated her with veiled impatience. It hadn't occurred to her he'd be interested in sex. Theirs was a business arrangement.

'Come to my room. Don't lie there looking at me as though you're stupid.'

'Your room? Why?'

'Why d'you think? I'm your husband, aren't I? You insisted I should be.' He pulled the bedclothes off her, leaving her shivering. 'Well, come on, there are obligations to marriage.'

'With you, Percy? I didn't think you'd be interested. I mean, you've never shown—'

'Couldn't muscle in on Laurence Oxley's territory. He wouldn't have liked that. It's different now he's cast you off.'

Elin shivered again. That was hurtful. She addressed the knobs on her iron bedstead. 'He didn't exactly cast me off.'

'What would you call it then? You shouldn't have let him get away with it. Getting you pregnant like that, and you only sixteen. You're too innocent for your own good. Unworldly. You'll be telling me next you did it for love.'

Elin blinked back the tears. It had happened without her consent. She hadn't been able to stop it. Yet she had felt love.

'Anyway you wanted to be my wife, so come on and try it. If I'm to have the responsibility of looking after you, I might as well have the advantages too.'

'No,' she said as firmly as she could. This had not been part of the bargain. But they hadn't discussed anything but the practicalities of getting a house and finding work.

He grabbed hold of her arm, pulling at her, so she almost fell out on the floor. She didn't see his other hand coming up, but the sharp clip against her ear sent her spinning.

'Don't you dare refuse me. It's my right. Now come on.' She pushed herself upright against the wall and, half blinded with pain, stumbled to his room. She felt dizzy.

His bed was cold and small for two. His breath smelled of whisky and onions, and the stubble on his chin was sandpaper rough.

After that she didn't expect any show of affection from him. She didn't get it. He wasted no time on kissing or fondling. No preliminaries at all.

'Open your legs,' he said, rolling on top of her. He was brutal. Percy wanted straight sex and plenty of it. Several times she thought he'd finished, but he found renewed energy. At last, he rolled off and pushed her away. With Percy it wasn't an act of love at all. In no time, he was snoring.

Elin felt bruised and sore, the side of her head ached. It took her a long time to get back to sleep. She'd exchanged Laurence Oxley for Percy Peck, and of the two she much preferred Laurence. He'd said to her more than once: 'You enjoy it too, you might as well admit it. We're good for each other, Elin.'

Percy didn't care whether she enjoyed it or not. Neither did he care that she was six months pregnant with another man's child. In that respect, Elin decided, the married state was worse than the single.

CHAPTER EIGHT

Elin heard the knock on the door and flung her duster into a cupboard. Bridie was on the doorstep, smiling but looking unfamiliar out of uniform.

'Oh, this is nice, Elin! You've got it lovely.' She took off her hat.

'Oh Bridie, you've had your hair bobbed!'

'Yes, everybody's having it done now. One and six, at Miss Wallis's in Grange Road.'

'You look so different. All neat and short.' No longer would the long strands of hair escape her bun to hang down her face. 'It suits you.'

'Shows the grey a bit, doesn't it? Wish I was blonde like you. I might have a perm next month. You didn't tell me I'd feel lightheaded without my bun.'

Elin took her matronly coat and hung it behind the curtain on the front door. 'This is our parlour. Do you like it?'

'Yes, you are lucky to have a place of your own.' Her brown eyes darted round, storing up every detail to recount to Mrs Dooley. 'I always liked this light oak table and sideboard when they were in the housekeeper's room. That was when we had a housekeeper. Mr Laurence decided to turn her room into an office. That's not old Mr Oxley's chair?' She stopped in front of it aghast.

'Yes, from his study,' Elin nodded. 'Percy wanted it, said leather looked expensive.'

Bridie sniffed, she looked stout in her flowered rayon dress. 'I wouldn't have let him bring it. I can see old Mr Oxley slumped dead in it now. It would always remind me.'

'Yes, I know what you mean.'

'It's like having his ghost here with you.'

'I told him any other chair would suit me better.'

'Peck's very money-minded,' Bridie said. 'He'd want it if he thinks it cost more.'

Elin stifled a smile. 'He wanted to bring old Mr Oxley's roll-top desk, but Mr Laurence vetoed that. Decided it was good enough to go to his new house.'

'We're moving on Monday. It's a palace, Elin. You wouldn't believe it.'

'Have you seen it?'

'No, it's out at Caldy. Eight miles away. All right for them that has a car. Won't be as good for shopping on the day off. It's what he says.'

'Oh, Mr Laurence is full of talk.'

'Mrs Oxley too, they're quite excited about it. We hear them talking. There's views across the River Dee from the drawing room. Is this your kitchen?'

'Yes, the kettle's on the boil, and I made some scones to Mrs Dooley's recipe.'

'The grate's come up a treat.'

'Black lead and elbow grease, like you said. I'm pleased with it.' Elin had thought it rather old fashioned. 'Cooks a treat, once you get used to the dampers. Uses a lot of coal though. Have a seat.'

'Here I am and not telling you the news.'

'What news?'

'Mrs Oxley's had her baby.'

'What? Already?' Elin straightened up and hoped her baby would come with so little waiting. 'I thought they planned to be in the new house?'

'Planned, yes, but she was taken into hospital suddenly last night, some complication. She had a Caesarean. She's all right though, and so's the baby. They think it's normal.'

'What did she have?'

'A girl, to be called Jane. You'd think they'd choose a better name wouldn't you? It's so plain and ordinary. I'd have called her Charmaine.'

The front door slammed shut. Elin half rose from her chair in surprise. Percy stood in the doorway as Bridie's voice went on, 'You've got a light hand with scones, I must say. Just as good as Mrs Dooley's, and she's a proper cook. Six pound six ounces she was.'

'What's the matter?' Elin asked Percy, her heart turning over with fear. He looked different, as though he'd had a shock. His arrogance was dented.

'Good God, Bridie! You round here gossiping as soon as I turn my back.' Elin could see the effort he was making to appear normal. 'What have you done to your hair? You're dressing mutton up as lamb.'

'Something's happened,' Elin said; she knew it wasn't anything good.

'I've come to give your house the once over,' Bridie said. 'Jolly nice. Don't you have all the luck!'

'No, I don't. I'll have a cup of tea, Elin.' She got another cup and saucer from the scullery.

'And I bring you all the news. The baby's arrived.'

Elin saw his eyes go to her abdomen. Oh God, he might as well tell Bridie in words. She surely wouldn't miss that?

'You mean the Oxley baby?'

'Of course. Three weeks early, she was. She's to be called Jane.'

Elin busied herself pouring tea. She was having difficulty holding the pot straight, some went in the saucer. She knew her cheeks were scarlet.

'What are you doing home from work at this time?' Bridie turned on him. Elin let out a long pent-up breath. He'd not be able to sidestep Bridie.

'What do you mean?' he was blustering.

'Elin said you were at work all day.'

'Well, she's wrong, isn't she? From now on she's wrong. I've walked out.' He was smoothing his hair back though it didn't need it. The Brylcreem made it look like patent leather.

'Why?' Elin demanded. She felt sick. 'Jobs aren't that easy to come by.'

'I'm not working for the likes of Mr Croft. He accused me of stealing. Just because he found me having a glass of claret in the pantry. Would you believe it?'

Elin sat down with a bump, remembering the steak he'd brought home.

'Perks of the job,' I told him. 'Normal practice to finish off what's left in the bottles. I was having it with my lunch, too. The agreement was I'd have my food there.'

'Then why?' Bridie wanted to know. 'Did you open a new bottle? You must have known you wouldn't get away with that except with old Mr Oxley.'

'I told him I didn't want his precious job. I could get a better one. It's true, and I didn't like working there anyway.'

'What will we do?' Elin worried.

'We'll be all right, you'll see. I'll get another, and we've got a bit behind us anyway.' He winked at her theatrically. Bridie could hardly miss that either.

'Another scone, Bridie?' Elin was feeling quite fluttery. Why did this have to happen while Bridie was here?

'Come on then.' Peck lowered himself on the other chair and reached for the scones. 'What's the rest of the news from Birchgrove?'

'Nothing to match yours, Peck. Mr Laurence has started his new business. He's expecting to make his fortune.'

'He already has,' Elin said making an effort. She wanted to appear normal too.

'Another fortune,' Bridie repeated her eyes round. 'He says everybody will have a car soon and they'll all need petrol. He says he's going to sell it from pumps, and he's going to have mechanics to mend the cars when they go wrong.'

'He's giving up old Mr Oxley's African business then?' Peck asked. 'These scones need more sugar, Elin.'

'No, he's got some big scheme going in the Niger delta too. You know that. Mr Laurence means to be rich rich.'

'Any sort of rich would suit me,' Elin murmured.

'Oh, we've got a bit behind us,' Percy said again. 'We'll be all right.'

'Perhaps I can get a job,' Elin said. Then she wanted to bite her tongue off.

'You! Hah hah hah!' Peck peeled out. She kicked him under the table. Did he have to tell Bridie everything?

'You're a fool, Percy Peck. It was a good job.' Bridie was making no move to leave. 'You don't know when you're well off.'

Elin was glad Bridie was speaking her mind. He might listen to her.

'I can do better.' Percy's air of superiority had gone. It had shaken him.

'It's one thing to get a job, it's another to keep it.'

'Damn it, I was with the Oxleys for nine years.'

'You lived on them, Peck, not worked for them. Another job like that would be a miracle.' Bridie patted her new hair style. 'You should see the baby clothes she's got, Elin. Little gowns of silk and lace. Shawls of soft cobwebby wool.'

Elin had a sinking feeling. Percy had let her down. She felt insecure without a steady wage coming in, vulnerable. She'd married Percy to provide it while she couldn't work. Now, after only three weeks, he'd thrown it over.

'She'll never use half the clothes before the baby grows out of them,' Bridie gossiped on, unaware that they were both waiting for her to leave. Elin was afraid Percy would suggest it, and upset Bridie.

Bridie had a half day and would be free till ten tonight. If she didn't leave soon Elin would have to offer her supper.

'I don't like the monthly nurse. She moved in last night, though Mrs Oxley won't be home for a while. Everything has to be just right for her. Thinks she's too good to eat in the kitchen. Never considers the extra work she makes.' Suddenly Bridie looked from one to the other. 'A lovely tea, Elin, thank you. I'll come again some time when Peck is out. Are you going to show me upstairs before I go? I want to see all over your love nest, Peck!'

Elin was on her feet in an instant, relieved by Birdie's hint of departure.

'Love nest you call it?' Peck had to get up to clear the way to the stairs. Elin held her breath, expecting to hear him say: Precious little love here.

'This way,' she said unnecessarily, glad to leave Peck downstairs.

'You've got it nice,' Bridie peered into every corner, 'I

do say that. But you'll have to stand up to Peck, or he'll walk all over you. Giving up his job like that! He never did like work. You'll have to get tough with him.' Elin led the way down again, feeling washed out.

'I've brought a little present for your house.' Bridie delved in her shopping bag while Peck found her coat. She brought out a blue Delft cheese dish from her shopping bag. 'I don't suppose you've got one of these yet?'

'No, we haven't, thank you.' Elin took it. 'It's nice, and it goes with our blue plates.'

'Hope we've got cheese to go in it,' Peck said. 'Did it come from the Oxleys?' Elin felt lightheaded, Percy seemed to be goading Bridie.

'No, I bought it in Courtneys.' Her tone was cold, and she turned her back on him, watching Elin. 'How do you put up with him?'

Elin felt the room spinning round. She'd been on her fet all day preparing for this visit. Percy had delivered a body blow, as well as making the going difficult.

'Are you all right?' Bridie's voice sounded a long way away. She knew she was falling.

Bridie's strong arms wrapped themselves round her, holding her upright. She could feel Bridie's corsets pressing against her swollen abdomen. Then she was being guided into old Mr Oxley's chair. She felt herself slump down on the slippery leather, as he used to.

'Elin! Elin, what's the matter?' Bridic was rubbing her hands.

'She's fainted!'

'She's . . . she's having a baby!' Bridie's voice was awestruck.

'I'm all right.' Elin tried to pull herself up the chair.

'When?' Bridie's mouth wouldn't close. 'When?'

'September,' Elin whispered, putting her hands over her face.

'Oh God, Peck! She's only a child herself. How could you?' Condemnation was thick in Bridie's voice. 'Only just seventeen, and an innocent country girl. You men are all the same.'

Elin wanted to scream a warning to Peck. 'Don't tell her!' Laurence had been very insistent, nobody at Birchgrove must know.

'You're blaming the wrong man.' Peck's voice was supercilious. 'But then you never did like me. I'm picking up the pieces, Bridie. Doing my best for her.'

'You mean Mr Laurence?' The horror in her voice hung between them.

'Who else?'

'Oh my God!'

Elin turned into the chair and began to cry. She'd promised him, and now Bridie had found out.

'That won't help,' Peck snapped irritably.

'Ah, love, why didn't you tell me?' Bridie was gathering her into her arms, rocking her backwards and forwards. It made her feel sick. 'What can I do to help?'

'There's nothing . . .' Elin shook her head miserably and then blew her nose on the handkerchief Bridie held out. Damn Laurence, probably she'd never see him again. Why should she worry about letting him down? Wasn't all this his fault? He'd let her down.

'It would help if you went, Bridie,' Peck said. 'You've done enough.'

Elin felt the long pause, the indecision. 'I'm all right,' she whispered.

'Goodbye then, Elin.' She felt Bridie's kiss. It made her want to cry again.

'Don't come again,' Peck said. 'You've upset her.'

'No,' Elin protested. 'No Bridie, it's not you. But don't say anything, at Birchgrove, please.'

Bridie turned, her eyes anguished. 'If that's what you want.'

She nodded. 'Please.'

'Thank God she's gone,' Percy said the moment he'd slammed the door behind her. 'You mustn't encourage Bridie, or she'll be here by the minute.'

'I like her. Bridie's kind and the only person I know round here. Percy, what are we going to live on?'

'Don't start that again. What's for dinner?'

'I don't know. Scrambled eggs?'

'That's all?'

'I didn't expect you.'

'Let's go out for supper.'

'Percy! No, I don't feel like it, and we can't spend money like that!'

'Course we can. We deserve a little treat. It's been a hard day. We could go back to the Woodside and eat in the dining room. That would show Mr Croft just how much I need his rotten job.'

'No, I'd be too embarrassed. No, Percy, there's no sense . . .' She began putting the cups and saucers in the sink.

'All right, we'll go somewhere else then. Get your hat and coat.' Elin hesitated, they couldn't afford to spend more money, but he'd never be satisfied with eggs. She did as he asked, and felt better once she was out in the fresh air.

As they were passing Talbot's newspaper shop, Percy said: 'I'll get a paper. See if there are any jobs advertised.' Elin waited outside, reading the notices in the window.

Percy could advertise here, she thought. Or they could advertise for a lodger for their spare room. She was feeling quite buoyed up by the idea, when another notice caught her eye.

'Required on these premises. Woman experienced in housework. For three hours on three mornings weekly.'

For a moment she was tempted to apply. She could still do that, three mornings a week was nothing. With that and the lodger, she'd survive. What did she need Peck for? She'd be better without him. Percy had come out and had the pages of the *Liverpool Echo* opened up.

'Here's just the job for me,' he chortled. 'Listen to this. "Honest, well-spoken male to work in Gentleman's Outfitters with a view to taking charge." '

'Apply for it then,' Elin said, rejecting the idea of a lodger. They couldn't have a lodger in a bedroom they had to pass through to reach their own, and anyway, she'd need it for the baby. There was no space for a cot in the front.

With the baby so close, she had to rely on Percy to bring in a wage.

Elin manoeuvred the sewing machine slowly round the neck of the tiny nightdress, and felt a glow of satisfaction at the neat line of stitches. She'd had a pleasant day, getting up with Percy and waving him off, smartly dressed, to the shop.

Percy was enjoying his new job, and was easier to cope with. He said shop work was much more his style. It gave him pleasure to see rows of garments swinging on their hangers, and to discuss the latest wide lapels or plus fours with customers.

For Elin, tidying and polishing her own little house was more an enjoyment than a chore. When she'd finished this morning, she'd taken last week's copy of *Home Chat* and gone down to the market to buy the cloth recommended for use with their free paper pattern. She'd spent the afternoon making up four nightdresses for the coming baby.

Feeling pleased with what she'd achieved, and pleasantly tired with her exertions, she filled the kettle, and put it on the hob to boil. Percy was due home. His key was scraping in the lock before she'd picked up the snippets of thread from the floor.

'How do you like this?' She held up one of the nighties to show him.

'Baby clothes,' Percy sniffed, flinging himself down in his chair. 'Is there any tea?'

'I've got four nighties out of two yards of flannelette at ninepence a yard, and I found enough lace to go down the front of each for twopence.'

'Very nice.' Percy was noncommittal, glancing at them briefly.

'I also bought four yards of terry towelling at sixpence a yard. Not the best quality, but it'll do. Napkins are easy, just a matter of hemming, and quite a saving. What's in your bag?'

'I bought myself a pair of Oxford bags.' He reached for the paper carrier. The name of the shop where he worked was printed on it, Robinson's, Gents Outfitters of Distinction.

'Pearl grey flannel, the very latest fashion, and a trilby to go with them.'

'There's enough material in each leg to make a dress for me,' Elin said with wonder, testing it between her finger and thumb. 'Lovely material.'

'Best wool flannel. Thirty shillings the pair.'

'Thirty shillings! You'll look like you're wearing a skirt.'

'Nonsense. Everybody's wearing them.'

'You already have smart clothes, Percy.' Elin felt the sting of resentment. Thirty shillings would buy the baby a magnificent layette.

'I need them, can't work in a fashion shop and look dowdy. There's special terms for staff. Quite a saving.'

'Where's the jacket?'

'There is no jacket, silly. My navy blazer will go well.'

'Don't you have to wear a suit to work?'

'Yes, well . . .'

'I need things for the baby, Percy.'

'You're making them.'

'I mean a cot and a pram.'

He looked at her coldly. 'I don't see why I should pay for things like that.'

'Mr Laurence's money . . .'

'That was paid to me. For marrying you.'

'He meant us to share it,' she returned tartly, resentment getting the better of her. 'He meant us to buy a house, not fancy clothes for you. Buy it now, Percy, you still could. Two hundred and ten pounds, and we'd be saved paying rent for ever.'

'We'd have to pay for repairs then, and the money's too useful as a nest egg.'

'You'd have enough over for a nest egg.'

'I'll think about it,' he said, but she knew he wouldn't.

'I must get a cot. Perhaps I could pick one up secondhand.'

'You still have money of your own.'

'It's dwindling fast. I ran out of housekeeping last week again, and I spent some on steak for you.'

'Then you must learn to manage your money better.'

'About the cot—'

'Use your own money, Elin. When am I going to get a cup of tea?'

She measured three spoonfuls from the caddy, and tipped the kettle over them. 'There's stew and dumplings for dinner.'

'I'm not too hungry tonight. Went to the Woodside for my lunch. Their steak and kidney pie is good.'

Elin looked at him, shocked. 'That would cost another shilling! What a waste of money, when we need—'

'More, I had half a bottle of burgundy to go with it. It was worth every penny to see Croft's face. I told him I'd got a better job.'

'If you manage to keep it,' Elin flared. 'Drinking in the middle of the day. I bet it took longer than the half hour you're allowed. You're a fool, Percy Peck. You don't know when you're well off.'

'I'd be better off without you, I know that. I'm going out.' He grabbed at his new clothes and went upstairs.

'Have your dinner first. No point in spending on a meal out when I've got one ready for you,' she called after him.

'You nag too much, Elin. A man needs a bit of relaxation when he's been working all day.'

She sat at the table waiting for him, the sewing machine still out. When he came down, his hair had been re-slicked back, his dark eyes glittered with pride and his new trousers flapped in huge folds round his legs.

'You wanted to marry me,' he said arrogantly. 'This is my compensation. My money to spend as I like.'

'Do you want your dinner first?'

'No. It'll keep till tomorrow, won't it?'

The door slammed behind him. Elin dropped her head on her hands. Laurence had meant her to have a share of the money. She had only four pounds left of her own, and would have to earn more. It was no use relying on Percy.

She ate some of the stew; if she added more water, it

would do for both of them again tomorrow. She'd been in bed for hours when Percy came to lie beside her. He was cold and smelled of whisky. Elin pretended to be asleep.

By the next morning, Elin had decided she'd advertise for a secondhand cot. She wrote her requirements on a card, which she'd pay to put in the newsagent's window. She was afraid four pounds would not be enough for a pram too, but if she had definite prices, perhaps Percy would help. When she reached Talbot's, she paused to read the cards already on the board. There was nothing suitable offered for sale.

On the step she hesitated again, there was a commotion inside. She almost retreated. A fat woman in a stained coat with the hem undone on one side was shouting at the top of her voice: 'Bloody fusspot you are, wanting the place like Buckingham Palace. It's a dump. Hasn't been cleaned properly for years. It stinks.' The shocked faces of the proprietors stared back at her from behind the counter. 'Think you're Lady Muck, don't you, Mrs Talbot?' Elin was elbowed against a magazine rack, the shop door slammed and the bell above jangled violently.

Mr Talbot recovered first, and attempted a smile in Elin's direction. He was tall and balding, his few grey hairs spread carefully to cover as much scalp as possible. 'What can I get for you, dear?'

'I've brought a card to put in your window.'

'Twopence a week,' Mr Talbot said, but it was his wife who took it.

'I asked her not to sweep dirt under the mats.' Her over-genteel voice was faint. 'I do want the place clean, but I'm not fussy, am I, Donald?'

'Women starting and then storming out. You'd never believe how hard it is to get reliable help,' he said, hobbling out from behind the counter. He was wearing carpet slippers.

'I'm not that hard to work for.' Mrs Talbot had the look of a woman who felt she was a class above her customers. Her permed grey hair was set in rigid waves. 'I'm getting desperate, it's been going on for weeks.'

'I'd like the job,' Elin said. 'Three mornings a week, isn't it? I'm very clean in my work.' Mrs Talbot's small round eyes seemed to see her for the first time. The shop door pinged and another customer came in.

'Come through.'

Elin followed her to the living room behind the shop, where a lad with a thatch of flaming red hair was sitting at the table reading *Picture Post*.

'Tom, go and help your father,' she said sharply. He got to his feet but his shoulders remained hunched, as though embarrassed by being six foot tall and as thin as a piece of string. She turned back to Elin. 'With the shop and everything, I have to have help.'

'I can start right now, this morning.'

'Good, I'll show you what needs doing.'

'I'm having a baby.' It was the first time Elin had spoken of it like this. But Mrs Talbot knew nothing of her circumstances. 'So I'll have to have a break, but I'd like the job permanently.'

'Well, I don't know.' She was eyeing Elin's abdomen.

'By then you'll know if I suit.'

'If you do,' she glanced down at the card in Elin's hand, 'then I suppose it'll be all right. Though I won't be able to manage long without anybody.'

'Thank you. I'd like this card to go in your window.'

Mrs Talbot continued to stare at it. 'I've got a pram and cot up in the loft. I'm passed needing them again. They'll need cleaning. Been up there a long time.'

Elin smiled. 'That'll not worry me.'

'I'll get our Tom to bring them down. There's other things, a high chair. I'll let you have them cheap, or you could work for them instead?'

'Yes, I'd like that.' Elin's golden eyes lit up. It would be marvellous not to have to hand over her last four pounds.

She started working with the minimum of fuss. Wearing a loose pinafore over her jumper and skirt, her pregnancy was not all that obvious, though she had difficulty bending over. It gave her heartburn to scrub floors, but she knew she'd find enough energy to work three mornings a week, from nine till one.

During a slack moment in the shop, Tom went up to the loft. When Elin saw what he was bringing down and stacking in the yard, she felt she'd had her first stroke of luck.

'What a big pram!'

'That belonged to a friend. She had one baby and then twins. Emigrated to Canada, she did,' Mrs Talbot told her. 'Had a bit of wear but it's not all that old.'

Elin appraised it. It was shabby, but heavily built and strong. The wheels were small and the body deep.

'A big pram's a blessing, if you have another. Plenty of room for one each end. Get a bit of oil on these wheels, Tom.'

'I'm thrilled.' Elin opened a cardboard box and found bedding for the cot, and baby clothes. 'Thank you.'

'You won't need to buy a push chair either. The mattress comes out.' Mrs Talbot demonstrated. 'And there's a false bottom. If you remove this middle section, a toddler can sit with his legs down the well. Plenty of room for two toddlers face to face. Better than a push chair, warmer in winter, and room for shopping.'

Elin smiled. 'I'm delighted with it all.'

At dinner time, Tom collapsed the cot, lifted it on top of the pram and wheeled it home for her. He seemed shy, having little to say.

'You work in the shop, Tom?'

'Just helping out for a few weeks. I've got a place on the *Conway*.' She heard the note of pride in his voice. For a moment, he straightened his shoulders, lifting his fiery head another two inches.

'What's that?'

He looked at her in astonishment. 'You know, HMS *Conway*. You must have seen her anchored in the Mersey. A wooden sailing vessel dating from the Napoleonic wars.'

'Sort of black and white squares?'

'That's right.'

'It's a training ship?'

'Yes, for officers of the merchant navy.'

'I didn't know, but I've seen boys rowing out to it.'

'One of the best training schools in England.' He marched on, bending his height over the pram.

'There's another ship. An iron one, black and yellow,' Elin said. 'I've seen lots of boys rowing out to that too.'

His red head nodded. 'The *Indefatigable*. Not in the same class. Trains seamen. Ordinary seamen.'

Elin heard the touch of snobbery in his voice, and knew he'd got that from his mother. 'Oh, yes,' she said.

He took the pram home again so he could wheel round the high chair and mattress. Elin was delighted. She tipped Tom sixpence for helping her carry the things upstairs.

She didn't tell Percy she had a job. He found out when he got the sack from Robinson's. She'd already gone when he shouted down for morning tea.

Elin was at work when she felt her first labour pains. The baby was two weeks early.

'I didn't know you were so close to your time.' Mrs Talbot was anxious. 'It's wrong you working.'

'I'd like to keep the job. I'll come back as soon as I can.' Elin held on to the mangle as the next pain came; it made her groan.

'Have you booked a midwife? I could send our Tom to tell her.'

'Yes, please.' Elin could feel the perspiration on her forehead. She pushed her golden hair back, it felt damp and stringy. 'Ask him to hurry.'

'Will you be all right walking home?'

'Yes.'

'You shouldn't have come in today.' Mrs Talbot was getting worked up.

'I'll be all right. I've finished the washing.'

Elin was frightened, though trying not to show it. The five-minute walk home took longer. She had to stop when a contraction creased her. Peck was still in bed. He got up in a hurry and made her a cup of tea.

She was glad when the midwife came upstairs and took charge. She said it was an easy birth.

Afterwards Elin looked down at her daughter as she lay in her arms. She weighed seven pounds two ounces, with every limb rounded and pleasing. She had pretty, even features, and a shading of fair down over her head. She was perfect in every way, except that her mother had narrowly missed being a fallen woman, and her father wouldn't even acknowledge her existence.

That night Elin dreamed Laurence had come to see her, bringing a silver rattle for the baby. He'd bent his bronze head to kiss her and she'd caught again the scent of his spicy aftershave. Then, thrilled as she was, he'd perched on the side of her bed and unwrapped the baby from her swaddling blankets. His intense blue eyes had been filled with love as he congratulated her on producing a more beautiful baby than Sybil. She wished she could have the Oxley name.

If the baby had been a boy, Elin had planned to call him Laurence. For a girl it wasn't quite so easy. She could be Laurel or Laura, or perhaps Lauren.

'Call her Laura,' Percy said irritably when she asked his opinion. 'The others are too bloody fancy. Laura Peck.'

'Laura it is,' Elin agreed, hugging the child to her. She hadn't expected this glow of pleasure in her child. From the first moments, love came into Elin's life.

As soon as she turned into Jubilee Street, Elin saw Beattie Higgs hovering on her front steps, wearing her husband's mackintosh with her old slippers.

'Your baby's crying inside,' Beattie called, but Elin could hear her already thirty yards up the street. 'Been at it for hours. I'd have seen to her but the door's locked.'

Panic-stricken, Elin broke into a run with her key at the ready. In the rush of anguish, she was clumsy and couldn't make it turn in the lock.

'Percy,' she shouted the moment the door opened. 'Percy!'

'He went out hours ago,' Beattie answered indignantly, from outside. 'I'd have looked after the little mite, if you'd asked.'

Laura's piteous cries tore at her heart. Elin rushed

upstairs, stumbling on the top step, to see Laura's legs and arms flailing, her cot covers long since kicked off.

'Laurie love.' At the sound of her voice the baby stopped in mid-scream and turned to listen, her face scarlet and awash with tears.

'Mam's here, love,' Elin sobbed, overcome with guilt that her baby had been neglected. She was lying on her rubber sheet wringing with sweat, tears and urine. Her nappy was sodden and had soaked her nightdress, binder and vest. Her sheets had twisted into a damp knot and been kicked to the bottom of the cot. She hadn't been changed since Elin had left home this morning. Hadn't been fed either, though Elin had expressed milk and left it for her. Laura had had no attention for seven hours. Elin snatched her up in a hug.

'Oh Laurie love, I'm sorry.' Her tears mingled with those on the baby's face.

A tide of guilt washed over Elin as she slumped down on her bed, unbuttoning her blouse. The infant grasped her nipple as though she hadn't been fed for a week, took a few mighty sucks and then released it to whimper softly, sucking in breaths that shook her whole body. It was some time before she would settle down and feed.

Damn Percy! Elin was crying with rage too, every bone in her body aching with fatigue. He'd promised to look after Laura while she worked; instead he'd gone out and left her.

Laura had exhausted herself with crying. Her eyelids were closing, her lips slipping off the nipple, her little body still shaking with an occasional sob. Elin lifted her onto her shoulder and took her down to the kitchen. She set a kettleful of water to heat on the stove, got out the big enamel bowl, and found some clean clothes. She'd not had time to iron; the crumpled baby nightdress seemed another example of neglect.

Gently she slid off the baby's malodorous clothing and lowered her into the warm water. She was rewarded by Laurie's gurgle of delight and shining green eyes. Afterwards, she sat rocking her to sleep in her arms, reluctant even to put her in her cot.

'Laurie love, I won't leave you again ever.' A wavering

smile parted the baby's lips as though she understood. 'I'll make it up to you, I promise. You'll have a good life.'

She felt a bitter rolling fury for Percy. What a fool she'd been to trust him. 'I could kill you for this,' she spat out, as though he could hear.

He didn't come home at the usual time of five o'clock for his evening meal. That added more fire to her fury. It was ten thirty when he came in.

'Where've you been?' Elin rounded on him, not surprised to see him dressed in his Oxford bags and trilby. 'Out enjoying yourself, that's for sure.'

'Been to Haydock races, if you want to know.' She could smell the whisky on his breath from the other side of the room.

'You left Laura. She was crying—'

'She was asleep when I went. Didn't want anything. Didn't miss me for hours, I'm sure.'

Elin put her face close to his. 'Don't you ever do such a thing again, Percy Peck. You are the lowest of the low. You promised to look after her.'

Percy's face leered at her. His fist came up and sent her flying into the corner, knocking the breath from her body. She screamed with shock and pain.

'Shut up woman. Stop whining. You wanted this, don't forget.'

Percy was drunk. He was always more quarrelsome when he'd had a drink, but she hadn't thought he'd attack her physically. Not like this.

She ran upstairs to the baby, snatching her out of the cot to hold her close. Laura stirred, opened her green eyes and smiled again. It was a comfort to hold the bundle of blankets. Love for her baby brimmed over.

Percy had hit her and meant to hurt her! Elin was shaking all over. Her cheek bone throbbed. She crept into the bedroom she shared with Percy to look at her face in the wardrobe mirror. Already it was swelling on one side. Her eye was red and puffy, and she'd bitten her own lip till it bled.

What a drudge she looked! Her hair was stringy and

needed washing, her eyes dull, her skin pasty. Her clothes were an untidy mess. Once, Laurence Oxley had called her his golden girl, but there was no glistening of gold about her now. Her energy was leaking away. She couldn't keep on top of the chores. She was perennially tired.

What a mess she'd made of everything. Running away from Llanddolfa to this. She hadn't known when she was well off. She'd had a good home at Tonteg. Why hadn't she stood up for herself? Told everyone her father was a despot, and their relations were severed. Bessie Roberts wouldn't have minded giving her time off on Saturdays.

She'd have been all right in Birkenhead if she'd opened her mouth when Laurence Oxley first came near her. What if she had lost her job? She could have got another. Ruby had had more sense.

The baby whimpered and stirred in her arms. Elin sat down again, hugging her close, studying the lines of her face. Laurie would not grow up to resemble her. The slanting almond eyes were not there. Laura's eyes were green and shining with intelligence. Already there was determination in her bobble of a chin, and tenacity of purpose in the twist of her smile. Elin paused and looked at her from a different angle. She was seeing a likeness to Laurence Oxley.

It would be a good thing if Laura were like him. Elin didn't want to see Laura in her position twenty years from now. She was going to need all her father's drive to survive.

Elin was filled with a desperate need to let Laurence know how much she needed his help now. He'd believed marrying Percy was in her best interests. He wouldn't knowingly have let her in for this violence and drunkenness. And she couldn't believe Laurence wouldn't care about his own daughter. He'd want to see her. Her mind was crowding with schemes of how she would bring about such a meeting. He would offer enough money to allow her to stay at home and take care of Laura herself.

Then she thought of him living with his family round him in a different house in Caldy occupied with his businesses. She didn't want to jeopardise any of that for him, and he'd probably have forgotten her by now. Where would she find the courage to contact him anyway?

After an hour, she crept halfway downstairs and saw Percy asleep in his chair. She crept back, undressed and crawled into the single bed in Laura's room, hoping Percy would stay where he was.

She had to think. It would be like this until Laura went to school, unless something happened to Percy. She wished he'd go away, find another woman, get run over by a bus. Anything.

Perhaps she could take Laura with her to work. She had managed to find herself five different domestic jobs since Laura was born, and worked a few hours at each, every week. Some of her employers wouldn't mind. Laura was a contented baby, she didn't cry much for attention. Mrs Talbot wouldn't mind, she could leave the pram in the yard. Mrs Black wouldn't either. If she had to spend time changing or feeding, she could make it up. Beattie Higgs would look after her, if all else failed, though on a regular basis she'd expect to be paid.

She'd have to try it. She couldn't risk leaving Laura with him again. Elin turned her face into the pillow weeping silently.

Book Two – 1938

CHAPTER NINE

Laura Peck rinsed her cup at the scullery sink, her anger boiling up. She'd found it impossible to concentrate at school. Mam's face, shocked and bleeding, came between her and everything else. Da must have been battering her for years, and she hadn't realised. How could she have been so blind?

Mam had looked ill this morning, with bruising under her golden eyes, her lip cut and swollen. How could she stop him?

'Don't go to work today,' she'd whispered, her arms round Mam's thin body.

'We need the money, love.' Mam had pushed her golden hair from her forehead with a desperate gesture. The scar showed where he'd hit her last month. Her blonde hair was fading, but it was still lighter and brighter than her own.

'Honey blonde is pretty too,' she often said, while Laura would feel her hands gently moulding it round her face. 'With enough natural curl to make it wave. It is pretty.' But she sensed Mam would have liked her to be more like her. Mam's golden almond eyes had once been truly beautiful. 'Green eyes are beautiful too,' Mam said, but Laura knew they were more ordinary.

'You're not like me, Laura. You're strong and single-minded. You'll make a success of your life.'

'You're a success. You're beautiful.'

Mam had smiled and shaken her head. 'No. Perhaps I was once, but it did me no good. I didn't have your strength. Look at me now. I'm a broken reed.'

Laura desperately wanted to help her, but how? She'd

rushed home from school to do a few household chores, but she usually did them anyway. She put the cup away and went to the parlour window to look down the street. It was raining hard. She didn't feel like going out again to do her paper round, but she didn't want to be home when Da came in. Good, no sign of him yet.

The fire was just beginning to make the kitchen warm. It had been difficult to light tonight. There were so few sticks left and she mustn't use them all, otherwise how would she light it tomorrow?

She lifted her coat from the chair where she'd left it to dry off after coming home from school. It felt wet enough to ring out. She held it in front of the flames till clouds of vapour rolled off it, but she hadn't much time. Last night had been truly terrible. She'd been woken by Mam's screams from the adjoining bedroom, and rushed in.

'What's the matter?' Her heart had been pounding with fright. Da's face had been purple with rage, veins throbbing visibly across his temple as he rampaged round the room, knocking brushes and glass off the dressing table. Mam had been cowering in a corner, clutching a pillow to her face.

'Get back to bed, Laura,' he'd raved. 'Stay out of this,' but she'd run to Mam.

'Do as he says.' Mam's wet cheek had brushed hers. 'Please, love. Go quietly.' She knew Mam was terrified he'd turn on her. More frightened of that than she was for herself. Boiling with anger, Laura had had to comply. She'd wanted to fly at him.

She darted back to the parlour window again. Da was coming heavily up the street, coat collar up, head bent against the weather. Seconds later, she was struggling into her hot, moist coat and pulling an old black beret on her head instead of her school hat. No one else from her school did a paper round, and she didn't want it known she did.

'Hello, Da.' She flung open the front door before he had his key out.

'Going already? I'd like a cup of tea.' His eyes were almost black and full of arrogance. His Brylcreemed hair was slicked back above the heavy lines on his forehead, droplets of rain stood in blobs on top.

'There's a cup in the pot.' He wouldn't like it because it would be stewed by now, but he'd drink it rather than go to the trouble of making another.

As she pulled the front door shut behind her, she could see the vapour still rising from her coat. The shop was five minutes' walk away, but she never allowed herself that long to cover the distance. She ran along the greasy pavement, thinking how different her parents were from those of the other girls at school. Why had it taken her so long to understand what was happening to Mam? She couldn't have been more than seven when she'd first overheard angry words and sobs from their bedroom, and next morning Mam had a black eye and dreadful bruising on her arm.

'Did you fall over?' Laura remembered asking. She could also remember the funny way Mam had looked at her.

'Yes. Yes, love. I fell over.'

It had taken her six more years to equate Mam's injuries with Da's bad moods.

A double-decker bus overtook her, spraying water across her black stockings; a few yards ahead it squealed to a halt at the bus stop. Several figures got out into the dusk and hurried away. One remained, huddling over a large package in the middle of the pavement. Laura, head down against the driving rain, was about to pass him.

'Hey, just a moment. Aren't you the paper girl from Talbot's? Mrs Peck's girl?'

'Laura Peck, yes.' She stopped, looking at him for the first time. His smile was friendly.

'You know me. I'm Tom Talbot.'

'Of course, yes.'

He straightened up to his full six foot three, and she wondered why she hadn't recognised him immediately. He was taller than anyone else she knew, his fiery red hair showed under his cap. Nobody forgot Tom Talbot. She remembered him going away to sea, wearing his mercantile marine officer's uniform.

'Sorry to accost you like this in the street, but would you

give me a hand?' He had gentle brown eyes, she thought him outrageously handsome. 'I've brought this home for my parents, and the cord broke as I got off the bus.'

'Shall I take this end?' Laura eyed it curiously. 'What is it?'

'A coffee table. I could manage if you took my bag.'

'Easier for you if I help with the table. Gosh, it's heavy!'

'It's an elephant table. Solid hardwood from the Gold Coast. The place is famous for them.'

'Australia, is that?' She was stumbling. He was so much taller than she was, it was hard to keep her end off the pavement.

'No, West Africa. Hot rainforest.'

'Is that where your ship goes?'

'Yes.' He was wearing a stout gaberdine raincoat, and had a rain cover on his uniform cap.

'Lovely sunshine?'

'Too much sunshine.'

'You can't have too much of that!' She was panting now. At least she felt warm, all except her left foot. She'd forgotten her shoe let in water.

'Nearly there,' he said. 'This is very good of you. I'd never have managed by myself. How old are you?'

'Nearly fourteen.' It was a terrible age to be, she was dreading it. Old enough to leave school and earn a living. She looked into his suntanned face, small lines radiating from the corners of his eyes. He had frown lines too. She wanted to ask how old he was, but some grown-ups resented that. She decided she had to know. The words came out in a rush.

He laughed. 'I'm twenty-seven.' Suddenly his face was alight, the frown lines gone. 'You'll be leaving school soon, then?'

'Yes,' she managed, through clenched teeth.

At last they reached the shop. She balanced the table on the step as he opened the door. It was warm inside and smelled deliciously of newsprint. Laura loved it. It was an Aladdin's cave of delights – desirable magazines that Mrs Talbot read in the back and returned to the racks for sale, tempting jars of sweets and bars of chocolate.

'Tom!' His mother shot from behind the counter where she'd been marking up the evening papers for Laura to deliver. 'We didn't expect you this early!' She gave a nervous laugh. 'Your father's gone into town to the wholesalers.'

Laura stood dripping water onto the red linoleum, watching Tom kiss his mother. Water had collected on his cap cover, and as he bent his head it splashed down onto her and the newspapers.

'Darling, look what you're doing.' Her voice was sharp. 'We can't sell that! Not now.'

He snatched off his cap with one hand and the top newspaper with the other. His hair was a glossy deep red. 'I'll buy it.' He shot behind the counter and rang up the till. 'The rest are only damp.'

'Ugh, you're wet. Do take off those things before you catch your death of cold.' Her fluttering hands caressed the stiff waves in her newly permed grey hair. 'Lovely to have you home again.'

'Lovely to be home. Sorry I missed your anniversary, but here's your present.' He was round the other side of the counter again, stooping to rip wet brown paper from the package. Laura dragged her gaze from his curling red hair and bent to help him.

'It's their twenty-ninth wedding anniversary,' he told her.

'Yes, your mother said, last week.'

'Oh Tom! I do like it.' A large carved elephant stood on a wooden base, supporting a glass table top, through which the beauty of the carving could be seen. 'It's lovely.'

'It's afrormosia, Mum.'

'Thank you, son. Take it through, and wipe it dry. I wouldn't want it spoilt.' She fluttered back to the pile of *Echoes* again. 'Put the kettle on and make a cup of tea.'

Laura shifted her weight from one foot to the other, wishing Mrs Talbot would hurry, so she could start her round. Today, none of Mrs Talbot's concern was for her. She would not be offered tea. Not that she minded, her stomach felt full of fluid. She'd made a pot at home and drunk three cups to fill herself up because there was no bread left for her usual bread and jam. She'd have loved cornflakes, but if she ate them now, there'd be none for breakfast. Thursday nights were always lean. Mam was paid on Fridays.

Her mother had left sixpence for her to get something for tea. It would buy sausages, though not bread as well. She'd peeled some potatoes in readiness before coming out.

The doorbell clanged and a customer came in.

Laura asked: 'Is my round ready, Mrs Talbot?'

'Not quite, dear. Yes, sir, what can I do for you?'

Laura sighed, she was going to be late starting, and she wanted to get home to Mam. Mrs Talbot was unused to marking up, only doing it when her husband was out. She was inclined to be slow and fussy, inclined to gossip, too, with casual customers instead of getting on with the job.

'A quarter of caramel fudge, and two ounces of lemon drops, please.'

Laura watched her unscrew the jar. The sharp scent of lemon drops came in a delicious cloud across the counter, making her mouth fill with saliva. But she wouldn't buy lemon drops, chocolate would be more filling. A bar of Double Six would cost twopence. Perhaps the butcher would have scrag end of neck? But no, that would take ages to cook. Her stomach rumbled noisily.

'I'm just going for some sausages, Mrs Talbot,' she said, deciding she must put temptation out of reach. 'For our tea.'

'We're having roast lamb.' Mrs Talbot flustered to the till as another customer came in. 'It's Tom's favourite.'

The newsagent was in a small parade of shops, and the butcher was two doors up. It was early closing day and the blind was down, but Laura knew if she rang the bell three times, the butcher's twelve-year-old daughter would come and serve her. The shop had been almost cleared. There was a little dried-up mince on one tray, a few tired slices of boiled ham on another.

'A pound of beef sausages, please.' It was that or three-quarters of thick pork, but it always had to be quantity over quality.

It was raining harder than ever. There were three

customers waiting when she got back to Talbot's, as well as Danny Holmes, the other delivery boy.

'Can I mark up my round, Mrs Talbot? I know I can do it.'

'Well, I don't know, dear. We don't want any mistakes.'

'I know it by heart, honestly.' That was true enough. She slid through the flap at the end of the counter where the pile of *Echoes* had been thrown.

'I've poured your cup of tea, Mum.' Tom Talbot was back. 'I'll serve while you go and drink it.'

'I can't now, dear, we're busy.'

'Don't fuss, Mum, I can manage.'

'You'll check Laura marks up properly, won't you? We don't want any complaints.'

'Course, Mum.' He pushed her into the living room. Instantly he seemed at ease in the shop, serving the customers rapidly. Most recognised him, but politely he cut gossip to a minimum.

Laura took the bag from where it hung in the passage and packed her round into it. She no longer felt impatient to get started. She wanted to stay with Tom. She watched him through her lashes. Glossy red hairs grew thickly between his eyebrows, so they almost seemed to join up. Another customer wanted chocolate caramels. The smell of chocolate as they were tipped onto the scales was overpowering. Her stomach rumbled again.

She was starting to mark up her second round when a bar of Cadbury's milk chocolate slid across the papers in front of her. She wanted it so much, it seemed at first a mirage.

'For you, Laura.' She could hardly believe her good fortune. 'For helping me with the table.'

'Thank you. Lovely, thank you.' She laughed while her fingers tore at the wrappings. Silver paper fell to the floor, but she swooped after it and put it in her pocket. She snapped the bar into bite-sized pieces and popped the crumbs into her mouth; the chocolate was deliciously thick on her tongue. She offered a piece to Tom.

He shook his head. She wanted to tell him how grateful she was, but his smile broadened, crinkling the skin round his brown eyes. She offered a piece to Danny Holmes who was reading this week's *Dandy* while he waited. His round wasn't made up either. He took it, of course, but sometimes he shared his sweets with her. Then at last she let a whole square melt on her tongue. It was bliss.

In the lull between customers, Tom Talbot parted the damp pages of the *Echo* he'd paid for and spread them across the counter. She saw him staring at a centre spread of photographs.

'What's that?' His mother came bustling back into the shop.

'Laurence Oxley, our landlord, is in the news.'

Laura was marking the papers with street and number, but her ears, like antennae, were picking up everything he said.

'Local businessman sells garage chain to Shell.'

'Did you say Oxley?' Laura went to look at the pictures.

'Yes, he's here with all his family.'

'Jane Oxley's in my form at school.'

'You go to the same school?' Tom's red eyebrows arched above surprised eyes.

'Yes, Birkenhead High.'

'But I would have thought . . .'

'It's the best school in Birkenhead. A member of the Girls' Public Day School Trust. I won a scholarship.'

'I remember now, your mother saying.' Elin still cleaned for the Talbot's three days a week.

'I'm the odd one out, not Jane Oxley. They look down on me a bit.'

'But if you won a scholarship, you must be the cleverest.'

'No. Jane Oxley's top as often as I am. She's very good at maths.'

'It's a good school,' Mrs Talbot agreed. 'Most pupils go on to university, don't they, Laura?'

She wanted to say yes, she was proud of her school. 'Well, most end up teachers, I suppose, or nurses, or they go into offices. Only the very clever ones get a degree.'

Tom whistled through his teeth. 'Will you?'

She shook her head sadly.

'So you've decided to leave? I thought you liked it there.' Tom's mother came to check what she was doing.

Laura had to blink hard. 'It's decided for me, Mrs Talbot.'

'That's a shame,' Tom said. His sympathy was almost as hard to bear as leaving itself.

'My wage is needed at home now.'

'Your mother said you wanted to be an accountant,' Mrs Talbot said.

'Well, that's what I'd hoped.'

'Couldn't you get a job in an accounts department somewhere, and work yourself up?' Mrs Talbot asked. 'You'll do very well, I'm sure.'

'I wouldn't be a professional accountant,' Laura frowned. 'Not that way.'

'Better start thinking about what's possible.'

'Yes,' Laura agreed.

'Jane Oxley looks like you.' Tom was studying the photograph again.

'Oh, she isn't, not at all.' Laura squinted at the picture. 'But we get weighed and measured at the end of every term, and we're always the same height. Five foot one last time. She's not so skinny.'

'You're both blonde.'

'Nothing like the same colour.' Laura shook her head sadly. 'She's got lovely flaxen hair, all feathery. Her sister has too. Mine's darker.

'Still honey blonde,' Tom said. 'Very nice.'

'And she isn't plagued with freckles.'

'You haven't many. Just a few across your nose.'

'You should see them in the summer.'

'I think they're pretty.' His face was close to hers as he peered at them.

'You'll be turning her head with all this talk,' his mother said. 'He's a one for the girls, Laura. Isn't it time you went on your round?'Laura heaved the bag of papers on her shoulder and set off. It was almost dark and still raining. She knew the round so well, she didn't have to think where she was going. Instead, her mind went over and over the same ground: if only Da went to work, like other fathers. If only he brought in a wage, and wasn't so brutal to Mam. He said it was impossible to get a job what with the depression; he was tired of trying.

She was wet through when she went back to the shop for her second round. One shoe squelched with every step, her foot was numb with cold. At least she wasn't hungry after the chocolate. Tom was kind, a lovely person to think of giving it to her.

Her round finished in Jubilee Street where she lived. Only Da's *Echo* was left in the bag, which she'd take back to the shop tomorrow. She put her key in the door and stepped into the parlour. Here the grate was cold and empty; they only ever lit the fire in the kitchen. What was the sense in stoking two fires, with coal the price it was?

The kitchen light was on and the warmth leaked across the darker parlour. Laura was pulling the curtain over the door to cut off the draught, when she heard his voice.

'I'm sick of waiting. Where is she?'

Laura shivered, there was never peace when Da was home. Every few days a row would erupt, and there was no knowing what would trigger it off.

'Why can't you cook? Are you helpless?'

Laura held her breath. Tell him, Mam, you've been working all day. That you ache with the bruises he's given you. Ask him why he can't cook. He's been sitting in the pub most of the day.

'Laura won't be long.'

'I'm here, Mam,' she said going through to the kitchen. The bruising on Mam's face was more marked now. She looked exhausted. She was not all that old, though her hunched shoulders and tired face made her seem so. Laura went to kiss her cheek.

'I've brought sausages for your tea, Da.' Nothing pleased him. He had the look of a man who had a bad smell under his nose.

'Dinner is what I want,' he said. 'But the way your mother's dragged you up, you wouldn't know the difference.'

She thought of Da as a parasite feeding on Mam. He was twenty years older, and he drained her. He made her wait on him hand and foot, care for him, work for him.

'Dinner then,' Laura agreed, sitting at the table to take off her wet shoes and stockings.

Da liked to put on an act, pretend he lived in comfortable circumstances, where all he had to do was to ring a bell when he wanted service. He seemed to think meals could be spirited out of air. Mam leaned back in the chair and closed her eyes. 'I put the potatoes on to boil, Laura.'

She found a pair of clean black stockings in the oven. The dampers had blocked with soot years ago, it was used as an airing cupboard now. Poor Mam, she was worn out tonight. The stockings felt blissfully warm.

'Don't put your shoes in the oven, Laura,' Da snapped. 'You'll ruin the leather.'

'They're already ruined, one's leaking. It's been squelching with water tonight.' She latched the oven door tight closed.

'Bloody hell! I suppose that means you want another pair?'

'Need,' she said. 'It means I need to dry them before morning. Yes, it means I need a new pair.'

'Don't speak to your Da like that, dear,' Mam protested without opening her eyes. Laura had told her a thousand times she was too eager to humour him, too quick to deflect his bad moods. 'You have to stand up to him, Mam,' she'd said many times.

'Where've you been till now? You're very late.'

'Mrs Talbot was late marking up, and Tom Talbot arrived home.'

'I did his room out for him yesterday,' Mam said.

'They should have more consideration. Keeping you so late.'

Laura went in to the scullery to light the stove and put the sausages in the frying pan. The potatoes had boiled almost to a mash. She turned the gas down as far as it would go, and felt in the cupboard for a tin of processed peas. She tipped the contents into a pan, and set it to warm.

'I brought your *Echo* for you, Da.' She put her head back into the kitchen. He already had it spread across the table she needed to set.

'Close the door,' he shouted. 'You make the room cold.'

'Yes,' Laura agreed, making no attempt to obey. Steam from the boiling potatoes had condensed into glistening globules under the corrugated iron scullery roof. She found a piece of old shirt and used it to wipe them off, otherwise they dropped on her head or, worse, into the food.

It was warmer now with all the burners in use, and the sausages sizzling and smelling delicious. She went back to set the table.

'Laurence Oxley's sold a chain of garages.' Da was reading the article that had interested Tom Talbot. 'He must have built it up since we left. Used to tell everybody he was one of the world's winners. Reckon he was right.'

'Reckon he could buy the earth now,' Mam agreed. 'You learned the wrong things when you worked for him, Percy. No good priding yourself on knowing burgundy goes with beef if you can't afford it.'

'You worked for the Oxleys, Da?' Laura leaned against the scullery door. 'I never knew that! You're always on about knowing how things should be done and being a butler, but I never knew it was for the Oxleys!'

'Your Mam worked there too. If anybody learned the wrong things from Laurence Oxley it was her.'

'Good gracious!' Laura felt astounded. 'Jane Oxley's in my form at school.'

'No!' Her mother was suddenly wide awake, her face anxious. 'Why didn't you say?'

'She's always been there. Since before I started. She came up through the juniors. I didn't know she was anyone you knew.' Laura looked from one parent to the other. 'You do know her?'

'No, she was born after we left.' Mam's face twisted with worry. 'I wouldn't say anything to her about us.'

Laura laughed. 'Don't worry, I won't. She looks down her nose at me anyway. So does her sister, Mary. She's our head girl, and a right snob.'

'Mary! I knew her.'

'Spoilt little brat,' Da said. 'I knew you should never have gone to that fancy school. It would be better if you left right away.'

'Da, no! I want to stay as long as possible. I'd get a better job if I stayed on for my School Certificate.'

'I can't afford to keep you in idleness till you're sixteen. Wanting new shoes, lacrosse sticks and God knows what. The Oxley girls there too! I can't get over that.'

'I wish they weren't,' Mam fretted.

'What difference does it make?' Laura wanted to know.

'Just the fact that once you both worked for the family. I certainly won't tell them. They'd have a field day.'

'You aren't burning those sausages, are you?' Da sniffed suspiciously.

Laura caught them just in time. She was surprised how concerned her parents were that the Oxley girls were at her school.

'How long did you work for them?' she asked as she dished up.

'Nine years,' Da sniffed. 'You've overcooked everything, and us waiting.'

'Is that where you met? How long did you work for them, Mam?'

'Nine months.'

Laura frowned. 'They made a big impression on you, in a short time.'

'You could certainly say that,' Da agreed, forking sausage into his mouth, his dark malicious eyes goading Mam.

'Why?'

'Eat up while it's hot,' her mother said, addressing her burnt sausage, and Laura thought she saw a tinge of embarrassment in her bruised face.

'What were they like? The Oxley parents?'

'Rich,' Da grunted.

'I know that. They're richer than anybody else in the school.'

'It's so long ago.' Mam was putting the dirty plates together. 'We know nothing about them now.'

'How long?'

'How old are you?'

'Thirteen and a half.'

'Then it's thirteen and a half years.'

As soon as she'd finished eating, Laura took her cup of tea to the parlour. It was cold there, but easier to concentrate on homework. Da had the wireless on in the kitchen.

Tonight, her mind buzzed with worries. Mam was discounting her injuries, pretending nothing had happened. Da was nagging about her leaving school, and she couldn't imagine why the Oxleys were important to them after thirteen years. It took an act of will to keep her mind on algebra and history.

She worked for an hour, by which time her hands were so cold her writing was growing spidery. It was March, but the weather was wintry. She was putting her books away when Da clumped noisily through. He usually went down to the pub in the evening.

'You're to leave that school,' he growled. 'The sooner the better.'

'Dad! I can't. Not before my fourteenth birthday, it's against the law.' Laura knew she was safe till the end of September.

'You could leave now. Go to the Council School for a few months.'

'Da, no, please.' She was wheedling she knew. She hated herself for begging. 'Let me stay where I am. I can learn so much—'

'What difference will that make? Just a few months?'

'I like it there. I'd have to get to know new teachers and everything. The lessons would be quite different.'

'Your Mam's bothered about the Oxley girls being there.'

'I can't see why. It makes no difference.'

'Take a letter in. Let them know you're leaving. Make it definite.'

Laura sighed, she knew one term's notice was requested before a pupil was withdrawn. She'd seen it written on documents she'd brought home.

'Why bother?' Da had said at the time. 'They can't stop us taking her away.'

Laura didn't want it made definite. Until it was, she could hope. At the same time, she felt Da should comply with the rules.

'You mean right away?'

'Tomorrow.'

'Have you written it?'

'Mam will do it.'

'She's tired, couldn't it wait till the weekend?'

'Laura, listen to what I say. She'll do it now, tonight. Let's make it definite. You don't need any more of that education. It makes you question everything I say.' There was a cold blast of air as he opened the door. The rain blew in on the mat. He was gone.

Laura went into the kitchen. Mam was asleep in front of the dying fire, her bruises livid. Laura raked out the ash to revive it, put on two or three small pieces of coal. Mam stirred, it was nearly time for bed. They never waited for Da to come home.

'Have the Oxleys got some hold over you and Da?'

'What?' Mam pulled herself up in the chair and yawned. 'No, of course not. What hold could they possibly have after all this time?'

'You seem afraid of them.'

'No,' Mam denied. 'No.' But fear seemed to hang round her in curtains.

She was afraid of Da, but with good reason. Though Laura caught the sharp edge of his tongue often enough, she knew Mam was his main victim. She was as completely in his power as the fly caught in a spider's web. Hate for Da welled up in Laura's throat every time she thought of what he did to her. It made her love Mam more.

The violence her mother suffered was not always physical. Laura had long been able to pick out the barbed thrusts he made to hurt her in other ways. Always he had some complaint about her cooking. The food was too salty or not salty enough, overcooked or undercooked. Everybody he knew could do it better. His shirts were never washed to his liking and her ironing didn't please him. He pointed out all the faults with her sewing when she made clothes for herself or Laura. He preferred a proper tailor to make his clothes, but as an economy because he had so many mouths to feed he was prepared to buy ready-made.

He insisted Mam cut his hair, but always she'd taken off too little or too much, or it didn't sit properly afterwards. Laura saw him sapping Mam's confidence. Child as she was, she could see her mother being destroyed before her eyes.

'Stand up to him, Mam. Tell him to go and get his hair cut at Hale's.'

'They charge a shilling, love. They're expensive.'

'Let it come out of his beer money.'

'He'd expect it from the housekeeping.'

'Mam, he gives you no housekeeping. You let him walk all over you.'

Mam shuddered. 'Sometimes I swear I'll kill him.' But Laura knew she'd never dare lift a finger against him. It had been going on too long.

Laura was twelve when he lifted his hand in temper and slapped her across her face. She remembered Mam screaming and throwing herself between her and that vicious swinging arm.

'Stop it! Don't you dare.' She'd never seen Mam stand up to him before. 'If you lay another finger on Laurie I'll—'

'What'll you do?' he jeered, confident of his power.

'I'll kill you,' Mam sobbed, picking up the bread knife from the table. 'I'll kill you. I swear.' He took her wrist, pushed it backwards, prising the knife easily from her fingers, laughing at her frustration.

Mam sobbed louder. 'I'll go to the police. I'll tell them what a fiend you are. I'll go to the NSPCC. If you lay a finger on Laurie again, I will. I promise you that.'

She had seen Mam walking along the road one day, on her way from one job to another. Holding herself stiffly, seeing nothing, not even Laura. Shuffling along as though she had no energy left. It made Laura more determined to stand up to Da. He wasn't going to destroy her.

'Da wants you to give notice at school.' Laura crouched over the fire, her hands outstretched to the puny heat.

'I'd better,' Mam sighed. 'We'll be liable for a full term's fees if I don't. It doesn't matter that you've got a free place. Map out a few words for me, Laurie. You're better at it than I am.'

Laura found a piece of paper in her satchel and wrote: 'I hereby give a term's notice of my intention to withdraw my daughter Laura from school. Her fourteenth birthday falls on September twenty-eighth, after which it will be necessary for her to earn her living.'

'Will that do, Mam?'

'Yes. No, you haven't said which day you want to leave.'

'They may not want me back for three weeks. The new school year starts on September ninth.' Her spirits spiralled downwards at the thought. Why should they?

That night, Laura was awakened out of a deep sleep by voices. She was often disturbed. The front bedroom opened directly off hers, and now a band of light was showing under the door.

Not again, she thought, but Da's voice was filled with contempt and cold dislike, not fury.

She wanted to call out: 'Mam, tell him to shut up. Stand up to him.'

Should she get up and throw open their bedroom door? It had stopped him last night, but Mam had asked her not to do it again. She was terrified he'd turn on her.

'It's all your fault.' Da's consonants were slurred, but he wasn't fighting drunk. He wasn't beating her up. Laura pulled her blankets about her ears.

'You're a pain, woman, you always have been. I should have had more sense than to take you on.' Da's voice grated on for half an hour, full of complaint. She thought she heard the name Oxley, she certainly heard her own name. 'Laurence Oxley got us both into this trouble.'

Sickened, Laura buried her head deeper in her pillow. Afterwards she thought she must have misheard. The Oxleys were on her mind. She must have been dreaming about them.

CHAPTER TEN

Laura ran up the steps of Belgrano, the large Victorian house in which her school had been housed since the turn of the century. Mam couldn't understand why Birkenhead High School, with its reputation for academic excellence and fees to be paid, should be a jumble of assorted buildings, while purpose-built schools should be free to all and have no status.

Laura's stomach was churning; for once she hadn't wanted to come. Mam's letter was in her satchel, and she'd have to hand it in.

She was late and her feet hurt. Her shoes had dried uncomfortably hard, and then as she'd pushed her feet into them, she'd seen a hole in the heel of her black stocking, a white circle no eye could possibly miss.

She'd run up Devonshire place with Phyllis Jones, who had been off school for three days with a cold. As they neared the school they'd seen the Oxley sisters getting out of a highly polished Alvis, driven by a uniformed chauffeur.

'Lucky them,' Phyllis panted, tossing a thick brown plait over her shoulder. 'They don't have to run for buses.' What Laura envied was the patina that a sense of privilege gave them, and their school uniform which always looked new. Jane recognised her, and gave a limp wave from the wrist, rather like Queen Mary's.

In the cloak room, Laura opened her bottle of black ink and with a corner torn from her blotting paper dabbed some on the circle of flesh to make it less noticeable. A bell rang, and she hurried to her form room. Ahead of her, Phyllis put the obligatory letter explaining her absence on Miss Powell's desk. Laura slid her own letter under it, and sat down.

The daily routine began. Miss Powell appeared, dumpy in twin-set and pearls, and proceeded to call the register. Another bell, and they were filing out to assembly in the school hall.

'Onward Christian Soldiers,' she sang, and her voice was lifted and lost in hundreds of others. Laura wondered how long it would take Miss Powell to read the letter. Perhaps she already had. The upper school knelt on the hard floor for prayers, stood for another hymn, then sat cross-legged for the notices.

'I want to tell you about an essay competition,' Miss Pleat the headmistress announced. She looked every inch an academic with Eton crop and pince-nez. 'It can be on any aspect of our West African colonies.' Laura felt a trickle of interest.

'The object is to increase awareness of our colonies. The Lower Fifth who are currently studying West Africa will be specially interested, but it's open to every member of the Upper School.' Her raised voice carried to every corner of the hall. 'You have till half-term to write it, and the winner will be presented with her prize on Speech Day. The competition has been set, and the prize donated by Mr Laurence Oxley, who as you know is a Governor of this school.'

Laura gripped her ankles, she hadn't known that. It seemed suddenly there was no escaping the Oxley name. It was coming at her from every angle. Half the school was looking at Jane, her face shone with pride. Laura caught her eye, and immediately looked away. Impossible to imagine Da doing anything like that, even if he were rich. She could not compete with Jane on this.

As she left with the rest of the Upper Fourth, Miss Powell beckoned her out of the line. Laura felt sick with anxiety.

'Laura, Miss Pleat would like to see you at first break,' she whispered. 'I'm so sorry.' The hand on her shoulder was meant to comfort. Laura found herself fighting for self-control.

After that, she couldn't concentrate on the first two lessons. She was dreading what Miss Pleat would say. She had to blink furiously. She couldn't return to the form with red eyes, or everybody would know how upset she was, even Jane Oxley. No good then pretending she didn't mind.

She'd always known it would happen. When she'd won the scholarship, Da had grudgingly agreed she might as well go to the High School since she could go for nothing, but he'd said she'd have to leave to earn her keep as soon as she was fourteen.

Three years at the High School had changed her. All the teachers agreed they were being given the best education possible, and they must make the most of it. A pupil's choice of career was all-important, though of course they'd have to give them up if they got married. Wives and mothers found their outlet in making a home for their families.

That made Laura feel she belonged to a different race. Mam went out to work, though she was married. She had to, to meet the cost of food and rent.

At break she went reluctantly to Miss Pleat's study.

'Come in, Laura.' Her gaunt lips pursed. 'I'm very sorry to see this.' Miss Pleat's manicured nails indicated Elin's letter spread before her on the desk. 'You're an apt pupil, but you must go on if you're to achieve anything.'

'Yes, Miss Pleat.' Wasn't she well aware of that?

'Is this your idea?'

'Oh no! I want to stay on. My father—'

'It's your mother who has written.'

'It's not her wish.' Laura was stony-faced. How could she explain to Miss Pleat, who believed women now controlled their own destiny?

'Before you entered school, your father signed an undertaking not to withdraw you until July 1940.' She pushed the document in front of Laura, who hadn't known about it. Hope flickered into life.

'In two more years you could matriculate. Anything less is a waste of your time and ours.' Miss Pleat's grey eyes looked at her through her pince-nez. They had lost their normal steely glint.

'We've had this problem before with scholarship girls. Unfortunately, the undertaking is not legally binding.'

Laura's spirits plummeted. 'However, you may not leave until the end of the term in which you have your fourteenth birthday. That is the law. So Christmas would be the earliest.'

'Really?' Laura lifted her green eyes to meet Miss Pleat's for the first time and her lips widened in a beam of pleasure. Another whole term! It was almost a reprieve.

'I shall write to your parents to that effect.'

'Thank you, Miss Pleat.'

'Perhaps they can be persuaded to let you stay on. I'll ask them to reconsider.'

Laura went to get her bottle of milk feeling cheered. Not that Da would be persuaded, she knew him better than that, but at least she could stay till Christmas.

When Laura went to do her paper round that evening, Tom was helping behind the counter. His height and his bright red hair drew her eye. His presence seemed to fill the shop.

'Hello, kid.' The electric light deepened his suntan, he looked relaxed in brown corduroys and a polo-necked sweater. The evening deliveries were all marked up and ready.

Friday was the heaviest day of the week. There were magazines and weekly papers to be delivered as well as the *Echoes*. Her bag was crammed to capacity; it seemed to weigh a ton as she heaved it over her shoulder. When she returned for her second round Mr Talbot was in the shop. She'd never noticed before how tall he was, only an inch or so shorter than Tom. He looked worried, his fingers plucked at his sparse hairs, smoothing them across his pink scalp.

'Danny hasn't turned up again. He's not reliable. Tom, do you think you can remember his rounds?'

'I can do an extra one,' Laura offered. 'I've got time tonight.'

When she returned to the shop again, Danny's rounds had been split. Tom heaved one of the bags over his shoulder and set out with her. He pushed the papers through the doors on one side of the street, while she did the other.

He said he wanted to get used to working in the business again, because now he'd changed his job he'd be home every six weeks.

'The ship carries passengers as well as freight, so it runs to a timetable. Next time I come, my parents are going away for a few days rest, and I'm going to run the shop.'

Sometimes there were fewer papers to deliver on her side of the street and she finished first. Sometimes Tom was waiting on the corner smiling at her, the breeze fluttering at his red hair. They raced each other. She was sure he let her win. She told him about the essay competition, and how much she wanted to win that.

The evening light was drawing in, the streets of small terraced houses were quiet. Tom took her bag from her in Jubilee Street, handing her Da's *Echo*.

'Done in double-quick time.' His gentle eyes lit his face with friendliness. He turned to go. 'Thanks.'

Laura was glowing with the fresh air and exercise. Tom's company seemed to heighten her senses.

'Tom, will you help me?' She knew it was an excuse to keep him. 'With the essay?' He bent from his six foot three to hear her. 'You've been to West Africa, you can tell me things I couldn't find in a book. Facts nobody else will have.'

'What do you want to know?'

Laura warmed to him. He hadn't said: 'Why bother about an essay competition if you're leaving?'

'Come inside, I need a notebook and pencil.' She sat with him at the parlour table. 'Tell me all about Freetown and Lagos.'

He laughed. 'They're thousands of miles apart, and very different. Don't you have a fire?'

The kitchen door crashed back. Percy Peck, a picture of outraged arrogance, filled the doorway. 'Who are you? What are you doing here?'

Laura went cold inside as she saw Tom flinch. 'It's Tom Talbot, Da, from the shop. He's helping me with an essay. It won't take long.'

Mam's voice hissed: 'Please don't make a fuss, Percy.

He's from the shop.' Laura knew Tom heard too. He moved uneasily in his chair.

'Start to cook,' Percy told Elin. 'I'm hungry.'

Mam's blonde head came round the door. 'It's herrings, Laurie. They won't take long. Will you be ready?'

'Yes. We're going to the pictures as usual?'

'Usually do on Fridays. Barbara Stanwyck's on at the Regal.'

'Oh, good.' Laura turned to Tom. 'Sorry,' she said, dropping her voice, embarrassed. Da was always the same if she brought anyone in. 'Which do you know best, Lagos or Freetown?'

'Lagos, I suppose, the boat turns round there, we stay longer.' He ran his fingers through his thick hair; it stood up against the light in a red-gold halo.

'Right, your impressions of Lagos as a town.'

'It's a city.'

'I want to know everything. What your ship is like, the cargoes you carry and lots more.'

Laura scribbled away, while the aroma of frying fish slowly invaded the parlour.

'I'd better go,' he said awkwardly after ten minutes. 'If there's anything else you want . . .'

Laura decided the day she'd dreaded hadn't turned out too badly after all.

She wanted her essay exactly right, and spent the whole weekend knocking it into shape. West Africa fascinated her, and so did Tom.

Monday at school was back to normal, none of her form knew she would leave at Christmas. That evening, before setting out on her paper round, she showed Tom the second draft of her essay. He remembered a lot more detail she could use. She scribbled and told him one day she'd love to see West Africa for herself.

Mr Talbot, wearing a brown drill coat over his pullover, was marking up rounds behind the counter. He shuffled over to fill her bag with papers.

'We need a new Saturday girl, Laura. Tom thinks you might be interested.'

'Tom?' Her heart lurched with pleasure.

'Do you fancy working on Saturdays?'

She knew she was grinning. There was nothing she'd like more! True, Tom was leaving on another trip, but he'd not be away long. It meant she'd see more of him when he was home. Then there was the money.

'I pay three shillings for Saturday help.' Laura's green eyes danced. She could save up and perhaps afford shorthand and typing lessons. Working in an office would be better than working in a shop or a factory. She felt heady with excitement.

Laura felt grown up on Saturdays, going to the shop in her grey twill dress, with Mam's apron on top to keep it clean. She loved the snatched moments on magazines she'd never be able to afford. This week, *Home Chat*'s free paper pattern was for a girl's dress. Laura studied the pictures and wondered if Mam could make it for her. She allowed herself the treat of spending 2d on *The Schoolgirl*. It provided hours of reading in bed.

The shop was a cheerful place with lights shining on brightly coloured packets of cigarettes and chocolate. She enjoyed serving sweets to the local children, *Home Notes* and *Home Chat* to the women who came in with their heavy shopping bags full of food, and sporting papers and Woodbines to the men on their way home from a morning's work.

If business was slack, Mr Talbot would disappear into the back room, leaving instructions she was to give the bell push two quick jabs if she needed him, but that didn't often happen. It was a thriving business, a little gold mine, Mam said. The customers liked to gossip with Mrs Talbot, but often all three of them were kept busy.

'When's your Tom coming home again?' a customer wanted to know as she settled her paper bill.

'Be back for Whitsun,' Mr Talbot grunted, and Laura felt a trickle of anticipation. 'Going to look after the shop for a day or two.'

'Give you a break, Mr Talbot.'

'Aye, we need it. It's all go, you know, from six in the morning till six at night.' Laura knew only Mr Talbot got up to open at six. Gert helped him; she was known as the early morning girl, although she was a grandmother. Tom's mother got up in time to cook breakfast for them both at nine o'clock.

'We're going to Ripon, to stay with the wife's sister for a few days.'

'Do you good, Mr Talbot.'

'Do Mrs Talbot good,' he sighed wearily. The till pinged and the money rattled into the drawer.

'I hope Tom'll manage,' he said to Laura, when the door clanged behind the customer.

'He will,' Laura assured him. 'He seems very much at ease in the shop.'

'It's the cashing up and the deliveries – he doesn't know them.'

'I know the deliveries, I could help.' Laura said.

'Won't you be at school?'

'Not at Whitsun, Mr Talbot. It's our half-term.' She saw his face brighten.

'Of course! Yes, I'd be glad if you would. Tom'll need a hand, it will give him time to think.' He hobbled up the counter in his carpet slippers. 'We're going after dinner on Sunday, and staying till Thursday. That's our half day, you see. If we're back for Friday and Saturday, the busiest days, Tom should cope.'

Pleasure spiralled through Laura. 'I'll be off school all week. I'd be very happy to work here.' She was careful not to add with Tom, but that was the thought that overcame all others. Tom would be here with her. She could think of no better way to spend her holiday.

'Monday to Thursday then, three and a half days extra,' Mr Talbot said.

The afternoon seemed long, and her legs grew tired with the unaccustomed standing, but on the whole, she decided, she enjoyed working at Talbot's, though shop work was not what her teachers meant when they spoke earnestly about careers.

Laura felt her last months at school were slipping away. When she was feeling low, she made herself think of being with Tom; it gave her a warm glow. Half term came before she was ready for it.

Saturday morning started like any other.

'Hello, kid,' Tom grinned, the shop lights glittering on his red hair. Laura grinned back, feeling a bemused fool.

The scent of frying bacon fought with the smell of newsprint. The Talbots withdrew to their living room for breakfast. Gert stayed till ten, to bridge the gap. She'd been doing it for years and could run the shop. Her hair had been peroxided and permed too often, and was now a halo of pale yellow fluff round her wrinkled face.

The flow of children and housewives never stopped. It was raining, wet stains on the red linoleum spread across the floor. Gert switched on the one-bar electric fire that was supposed to keep them warm.

When the family filed back, Gert put on her coat, and Mr Talbot switched off the heater. Tom was at his father's heels, being given minute instructions about orders for reps expected to call in his absence. He winked at Laura over his father's head.

Mrs Jack came in for her *Daily Mirror*, her curlers bulging through her head scarf. She said it wasn't worth paying a penny a week to have it delivered since she only lived round the corner.

'My, Tom Talbot, you've grown.'

He laughed. 'Six foot three, Mrs Jack, and I finished growing years ago. Except round the middle.'

'You've grown a handsome lad. You'll be proud of him, Mrs Talbot.'

'I am that.' She patted at the rigid grey waves of her perm.

'Not married though? Isn't it time you got yourself a girl friend?'

'No need when I've got my Mum.' He put an arm playfully round her shoulders.

'At your age you need a girl friend. Someone young, to have a bit of fun with.'

'I've got Laura.' He moved to her side. 'She's young

enough for anyone. Not fourteen yet.' His arm felt heavy across her shoulders as he pulled her close. She felt herself blushing. 'Good fun too.' He did like her then. She felt overcome with happiness.

Even Mrs Talbot laughed, but it had an uncomfortable edge to it. 'Old harridan,' she said when Mrs Jack had gone, and Tom's parents both seemed very tightlipped.

When Laura arrived at the shop on Monday morning, Tom was busy behind the counter with Gert. Laura hung up her coat in the passage to the living room and went to help. Tom's friendly brown eyes twinkled at her, making her heart turn over.

'Laura, could I ask a favour?'

'Of course.' There was nothing she wouldn't do for Tom.

'Would you get me some breakfast? I'm starving.'

She nodded, smiling.

'I fell straight out of bed at six this morning and started marking up. We've been busy, haven't we, Gert? I've been at it for three hours on an empty stomach.'

'What do you want?'

'A fry-up. Whatever you can find in the larder.'

She went through into the living room behind the shop. Mrs Talbot didn't encourage her to come in here more than she had to, but it wasn't possible to keep it private. Stacked high all round the walls were boxes of sweets, crayons, pencils, and cards. Officially the stock room was three floors up in the attic, but most things didn't get that far.

It was rather a dismal room, Laura decided. Mam admired the grate because it made hot water come out of the taps. Today, however, nobody had got round to lighting the fire, and the room felt dank. The sash window looked onto a wet back yard, with a washing line and dustbin, just like their own.

She went to the kitchen. The larder was a revelation, stacked with food beyond anything she'd ever seen at home. It surprised her, as supplies could be bought at a moment's notice from the other shops in the parade.

'Found everything?' Tom asked from the doorway, but the shop bell pinged and he had to retreat.

The family cat rubbed against Laura's ankle as she stood at the stove. Tom was hardly likely to use two and a half pints of milk, so she filled a saucer and put it down on the coconut matting. The cat lapped softly, while the bacon frizzled. She called Tom when it was almost ready. He came to wash his hands at the kitchen sink.

'Newsprint is dirty stuff.'

Laura wasn't listening, she was concentrating on setting out the food as instructed by her Domestic Science teacher. Corners of fried bread peeped from behind the eggs.

'Very posh. You're looking after me better than my own mother,' he laughed.

Laura grinned. This is what it would be like to be married to Tom, she thought.

'Be a good girl and take a cup of tea through to Gert,' he said. 'And you'll have one with me?'

When the shop closed at lunch time, Laura made them both roast pork sandwiches with a fresh loaf.

'I ought to let you go home for an hour,' Tom said guiltily.

'I'd rather stay,' she said.

At two o'clock, Elin came through the shop for her regular three-hour stint, to make beds, light the fire and vacuum through. Afterwards, Laura found she'd peeled potatoes, chopped onions and laid them out with the steak for Tom's tea. She thought the dark little room had a shine to it now her mother had swept and polished.

Laura discovered there was another sitting room above the shop, much smarter, and also a bathroom. She knew all the girls at school had bathrooms, but no one had in Jubilee Street. She stood inside, marvelling at the bath on curving legs and the proper wash basin, too. She always washed in the enamel bowl they kept under the kitchen sink. Sometimes they took it up to their bedrooms, to get away from Da, but bath or hair wash, it was done in the enamel bowl.

Laura enjoyed working with Tom. Thursday lunch time came round very quickly. They were not busy during the morning, they'd been chatting between customers. She told him about going to the pictures with Mam every Friday. She had homework to do other week nights, but on Fridays it could be put off.

Mam loved the pictures and had told Laura that when she first went to the pictures in Wales they were known as flicks because they flickered so much. When she'd first come to Birkenhead she'd seen Rin Tin Tin, and Pola Negri. Rudolph Valentino had been in the very first film she'd seen, she'd thought him absolutely marvellous at the time, but he reminded Laura of Da, brushing his hair straight back, and slicking it with brilliantine.

'Do you fancy going tonight too?' Tom asked.

'Love to,' she beamed.

'*Top Hat* is on at the Liverpool Odeon.'

'Liverpool?' Laura was incredulous.

'Why not? We can go over on the train.'

'Marvellous. Mam and I never go further than Birkenhead. Oh, I'm thrilled, Tom.'

'One of the nice things about you. You're easy to please.'

'Am I?'

'I expect it's your age, older girls are more . . . Well, you know, demanding.

He was unlocking the shop door to let her out at one o'clock when his father's baby Austin drew up at the kerb. Laura would have liked to slip away before the flurry of greetings, but Tom had not said where they were to meet. Mrs Talbot, in flowing folds of Liberty print, wrapped Tom in a hug. He ferried suitcases from the car to the shop.

'Has everything been all right?' his father asked anxiously, walking with difficulty in shoes.

'Laura's been a great help.' Tom smiled down at her. 'I'm taking her out tonight, because I'd never have managed without her. She's really looked after me. I'll call for you, Laura, about half four. We'll go to first house.'

'How have the takings been?' Laura heard his father ask as the door closed behind her. She danced home to Jubilee Street. A real date with Tom Talbot! She couldn't believe her luck.

She wondered what she could wear. She'd been wearing

her best frock to the shop every day, and even with Mam's apron it had got grubby.

The house was silent when she let herself in. As she lit the gas under the kettle for tea, she thought of her mother's blue suit. It was hanging in her wardrobe. Elin lamented she'd never got her wear from it, and now it was too tight for her.

Laura took the stairs two at a time. She tried the jacket on, it fitted well. She pirouetted in front of the mirror on her mother's deal wardrobe, then stripped off her dress and reached for the skirt.

It felt all right, but looked old-fashioned. She should have known. Skirts were being worn longer again, but now they were cut in gores. They flowed elegantly. Mam's skirt was straight. But if she shortened it? It was that or wear the jacket over her grey twill dress.

Apart from her school gaberdine, the only other coat she had was three years old. She tried it on. It showed four inches of grey twill at the hem, and the sleeves were halfway up her arms. It was impossible. When she went to the pictures with Mam she wore school uniform.

She measured the skirt against the length of her dress, it was only an inch and a half longer; she could take it up. Mam had talked of making it fit her. Laura got out a needle and cotton. She'd have to wear her school blouse, but she could knot Mam's blue scarf at the neck instead of her tie. School shoes too, but she had new ones. Mam had bought them in the market for her. They still pinched a little, but they looked smart.

Laura scribbled a note for her mother and was ready. She'd peeled potatoes and chopped cabbage, so Mam wouldn't have to do it when she came in. She was taking off her covering pinny when she heard Tom's first drop of the knocker.

'Hello, kid.' Tom gave her the box of chocolates he'd been clutching. 'Couldn't bring myself to buy sweets anywhere but Dad's shop. My, you look grown-up.'

Laura laughed, she'd have liked to take his arm as they went down the road, but he didn't suggest it. Perhaps he thought her too young for that. He did look handsome. She felt proud walking alongside him, giving a skip every few steps to keep up with his long stride. At Hamilton Square station she stood back while he bought the tickets and wished half the school could see her now, with a real escort, taking her to the Liverpool Odeon.

In the auditorium, the crimson carpet felt lush enough to brush her ankles. It was a thrill to have a balcony seat, a luxury at two shillings. Mam paid ninepence and they always went downstairs. Best of all, they were early enough to sit on the front row. Laura leaned on the upholstered rail and looked down on the circle of plush seats below. She admired the gold corded pelmets, the ceiling decorated with plaster cherubs, and the wonderfully elaborate chandeliers. How she wished Phyllis was here to see her now. It was a lovely cinema, what Mam called a picture palace.

She let her eyes follow the curving balcony. The tiers of seats were filling up. There was something familiar about a girl, half turned away from her, her blonde head close to that of her escort. Neither looked in her direction, they were too engrossed with each other.

Laura opened the chocolates, but she was unable to drag her eyes from the blonde. Unable to swallow the coffee cream in her mouth, almost unable to breathe.

'Who's that?' Tom bit into chocolate marzipan.

'Mary Oxley,' she breathed.

'Good lord!' Tom's eyes honed in too.

Such a smart Mary Oxley, wearing one of the latest pill box hats on her feathery blonde hair, and a smart beige coat with a fur collar thrown open to reveal a beige dress. Her hand was stroking that of her escort. He caught her fingers and raised them to his lips. How romantic!

Mary was animated, talking and laughing at the same time, her blue eyes sparkling. Mary Oxley must be in love.

Laura craned a little further to see her escort. Not nearly as tall and handsome as Tom! Fair-haired and a mere lad. She smiled, for once she felt she'd done better than Mary Oxley, though she'd be eighteen. This must be a fine cinema if the Oxleys came here. Laura felt herself swell with pride.

At last the rich drapes swished open, and the lights dimmed. Laura settled back to enjoy Fred Astaire and Ginger Rogers. Her head was filled with impressions of skirts swirling in time to the music, heels moving like quicksilver, tapping out the beat on flights of marble steps. It was fast and wonderful.

She was walking on air as they came out into the street, with neon signs flashing in the dusk. Tom took her arm to cross the busy street, seeming to bend his height over her. Laura felt she was living at last.

A two-seater roadster in racing green came towards them with a laughing Mary Oxley at the wheel, her escort's arm round her shoulders. Her blue eyes met Laura's for a fleeting instant. The love went from them, they were a little shocked. It was almost as though Mary Oxley felt Laura had no right to be here. Laura shivered and turned her attention back to Tom. Smiling at her like this, he was as handsome as Cary Grant. She wished it had been Jane Oxley who'd seen her here. She could have made much of Tom as her boy friend.

Several weeks later when she and Phyllis were hurrying to catch their bus after school, she saw Mary Oxley's boy friend again. The Oxley Alvis with chauffeur was waiting at the gate as usual, but so was the green roadster, and the young man in the driving seat looked very smart in blazer and flannels. When he saw Mary running towards him still in her school uniform, though the Sixth wore plain black skirts that looked quite smart, he got out and held open the door for her to get into the driving seat.

'She can drive!' Phyllis gasped. 'Oh, the lucky thing! Bet Jane will have lessons too.'

'You should see my boy friend,' Jane Oxley boasted the very next lunch time as the Upper Fourth were changing after lacrosse practice. The Upper Fourth talked a lot about boy friends, but nobody else had one. 'He's staying with my family at the moment, we're taking him to the theatre tonight. You'll see him in the car when it picks me up.' Half the Upper Fourth hung on her words. Jane Oxley had everything. A boy friend conferred great status.

'Bet her father bought him for her,' Phyllis said behind

her hand as she flicked her pigtails back. Jane was popular, but many were envious.

'His parents are working for my father in Lagos. He's at boarding school, and it's his halfterm. He's got such lovely brown eyes, but you aren't interested in boys, are you, Laura Peck?' There was always this spirit of competitiveness between them, of straining to get on top of each other.

'No,' Laura said, tying her shoe laces. 'Not boys.'

'Going to be an old maid like Miss Pleat?'

'I hope not.'

'You will if you can't get a boy friend.'

'I wouldn't be interested in a school boy.' Laura pulled herself upright.

'He's in the Upper Fifth,' Jane said haughtily.

'Too young for my taste. My boy friend is twenty-seven, and very handsome. A bit like Cary Grant.' Laura smiled into the stunned silence.

'You're having us on,' Jane Oxley said.

'I don't believe you.'

'His name's Tom, he's a merchant naval officer.'

'Are you going to marry him?'

'He hasn't asked me yet,' Laura said. 'But I expect so.'

'Don't suppose he will,' half the form chorused.

'I don't suppose he exists except in your imagination,' Jane Oxley said, her blue eyes searching into Laura's face.

'He does,' Laura snapped back. 'Ask your sister if you don't believe me. She saw us out together in the Whitsun holidays.' She'd been longing to boast of this for weeks. 'Tom took me to the Odeon in Liverpool to see *Top Hat*. I saw Mary there.' The ring of faces surrounding her showed envy. Laura was delighted. 'She was with her boy friend.'

Jane's face broke into a triumphant grin. 'Now I know you're making it up. Mary was staying in Southport with our Aunt. Anyway she hasn't got a boyfriend.'

'She has, I saw her driving his car only yesterday.'

'Oh, Robert? He's our cousin. They can't stand each other. Mary,' she called, as she caught sight of her sister with two other Sixth Formers. 'Did you see Laura Peck out with her boy friend in the Whitsun holidays? She says you did, that you went to the Odeon to see *Top Hat*.'

'Ginger Rogers and Fred Astaire,' Laura added.

Mary's blue eyes came to rest on her, they were like ice. 'No, of course I didn't. I went to stay with Aunt Josephine. I saw *Top Hat* in Southport with her. You make stories up, Laura Peck.'

'Ha ha. Now you've been caught romancing.'

Laura knew her mouth hung open in astonishment. Why should Mary deny seeing her? 'You were with your boy friend at the pictures on the Thursday night. I saw you.'

'No, I wasn't,' Mary snapped. 'And I haven't got a boy friend.'

'But I saw him kiss you. He was holding your hand even before the lights went down.'

'Very romantic, I'm sure,' Jane giggled.

'One of the world's losers,' Mary said *sotto voce* to her Sixth Form friends. 'A peasant.'

'Must have been somebody else,' Phyllis said, turning to go.

'I saw you with him again yesterday,' Laura shouted. 'You were driving his car, both times.'

'I told you, that's Robert,' Jane said. 'Mary loves his car, but not him. Fight like cat and dog they do. Boy friend indeed!'

'You know you saw me,' Laura insisted.

'You're a liar, Laura Peck.'

'Boy friend of twenty-seven! Does it sound likely?'

Laura couldn't believe that Mary Oxley should go to such lengths to deny seeing her. It didn't make sense.

CHAPTER ELEVEN

Laurence Oxley had always known where he differed from his twin. Money fascinated him, he had a compulsion that drove him to strive for more. Leonard was more academic, content with a job he found interesting. Content with his salary, and the little more he had from private means.

'There is a limit to what one can spend on food and shelter,' he'd said earnestly. 'As long as I can afford pretty clothes for Catherine, a decent education for Robert, and have the cars and holidays I want, I can't see the point in slaving for more.'

That had made Laurence smile. Slaving indeed! He found making money more absorbing than Leonard found golf. Leonard couldn't see that money bought other things. It bought power over others, and freedom to have exactly what he wanted.

This new office, for instance. He'd taken a suite in the Royal Liver Building, which dominated the Liverpool water-front. The great towers at either end were each surmounted by a Liver bird, the mythical bird from which the city was supposed to take its name. Laurence thought they looked suspiciously like cormorants. Other office suites were occupied by the Royal Liver Friendly Society and Liverpool's biggest shipping companies. All were fitted out with ultra modern facilities.

For years he'd coped with office space in one or other of the buildings housing his new enterprises as they pulled themselves up off the ground. His father had worked from an office near Nelson Dock all his life. Laurence could think more clearly in this gracious panelled office overlooking

Princes Landing stage and the river. It had dignity and comfort.

He'd always had ambitious plans for his business. He'd started new enterprises and expanded those he had. Now he wanted to see it quoted on the Stock Exchange. It had taken years of obsessive work to reach the point when he might achieve it.

He was able to afford the services of a very able accountant, and for the past two hours they'd been discussing and trying to unravel the technicalities of going public. He'd told his secretary not to disturb them unless it was important. He had to stifle his impatience when the telephone rang on his desk.

'Laurence, you haven't forgotten about coming home early tonight?'

'What's that?' The sound of his wife's voice made him more abrupt than he'd meant to be.

'I'm ringing to remind you we have company for dinner. The Faireys and the Machins are coming, and of course Leonard and his family. I'd like you to be home in good time, to be sociable.'

'Yes, dear, I haven't forgotten, it's your birthday.' Damn it, he had forgotten! He had more important things to think about than Sybil's birthday today. 'I'll be home by six, we can have a drink first.' He buzzed for his secretary to come in.

'Miss Almond, I want you to go out and buy a present for my wife.'

'Yes, sir, what sort of a present?' Veronica Almond was his secretary's assistant, an attractive young redhead.

'Flowers . . . No, not flowers.' The new gardener was producing wonderful blooms in both the garden and the greenhouse. He was already plying Sybil with flowers. 'Chocolates. A big expensive box.' That wouldn't do either, he'd started taking her chocolates every Friday. Little gifts humoured Sybil, made him seem attentive. 'Get her a bracelet or something, as well. Gold, of course. Charge it.'

'Yes, Mr Oxley.'

'Don't take long, it's almost time I was leaving.'

'Time we were all leaving, Mr Oxley. It's after five, and the shops will be closing.' Miss Almond was able to take liberties other employees could not. She flashed a coquettish smile with her brown eyes as she went out. Laurence pursed his lips.

'Now, John, where were we?'

'You'll still be in control.' John Barker's pale eyes regarded him through thick bottleglass spectacles. 'Your family will retain most of the voting power.'

Family, the word struck a chord in Laurence's mind. Robert, Leonard's son, was already twenty, and had another year to do at Cambridge. He'd be ready to come into the business then. Robert was a good lad. Laurence regretted he had no son of his own. Of all the disappointments in his life, that was the greatest. Made more so because James, his firstborn, had at first appeared a normal child. It had taken them a year to realise he was not developing as he should. Even now, the words mentally retarded could make him shudder. It still hurt to think of James; Sybil had never got over it.

'We all knew it ran in the family,' she'd wept. 'But we didn't think. If only your father had spelled it out before we married.' Sybil was his first cousin, orphaned as a child, and Oxley blood on both sides had compounded the likelihood. 'He must have known the risk we were taking.' Theirs was not the first marriage of first cousins in the family. James was not the first Oxley to be mentally retarded. Laurence couldn't admit to Sybil his father had spoken of it. He'd chosen to ignore the warning. He'd had his reasons.

James had died of pneumonia when he was ten, but he'd been away in an institution since he was four. Sybil still felt guilty about sending him there, though Laurence knew it was the only way the rest of the family could have a normal life.

'Better this way, Sybil,' he'd said, when news of James's death reached them. They'd argued and worried about James for ten years. 'Perhaps now we can have peace.' But there never had been peace between him and Sybil, before or since. The tragedy was there between them still, one more thing to keep them apart. Having two healthy normal daughters couldn't compensate.

He'd always felt close to Leonard. He felt close to Robert too. He wasn't quite his own son, but he was the nearest he was going to get. He'd had to accept that.

His accountant's voice went on: 'Going public will raise more capital for you.'

'We'll be able to expand at twice the speed.'

'Yes, you've expanded rapidly since you've run the business, Mr Oxley. You haven't put a foot wrong. Even the depression, which bankrupted many, hasn't slowed down your business, you've gone against the trend.'

'Yes, but I feel we've reached a plateau. I need the impetus more capital will bring. Timing is important.'

'In the autumn. Shall I apply for a quotation?'

'Yes. Start the ball rolling. And I want to buy out Betta Oils.'

'We can start buying their shares a few at a time. We've enough liquidity. Pick them up cheap now.'

'And start a West African Petroleum Company?'

The internal telephone buzzed again. Miss Almond's voice said: 'I've got a gold slave bangle, they're the latest thing, and chocolates. I've had them both gift-wrapped. They're on my desk. Is it all right if I go home? Everyone else has.'

'Thank you, yes. Good night.'

'We'll raise money for that in the market. It's perfectly feasible.' John Barker adjusted his spectacles.

'I want Oxley's to be a holding company comprising my six different businesses here and the West Africa imports and exports. I want to be able to add or subtract companies as I see fit.'

'Much the best arrangement.'

'I might sell off the clothing factory, it isn't doing much at the moment.' Laurence looked at his watch. 'I'll have to go home.'

'The rest of the business can carry the clothing, Mr Oxley. It's very healthy, and the clothing could come right.'

'I don't want anything carried. Every facet should pay

its way. I've got to go, I'm going to be late. Mustn't upset Sybil.'

Laurence Oxley hurried down to his car, grateful that at last the Mersey Tunnel had been opened and he could be driven between his office and his home. Until the last year or so, he'd had to take the train from James Street out to West Kirby, with all the frustrations of waiting about on station platforms. Even so, he resented having to tear himself away from John Barker. Business interested him more than Sybil's social life. Her friends, especially the Faireys, bored him.

The house he'd had built thirteen years ago still gave him enormous pleasure. He loved the first glimpse of it at the end of the drive, its traditional pink brick weathering now. Sybil had wanted a modern marine place, white and with flat roofs; he was glad he'd had his way.

As he let himself in, the hall clock was striking six thirty. Not too bad for time. He did what he always did when he arrived home, went straight to his study to see if he had any mail. He ripped open the large manila envelope he found on his desk. One of the girls must have brought it home from school. Miss Pleat's letter read: 'There were even more entries for the West Africa essay competition than I'd hoped for, and the standard was high. However, one stood out above the others. Laura Peck at thirteen is one of the youngest entrants. A member of the Upper Fourth, and the holder of a Local Authority Scholarship. She is so obviously interested in the subject, and has packed her entry with facts.'

Laura Peck. Laura Peck. There was something about that name. . . . He got up and poured himself a finger of whisky from the tray put in his study each evening. He sipped it slowly, standing at the window looking over the Dee estuary and out to the Irish Sea. The water was blue and calm, it was a lovely summer's evening.

He was frowning. Laura Peck? The name struck a chord somewhere. Perhaps the daughter of one of his employees? But a scholarship girl? Suddenly it came to him like a kick in the stomach. Peck! That rogue his father had employed as a valet, and what was her name? Elin? The child would be thirteen now, a few months younger than Jane. He could feel his guts churning.

Sybil would shake hands with the girl when she presented the prize. Would she remember? Would she recognise her? He tossed down the whisky in his glass and went upstairs to bath and change, feeling suddenly sick. He lathered himself briskly, deciding he'd have to arrange for Sybil to be somewhere else that day. He didn't want her at the school.

She came to his dressing room and was delighted with the bracelet. Guilt made him make a fuss of her, complimenting her on her new grey lace evening dress.

'You're as lovely as the day I married you,' he said, kissing her cheek. It wasn't true. Sybil's features had grown sharper. There was a sour look about her now, as the lines of discontent cut deeper. Her hair was a brighter gold than it had been in her youth. Her hairdresser must be touching it up when he set her curving waves.

He opened a bottle of champagne to toast her birthday, made a ceremony of it, giving a glass to each of the girls. They were having half an hour together as a family before the guests arrived. This was what Sybil enjoyed. The tragedy of James had made her appreciate the girls. There was no way she'd let them go away to boarding school. She wanted to see them growing up around her.

'How old are you, Mummy?' Jane wanted to know.

'You must never ask a lady how old she is, Jane.'

'Why not? I don't mind everybody knowing I'm fourteen, and Mary doesn't mind everybody knowing she's nineteen.'

'You're safe to ask up to twenty-one,' Laurence smiled.

'How old are you, Daddy?'

'I shall be fifty soon.'

Sybil was a year older, and looking every minute of it.

'Who won the essay prize, Dad?' Mary shook out her feathery flaxen curls. Frizz, Jane called it when she was being less than kind. Her own hair had more body and was the pale gold colour Sybil's had once been. 'I brought the envelope home from school.'

'Laura Peck.' He found it hard to say her name, but he had to pretend it meant nothing to him. His voice sounded strangled.

'Laura Peck!' Jane's blue eyes showed shock.

'You know her?' He gulped at his champagne. Was he trying too hard to make it appear he did not?

'Of course we know her.'

'Peasant,' Mary said. 'She's not the sort to win anything.'

'I don't like her.' Jane's nose wrinkled. 'Why did you choose her?'

'I didn't. I asked Miss Pleat to pick the best.' He hadn't wanted to waste his time trying to evaluate schoolgirls' essays. Anyway, Miss Pleat enjoyed doing it.

'She can't be the best! Unless it has to be one of the scholarship girls? To encourage them?'

'No, they've sent me her essay. It's very good.' He'd been surprised at her knowledge. There were things in it he hadn't known himself.

'I want to read it,' Mary said.

He hesitated.

'Oh, come on, Dad, it's not covered by the Official Secrets Act. It's only a tuppenny ha'penny school essay.'

He didn't know how to treat Mary these days. She was hell bent on having her own way about everything. Difficult to cope with. He'd wanted her to come into the business. Part of it would be hers one day, she needed to know how to run it. He'd steered her through the school curriculum, so she studied the right subjects. These days girls expected to have careers.

'Of course I want a career, Dad,' she'd spat at him like a cornered cat, three years ago, when she was moving up to the Sixth. 'I want to go to Cambridge.'

'Then what's the fuss about?'

'Why don't you listen? I've told you twice. Maths and economics are not the right subjects for me. I'm struggling to achieve average marks. I won't get to Cambridge with maths. I'm more interested in history and literature. My best grades, too.'

'History? What good is that in business?'

'It's all education. Or I could teach—'

'Teach! There's no money in teaching! I want you to read a balance sheet. Become a chartered accountant.'

'I can't, Dad.' Her eyes had been like blue steel.

'Then read law. That would be useful.'

'No. It's my life, Dad. I have to do it my way.'

'But the advantages of—'

'No, Dad.'

And he'd had to pretend to accept it. He'd bided his time, kept on at her, and eventually she'd seen sense. She'd changed courses, and was having to do three years in the Sixth to get her university entrance. That in itself meant a wasted year. He certainly wouldn't have put up with it from anyone else.

'Laura Peck's essay, Dad.'

He went to his study to get it. What did it matter, after all? Better to give in gracefully than have a confrontation with Mary tonight. He came back, refilled Sybil's glass as well as his own, and settled in the chintz armchair. He would read it to them:

'*Beware and take care of the Bight of Benin*
Where few come out though many go in.

'A sinister jingle largely ignored by Europeans in search of trade and fortune. First it was slaves, then it was palm oil Europe wanted, from *Elaeis guineensis*, a plant indigenous to West Africa, used to oil the great Victorian machine age, and to make soap. There was also timber, gold and ivory. The West African Coast was a pot of gold. . .'

Laurence paused. He had seen it as a pot of gold, she was right. It had provided raw material for industry for the last two centuries, but this was 1938. His father had been successful in the West Africa trade, but he'd not foreseen that countries like Nigeria and the Gold Coast would have money to buy European manufactured goods in return for their palm oil, cocoa and timber.

He was doing extremely well. Hadn't he been selling them kerosene refrigerators since 1928? Every European considered them essential in the god-awful climate, enabling them to keep their food fresh and stay healthy. Food shops had to have them if they were to sell to Europeans, so had hotels. He was selling them cars, petrol and oil, and tools of every sort. The market would grow, and his companies prosper.

Leonard arrived with his family. To look in Leonard's face was like looking in his own. His identical twin was his exact mirror image. He had a mole on his right cheek, Leonard had his on the left. He was right-handed, Leonard left. Their wavy bronze hair was parted on opposite sides. Leonard had a few new grey hairs, and his frown lines were prominent. As he passed a mirror, Laurence checked on his own. No, not yet. Leonard had put on more weight, too.

Leonard had never had his energy, and he didn't push himself. He had longer fuses on his temper and his patience. Laurence loved Len, and was glad he hadn't harboured a grudge over the way he'd handled Father's money. Time had eased that.

He watched Robert kiss Sybil and proffer a gift. 'Happy Birthday, Aunt Sybil.'

How he envied Leonard his son. Robert was exactly the son he should have had, healthy and intelligent. Already he was stockier than they were, and he was certainly taller. He had the same wiry hair, perhaps a shade or two darker, but still fairish, and the pale Oxley skin which burned so easily in Lagos. Laurence studied Robert's eyes, searching for his father's tranquillity. It wasn't there, and he was glad. His Oxley eyes of cornflower blue burned with ambition and competence; he hadn't inherited his mother's need of glasses, thank goodness. Robert had boundless energy, too. It gave Laurence immense pleasure to see more of himself in Robert than of his father. It made him more his.

Robert was coming over to greet him. He appeared uncomfortable under Laurence's scrutiny, almost as if he were trying to draw a veil across something.

Laurence rang for the housekeeper to bring more champagne.

'We must all congratulate Laura Peck on winning the West Africa essay prize,' Miss Pleat announced after morning prayers towards the end of term. Laura felt a surge of triumph. 'It's specially pleasing to see so young a pupil win. Well done, Laura.' The teachers clapped, the school took up their lead. Laura couldn't keep a smile from pulling at her lips.

Jane Oxley's blue eyes were needling her as they returned to their form room. 'Aren't we satisfied with ourself.'

'Of course I'm satisfied. I set out to win the prize and I did. It's more than you managed.'

'Think you're clever, don't you?' Jane mocked. 'Daddy made me enter, but he told me straight I wouldn't get the prize, not if my essay was ten times better than any other. He said he expected mine to be good, but he couldn't acknowledge it. He told Mary the same, but she said she wasn't going in for it because she's doing her Higher. He wants to spread interest in West Africa, since he's got business there. He's taking us out for the holidays. We sail three weeks tomorrow.'

'I'd rather go to Rhyl.' Phyllis Jones was retying the ribbon on one of her plaits. 'You're going to the white man's grave.'

Laura bit back an inanity about hoping it would be a white girl's grave too. She knew she was envious. She'd love to go to Freetown on the mail boat and see the big harbour and the gorgeous beaches. Then come back and work at school for matriculation. She was green with envy for everything Jane had and she had not; she was especially envious of a father who was so rich he could give prizes. She must not let Jane see that.

She tried to fix her mind on pleasanter things. Tom was due home again soon. She was looking forward to that. Perhaps he'd take her to the pictures again.

The house was quiet when Laura returned from doing her paper round the following Tuesday. She found Mam dozing in front of the fire.

'Isn't Da home?'

'No, I don't know where he's got to,' Mam's golden eyes looked puzzled.

The pub closed at two; where he went after that, Laura didn't know. He usually came home before she set out for her paper round, and he always had tea with them before going out again.

'Tea's ready,' Mam stretched in her chair like a kitten. 'But we'll give him five minutes.'

They gave him twenty before going to dish up. Laura expect Da to come in and be cross because they hadn't waited.

Afterwards Laura asked: 'Will you want the wireless on?'

'Not till half eight, there's a play then.'

'I'll do my homework here then, where it's warm.' While she enumerated the different aspects of Victorian economic prosperity in her history book, she was conscious of listening for Da's key turning in the lock. The sound didn't come.

'Can something have happened to him?' Laura was asking when the knocker thumped on the front door. She saw the look, half dread, half hope, on Mam's face as she got up to answer it.

'It's Beattie Higgs from next door,' she called to set her mother's mind at rest.

'Is your Da in?' Beattie carried a large package tied up in brown paper.

'No, come on in,' Laura invited. 'It's safe.' Beattie's grey hair was still in curlers; Laura wondered if she ever took them out. Elin got to her feet to greet her.

'I've been clearing out me sister's house. Told you she died last week, didn't I?' Beattie was pulling on the string, trying to break it. 'She had smashing curtains for her french windows. Red velvet. Do lovely behind me doors, stop them draughts.' Beattie's fingers tried to fasten up her grey cardigan but there were two buttons missing. 'I've got them up, but they're dragging the floor too much. I've come to ask if you'll shorten them for me.'

'Will you have a cup of cocoa, Beattie? Laura usually makes us one at this time.'

'Cocoa? I'd rather have tea.'

Laura hated to see her mother faced with more work. She went to put the kettle on.

'I could do it Sunday,' Elin offered.
'There, luv, I knew you would. I brought some of her clothes for you. She had good things, not like me. You're clever with the needle, Elin, you could make something of them. Make them fit Laura.' She was opening the brown paper parcel.
Laura stood in the scullery doorway looking at the drab garments as they came out one by one. Elin's eyes flashed golden arrows of sympathy in her direction.
'A bit old for Laura, too dark, do you think?'
'Not this,' Beattie said, pulling out a dress checked in greens and fawns. Laura brought in three cups of tea and fingered it.
'Lovely wool cloth,' Elin said. 'Hardly worn. Would you mind . . . that they belonged . . .'
'You'll look a treat in it.' Beattie turned to Laura. 'The fawn'll bring up the colour in your hair. The green'll match your eyes. Young, too.'
'Old-fashioned style,' Elin murmured. 'Dropped waist, very fashionable in the twenties. I'd have to put the waist back in the right place, and that shortens the dress by six inches.'
Beattie held it against Laura. 'Our Ethel was very big. Wouldn't it do?'
'It's got a big hem,' Elin said hopefully. 'It might.'
When her mother went next door to see the curtains that needed shortening, Laura began to unpick the check dress. She usually helped with the parts needing less skill.
Afterwards, they listened to the play on the wireless, while Elin cut into the bodice and showed Laura how to tack it together again. By the time the nine o'clock news finished the main parts were tacked up, and Laura could try it on.
'Looks fine,' her mother assured her, yawning. 'Pretty material. Makes your eyes look like emeralds. Have a look in the mirror.'
Laura raced upstairs. She had a mirror on top of a chest of drawers to serve as a dressing table. She sat on her bed and looked at the dress. It pleased her. Elin had had the sleeves out to make it narrower across the shoulders. She

was getting up to look in the full length mirror on Elin's wardrobe when the box on her bedside table caught her eye. She froze, full of suspicion, examining it in the mirror.

Once it had held several layers of expensive chocolates; the scent of them lingered inside. Mrs Talbot had given her the empty box, saying it was too pretty to throw away. She'd kept her treasures in it for the past year. It was deep, of strong cardboard covered with silvery pink paper, with a pink satin bow on top. She'd not left it with the lid caught on one corner, a strip of gold showing round the rim.

She rolled across her bed to grab the box, dreading to find her money gone.

Her best art silk stockings were still there. She tossed them onto the bed. Her bead purse followed, and her diamanté hair band. The four pounds, three shillings and two pence she'd counted into it on Saturday had gone.

'Mam,' she shouted wildly, tears stinging her eyes. 'Mam!' The wireless was still on, she couldn't hear. Laura grabbed the empty box and raced down the stairs.

'He's taken my money, Mam, he's taken my money!' Elin's shocked eyes stared back at her. She saw her mother's hand go slowly up to switch off the Welsh choir. It didn't occur to either of them that anything else could have happened to the money.

'How much?' Elin's voice was scarcely above a whisper.

'Four pounds, three shillings and two pence. All gone!'

'Enough for him to stay out overnight.'

'It was for typing lessons. Oh, Mam!'

'You'll need new clothes too. Can't wear school uniform.'

Laura felt her mother's arms go round her. She put her head down on her shoulder and wept.

'I nearly bought a pair of sandals,' she sobbed. 'I wish I had now.'

Elin was shaking. It had taken her an hour to calm Laura and get her to bed. To take the money Laura had worked for and saved so carefully was the worst thing Percy had ever done. He'd be throwing it away on a few drinks or the horses, what he called having a bit of fun.

She had to get Laura away from him. Why hadn't she left him years ago? Percy was a hateful parasite. Her money would go further if there were only two mouths to feed.

She snatched at his copy of the *Echo*, unopened till now. She'd find another house to rent. At the other end of town. She'd like to go to the back end of Liverpool, but Laura would want to stay on at school for as long as possible. With a bit of luck, they could leave without him knowing. The paper opened at the situations vacant page. Her eye came to rest on one small advertisement.

'Live-in companion housekeeper for elderly widow. School child not objected to. Oxton area.'

She stopped and read it through again. It was exactly right for her. Laura would be no trouble to the elderly widow. She was at school all day, and was very quiet in the evenings doing her homework. Could this be the answer? She tiptoed upstairs.

'Are you awake, Laurie?' She pitched her voice at a whisper in case she was asleep.

'No,' a strangled choke came. 'No, Mam.'

Elin switched on the light. Laura, looking red-eyed, red-nosed and utterly miserable, blinked from a damp pillow. It made Elin catch her breath.

'Laurie, love.' She gathered her daughter into her arms to comfort her. She should have guessed this would happen.

'All that money, Mam,' Laura gulped. 'All those Saturdays worked . . .'

'Look at this.' Elin rattled the newspaper, pointing out the advertisement. 'Wouldn't it be a good move?'

Laura stared at it, sniffing. 'Do it, Mam! Apply for it.' The tears had dried, her eyes were puffy with a feverish sparkle, but there was hope in her voice.

'Do you think I stand a chance of getting it?'

'Mam! Of course you do. Who knows more about running a house than you?'

'Companion, though.'

'She just wants somebody to talk to.'

'But what will I talk about?'

'Listen to her. That's what she'll want.' Laura was out of bed, taking paper and pencil from her school satchel. 'I'll help you draft the letter, shall I?'

'What if she wants cooking too?'

'You're a good cook.'

'It's a long time since I did much.' Her confidence was ebbing.

'It's not easy to get live-in help. Try, Mam, you must.'

Elin sighed, it was a way of escape, but Percy would be back before any reply came. Four pounds wouldn't last him long. She wrote her letter from Laura's draft, and went to bed.

Twenty-four hours passed with no sign of Percy.

'Perhaps he won't come back.' Laura looked at her mother over the rim of her cocoa cup. She could see Laura half believed he wouldn't, but Elin knew it was only a question of time.

The following evening, while Laura was doing her homework at the kitchen table, she dozed in her chair. At the first scrape of his key in the lock, she was wide awake. The frustration and anger she saw in Laura's green eyes frightened her.

'Hello.' Percy collapsed in his leather chair and stretched out his legs. 'What's for dinner? I'm hungry.'

'Nothing,' Laura said. 'We thought you'd gone for good.'

'You knew I'd be back.' His hair was light on brilliantine; for once it looked faded and untidy.

'Where've you been?'

'Never you mind. Get me some toast, Laura. Is there any cheese?'

'No, there isn't. You stole my money, Da. My savings. Four pounds, three shillings and two pence. I want it back.'

'You'll get it. I only borrowed it. I had to have a stake. I was fifteen pounds up at one stage,' he said unlacing his shoes.

'Haydock races. You were right, Mam.'

'The money's all gone? I'll be right about that too.'

'Yes, but—'

'This time you've gone too far.' Elin knew she had to

stand up to him. 'It was Laura's money you took. I told you I wouldn't stand for anything that hurt Laura.'

'For God's sake, woman. I haven't hurt Laura. She'll get it back.'

'It was for typing lessons so she wouldn't have to work in a shop.'

'I was going to double it for her. Make me some tea and toast.'

Laura went into the scullery to put on the kettle. Elin followed her out, knowing Laura had gone so she wouldn't have to.

'I'll get the money for you, Laurie,' she said fiercely, cutting two slices off the loaf. 'I'll get it. I don't want you to end up like me, working your fingers to the bone.'

'Shop work isn't too bad.' Laura's face was white, her eyes burned like emeralds.

Elin thought the Oxley likeness was stronger tonight. Laura might yet grow up pretty, but she was too thin, undernourished, and down-at-heel. The stamp of poverty was on her. Elin felt fiercely protective.

'Not if I can help it, love.' She hugged Laura, hiding her own tears, until Percy shouted to ask if they were burning his toast.

Laura had forced everything out of her mind but the fact that Tom would be home next week.

On Thursday she'd finished her paper round and he hadn't arrived. The shop was about to close, she couldn't hang about. She walked slowly to the bus stop, looking into every bus as it lumbered to a halt. There were a lot of passengers at this time of the evening, but nobody in merchant navy uniform. She went home, telling herself to be patient. She'd see Tom tomorrow.

The next evening, she was early getting to the shop, eager to see him. Mrs Talbot was gossiping to a customer when she went in.

'Yes, a girl friend. We're delighted.'

'It's serious then?'

'Yes, says he's asked her to marry him. He's bringing her to meet us tomorrow.'

Laura froze, hardly able to believe they were talking about Tom.

'She was a passenger on his ship,' Mrs Talbot's voice, deliberately genteel, went on. Laura couldn't look at her. 'Her parents are working in Lagos, and she'd been out on a visit. Rosemary, her name is, and according to Tom she's very . . . She's very beautiful, isn't she, Tom?'

'Certainly is.' Tom was there, beaming at her from his great height.

'Congratulations.' The customer picked up her newspaper and cigarettes. 'Time you settled down, Tom.'

'Everybody keeps telling me.' He was triumphant, laughing.

'What's she do?'

'Got a dress shop in Liverpool.'

'You've fallen on your feet, young man.'

'Yes, I'll be selling ladies' gowns instead of papers.'

'I hope you'll be very happy. When is it to be?'

'Soon, we haven't set a date.'

The doorbell pinged as the customer went out. Laura felt her stomach churning. She was afraid she was going to be sick. Tom marrying someone else! She couldn't believe it. Somehow he'd seemed so . . .

'Well, Laura, what do you think of my news?'

They were both looking at her. She had to say something. The blood was thundering in her ears. She couldn't say she thought it dreadful, a sickening disappointment. She'd relied on Tom, trusted him. It seemed like a stab in the back.

'Congratulations.' She choked the words out. It didn't sound like her voice. 'I hope you'll be happy.'

She didn't! She hoped he'd be utterly miserable with his Rosemary. As miserable as she was going to be without him.

'You must come to the wedding,' he said. The shop lights sparkled on his red hair, his brown eyes were luminous.

That was the last thing she wanted, to see him promise to love and nurture someone else. The thought of it brought a lump the size of a golf ball to her throat. She was blinking madly. She mustn't let him see her disappointment. Or just how much she loved him. She'd thought he liked her enough . . . She had to make them talk about something else.

'I won the essay prize.' Her voice still sounded strangled, she should have said it with pride not as though she was telling them she'd caught a bus.

'Congratulations. I'm proud of you, kid.'

Kid! That was how he thought of her. Just a kid. 'You told me all the right things,' she choked. 'You did it for me.'

'No, Laura. I couldn't write an essay now.'

'What's the prize?' Mrs Talbot pushed at her grey perm.

'A book.'

'I should have thought the money would suit you better,' she sniffed.

'I'll be asked which one I'd like,' Laura tried to explain. 'It's the winning that counts really.'

'Of course it is,' Tom said enthusiastically. 'Mum doesn't understand about prizes. You'll be able to keep a book all your life.'

The lump in her throat was becoming impossible, she must not cry. She only just managed: 'Is my round ready?'

'Yes, dear.'

Laura was glad to get out in the street. Not that she could cry there, but she could run and turn her face away from other people. This was awful. Worse than Da taking her money. She'd felt so sure of Tom.

CHAPTER TWELVE

Elin felt overwhelmed. She was failing to give Laura a decent life, though she'd vowed she would. She wasn't providing enough to eat, and what Laura got was cheap and sometimes stale. When Beattie Higgs had come into her scullery the other day and seen the cheap bread and tired vegetables she was unpacking from her shopping bag, she'd said: 'What won't fatten will fill.'

As a child, Elin had never gone hungry. There was always abundant fresh food grown on their smallholding. She had been the best-dressed child in the school, not the shabbiest. Her mother had made her pretty dresses and pinafores from the offcuts from her dressmaking. The best she could offer Laura were cut-downs from a dead woman's clothing. To think of that brought choking guilt, but Laura had to have something other than school uniform if she was going to start work.

'It's good wool material,' she'd tried to justify it. 'Don't think about anybody wearing it before you.'

'I won't.' But Laura's smile had wavered. 'After all, a sheep will have worn even the most expensive cloth first.' Elin hugged her for that; Laura had greater resilience than she had.

She'd hated Evan Jones, but he'd never been drunk and violent like Percy. He'd contributed to the running of the home.

Elin usually looked forward to Friday nights. Her weekly treat was taking Laura to the pictures. Tonight she felt low.

Laura had returned from her paper round with eyes glittering like emeralds. She'd bolted her food, seeming keyed up. Before they'd drunk their tea, she was on her feet clearing the table and starting to wash up.

'We've got plenty of time to walk to the Palace in Rock Ferry for the second house,' Elin was saying when the crash of breaking crockery made her rush to the door. 'What's gone?'

'Sorry, Mam. A plate. A big one.' Usually Laura was very careful. Elin could see suppressed excitement in her face.

'It doesn't matter.' She picked up the pieces. 'I can get another in the market.' She began drying the dishes on the draining board. 'What's the hurry?

Laura shook her head and nodded towards the kitchen where Percy's head, glistening with brilliantine, could be seen over the pages of the evening paper. He leaned across and switched on the wireless. Under cover of the new sound, she whispered, 'Tell you later.'

Laura didn't allow her to waste a moment. Already she was putting on her coat. Elin took her own hat and coat from behind the kitchen door and followed.

Once out in the street, Laura tucked her arm through her mother's and hurried her round the corner.

'You've got a reply, Mam! To your application.' Laura's excitement came bubbling out now she no longer needed to hide it. 'I picked it up off the mat when I came home from school. Da hasn't seen it.'

'Thank goodness it didn't come by the morning post,' Elin smiled, feeling a surge of adrenaline as she ripped it open. They both stopped walking.

'She wants me to go for an interview on Monday.' She felt her first misgivings. The whole idea was crazy. 'I can't, I'll be working at the Crown.'

Laura snatched the letter from her fingers to read herself. 'You'll have to go if you want the job.'

'I can't on Monday.'

'There's a telephone number, Mam. Why don't you ring and ask if you can see her tomorrow or Sunday?'

'For an interview?'

'She's at home all the time. What difference does it make to her?'

'I can't ask for an interview on a Sunday. Anyway, I don't like the telephone. I'm not used to it.'

'I'll dial the number for you.'

Elin shivered. 'Now Da's back, we'd never get away.'

'Why not? We know when he comes and goes. He spends hours in the pub.'

Elin felt paralysed with fear. It was a big step. What if Percy found out?

'We wouldn't be able to take much with us,' Laura said.

'I must have my sewing machine.'

'Just clothes and your sewing machine. It won't take long to pack. Leave no trace.'

'I don't know.'

'Yes, we could. Don't get cold feet now, Mam.'

Elin sighed. Laura was very determined. 'What'll I tell them at the Crown and Talbot's?'

'Nothing.' Laura was at her most decisive. 'Da will go round and ask. Just disappear. That's the safest.'

'I thought you liked working at the Talbot's. Then there's Tom . . .'

She was aware of Laura's reluctance to talk about them. She was walking fast, staring straight ahead.

'I do, but it would be silly to tell them anything. Da will worm it out of them.

Elin thought it was one more sign of Laura's strength. If she had to cut herself off from Tom to get away from Da, then she would.

'He never goes to the Rose and Crown.'

'Not to drink, because you clean there, and he likes to pretend he's a man of means. But he'd call round and ask about you. He'll think we've found rooms somewhere, and you're still working there. Don't you see?'

'But we won't have taken any pots or pans or anything. I don't know, Laura, perhaps we'd better leave things as they are.'

'Mam, no! This could be our chance. We'd be far better off without him. Look, here's a phone box. Let me ring the number for you.'

'But what shall I say?'

'Tell her you're working, and you don't want to compromise the job you've got if you don't suit her. She'll understand. Ask her if she'll see you tomorrow when you're free.'

Elin took a shaky breath. She was being rushed into making a big decision. 'I'm not ready. I want to think.'

'Strike while the iron's hot.' There was no stopping Laura. 'And try to sound keen, Mam.'

She was stiff with apprehension when Laura pushed the phone in her hand. She found herself stammering, trying to phrase it as well as Laura had, straining with concentration not to miss what was being said to her.

Laura was dancing round the phone box like a puppy; Elin had to fix her eyes on a Woodbine packet on the floor. Then it was over, a weight off her mind. She pushed open the door.

'What was she like? What did she say?'

'Pleasant enough. Quite willing to make it two o'clock tomorrow.'

'I told you so. That's splendid. Give you time to finish work, have something to eat, and smarten yourself up first. Oh, I am excited.'

'Too excited, I haven't got the job yet,' Elin said, but she felt flushed with success herself, exhilarated because she'd made the effort, full of hope that things would change. The feeling of euphoria lasted throughout the evening. Jean Harlow was magnificent.

By the following lunch time, her nerve had gone. 'Don't let Da come upstairs while I'm changing,' she told Laura. 'He'll ask where I'm going if he sees me in my new red dress.'

'He won't come back yet,' Laura seemed full of confidence. 'He never does. But if you're worried, take your old coat up to cover it. I'll tell him we're going shopping, and I'll bring your coat back in the bag.'

They left the house together rather early, because Laura had to return to Talbot's shop to work. At the bus stop, Laura kissed her cheek when she saw the Woodside bus coming.

'Good luck, Mam. Da won't see you now.'

Elin climbed into the bus feeling she was over the first hurdle. By the time she changed to the Oxton bus, she felt more positive. The sun was shining, it was a warm summer day. Oxton was green and leafy, and the gardens delighted her. She couldn't remember seeing so many gladioli in full bloom.

She found the house, a big Victorian semi, prosperous but not over-grand. A woman with bushy grey hair opened the door and turned immediately to knock on the nearest door down the hall.

'She's here, Mrs Redman.' Elin was being beckoned forward.

'Do come in, Mrs Peck.' She was invited to sit in a chintz armchair. She liked that, most of her employers had kept her standing while they decided whether she'd suit.

Mrs Redman had white hair swept up in a bun, and soft, lax skin. She wore a black dress in a style fashionable at the turn of the century. She was older than Elin had expected, and walked stiffly with a stick. The sitting room was square with a high ceiling and a bay window overlooking the front garden.

'I'm a widow. I want someone else in the house at night.'

Elin relaxed a little. She could understand that, it was such a big place. She'd been wondering what she should say about her own circumstances. On the spur of the moment, she said she was a widow too.

'Then we have that in common.' For a moment Elin was afraid she'd ask the cause of her husband's death. She'd have to think of something. The question would come sooner or later.

'I employ a daily woman. Mrs Jones has been with me for five years. She's a good worker and does the heavy cleaning.' It was an old-fashioned room with a Turkish carpet and a surround of polished boards, comfortable with expensive china in a glass-fronted cabinet.

'Can you cook, Mrs Peck?'

'Yes.' Laura had impressed on her the need to sound confident. 'Plain cooking, stewing and roasting.' It would only be for three, and Laura would help when she was here. 'I enjoy baking cakes, pastries, scones and all that.'

Mrs Redman seemed impressed when she told her Laura was at Birkenhead High School. It was definitely a mark in her favour. Elin knew she'd get the job before it was offered. She had brought the references she'd collected over the years. A glowing one from Laurence Oxley, and several more recent ones. She explained how she worked now.

When the offer came, the wage was more than the combined total of the jobs she did now. She'd be a fool not to take it. It was like watching another part of her when she accepted the job and made arrangements to give a week's notice to her employers and move in the following weekend.

'I find the stairs a little difficult now,' Mrs Redman explained as she rang for Mrs Jones, the daily, to show her the rest of the house.

The woman with the bushy hair said: 'She's very nice to work for. Getting frail now. I usually finish at half one, but she didn't want to be alone in the house when you came. She didn't know you, you see.'

There was a formal dining room, a morning room and kitchens on the ground floor, with four bedrooms upstairs. She was shown the one she would use, and a separate smaller one for Laura. It all looked well cared for.

A week after she'd moved to Shrewsbury Road, Elin began to relax; she felt she'd done the right thing. Mrs Jones did most of the heavy cleaning. Mrs Redman wanted her to cook and serve meals, but since she was expected to sit down at the table and eat with her, Elin enjoyed doing it. Mrs Redman didn't feel steady on her feet and was afraid of going out alone. Now, with Elin's arm to hold on to, they went shopping together or for short walks in the park. If the weather was bad, Elin shopped alone. What the old lady wanted most was her company.

Laura was fitting in well, she read to Mrs Redman after supper each evening, and was quiet and polite. The old lady seemed to take a liking to her. There were roses in Laura's cheeks Elin had never seen before, and her honey-coloured hair lightened in the sun and had a new shine to it. She couldn't help but notice she was picking up a middle-class accent from her school.

Best of all for Elin she was no longer dogged by Percy's moods. It was such a relief not to share his bed, and not be afraid for her own skin, or Laura's.

'Are you happy here?' Elin was in Laura's room. She'd gone up to say good night.

'Oh yes, aren't you? Lovely to have a bathroom upstairs. You know, Mam, you look better already.'

She looked at herself in the mirror on Laura's dressing table. She'd had her hair cut properly for the first time in years, it was a golden cap again. She looked years younger.

'I'm putting on weight. Better food.'

'More of it,' Laura said. Mrs Redman liked her dinner at midday. Elin had not had two cooked meals a day for years.

'I told you it was the right thing to do,' Laura said.

'You know, we could manage to keep you at school after all.' Elin perched on her bed. 'Why not? We're in clover without Percy, no rent to pay, or food to buy from my wages.'

'Oh Mam,' Laura hugged her. 'I'd love to take School Certificate.'

'Even longer, your Higher, if it's what you want.'

'Oh, I do,' Laura breathed, her green eyes shining. 'That's wonderful.'

'You're not missing your paper round or Saturday job at Talbot's?'

'Like I'd miss a broken leg.'

Elin laughed, but she wasn't sure it was the truth. She'd expected Laura to miss the Talbots, especially Tom.

Mrs Redman had been in the habit of taking her afternoon tea, a meal of bread and butter, jam and cake, set out on the dining table at four o'clock. On the first few days, Laura had come from school and joined them while they were drinking their second cup. Mrs Redman said nothing to Elin, but contrived to delay the meal, so that they could all sit down together.

It was cool and rainy the next afternoon. Elin had lit the dining room fire and the reflection of the flames flickered on the brass scuttle. She'd made a sponge cake and scones, and set the teacups out in readiness on the dining table. She'd just gone into the kitchen, where the kettle was beginning to blow out steam, when she heard the front gate clang shut. She reached for the tea pot to soak the tea. The back door opened, and Laura came in with her satchel on her back.

'Hello, dear.' Elin kissed her cheek. 'Just wash your hands and come. Tea's all ready.'

As Elin carried the tea pot and hot water jug to the dining room, Mrs Redman was pulling out her chair. She'd been watching for Laura and seen her come up the garden path. 'I'm going to be very naughty and have no bread and butter today,' she announced cheerfully. 'I shall start with one of your lovely scones, and then I'll still have room for cake.' Mrs Redman had been a school mistress before she married fifty years ago, and was always interested in what Laura had done at school that day.

'In literature this afternoon we read more of *Midsummer Night's Dream*.' Elin began to pour out tea, but paused hearing a noise she couldn't identify.

'We've got as far as Puck—'

Suddenly the dining room door was thrown back with such force it crashed against the wall. Percy Peck, arrogant dark eyes surveying them, filled the doorway.

Elin felt the blood drain from her face. The teapot dropped back onto its stand with a crash. Mrs Redman gave a little scream. 'Who are you?'

Elin couldn't get her breath, her heart was thumping fit to burst. This was worse than anything she'd ever imagined. Laura was transfixed, her mouth open.

'I've come to take you home,' Percy said, looking down his Roman nose. 'You'd no business to walk out on me.'

'No,' Elin protested. 'No, you don't want me. You don't even like me.'

'I want you to take care of the house and see to the meals.'

'Who is he?' Mrs Redman demanded. 'What does he want?'

'Leave us alone, for pity's sake,' Elin said.

Laura's face was stricken. 'How did you find us?'

'Followed you, Miss Clever. Knew you'd still be going to that fancy school. You led me straight here.'

'Oh no,' she moaned, covering her face with her hands.

'Get out of my house! You've no right to come in here.' Mrs Redman was struggling to her feet; her stick slipped and she flopped back into the chair.

'Not without my wife,' Percy said at his most haughty. He was smartly dressed. 'I've come to fetch her back.'

'Mrs Peck? You said you were a widow!'

'Wishful thinking on her part. You don't get out of your vows that easily, Elin.'

'We're not coming,' Laura told him white-faced.

'I'm going to call the police,' Mrs Redman gasped.

'Go and wait at the gate,' Elin shouted at Percy. 'Can't you see you're upsetting her.'

'I've got every reason to be upset,' Mrs Redman cried. 'In my own house, such a scene.'

'Get your things together, Laura.' Elin felt she was reeling. Her knees felt weak.

'I don't want to go.'

'You can't stay here.' Mrs Redman was indignant. 'I can't have strange men bursting into my home like this.'

'Absolutely not,' Percy agreed.

'I can't put up with it.' Mrs Redman's anger was rising, her soft skin suffused with rage. 'You can all go. Fight it out somewhere else.' She turned on Elin.

'You told me lies.'

'She's all lies,' Percy said.

Elin was close to tears. 'Wait outside,' she snapped at Percy. 'We'll come. Just get out.'

'You took advantage of me,' Mrs Redman was incredulous. 'I believed you.'

Elin took a deep breath. 'I'm sorry, we'll go. Would you like Laura to stay with you overnight?'

'No, no, I'll be all right. Just go. All of you. I'm far too trusting. A man like that walking into my house!'

'I'm sorry.' Elin put an arm round Laura's shoulders drawing her out of the room. 'We'll pack our things.'

'Oh Mam, it's my fault! I never thought of him following me back. I've ruined everything.'

'It's not your fault, love.' Elin wanted to protect her daughter. She'd known it wouldn't last.

'But it is,' Laura wailed.

Elin hardly knew what she was doing. She pulled her suitcase out from under the bed and threw everything that looked familiar into it. She could hear Laura sobbing in the next room.

When they went down together, Mrs Redman was waiting at the front door. 'Here's what I owe you, though you don't deserve it. I thought you liked me, but all the time you were telling lies, taking me in.'

Percy was waiting at the gate. He swaggered behind them to the bus stop, not offering to carry anything. Laura had her school satchel on her back, and two shopping bags full, as well as a small case. Elin staggered with her case, her hatbox and her sewing machine.

'You're not as bright as you think you are,' Percy taunted Laura. 'Following you from school was the obvious way to find where you'd hidden yourselves.' Elin could see her daughter's green eyes glittering with hate for him.

Jubilee Street looked worse than she remembered. Even a couple of weeks away had softened her. Made her think leafy gardens were normal. Inside the house was worse, it was shabby. The kitchen grate was full of cold ash, the scullery sink full of dirty pans and dishes. There was dust everywhere, and no food in the house.

'I need you here. It's a comfort to be needed, isn't it, Elin?'

'No.'

'You wanted to marry me, don't forget. It wasn't my idea. I'll always find you, you know,' Percy gloated. 'I'm not such a fool as you think.'

Elin pushed a shopping bag and some money at Laura. 'Quick, love, run to the shops before they close. Milk, bread, tea, eggs.'

'Butter,' Percy added. 'And I fancy some sausage.'

Laura ran down the street, hardly able to see where she was going for tears. It had been a mirage. The comfortable life without Da, where she could stay on at school. It had gone; worse, it was her own fault it had gone. How could she have been so careless? So stupid?

She ran past Talbot's newsagent with her head down, hoping they wouldn't see her. The nearest grocer's was in the same parade. She had to wait at the counter, fidgeting with impatience, while another customer was served. She'd been afraid to come out and leave her mother with Da. She'd run till there was a stitch in her side so she could get back as quickly as possible. Da was in a mood when he might do anything. He'd been exhilarated by his victory, glorying in the power he had over them.

What did Mam want? Bread, butter, tea, eggs and milk. There was no fresh milk so she bought condensed instead. Now the sausages. The butcher's was farther along the parade. She ran out, straight into Tom Talbot's arms.

'Hey, kid. Where did you disappear to?' She tried to break free, but he held her in a bunny hug. 'Your father came round asking.'

Laura could stand no more. Her head went down on his shoulder and the tears flowed unchecked. He took her through the shop into the living room. 'Come on, you can tell me.'

He was being kind and she felt full of love for him. Looking up into his concerned gaze, she could almost believe he felt the same way about her, that Rosemary didn't exist. It all came out, a bit at a time, interspersed with sobs. The need for secrecy, the way Da beat Mam up. That he'd taken her money. The only thing she kept back was the worst, the searing disappointment she felt that Tom had a new girl friend. She was well into her tale when she looked up to see Mrs Talbot had come in from the shop and was listening too.

'There,' she clucked sympathetically, 'I thought it might be something like that when your dad came round. You should have told us.' She poured a cup of tea for Laura from their pot.

'Do you want your job back?' Tom was asking.

'Yes, please.' She'd been worrying she'd lost it from the moment she knew they were coming home. She'd let the Talbots down. They rated reliability high, and she'd just disappeared. 'I'm sorry . . . He found us, after all.'

'I did your job on Saturday,' Tom said gently. 'So Dad will be glad to have you back.'

'We've taken on another paper boy, but we're getting more deliveries,' his mother added. 'We can use you too.'

'Thank you, thank you.' She hardly liked to press further, but Mam would be desperate if she lost all her jobs. 'And Mam?'

'I took on another woman, but she's not clean. Not nearly as good as your mam. Tell her to come back.'

That was good news anyway, Laura felt a little better. 'Thank you, you're very kind. They're waiting for me to bring their tea. I'll have to go. Do I look awful?'

'Go up to the bathroom and wash your face first,' Tom suggested, pushing her up the stairs.

When she reached home, Laura opened the front door cautiously. The shouting had stopped, Mam was huddled into her chair with her face buried in the cushion.

'You've taken your time,' Percy said. 'Get it cooked. Fried egg and sausage. I'm hungry.'

'Omelette, Da, they didn't have any sausage left.' It was her way of showing defiance. It was only then she noticed Mam's face was bruised, and her lip cut and bleeding.

'Mam!' She threw her arms round her and hugged her. 'What have you done to her? You're a monster to hurt her like this. Get your own tea. I'll not wait on you.'

Percy tore her away, his hand came down against her bottom but not with any degree of force. He pushed her into the scullery. 'Do as I say, unless you want to feel more of that. Your mother wants to eat too.'

'Please, Laurie,' Mam implored.

Laura had no appetite, and neither had her mother, but once Percy had eaten, he went out as usual to the pub. It meant a few hours of peace.

Laura told her they both still had jobs at the Talbots.

'I raised your hopes,' Elin mourned. 'You won't be able to stay on at school after all.'

'I should have been more careful,' Laura said. 'I let him follow me.'

'I think I know where I can get money for your secretarial course.' Mam's sun-gold eyes were showing fight again.

'Where?'

'Just leave it to me. I'll try.'

Laurence Oxley had considered cancelling his visit to the school on Prize Day. He was alternately sorry he'd accepted the invitation to be the main speaker and glad of the opportunity to see the girl. At times, he was overcome with curiosity about her, wanting this moment.

The sea of girls' faces swam in front of him as he made his speech. Then Miss Pleat rose to her feet beside him to announce the prize winners.

'Essay prize, Laura Peck.' His heart gave a sickening jerk against his ribs as he saw her get to her feet and come forward. The Oxley blood was quite obvious in her fair hair, her high cheek bones and strong chin. How had Mary not recognised it? Sybil certainly would; he'd been right to persuade her to visit Violet today.

She held her head proudly. Her green eyes were searching his face. Would she see? No, no, his secret was safe. Her hand was cold and shaking in his, her school uniform shabby. He felt suffused with guilt as he handed over her prize, a book on West Africa. He tried to smile, his vision was clouded. Then she was stumbling away. There was a hole in her stocking. Mary came to receive her history prize from him. Well groomed but startlingly alike in features. It was incredible nobody had noticed.

It was only afterwards, when Miss Pleat led him away to take tea with the teachers and parents, that the possibility he might meet Elin occurred to him. He considered making some excuse to leave immediately, but Jane was there with his cup of tea. Laura Peck was handing round a plate of cucumber sandwiches.

'I found your essay very interesting,' he told her. 'I even

learned something from it.' But she was too shy to stay and talk to him.

'A pity about Laura Peck,' Miss Pleat said, drawing him aside. 'She's leaving school at Christmas.'

'Leaving! Why?'

'Her parents say she must start to earn her living.'

'Are they here today?' He had to find that out. Be prepared.

'No, they never come to any school function. Not even the mother. She works, I believe.'

He could relax, he wouldn't have to face Elin Jones after all. She might know he'd be here, of course.

'Such a bright girl too.' The light glinted on Miss Pleat's pince-nez. 'A terrible waste.'

'I'd like to help. Her fees . . .'

'That's extremely kind of you, Mr Oxley, but there's nothing to pay. She has a scholarship from the Local Authority. They pay her fees, her books and give a grant towards her uniform and transport. She even has free lunches.'

'Then why take her away? It doesn't make sense.' He felt angry with Peck. He'd never known which way his bread was buttered.

'She could be earning a wage, serving in some shop or working in one of your factories.'

'At fourteen years of age? She'd be lucky to get a pound a week. Fifteen shillings is realistic.' Laurence Oxley chewed on the sandwich, it tasted like sawdust in his mouth. 'No lunches, no clothes, no bus fares to work, and no future. If they gave one thought to the girl's future . . .'

'The poor don't value education, Mr Oxley, and it can divide the family. Make her more middle class in outlook.'

That made him squirm. Ridiculous for her to leave now. The girl showed promise. He ought to do something for her. He nearly opened his mouth to ask Miss Pleat to arrange some special bursary for her. But it would not be for fees or books. If he were to pay her living expenses, how could he deny she was his daughter? It would leave him vulnerable, his defences down.

Oxley accepted another cup of tea. He felt he was failing her. His eyes searched among the tide of pupils, trying to pick her out. It wasn't possible.

Elin felt scared, there was no point in pretending she wasn't. It would be putting her head into the lion's den. She hadn't seen Laurence Oxley for nearly fourteen years. She was dreading coming face to face with him but she had to do it. For Laura's sake.

Over the years she'd schooled herself not to think about him. But it was his fault Percy Peck was on her back now. It made her bristle with hate and frustration when she compared Laura's circumstances with his.

Once, she'd believed herself in love with Laurence, but no one can stay in love with a man they hadn't seen for fourteen years. Anyway, what did she know of love? She'd never had it, except from Laura.

Would he even recognise her?

She'd wear her red dress if the day was warm enough. It was the smartest thing she had, even if she had made it herself. Her black felt hat didn't go with it; perhaps she should get herself another.

He had an office somewhere in Liverpool. Laura would know how to find the address, but she couldn't ask her. Laura was already too curious about her connection with the Oxleys.

The telephone book of course. She went into a kiosk with pencil and paper and wrote it down. The Liver Building! Everybody knew where that was. She'd call and ask to see him. Take him by surprise. She couldn't risk asking for an appointment. Even so, he might refuse to see her. She shivered at the thought, but she had to try. And it had to be soon before the mild autumn weather went. She didn't own a decent coat.

Percy was never in a hurry in the mornings. He slept late and got up between nine and ten to make himself tea and toast in a leisurely fashion, listening to the wireless. Then he'd wash and shave and walk down to the pub about eleven.

Elin always got up with Laura when she was going to

school, and usually they left the house about the same time. Today she went into Birkenhead and bought herself a fashionable pill box hat in the same shade as her dress, with a bit of veiling that came down over her eyes. She bought a pair of black cotton gloves too, to hide her work-worn hands. It took most of next week's rent money.

Percy had gone by the time she got back home, so with the house to herself she set about curling her hair with curling tongs borrowed from Beattie Higgs, which she heated over the scullery gas stove. Then she changed into her red dress and studied her reflection in the wardrobe mirror. Not too bad, with her hair done like this. The dress would have hung better without the pockets set into the side seams. She hadn't stitched them in right. It would improve the whole thing if she took them out and stitched the seam flat, but it was too late to do it now.

She paused, asking herself why she was going to so much trouble with her appearance. If she was honest, she wanted him to like what he saw. He had once. Perhaps he'd suggest taking her somewhere for lunch? She tingled at the thought. No, she was being silly, it would be after lunch when she got there. Dinner then; he might suggest meeting her for dinner. She wouldn't mind if it became a regular thing again. A man like Laurence Oxley would think nothing of renting a hotel room. He'd want it often, she could safely bet he wouldn't have changed in that respect. He knew how to make a girl enjoy it too. Not like Percy. Laurence Oxley would always have another woman on the side.

She made herself eat something although her stomach was churning. She mustn't let hunger sap her energy, as she knew it could. It cost more to buy a snack once she was out. She caught the ferry to Liverpool, travelling in the saloon so the breeze wouldn't spoil her hair. The Liver Building dominated the city waterfront. She watched it coming closer as the engines pounded beneath her feet. Its four dial clock was one of the three or four largest in the world. With seventeen floors, it was almost an American sky scraper. To Elin, it emphasised Laurence Oxley's wealth.

The Liver Building was palatial inside. Her footsteps

echoed on the ornate floors. From the board in the entrance foyer, she saw Oxley Enterprises occupied the whole of the third floor. She looked at the express lifts presided over by uniformed attendants and headed for the stairs.

There was a ladies' cloakroom on the way up. She went inside to comb her hair again and make sure she looked her best. The curls she'd made had dropped a little. She put a hair clip in. Not as good as they had been, but not too bad. Her breathing was uneven. She was nervous, but she had to do it. It was for Laura. She made herself take deep steadying breaths. One more deep one, and she walked into the outer office.

'I've come to see Mr Laurence Oxley,' she announced. She was escorted along a corridor to another office. There were two secretaries, one young and attractive, one middle-aged, wearing glasses. Both were typing.

'I'd like to see Mr Oxley if he could spare me a few minutes,' she said to the younger one. She was quaking inside, but she had to look as though she did this every day. 'I don't have an appointment.'

'I'll ask him. May I have your name?'

'Mrs Peck.'

The girl hesitated. 'Is it about . . .?'

'It's a personal matter. He knows me.' That, she had decided, should get her past the secretary and make it harder for him to refuse. The auburn-haired girl picked up one of the phones on her desk and spoke into it. Elin's heart plummeted when she saw it was being put down immediately.

'He'll see you if you wait, Mrs Peck. He's busy with a client at the moment.'

'Thank you.' He hadn't had time to say all that, but it was what she'd hoped for. She took the seat indicated and watched the girl return to her typing. She was the sort Laurence Oxley would like.

Elin felt her confidence draining away with the minutes. She wished he'd hurry up. A uniformed messenger came in with a book and a thick envelope. Elin took more deep breaths while the senior secretary pulled out two bundles of currency notes and began to count. Elin stared fascinated at the five pound notes. She'd never seen one before. The one pound notes were more familiar, but the sight of so many was not.

The woman initialled the book, placed the envelope inside it on the edge of her desk, and the messenger left. Typing resumed. If she could get Laura trained for a job like this, where she could sit down all day and be nicely dressed, it would give her a much better life than shop work or cleaning.

The waiting was terrible. Her nerve was going.

The door to an inner office opened. She heard Laurence Oxley's laugh; she'd know that anywhere. The strength seemed to ebb from her knees. This was it.

She watched him shaking hands with the man who was leaving. He was more heavily built than she remembered. Stouter and broader in his formal grey pin stripes. His bronze hair had faded, there was silver in it now.

'Mrs Peck to see you,' his secretary reminded him. 'And the cash you asked me to get.' The book with the envelope inside changed hands. The intense blue eyes she remembered so well swept over her. She saw his jerk of recognition, his air of bonhomie fading. He didn't want to speak to her. For a moment she thought he was going to send her away.

'Come in,' he barked and turned back to his office. 'Do sit down.'

The room was impressively panelled, with a large mahogany desk. She could see storm clouds gathering over the river through the two tall windows that overlooked it.

'What brings you here?' His face was stern, his eyes coldly resolute. He had the look of a man used to wealth.

'I need help.' She saw his gesture of dismissal and went on quickly, 'I wouldn't have come if I hadn't thought it absolutely essential. I haven't bothered you over the last fourteen years. Laura, my daughter, needs help.' She lowered her voice. 'Your daughter.'

'What sort of help?' He still couldn't sit still; there was a bounce in his step as he strode between his desk and the windows, backwards and forwards.

Elin did her best to explain. 'Peck wants her to leave school at Christmas and get a job. He's thinking of the Maypole. Butter and cheese shop, you know?'

'Yes,' he said impatiently.

'She was saving money from a Saturday job to take typing lessons, so she could get office work. Peck stole it. If you would pay for a year at a secretarial college, it would make all the difference for her.'

'Elin.' He swung round from the window like a caged animal. Her name rolled off his tongue so easily, it made her hopeful. 'Elin, she's too bright to be a typist. She's at a good school. I'll help you keep her there. It's the best thing for her.'

'It's Percy,' she stammered. 'He wants her to leave, not me.'

'Then change his mind for him.' He ran his hand through his pepper and salt hair. 'When the time comes, I'll help with further education too, professional training.'

'It's too late. Percy's given notice. She's leaving at Christmas. There was no changing his mind. He thinks she'll earn her keep this way, and he'll live better. He's a parasite. He beats me.'

He held up his hand and looked at her pityingly. Elin could see he thought she was laying it on thick. Impossible to make him believe it was true.

'If she's to get anywhere, she really must stay on at school, believe me. If, then, she wants a secretarial course, I'll even help with that. But not now.'

He turned and paced towards the windows again. Elin felt her spirits spiral downwards. She couldn't make him understand, it was hopeless. Her eyes came to rest on the envelope containing all that money. It was slipping out of the book. He'd put it on his desk alongside the cut glass and silver inkstand. Within her reach.

'The worse thing you ever did was to shackle me to Percy Peck.' She shouldn't have said that, it wouldn't get her what she wanted. Her accent was slipping, she sounded like a fish wife.

'It isn't in her interest to leave school at fourteen. It would put her at a disadvantage.'

She moved her handbag to her left hand as he turned and swung back towards the windows again. Her right hand shot out and grabbed the envelope, pushing it down into the deep pocket in the side of her dress. The book slapped shut, with a noise she hadn't expected, and she'd pulled it forward a few inches.

'You'd do better to work on changing Peck's mind. Get him to see sense.' She was shaking all over as she stood up. It was for Laura. She couldn't let her down over this.

'I thought you'd want to help her.' The room was spinning, she had to get out.

'Don't ever come to my office again. Ever, do you understand?' He bent down so his face was near to hers. There were a few wrinkles on it now, but his iron will still showed.

'Yes,' she choked. There was no danger of that, she'd never dare look him in the face again after stealing his money.

'Write to me if she needs help when she's finishing school. Post it here. Be sure to mark it personal. Above all, say nothing about me to the girl.'

It had been the right thing to do, she told herself as she hurried down the stairs. It was the only possible way to help Laura. The envelope was fat beneath her fingers. She'd hide it when she got home. Keep it till Laura had left school. She wouldn't tell her how she came by it. It would be her secret. She'd give her what she needed. Percy must never know about it.

CHAPTER THIRTEEN

As the door clicked shut behind Elin, Laurence Oxley collapsed into his chair. To see Elin Jones walking in after all these years had been a real kick in the gut. He wouldn't have believed her capable of coming. She'd been a shy little thing.

The fact that she'd found him took away his sense of security. Sybil wouldn't believe he'd had no contact with her. She'd been suspicious once.

Elin's face had lost the rounded youthfulness he remembered so well, and the rosy cheeks. It was even a little pinched. He'd found himself searching out the changes, trying to remember exactly how she'd looked. Her slanting gold eyes had blue shadows under them now, giving her a haunting beauty. Yellow cat's eyes, Sybil had called them in a fit of jealousy.

How old would she be now? Thirty-three? Her waist hadn't thickened as Sybil's had but she didn't look in good health.

He'd had a lot of women on the side since, but none had pleased him more. It was a pity he'd lost sight of her. He'd been a fool not to set her up in a small house where he could visit. He was getting too old to keep making new conquests. Still, she'd wanted to marry the valet, and he'd gone along with that.

Laurence sighed and pulled himself up in the chair, taking out his wallet in readiness. He was reaching for the envelope he'd put on his desk when his hand froze in mid-air. He moved a file, unable to believe his own eyes. The blood was draining from his face.

The bitch! He snatched at the book. It was all she'd left

him. The little bitch, she'd come for money and she'd got it. He closed his eyes, took a deep breath. Tried to still the growing fury within him. He'd seen the disappointment flood into her golden eyes when he'd refused her. Damn it, he'd even felt sorry for her.

There was nothing he could do about it. The last thing he needed was to draw attention to her visit. What did £50 matter anyway? She'd know that and feel safe. But he'd believed Elin Jones to be honest.

She'd said she was short of money, but she didn't look it. Her dress looked new and was very becoming. She'd found money for a smart outfit from somewhere. She wasn't starving.

When Neville Chamberlain returned from Munich bringing peace with honour, Miss Pleat said a special prayer of thanksgiving in Assembly. But before long, people were talking of war again, and Miss Powell said the storm clouds were gathering.

Laura had been feeling low all day. It was an effort to get up from the tea table to do her homework. There seemed little point, now her school days were definitely ending. Except that Miss Pleat had sent for her today and talked as if she expected her to carry on with her studies and matriculate. She'd advised her on night school classes, and had written down the date and place where she must enrol. It sounded like pie in the sky.

Da paused at the parlour table to speak to her on his way out. 'I called in at the Maypole today. The manager needs a school leaver to help on the counter over Christmas. He said you could call in and see him ten o'clock on Monday.'

'I'll still be at school on Monday. I don't break up for another three weeks.'

'For God's sake! Don't be so stupid. The job's there now. Nobody takes on staff after Christmas. You need to start thinking which side your bread's buttered.'

The front door slammed behind him. Laura banged her history book shut and packed her notebooks back in her satchel. What was the use? She'd go and help wash up. Mam was emptying a kettle of boiling water into the brown stone sink and swishing the cage that held the ends of soap tablets in the water.

'That secretarial course,' Mam said confidentially. 'It'll be all right.'

'What?' Laura's mind was still on the job at the Maypole.

'You'll be able to go to college when you leave school. I've got the money for it.'

Laura stared at her in disbelief. There was a new vigour about Mam's shoulders as she continued to stack plates on the draining board.

'You've got money for it? Where from?'

'Never you mind. I've got it.'

'Typing lessons?'

'A full secretarial course. Shorthand, bookkeeping, whatever you want.'

'But that's going to cost more than staying on at school.'

'You'll have a skill at the end of it. You won't have to do shop work.'

'What about Da? And the Maypole?'

'You leave Da to me. I'll make him see you'll earn twice as much this way.' Mam pushed her golden hair back from her forehead leaving a few soap bubbles on it. There was determination in every line of her face.

'Where did you get the money, Mam?'

'That's my business, I've got it, but don't say anything to Da. It's our secret.'

'I can't believe . . .'

Elin turned, and Laura saw the shadow cross her face. She knew her mother had pushed herself to the limit to get it. Mam loved her enough to do anything for her.

'Don't mention it to Da, whatever you do. Get yourself a place in college. Decide which one.'

'I've heard Skerry's is very good, and Bateman's. I'll find out. Write for brochures.' Laura felt a shiver of elation. 'Oh Mam!' She wrapped her arms round her mother's thin shoulders, pulling her close. 'Thank you, I am grateful.'

'I have to try for you,' Elin gasped. 'You've got to have your chance. I never did. I don't want you to end up like me.'

By mid-December, Laura had made arrangements to start her secretarial course at the beginning of January. She had been surprised how quickly Mam had settled the matter by paying the first term's fees. There had been terrible row about it, but for once Mam had stood out against Da's wishes.

Elin had been complaining of a headache and a sore throat for some days, though she'd continued to go to work. On Tuesday, Laura came back from her paper round to find her asleep in her chair, unable to eat her tea.

'I feel terrible, I ache all over.'

'You've got 'flu,' Da said. 'You'd better go to bed.'

'I think I will.'

Laura watched her drag herself up stairs before going to heat some milk for her. 'Don't go to work tomorrow, Mam,' she said, looking for the aspirins. 'You aren't well enough.'

'I'll see how I feel. I might be over it by tomorrow.'

In the morning, Laura thought she looked worse. She put her hand on her mother's forehead; she was burning hot. 'I'll get the doctor.'

'No,' Elin said hoarsely. 'I'll be all right. Can you run up to Talbot's before you go to school? Tell them I won't be coming. It's Mrs Mount this afternoon, perhaps I could get there.'

'No, Mam. I'll call there too. You aren't well enough. Or do you think,' Laura hesitated, 'do you think I should do your cleaning for you? Keep your jobs? Then we'd still have your money.'

Mam closed her eyes to think. Laura could see beads of sweat on her nose. 'What are you doing in school?'

'I've a history exam this morning, and biology this afternoon. End of term exams.'

'Could be important to you, Laura, if you want to go on studying. Go to school.'

Laura bent to kiss her hot sticky face. 'I wish you'd let me fetch the doctor.'

'I'll mend without him. Bound to, staying in bed all day like a lady.'

Elin was off for the rest of the week, and even then she had a hacking cough.

'Stay off another few days,' Laura urged.

'We need the money, we'll be short this week as it is.'

'You look downright ill. Everybody will be afraid of catching it from you.'

'I'll tell them it was just a heavy cold.'

Laura put her paper round money towards the rent at the weekend and settled with the milkman from her savings.

Da came in whistling at tea time. Laura put her head round the scullery door when she heard him, in time to see him take a bottle of sherry from his overcoat pocket.

'This will help you pick up, Elin. Bring some glasses, Laura.'

She managed to find one sherry glass and brought a small tumbler as well.

'There now.' He half filled the sherry glass and put it into Elin's hand. 'See if that does you good.'

'Food would do her more good,' Laura dared. Da had been increasingly difficult since he'd fetched them back from Mrs Redman's. She felt permanently on edge when he was home in case she should trigger another row, and yet she couldn't stop herself niggling at him. 'Eggs and oranges and things like that.'

His domineering dark eyes held hers. Slowly he took out a bulging wallet and pushed a ten shilling note across the oil cloth covering the table. 'Get her some oranges, whatever she needs. You can't say I'm not generous.'

Laura gasped at her unexpected success, while Mam looked up from her sherry to ask: 'Come into a fortune, Percy?'

'Managed to make a bit this week,' he said loftily, rubbing his hands.

'Good,' Laura said. 'Mam's had a short week.'

'I thought all her weeks were short now,' Da said, his patience gone, 'since you persuaded her to throw her jobs away.' Elin hadn't been able to fill all her hours since her return from Mrs Redman's.

'Being off sick only makes it worse.' She waited, hoping

he would put some more notes down. It didn't happen. 'Please, Da, could you give us money for coal?'

She watched his hand go towards his wallet. Then slowly he withdrew it. His nose rose to its most arrogant angle, daring her to press him further. 'Coalman will let you put it on the slate.'

But they wouldn't put it on the slate; Mam hated owing, and it had to be paid sometime.

She'd take the old pram round to the gas works and collect a hundredweight of coke. It was a by-product of gas-making, and sold cheaply on the spot. Some thought it demeaning to push coke through the streets, but plenty could be seen doing it in carts made from wooden boxes and old wheels. The old pram had been kept for the purpose. She'd gone with Mam many a time and helped push it back up the hill with the sack on top.

Elin went back to work on Monday, but only managed to work for two days before taking to her bed again, feeling worse.

'You went back too soon,' Laura said, worried. 'You've got a raging temperature.' She took up a bowl of warm water to sponge her down. 'I wish you'd have the doctor.'

'It's the money, and Christmas nearly here.'

'Go to see him then, we can afford half a crown. I'll come with you tonight.'

Elin was unsteady on her feet and covered in perspiration but she agreed. It was a busy surgery, they had to wait a long time. Laura tried to think of something cheap she could cook for tea. The doctor prescribed cough medicine, told Elin she had 'flu and sent her back to bed.

'I told you it'd be a waste of money,' she fumed on the way home. 'Sixpence for cough mixture, too!'

'It's set my mind at rest,' Laura said as she walked home with her, but she had to rush out again to do her paper round.

Mam hadn't moved when she got back. She was still sitting by the fire with her eyes closed. Laura went into the scullery and got out the frying pan.

Da came in whistling. She knew immediately he'd had

another good day. His jacket swung open as he took it off, and she could see his wallet bulging in his inside pocket. Laura half expected him to produce another bottle of sherry, but he settled down with the evening paper. She boiled potatoes and cabbage, and then mashed them together and fried them in leftover bacon fat. It smelled nice as she set it on the table.

'What's this?' Da prodded his helping suspiciously.

'Bubble and squeak.'

'It's very tasty,' Mam said hastily, pushing a tiny amount into her mouth.

'I don't like fried cabbage.' He crashed his fork down on his plate. 'Why don't you make a decent meal? You can make stew, can't you?'

'Meat costs money, Da. Mam's not been able to work.' Laura hesitated, but she knew she had to try. She pushed her fair hair back from her face. 'Could you give me some money? I could get you steak then.'

'I'm always giving you money,' he bristled.

'Da, you gave me ten shillings last week. We haven't enough for food.'

'You should get off your backside and work then.'

'It's all right, Laura. Leave it,' Mam said quietly.

She couldn't leave it. Da had a fat wallet and wouldn't part with a penny. He came home every day expecting a hot meal; he expected Mam's wages to keep them all, even when she was too ill to work. Fury rose in her throat.

'What else is there?' Da pushed his bubble and squeak away uneaten.

'Nothing,' she said.

He went into the scullery and started to open cupboards. 'There's one egg left. Fry me that. I'll have it on toast.'

Laura had meant to whip it into milk for Mam's breakfast. She could get that down despite her sore throat. She opened her mouth to say so, but her mother was getting to her feet.

'No, Mam, I'll do it. Finish your tea.'

She had to get money from somewhere. The rent was due on Friday and there was only six shillings left in Mam's housekeeping purse now. They needed coal. She couldn't light the fire with just coke, it wouldn't catch. Mam had to have a fire in the house while she was ill.

The toast was under the grill, the egg spitting gently in the frying pan, when the thought came to her. It was the obvious answer. Why shouldn't Da contribute to the running of the house? He had money and they had none. She crept to the scullery door. His jacket was still hanging on the chair. He was holding the newspaper wide open in front of his face. Mam had gone back to her chair near the fire and had closed her eyes.

Laura kept her eyes on the newspaper as she slid her hand inside his jacket and withdrew his wallet. She didn't take another breath until she was back in the scullery. Her fingers were shaking as she forced them under the stud that kept the wallet closed. There was thirteen pounds in it. Thirteen pounds!

She took four pounds out and folded the wallet. Where could she hide them? Her hand slid under the knife box inside a drawer. It fell back on the money with a rattle. Suddenly she realised black smoke was streaming from the toast. She rushed towards the stove.

'You thieving bitch!' Da bellowed behind her. 'Can't take my eye off my money for one minute.' He swiped at her, catching the side of her head. She was already bending towards the grill and the force knocked her face against the corner of the stove. Pain shot through her. She staggered and collapsed in a heap, her arm catching the handle of the frying pan and knocking its contents over her. She screamed in terror and pain.

'What is it?' Mam was supporting herself against the scullery door.

'She tried to steal my money!' Da shouted, waving his wallet triumphantly. The toast burst into flames. Mam stepped forward, turned the gas off, and bent to help Laura to her feet. She was shrugging out of her blazer. The egg had landed on her shoulder but fortunately most of the fat had been absorbed; the thick material had saved her. She felt terrible; pain sliced down her face, her head throbbed.

'You think you can take my money?' Da lunged at her and another slicing blow sent her reeling against the stove again. Laura put out a hand to save herself and it landed on the burner which moments before had been lit. Laura screamed again.

'Stop it, Percy! Don't you dare hit her.' Mam was standing protectively over her. Mam who had seemed faint with weakness moments before.

'She's taken my money. She's taken four pounds.' Da stood over her menacingly.

'If you lay a finger on her again, I'll kill you,' Mam said with icy determination.

Percy ignored her. 'What have you done with it?' He clutched at Laura's school tie, pulling her forward by the neck.

'It's under the knife box,' she sobbed.

'I mean it,' Mam breathed. 'Don't ever touch her again. I won't stand for Laura being hurt.'

'Then she'd better leave my money alone.'

'You took mine,' Laura spat, her green eyes blazing. 'You promised you'd pay me back, but you never did. You owe me four pounds, three and twopence.'

'Some other time,' Percy sneered. 'I'd have given it to you had you asked nicely. But not when you try to steal it.'

'You stole it from me,' Laura sobbed.

'Borrowed it.'

'If you want to eat, you'd better pay me back now.'

'I'm going out to eat.'

Laura closed her eyes waiting. As the door crashed behind him, Mam gathered her into her arms.

'Laurie, love! You shouldn't have tried.'

'I was only taking what he owed me. That's not stealing. You know he'll never pay me back. Not him.'

'No.' Mam took the face cloth that hung by the sink, soaked it in cold water and dabbed at Laura's face.

'We have to get money from somewhere. The rent—'

'I have a little hidden away.' Mam continued to sponge. 'I wanted to keep it for your college, but if some has to go on other things, then it has to.'

'You should have told me, Mam. How much have you got?'

'Enough. I'm afraid you might have a black eye by morning, the corner of the stove must have caught you.'

'What?' Laura shot up to her bedroom to look in the mirror. She had small cuts and bruising round her left eye, and the whole side of her face was grazed and sore. She parted her fair hair and saw a gash in her scalp. Her shoulder hurt, and her hand where she'd burned it.

'I hate him. He's horrible to us both,' she called. Slowly she went back downstairs. 'At least I can say truthfully I fell against the stove. I don't have to say Da pushed me.'

'Keep the cold flannel against your face,' Mam advised. She stood looking down at her. 'I do hope you don't marry someone like Da.'

'I'm never getting married,' Laura told her, thinking of Tom. There would never be anyone to hold a candle to him.

It had been a warm day. After being cooped up in the Liverpool office all day, Laurence Oxley looked forward to going home to a family dinner.

Leonard and Catherine were off to Washington on the *Queen Mary* tomorrow and were spending the night with them. He'd asked Robert over to join them for dinner.

It was a beautiful evening, they spent most of it on the patio, looking out over the garden to Hilbre Island and the sea. Leonard wouldn't find anything to beat it in Washington. Sybil was proud of her garden, it was looking lush now the trees and shrubs had matured. Laurence watched her take Catherine on a tour of inspection. Both of them were putting on too much weight. Their voices drifted back on the breeze, Catherine's larger frame and dark head outlined against the silvery water. She'd been very taken with the exotic blooms in the greenhouse.

The ladies returned from the garden and they all watched the sun set with a dazzling display of red and gold light, and finally disappear into the sea. Night had come, it was getting cooler. Beside Laurence, Mary shivered.

Robert stood up. 'It's time I went home, if I'm to feel

like work in the morning.' Laurence had had to persuade the Jennings to take him in after the trouble last year. He and Mary were seeing too much of each other, both living in this house. 'Thank you, Aunt Sybil, lovely dinner,' Robert said politely.

Laurence watched while he kissed his mother. He had inherited something of her build, Oxley shoulders had never been as powerful as his. Robert wished his father well in his new posting and said his goodbyes. Thank goodness all the bother between Robert and Mary was over. Laurence had managed to squash it before it went too far. He needn't have worried about asking Robert here. Mary had sat demurely between him and Sybil, and hardly said anything to Robert all evening.

They all trailed through the house with Robert to the front steps, and watched him drive off in his Morgan roadster.

'I think I'll go to bed,' Mary said when the front door closed behind them. He thought he'd never seen her look less tired; her blue eyes were wide, sparkling with life.

'A nightcap?' he suggested. Only Len took him up on it; Sybil and Catherine followed Mary upstairs.

Laurence rang for another bottle of brandy, and told his housekeeper to lock up. He led Len back to the patio. He didn't want to stay indoors, though the night was chilly now. A sliver of moon was climbing into the sky.

'How's Robert making out?' Len asked, settling back in his armchair. They were not as much alike as they used to be. Len was greyer and had developed the distinguished bearing of a diplomat.

'I've no worries about his work. He's very able.'

'Catherine's worried stiff. If this damn war comes, he'll have to go and fight. He's that age.'

Laurence cradled his glass and sighed. 'Will it come? What's the view of the Diplomatic Service?'

'Half say yes, half are still hopeful.' He paused. 'I don't think there's much doubt myself. What will you do?'

Laurence sighed again. 'I've had plenty of time to think. I've made my plans.' War with Germany would split his business empire in two. He wouldn't be able to travel backwards and forwards between Liverpool and Africa.

'I want a reliable man established in Lagos. He'll have to manage everything at that end. Probably have to stay for the duration.' He looked at his twin, splashed a little more brandy into his glass. 'I'm thinking of sending Robert.'

'Really?' Leonard looked up, interested. 'That would please Catherine very much. To have him away from the trouble. We might get stranded in America, you see.'

'I don't want him blown to smithereens either. The business needs him. I'll put it to him in a day or two. Get him out there before anything starts.'

'He wouldn't know there was a war on.'

'He'd have to cope with shipping palm oil back. That won't be easy in a war.' Laurence had already discussed it at government level. Edible oils and other raw materials for food and industry would have top priority. The government wanted his trade to continue. Hitler would want to stop it. It depended on who had sea supremacy.

'You wouldn't want to go yourself? Take Sybil and the family?'

'No.' Laurence had decided immediately to stay in Liverpool. 'War will bring new opportunities. This is where the money will be made.'

'Catherine will be very grateful. Me too.' Leonard stood up. 'Better get to bed. Thanks, Laurence.'

Laurence poured himself another measure and sat on a little longer, till he could feel a dampness on the fabric of his chair. He still wasn't ready for sleep.

Sybil enjoyed the garden, though he hardly had time to look at it. The five acres kept her occupied, she always had plans for something new, and the girls loved the swimming pool and tennis court.

He went slowly down the steps and through the rose garden. Beyond, in the country garden, the flower scent was heady. He must ask his gardener what it was. The pearly grey sky and the silver half-light made everything look beautiful. He strolled on towards the greenhouse wondering if there was enough light to see the aster Catherine had raved about.

Suddenly he froze. There was no mistaking that intimate giggle. Mary was here somewhere. Another, deeper, voice whispered gently. Laurence went striding towards the greenhouse, wrenched open the door.

'Mary! What do you think you're up to?' He was fuming as he watched them scramble to their feet, Mary rebuttoning her dress, smoothing her flaxen hair. 'This is underhand, Robert!' He knew exactly what they were up to, and he'd forbidden it. 'Come to the house.'

He led the way, stepping out angrily, before he realised they were falling further and further behind. Why couldn't they see sense? Every time he thought about it another wave of fury washed over him. He went back like an irate sheepdog to hustle them on. Damn damn damn both of them! He'd explained it all last year, in words of two syllables.

Mary blinked in the bright lights of his study, smoothing her crumpled dress. Robert had the grace to look ashamed.

'I'm sorry, sir, but I love Mary.'

Laurence took a deep breath. 'This is entirely for your own good. You don't understand how it can ruin your lives.' He looked from one to the other, Mary sullen, Robert rebellious.

'Let me put it to you both again. You know about James? Your brother, Mary, and your first cousin, Robert? Mentally handicapped, and you know he's not the only Oxley to be thus afflicted. You both knew your Aunt Edwina and Uncle Hubert. And there was Alec and Rosie. It's in the Oxley blood. In your blood. Your mother and I are first cousins, Mary. We Oxleys have made a habit of marrying each other. It compounds the possibility of it happening again. You, Robert, are the son of my twin brother. We tried to bring you up like brother and sister in the hope this wouldn't happen.'

'But it has.' Mary turned from the window, pale but determined. 'Dad, we only want to do what you and Mummy did. What's wrong with that?'

'I keep telling you,' he exploded. 'I want you to learn from my experience. To bring a child like James into the world is a very painful experience. It isn't something to brush aside and forget. It burns on inside me still. Even now I find myself thinking, if only James had been normal . . .' And for the mother of such a child, he believed it was even worse. Sybil hadn't been the same since. She hadn't been able to accept it. It took more courage than either of them had.

'We don't want children, Dad. We just want to be together.'

'You will want children for no other reason than to carry on the business you'll inherit. There are hundreds and thousands of partners to choose from. Charming young men with business aptitude. Pretty girls with nice manners. You will each be happier if you choose someone else. I've nothing against you, Robert. You're a fine lad, but you carry the Oxley genes.'

'I want to marry Mary,' he said quietly. 'Honestly, we'll do without the children.'

'No,' Laurence bellowed. 'I won't countenance it. Not for one moment.'

'But sir, I have a right to choose my own wife. . . .'

'Choose any one you like but Mary. You'll have my blessing.'

'I've chosen Mary,' he said stubbornly.

'I'm of age, Dad. You can't stop us.'

Laurence looked slowly from one to the other, pursing his lips. 'If you marry against my advice, then I'll disinherit you. Both of you. I have your wellbeing at heart.'

The silence lasted until the grandfather clock in the hall struck midnight.

'Think it over carefully, both of you. You might as well know now, Robert, I'm planning to send you to Lagos.'

'Oh no, Dad, not that!'

'It's a marvellous opportunity, Robert. You'll manage the business there, when you've had a bit of experience.'

'I won't go,' Robert said. 'Keep your opportunities. Keep your business.'

'Don't be so bloody stupid. Take time to think of your own interests. Now go home, and don't come sneaking back here again tonight.' Laurence moved to the door. He was shaking, he wasn't used to fighting to get his own way. He turned to look at his daughter. 'Get yourself to bed,' he snarled.

* * *

All through the summer months, Laura had kept her mind on her shorthand, typing and bookkeeping lessons. She didn't dare let up. She didn't want to think of Tom's wedding coming steadily closer, it filled her with dread. So did the thought of war, and everybody now believed it was inevitable. Hope that Tom would change his mind withered and died.

Today, sitting in church on his wedding day, she felt frozen inside. Rosemary was coming up the aisle on her father's arm. A picturebook bride in a white crepe de Chine dress, slim and clinging, smartly elegant, topped with a wide-brimmed white hat. Tom's back view drew her gaze as he waited at the altar in his tail suit hired from Moss Brothers, towering head and shoulders above his best man. As she watched, he smiled down at Rosemary. Nobody could mistake how he felt about her. It was a further hurtful turn of the screw.

'Marry for love, Laura,' Mam whispered beside her. 'Never for any other reason.'

Laura made herself smile her assent. Fat chance now, with Tom married to someone else. Nobody thought of her feelings, not Tom, not even Mam. At fourteen, they didn't think she was capable of love.

Her mother was dabbing at her eyes as the responses were being made. Laura thought her incurably romantic. Or perhaps she was thinking how different this marriage service was to the one she'd gone through.

'When you grow up, things will look very different,' Mam had said. 'It's hero worship, Laura. Tom Talbot isn't for you.'

Laura grieved silently. She couldn't bring herself to say: I was sure he was.

She still felt numb when two weeks later, war was declared.

Book Three – 1941
CHAPTER FOURTEEN

The sinister wailing of the air raid siren woke Elin from a deep sleep. Gripping fear brought instant cold-sweat wakefulness. She half fell out of bed, grabbing at her clothes.

Not again! How she longed for an undisturbed night. They'd already had heavy raids on three consecutive nights, a fourth had never happened before. She'd really believed tonight would be quiet.

'Percy,' she shook him. He'd been unable to buy Brylcreem recently. The substitute he'd bought had a sickly smell and made greasy stains on his pillow. She'd be pleased when the tin was finished. 'Get up.'

He groaned. 'Oh God, not again.'

'Laura, are you awake?'

'Yes, Mam.' She heard the floor creak as Laura got out of bed.

'Come on, Percy, you've got to get out.'

'Five minutes,' he gasped. Percy was their ARP warden and should have been out on the streets since ten o'clock. With the present labour shortage, he was holding down a job. Her eyes went to the alarm clock. It was half past eleven.

Percy had been cock-a-hoop when he'd first got the job. Once the blitz started in earnest, he liked it less.

'I'm stuck in a sandbagged shop they call an ARP post, instead of being in the snug at the Bull.'

It pleased Elin that he was finding less to drink. Percy was less likely to let his fists fly if he was sober. Most publicans spread their meagre consignments of beer and spirits thinly round their customers. Even at the Bull where his custom was valued he couldn't be sure of getting what he wanted.

The air raid warning continued to scale up and down; the sound itself was enough to make Elin shiver. She grabbed the eiderdown and pillows from the bed and rushed for the stairs. Laura had already gone.

In the cellar, two old deckchairs were kept set up close together against the party wall under the stairs. Percy said that was the safest place, away from flying glass and debris. The stairs would give them the best chance of not being crushed if the house was flattened.

Elin flung down her bedding and ran up again to the scullery. Laura already had the kettle on and was getting the thermos ready.

'I'll see to the tea, Mam.'

Elin fiddled with the teapot. She couldn't leave Laura in the scullery. With its rusting tin roof, it would be the first place to go.

She leaned across the sink, twitching the blackout curtain aside. There was enough moonlight for the house to cast a shadow across the yard. The old zinc bath hanging against the wall stood out starkly. There was too much light for safety.

The front door slammed. Percy had gone. It could be a nightmare out on the streets in a raid. She was always surprised when Percy returned unhurt. It would be such an easy way out. But things like that didn't happen if you wanted them.

Beyond the neighbouring chimneys, searchlights suddenly sent seeking shafts into the starry sky, lighting up the floating barrage balloons.

'Everything's ready, Mam.'

'Listen.' The throb of engines was growing louder.

'They'll be ours,' Laura said confidently as the water came to the boil.

Elin's gut began to churn when she heard the shrieking whistle. The next moment, she was hurling herself under the draining board, dragging Laura with her. The crump made the water spurt out of the kettle and the gas sizzled out. The electric light dipped and recovered.

'Quite a long way off.' Laura was jumping up, turning off the gas, tipping water into the teapot.

Elin could hardly breathe. She wished she was more like Laura, who coped incredibly well for a seventeen-year-old. Her green eyes were calm, reminding her of Leonard Oxley, as she stirred the teapot to hurry the brew. But she had Laurence's self-mastery, too. Her fingers were steady as she filled the flask and pushed it at her. Elin almost let it slip through her shaking hands as guns from the nearby battery began to roar. They stumbled down the cellar steps, Laura carrying two mugs of tea to drink straight away.

Elin wriggled into the blankets and tucked the eiderdown round her. The deckchair, with a stool for her feet, was not too bad but she hated the dank cellar smell. That alone was enough to make the hairs on her forearms stand erect. Beside her, Laura lit the candle and opened a book. She said it helped to study, kept her mind off other things. For Elin, it was calming to see Laura's honey-coloured head bent over a book.

She reached for her tea. Her mouth was always dry in an air raid. They always came down with the expectation that they'd sleep, but how could she settle when every moment could be her last?

Elin closed her eyes. She could hear the crump crump, and feel the house shake from time to time. She slept eventually, and awoke to the sound of the front door opening. Percy must be home. They'd survived another night. Beside her, Laura was sleeping. Elin tried to get out of her deckchair without waking her. Better now if she slept for the rest of the night where she was.

Elin felt stiff and aching as she dragged herself up the stairs to the kitchen. Percy was slumped in his chair, his face streaked with dirt.

'Was it awful? Out there?'

'We've had a party.' His laugh grated on her nerves. He rarely laughed unless he was drunk. 'A real party.'

'Not a bad night? It was noisy.'

'Liverpool got it mostly. Have a drink.' He brought out a full bottle of whisky from inside his navy battledress. 'Plenty more where this came from.' He gave an exaggerated wink.

'No thanks.' She peered at the clock. It was half past four. 'Where did you get it?'

'Some windows went at the C . . . Crown.' His speech was slurred.

'That's looting.'

'So what?' He lifted the bottle to his lips and took a swig. 'I went in the Crown for a drink yesterday and old Stubbs said he had nothing left.' He threw back his glistening head and laughed. 'All the time he had this cupboard loaded with two cases of whisky and a case of gin. Lots of other stuff too. Serves him right. Come on, have a drink.'

'No thanks, I'm going to bed for a few hours.'

'Press my grey suit for me first,' Percy said. 'I've heard they're looking for bomb damage assessors. Better job. More money.'

'Now?'

'I might go down and see about it tomorrow. Eleven o'clock, they said.'

'Then you'll have time to do it in the morning. I'm going to bed, Percy. I have to be at work by eight.'

She went to pass his chair on her way upstairs. His hand shot out with tremendous force, taking her by surprise. The punch caught her in the abdomen. She fell against the table, tasting the vomit in her mouth.

'The suit, woman. I want you to see to my suit.' His face was flushed, he stood up unsteadily, raising his hand at Elin. She tried to pull herself up, knowing she must obey when Percy was drunk.

'Stop it, Father.' Laura had come silently up from the cellar. 'Mam's got enough to put up with without you knocking her about.'

'Shut up, you little bitch, it's nothing to do with you.' Percy raised the bottle to his lips again. 'Get the suit, woman,' he said as his fist shot out and cracked into Elin's face. She tasted blood and pain shot through her head.

'Father!' Laura screamed. 'Stop it.'

'Don't you father me,' he shouted at her. 'I'm not your father.'

Elin, crumpling in pain, thought the pause would never end. At last, Laura asked hoarsely, 'Who is then?'

'Ask her.' He nodded in Elin's direction.

Elin felt she was choking, Percy had promised never to tell.

'I'm asking you.' Laura's voice was steadier.

'Laurence Oxley.'

Elin was aware of Laura's shocked gasp. She looked up. Laura's green eyes searched into hers, questioning, still not believing.

'Is it true, Mam?'

Elin swallowed. Damn Percy! Damn damn Percy. She managed a nod.

'He's the very Devil,' Percy leered.

'Compared to you, he's a saint,' Laura said.

'I'll get even with you, Percy, for this.' Elin felt hatred flare white-hot within her. He took another threatening step towards her.

'Come to bed, Mam, let him press his own suit.' Laura's tone was authoritative. She stood protectively between her mother and Percy.

Elin scuttled upstairs and Laura followed, dragging her eiderdown behind her.

'Come and sleep in my bed,' Laura ordered. 'You can't go in there with him.'

There wasn't much room for both of them, but Elin felt safe with Laura's firm young body curled round her. The soft whisper came.

'Tell me, Mam, about . . . my father.'

Her limbs would have threshed about the bed had Laura's arm not held her firmly. There were no words . . .

'I can't . . . Not yet. When you're older.'

There was a pause, and Elin thought she'd given up.

'At my age you'd already had me.'

Elin couldn't answer. Why couldn't she talk to Laura about it?

'I want you to know I'm not upset. I don't like Da. I'm glad he's not my father. Whatever made you marry him?'

Elin stifled a sob. Hadn't she said the same, on that terrible Sunday, to her own father?

It was Friday. Laura called at Talbot's on the way home from work to pay for the week's *Echoes*. The shop door pinged as she opened it. It was like stepping back in time to smell the newsprint and sweets.

'Hello, Laura,' Tom said rather self-consciously from behind the counter. She hadn't seen him for almost a year. He seemed taller than ever. A bean pole, topped with flaming hair fiercely cropped into a regulation hair cut.

'How's life?' It was an inane thing to say. With Tom, she was unable to be herself.

'Almost lost it. Ship sank in mid-Atlantic. Torpedoed.' His thinner, drawn appearance was unnerving. His mother had once whispered fearfully that Tom was with the convoys bringing food across the Atlantic.

'Four days on a life raft before being picked up. It was the worst thing I ever lived through.'

'Yes, I heard.' Laura tried to think back. The war had only just started when Mam had come back from the shop saying Tom had been shipwrecked, but he was safe. 'Mam said your mother was bursting with pride that you helped save some of the crew.'

'What?'

'Said you must have nine lives.' Her voice trailed away. For the first time she doubted the truth of it. There had been no mention of the frightened anguish he still showed. 'I'd have been terrified.'

'We all were. Thought our end was coming, and freezing cold.'

'Must have been awful, Tom. Still, you've got leave to look forward to now.'

'Reporting back on Monday. They gave me a week.'

'Oh.' She was surprised then to see him serving here, instead of at home enjoying himself. 'How's Rosemary?' His face seemed to close up as she asked.

'All right.' His tone was noncommittal, the pause dragged out. She could see a tremor in his fingers as they rested against a pile of *Picture Posts*.

'I've come to pay the paper bill,' she said. Da's *Echo* was still being delivered, although she no longer did the round. Mam was now doing war work that paid better.

Tom was riffling through the book looking for her bill. 'Do you feel like coming to the pictures? For old times' sake?'

How many times had she imagined Tom asking her this? In the rush of pleasure and surprise, Laura didn't know what to think. 'What about . . . about Rosemary?' He met her gaze as she choked on the name.

'She seems to be busy . . . elsewhere.'

'She's joined the Wrens?' Laura asked. 'Your mother said she'd closed her shop.' Mam had suggested she might join the Wrens next year, when she was eighteen. It was definitely the popular choice to help the war effort.

'No,' Tom said hollowly. 'She's working in a munitions factory, but she has no time for me any more.'

Laura felt a tremendous surge of joy, of victory. A moment later, in the face of Tom's evident misery, she was ashamed of it.

'I think it would have suited her very well if I hadn't been rescued from that life raft.'

'I'll come.' The words came out in an eager rush. 'I'd love to. The cinemas all close at nine now, so we'd have to go early.'

'We always did.' He smiled and straightened up to his full six foot three inches.

'I work till five at the biscuit factory, and then I go to night school four evenings a week. Did you know? Saturday is the only day of the week I could manage.' And even that meant letting Mam down. But Mam wouldn't mind if for once she went with Tom instead of her.

'Tomorrow it is then. Let's see what's on.'

Laura felt like singing as she ran home. There was nothing she wanted more than to be with Tom, to help him forget his ordeal on the raft, forget Rosemary. She always looked forward to Saturdays; this one would be better than usual. She was elated about Tom, and about what Da had let slip.

Laurence Oxley her father! She couldn't get the thought out of her mind. Those snobs Mary and Jane Oxley, her half-sisters! They wouldn't be pleased to hear the news. She had no doubt they were as ignorant about that as she had been. Best of all, it meant she was no part of Percy Peck. She despised him.

The works closed at midday. On the way home she shopped for whatever food she could get. Liverpool was a good place for that, if she had time to queue. She managed to get enough potatoes and vegetables to see them through the coming week. When she got off the bus, she called at the pet shop to collect ten pounds of meal for the four Rhode Island Reds they now kept in the back yard.

Elin was home when she got there, setting out a meal on the table and pretending nothing momentous had been said last night.

There were a hundred things Laura wanted to ask about her birth, but one look at her mother's face told her this wasn't the right moment to ask. Sooner or later she would. Instead she told her about Tom and his offer to take her to the cinema. Elin was pleased for her. She didn't mind staying in. She looked exhausted.

In the afternoon Elin took the ration books and went shopping. Saturday was her only chance to stock up for the coming week. Laura put clean sheets and pillow cases on both beds, then washed the dirty ones with a few clothes in the scullery sink. She started the ironing from last week. It irked her to iron Percy's shirts, but she knew if she didn't Mam would have to.

She was washing her face in the scullery, getting ready to meet Tom, when she heard voices and knew both were back. A moment later, Mam came in to drop her two heavy bags against the cupboard.

'I can smell the drink on his breath,' she hissed, hiding Da's full bottle of whisky in the cupboard. Glazed with fear, Elin's eyes glowed darkly amber.

Laura was conscience-stricken. 'I wish we were both going

out as usual. I wish I'd never told Tom . . . Will you be all right?'

'Of course, love.'

Laura began unpacking the shopping. 'Perhaps you should come too. I don't suppose Tom'll mind.'

'Of course he will. I'll be all right.' Elin was smiling again. 'You go.'

Laura was reassured, it was just an attack of jitters. Nothing unusual for Mam.

As she went through the kitchen, Da was in his leather chair, wearing his grey suit. It didn't look as though anybody had pressed it.

'Get the new job, Da, did you?' she asked, and his eyes shot malevolently to her face. He didn't deign to answer.

Tom was late coming for her. She walked towards the shop to meet him with a spring in her step. She was going out with Tom again, after all these years. She saw him coming up the dusty pavement long before he saw her. He was slouching along, eyes downcast, looking miserable. She felt filled with love for him, wanting to comfort him.

'Tom?'

His smile was lopsided. 'Hello, you look grown up.'

She'd taken extra care with her appearance, pinning her fair hair up in the latest bangs round her face. She'd bought two or three outfits for the office with her clothing coupons, and she'd put on the newest, a blue serge dress with a darker blue collar and cuffs. The weather was fine and warm for May; she carried a dark blue cardigan over her arm, in case she'd need it when they came out of the cinema.

'I am grown up,' she laughed.

'It's happened quickly.'

'It had to. The war.' Tom's depression seemed even blacker in the face of her own elation. She took his arm, concerned about him. 'What's the matter?'

'Nothing.'

'Something is. Can't I help?'

'Well, if you must know, Rosemary wants a divorce. She's got another man.'

Laura had to stamp down the wave of exultation lifting

her; she'd always known Tom was meant for her. She tried to put herself in his position. He was very upset.

'Perhaps she wasn't right for you, Tom.'

'I've been away so much. This war . . . If I hadn't had to leave her . . .' Laura hadn't expected to feel sympathy too, but it was impossible not to be moved by Tom's agonising.

'She couldn't stand staying at home, night after night, by herself. She had to get out.' The bus came.

'Shall we have a cup of tea somewhere first?' she suggested. 'We've plenty of time.'

'I thought we could see the film and then have a drink.' Laura didn't like drink, she saw what it did to her father. Besides, she wasn't yet eighteen. She shouldn't drink in pubs, but she didn't want to remind Tom of that.

'Tea first at the Copper Kettle would be very nice,' she said.

'Then we'll have it.' Tom tried to smile as he handed her the bag of sweets he'd brought. 'Sorry, couldn't get chocs. Pretty scarce now. I miss you not working at the shop.'

'I meant to keep on Saturday afternoons, but it was too much. And better for your dad to get another girl, to do mornings too. These caramels are nice, thank you.'

'Rosemary liked them. She always wanted a good time, you know, parties . . .'

Laura decided it wasn't helping to let him harp on Rosemary. Perhaps it would cheer him if she talked about her own affairs. 'I'm still studying, you see. That's why I'm busy. I got my School Certificate, and I'm working now for my Higher at night school. It'll take me three years instead of two, but I'll do it.'

'Pity you had to leave school.'

'I don't regret it now.' She found it hard to believe Jane Oxley was still there, and would be for another year. 'I've learned a lot.'

'You're a shorthand typist?'

'No. The course included double entry bookkeeping, and I preferred that. I managed to get a job in the accounts department at Burdon's Biscuits. Have you heard of them?'

'Burdon's Best Biscuits, yes,' he nodded.

'It's a family business. Did you know it started two hundred years ago making biscuits to provision sailing ships? Hard tack, they called it. It's a smashing place to work, the scents of baking filter deliciously through the whole place. You can even smell biscuits in the street outside.'

'You were always obsessed with food.'

'I was always hungry!'

'So you're an accounts clerk?' Tom, she decided, had changed. He looked much older. His brown eyes had always seemed gentle and kindly, now they looked back at her full of pain. Laura ached to help him.

'I started as the most junior of four. Burdon's employed four hundred workers then. Now we're down to seventy-four.'

'The war? They got their call-up papers?'

'Yes, and those too old for calling up discovered wages were better in munitions factories. Did you know Mam was making aeroplanes at Ledsham?'

'Yes.'

'She loves it. Music while you work, and all the chatter.' She liked the money too, but it was better not to tell him how much better off they were. Laura didn't want to infer his mother had been underpaying Elin.

'Go on, about your job.'

'Even with a smaller work force, we couldn't keep them working all the time, because raw materials are so hard to get. Production was cut to the bone, and profits fell because of the overheads. Terrible, when we could have sold everything twice over.'

'But that's not your problem.'

'It has become so.'

'Really?' They got off the bus and walked to the Copper Kettle Tea Rooms.

'Yes, I keep the books for Burdon's now.'

'Tea and cakes, please,' Tom said to the waitress.

'Sorry, no cakes. We have biscuits, or toast and jam.'

'Biscuits then, please.' He turned back to Laura. 'By

yourself? You mean you're in charge of the accounts? You don't seem old enough for that.'

Laura laughed when the waitress brought their tea and four biscuits on a plate. 'Burdon's Biscuits too, and not our best,' she said. 'We don't make those any more, can't get the ingredients.'

'This war! It's bad for everyone and everything.'

'Not for me. It's given me enormous advantages.' Laura poured out the tea. The tremor of his fingers was more noticeable today. The biscuit he held was twitching. He looked ill.

'Advantages? I don't see how.'

'I haven't had to work my way up. The staff left wholesale, leaving me more and more responsibility. When I started, there was a financial director, a qualified accountant, and four full-time accounts clerks. Now there's me and old Mr Burdon who's seventy-one. He's come back as Financial Director, after retiring in 1935. He hated seeing the profit margins fall and was desperate to do something. He has to talk it over with someone.' Laura nibbled a biscuit.

'There's young Mr Burdon too, he's our General Manager. He's almost fifty, but he's been an invalid for years and comes only two or three days a week. He thought it better to close the business down before it lost money. Of the grandsons, Mr Anthony, our accountant, is in the Western Desert. Mr James, our General Manager, is now a pilot, and Mr Tom, our Marketing Manager, was killed in France.

'I suggested we tried to get war work. After all, the armed forces have to be fed. I found the addresses and wrote round. We've got a contract now to make survival rations for life rafts and aircraft. They allocate all the ingredients.'

'So everything's fine again?'

'We're making a profit, that's the main thing.'

'It wasn't too difficult, was it?'

'Not easy. Everything had to be thought through. We have to keep a bigger maintenance department – you know, carpenters, plumbers, electricians – to make good the bomb damage quickly, but we've liquidated the marketing department. The biscuits no longer have to look attractive or taste good. The aim now is to pack as much nutrient into as small and light a biscuit as possible. The packaging has to be airtight. It needs to keep well, but if there isn't anything else . . . I'm not boring you, am I?'

'No,' he smiled. 'You're doing me good. Taking me out of myself.'

'It fascinates me, and I count myself very fortunate to learn how to run a business. Old Mr Burdon has decades of experience. He'd never have got round to talking to me about it under normal circumstances. It's better than private tuition. I could run a business myself after this.'

He smiled, her enthusiasm was bubbling out. 'But will you get the chance when the war's over?'

'I might. I want to become a chartered accountant.'

'You'd have to be articled to a firm of accountants for that, and you'll never leave Burdon's. You're too keen.'

'I won't leave yet. I can't turn my back on valuable experience like this, and I need two more years to work for my Higher. I might even try to get a degree at night school. But I'll go when I'm ready.'

'You're quite the career girl, Laura.'

She paused with her cup halfway to her lips. He was right. Where did marriage to Tom fit into that? Somehow, it would have to.

Tom looked less down in the mouth. She took his arm as they walked to the Ritz to see Barbara Stanwyck in *Stella Dallas*. He was bending from his huge height to catch what she said, just like he used to.

Elin felt aching and ill. She had a bruise on her abdomen where Percy's fist had caught her, and a pain in her side where she'd fallen against the table. It jabbed at her every time she breathed in, and she winced as she slowly unpacked the shopping in the scullery. She hoped he had not broken her rib.

Her mind was in a ferment because Percy had told Laura, and in such a brutal way. Now Laura was even more curious about Laurence Oxley. The questions had been in her eyes at breakfast time and when she'd come home at midday; she would worm it out of her, sooner or later. Elin sighed. It was quite impossible to talk to Laura about how Laurence Oxley had become her father. She just couldn't do it.

Damn Percy! She'd never been able to free herself from the power he had over her. She'd always done exactly what he wanted. He was getting worse, like a volcano, threatening to erupt at any moment. She shivered with fear. Laura was going out of her way to taunt him, and would go further now she knew he wasn't her father.

Once again Elin had the feeling of history repeating itself. This had happened to her mother. She prayed Laura would find a loving husband. But nobody could make a worse husband than Percy. She'd hated him for years; now her hate was mushrooming into a huge cloud that blotted out everything else. She found it hard to think of anything but getting her own back, of seeing him squirm for a change. What she felt for Laurence Oxley paled beside her loathing of Percy. How many times had she dreamed of poisoning him? She had the opportunity since she cooked most of his meals, but which poison should she use, and where would she get it?

Laura might know something about poisons. Or if she didn't, she'd know where to get the information without anyone knowing. But she mustn't involve Laura. Nobody else must know.

'Get me some lunch,' Percy slurred from the kitchen.

'It's nearly four o'clock.'

'I'm hungry,' he bellowed.

'Scrambled eggs then?'

'I'm sick of eggs. Eggs for breakfast, eggs for dinner, eggs for tea. Get me something else.'

'There's nothing else. There's a war on. We're lucky the hens are laying well.'

By the time she'd got it ready, she could hear snoring. She looked around the scullery door. He was horizontal in his chair, his mouth open. She hesitated, it was a shame to waste food, but if he was asleep, it meant peace for her.

She tiptoed upstairs and lay on her bed, feeling downright ill.

She was woken by Percy's bellowing. She rolled quickly off the bed, heading for the stairs. She'd stiffened up. The room swung dizzily round her. She leaned against the banisters for a moment, unable to take a breath for the pain in her side.

'Elin, this food's cold! Elin, what are you doing?'

She staggered down the stairs. 'Of course it's cold now. You've been to sleep.'

'You've been to sleep, you mean.' He'd found the whisky bottle in the scullery and now it was half empty. He reeled across to the table and tipped more in his glass, raised it to his lips neat.

'This will still be all right.' She cut the toast in half. 'Try it.' He'd be paralytic if he didn't eat something.

'Don't like it cold,' he hiccupped.

'I'll do you some more then,' she said hastily, sliding the bottle into the scullery with the plate. Her heart was thumping, there was no saying what Percy would do when he was this drunk. She looked at the clock, she'd been asleep for three hours.

She put the kettle to boil, took the bowl from the sink she'd used to beat the eggs last time, and beat up two more. Would the pan burn if she used it again?

Percy suddenly filled the doorway. His dark eyes squinted at her, no longer able to focus. 'The bloody whisky! You keep hiding the bloody whisky.' He swayed past her to grab it. 'What d'yer do it for?' The neck of the bottle clattered against the tumbler, slipped and released a pool that darkened the wooden draining board.

'It won't take long.' Elin grabbed the unwashed pan. She felt his hand heavy on her shoulder, and shivered. The hand ran down her back in a gesture she recognised as the nearest Percy ever got to a caress. Oh God, she could do without that now. 'Go and sit down, I'll bring you the eggs in a minute.'

'Sod the eggs.' He spun her round to face him and the pan clattered back into the sink. 'Come on in here.' His face had degenerated into an evil mask, topped with hair greased into a black cap. The cheap scent of his grease made her gag; she'd throw up if she wasn't careful. His fingers scratched her skin as they tore her blouse open. The top button flew off and pinged on the lino. She tried hopelessly to keep the garment on.

'No, Percy!'

Now his fingers were tearing at her skirt, it was falling round her ankles. Her heart was pounding, her head felt as though it would split. He pushed her into the kitchen and held her down in the chair, while he took his trousers off. His scarlet face was leering at her.

'No!' she screamed as he pulled at her knickers.

'Come on, you whore. You can do it for me too. This is what you wanted. I'm your husband, aren't I?' Roughly he forced her legs apart. The weight of his body fell against hers, knocking the wind out of her lungs, sending needles of pain down her side. Her back felt as though it would break, bent across the armchair.

She wouldn't mind so much if he'd just do it and go to sleep again. But he wouldn't be able to do it. Not in this state. He never could when he drank too much. She knew that, though he never did. He always had to try and try, his fingers searching roughly, hurting her.

His whisky-laden breath panted into her face. Suddenly his full weight descended on to her broken rib. She screamed, finding the strength to jerk him off.

'You bitch!' He crashed his hand into her face, lost his balance and slid to the floor.

Freed from his weight, Elin leapt to her feet, sobbing and gulping in huge mouthfuls of air.

Blood was in her mouth and running down her face. 'I hate you, hate you.' She grabbed the shell case from the 1918 war off the mantelshelf and swung it at his head as he lay on the hearthrug. His skull cracked. The sound goaded her to frenzy. She swung the shell at his head again. The pent-up loathing she felt for him put weight behind it.

'I said I'd kill you if you touched Laura. You didn't believe me, did you? Didn't think I could do it.' She raised it again and again, bringing it down with all her might. She had broken the power he had over her. Rebelled at last. She swung the shell again.

'This is for bringing us back from Mrs Redman's. This for stealing Laura's money. I promised you this. You've asked for it over and over. You deserve all you get. You've been a bastard, a right bastard to us.' She went on raising the shell, again and again and again, till her strength was spent.

His skull cracked open in several places, blood and brain splattered everywhere. Percy's blood. He lay still, not moving, not breathing. The shell dropped from her nerveless fingers as she collapsed in sobs on the chair.

She cried till she could cry no more. She was still shaking when she raised her head to look at what she'd done. Hardly able to believe . . . Was it another of those dreams in which she wanted to hurt Percy, but never did? Realisation came; this was no fantasy.

She ran to the scullery to vomit in the sink. It didn't stop the nausea or the shaking. She left the tap running. The still horror on the hearthrug drew her back. She couldn't believe she'd done that. She had to clean up the mess. Before Laura came back. Get rid of him. Her skirt was under his head, soaking with blood. She couldn't pull it out, so she folded it back to cover his face, to shut out the sight.

The kettle was boiling itself dry on the gas, the scullery full of steam. She used what was left of the hot water to wash herself, and then washed Percy's blood off the clothes she'd been wearing. She went upstairs and dressed herself decently. She had to get rid of the body, but how? She couldn't think properly. She felt desperate.

The sudden banshee wail of the air raid siren sent a new terror through her. Surely it wasn't that time already? The Luftwaffe was early tonight and Laura wasn't home. Elin hated her to be out in a raid, and she needed her here to help. She didn't want to be alone in the house when the bombs started. Laura ought to be home by now, Tom Talbot had no business to keep her out. It wasn't safe on the streets in a raid.

CHAPTER FIFTEEN

It was a dark night without stars. The siren had gone but there was no other sign of a raid. Laura held onto Tom's arm. They almost had to feel their way along Jubilee Street in the blackout. He insisted on coming right to her door.

'A false alarm,' he said, his shoulders only just visible against the sky. 'There's heavy cloud tonight, the weather's changed. The German bombers won't be able to see us.' She sensed his fear; he was trying to convince himself. Poor Tom. His nerves were shot to ribbons.

'They won't come again tonight,' she agreed. She could just make out his face, white and anxious, his red hair made black by the night. 'They've been four nights on the run. They'll never come a fifth.'

'We could all do with a decent night's sleep.'

'Will you come in for a cup of tea?' She was torn, wanting to prolong the time she spent in his company, yet afraid of the reception he'd get if Da were home.

He hesitated. 'No thanks, I'd better go. Mother worries if I'm out in a raid.

Laura felt relieved. Mam would be on edge if she took him in. She stood on tiptoe and kissed him, he clung to her for comfort. He felt tremulous, and she held him till he calmed. Gently his lips came down on hers. Not a lover's kiss, more a token of gratitude, but her heart seemed to somersault. Tom could make her feel wonderful. He'd kissed her!

The all-clear sounded.

'I knew it was a false alarm,' Laura smiled.

'Yes, but it's getting late, I'd better go.' He hesitated again. 'Come out again tomorrow, Laura?'

She laughed, filled with pleasure, though normally she reserved Sundays for studying. 'The pictures again?'

'For a drink.'

'Oh!' He'd persuaded her to call in the Rose and Crown on the way home tonight. There had only been beer. Tom had had two pints to her glass of lemonade before the siren wailed.

'A cup of tea, and a walk in the park, then. I just want to talk to you.'

'I'd like that. Four o'clock?'

He kissed her cheek. 'Good night, let's hope it's a quiet one.' He put her key in the door and pushed it open before going. Laura stepped into the blackness of the parlour.

The house had an alien silence. She knew at once something was very wrong. Then from the kitchen she heard something between a gasp and a groan.

'Mam?'

More a groan this time. It made her shiver. She stepped across to the light switch, knowing exactly where to put her hand. Her mother shrank from the sudden light. She could see Da's feet sticking out from behind the leather chair.

'What's the matter?' Laura could feel the hairs on the back of her neck standing erect.

Her mother looked like a cornered animal cowering against the wall. Her eyes burned like lamps in her grey face, her colourless lips moved but no words came. Laura took another step forward. Da's head was covered with navy serge which showed dark, wet stains. Stifling her repugnance, she put out shaking fingers and twitched it away. His skull was a matted mess of hair, blood and brains, still bleeding darkly into the hearthrug.

'Mam! What's happened?' Icy fingers clutched and squeezed her entrails. On the floor beside him was the blood-covered shell from the Great War. She knelt beside him. He wasn't breathing.

'You've got to help me, Laura.' Mam's voice twisted and choked. 'I can't lift him.'

'He's dead! What have you done? He's dead, Mam.'

'Yes.' Her face was a ghost's. 'I hit him with the shell.'

Laura stared at the body. 'Oh Mam!' Her mouth was dry. She couldn't swallow. Thank God Tom hadn't come in!

'I want him in the pram. You've got to help me.' It was only then Laura noticed her old pram had been brought from the shed. 'I'm going to take him away.'

'What for?' Laura felt she couldn't breathe. Couldn't think properly.

'Murder,' Mam gasped. 'Murder it is I've done. I'll hang. You've got to help me.'

'No, not murder, Mam. He's gone for you many times. I'll tell them that. Self-defence. Manslaughter at the most. You'll not hang.'

Elin's face was wet with tears, her eyes gaping red holes. 'Years in prison. Everything dragged through the courts. No, you've got to help me take him away.'

'Where to?'

'Another air raid, and who's to know how he died?'

Laura swallowed, trying to draw some saliva back into her mouth. 'But what if we're seen? Air raid wardens, and fire-watchers . . . What if there isn't a raid tonight?'

'The siren, I heard it. Just before—'

'The all-clear too. There hasn't been a raid. Could have been a reconnaissance plane. Or nothing at all. Besides, the weather's changed. No moonlight.'

'Please, Laura!'

'But where to?'

'He usually goes to the pub. He ought to be at his ARP post. Somewhere round there.'

'Mam, I don't think it's the best thing to do. If you say it was self-defence . . .'

Already her mother was dragging the pram closer to the body. 'Come on.'

'We'll never lift him in.' Laura could hardly bring herself to look, it made her feel sick. The bloodstain was spreading.

'We can.' Her mother tugged at his coat. He hardly moved.

Laura turned the pram on its side, propped it a little off the floor on cushions. Together they rolled him against it, lifted his legs, pulled at his hips and finally managed to rock the pram back on its wheels with him inside.

It had long since lost its hood, and also its bed. It was old-fashioned and deep. Laura, swallowing back the vomit rising in her throat, bent his knees and pushed him down as far as he'd go. As she snatched up the rag rug from the floor to cover him, blood dripped audibly on to the lino.

'Come on then.' The pram was heavy and difficult to manoeuvre through the scullery. 'Get your coat, Mam.' Laura switched off the lights before opening the back door, and hesitated again. 'Wouldn't it be better if I just went for the police?'

'No, no,' her mother choked. 'Down the entry.'

'Thank God for the blackout.'

'Sssh. Don't make any noise. We don't want the neighbours to hear us.' Laura tiptoed into the yard and looked back at Beattie's windows. They were all in darkness, but that didn't mean she wasn't there behind the blackout watching. Mostly there was no malice in Beattie's interest. She liked to know what everybody was doing and pass it on as gossip. Even details of the washing on the line. 'Mr Jones at forty-one has changed into his winter combinations. Alice has got a new nightdress, pink flannelette,' were grist to her mill. But she didn't like Percy, and enjoyed reporting his misdemeanours to the neighbours. Laura felt all Jubilee Street pitied her and Mam as a result. She knew Beattie watched diligently for further proof of Percy's villainy.

As she passed the hen house built of rusting corrugated metal, Laura heard fluttering and anxious gurgling. She froze, her heart thumping in her chest. They had heard her, and knew something was going on. Elin moved wraith-like, her finger against her lips to stop even whispering. Opening the back gate carefully, Elin eased the latch down without a sound. The pram was difficult to push over the back entry setts and rocked from side to side.

This is crazy, Laura thought, and then, worse, it's criminal. I could end up in prison too. Why do this if it wasn't cold-blooded murder? Now nobody would believe it wasn't. Oh God, what were they doing?

Laura went ahead before they pushed it out into the street. Hurrying steps were coming along the pavement towards her. She saw the shadow of a man and managed to shrink back against the wall in time. He went into number three. Mr Floyd then. She listened, more steps were coming. Somebody else went down the opposite pavement, then silence.

'Now, Mam.' The pram ran more smoothly on the road, with both pushing on the handle. It never travelled this fast when filled with coke.

Suddenly the air raid siren was wailing out its fearsome sound again. Laura's stomach muscles contracted with tension.

'Here they come,' Elin grated through clenched teeth. Tonight they needed the raid, but their presence on the streets was more likely to be questioned now. An air raid warden would direct them to the nearest shelter. They'd have to go. She'd say the pram contained their bedding, but they'd be expected to lift it out and leave the pram outside. Still the warning wailed up and down.

'Won't this do?' Laura asked. 'We can't go past the church, there'll be fire-watchers there.'

They were level with a bomb site. It had happened only last week. Four or five terraced houses gone, and another abandoned because it was no longer safe.

'Lightning never strikes twice in the same place,' Mam hissed.

'Come on then,' Laura urged. She wanted to be rid of him. Wanted to get as far as possible away from him. She'd never feel safe again, but she couldn't breathe while he was this close. 'This will do.'

The sky suddenly throbbed with life as the Luftwaffe swept overhead in steady waves. Brighter, too, with flickering searchlights criss-crossing it. That made it even more urgent to dump the body. Across the river they could see chandelier flares dripping down like Chinese lanterns, bathing buildings in a pure white glow. Already two or three fires had started and were gathering strength, fanned by the stiff breeze. There was a ghostly beauty about the leaping yellow light, reflecting on the water.

'Here,' Laura said desperately. 'Please, Mam, here.'

'They'll be aiming for the docks. Or for Laird's. They always do. We could get closer, go behind the church.'

'No, it's Liverpool's turn tonight.'

'Liverpool got it last night. The river's only a mile wide here. What's a mile when you're aiming a bomb?'

'This will do as well as anywhere. We mustn't pass the pub, remember? What would he be doing near Laird's at this time of night?' She knew Mam wasn't thinking straight. 'Now, before the flares come again. There's nobody about.'

They upset the pram against the pavement. The body rolled out. Elin righted the pram and Laura tugged desperately at the hearthrug; part of it was underneath him. It came at last. His legs were bent at a strange angle. Laura made herself straighten them till they looked more natural. Was there anything else?

'Money,' Mam said. 'He had three pounds last night. He can't have drunk all that.'

'No,' Laura almost screamed, snatching at the arm that went to his pocket. 'You'll make it look like theft. There must be no sign of crime. Leave it, Mam.'

They were running, the pram squeaking with every turn of the wheels. Squeaking loud enough to attract attention. The night was alive with eerie noises. Far away in Liverpool, distant bombs sounded like a truck unloading bricks. The sky was flushed with fire, and the acrid smell of burning was coming across in a choking pall. Guns thundered all around them. Who would take any interest in a squeaking pram while Liverpool burned? The sky throbbed with engines. Soon it could be their turn. Elin didn't dread it tonight, she wanted it.

Laura felt her legs go weak when she saw two men hurrying towards them. One shouted: 'Take cover. Get to a shelter.'

She heard Mam rasping for breath as they raced silently on, both hanging onto the pram handle. Her mother needed something to keep her upright, she was swaying wildly. Laura felt sick. What had they done?

Miraculously, they were rocking back over the setts in the

back jigger. Elin was scraping the back yard gate open. They got the pram back in the shed, and the back gate bolted.

Laura could barely stagger the last few steps to the scullery door. She felt safer with that locked too. Her mother was half lying on the big leather chair, sweating and grey, shaking with terror. There was a big bloodstain down the front of her coat.

Laura poked the last of the coals to life, and made up the fire. She shivered, she couldn't remember when she'd last felt so cold.

'Mam!' Her mother's teeth were chattering, then she threw up, adding vomit to the blood on her coat. Laura felt numb with horror.

'We need tea.' She put the kettle on, came back and started to rub her mother's hands. There was blood on them. Blood on her own. She stumbled back to the scullery sink and washed it off with icy water. What if someone should come and see it?

'Off with that coat. Come on, Mam, you must.' Laura pushed her to the sink, made her wash her hands and face. There was even blood darkening her golden hair. Laura sponged it off. There was blood on the towel now! She ran more water into the sink and cleaned it, then left the towel soaking. She found a warm cardigan for Elin, and another for herself.

She got her mother's dressmaking scissors and hacked the coat to pieces, tossing them one by one on the fire. She made herself cross the yard again and fetch the rug to do the same. The smell of burning was horrible. Tomorrow, in daylight, she must clean any telltale signs off the pram. The tea served to thaw her hands. The fire was blazing up.

'Too far away, the bombs.' Elin's face was stiff and frightened. 'I wish they'd come closer.'

Laura took a shuddering breath, knowing how terrified Mam was of air raids. Tonight she was more frightened of Percy being found where they'd dumped him, with nothing to account for his death. Suddenly the house shook on its foundations. A tidal wave set up in her cup, tossing tea into the saucer. A piece of plaster plopped down from the ceiling.

'That's better. Close enough, surely, Mam?'

'I don't know,' Elin said, bursting into tears. That was the trouble, they had no way of knowing whether it was close enough unless they went back to see, and Laura knew she wasn't capable of that tonight.

Gradually she felt herself thawing. She heaped more coals onto the fire; they needed warmth. For once, economy must be forgotten. She poured more tea.

'But I'm glad I did it. He deserved to die, didn't he, Laurie?' Her mother was thawing out too, and with the thaw came venom. 'I told him I'd kill him if he touched you. I promised him I'd do it. I did warn him.'

'Oh Mam!' Laura found it disturbing to see her mother excited like this, her slanting eyes shining feverishly. 'Let's go down the cellar and get some sleep.'

They fetched their pillows and eiderdowns, but Elin couldn't settle. The candlelight flickered on the underside of the cellar steps as her voice droned on from the deckchair.

'He deserved it, Laura. He deserved all he got. He was no good.'

'You shouldn't have married him, Mam.'

'I had to marry somebody. Things were different in those days.' Suddenly she sat up and grabbed Laura's hand, her face twisting with anguish. 'We'll be better off without him, won't we, Laura? Much better off.'

Laura couldn't say the words, 'Providing we aren't found out.' She knew they must be uppermost in Mam's mind too.

She hardly slept all night. She heard her mother tossing restlessly, moaning in her sleep. She heard the Luftwaffe come, wave after wave of them, dropping bombs, but that wasn't what kept her awake.

Laura was worried about the state in which they'd left the kitchen. There were so many pointers to the way in which Da had met his end. She thought about the work she must do. It kept going round in her head. She was stiff with tension when the all-clear sounded again. When she decided to make a start, Elin was sleeping at last.

Laura crept up the cellar steps without waking her mother, and drew the blackout curtains. The first fingers of light were in the sky. The stench of burning cloth hung about the kitchen. She opened the window wide, and rekindled the fire, careful to put any unburnt bits of rug back into the blaze.

There were several blotches of dried blood on the kitchen lino. She boiled the kettle and set about cleaning them off, washing down the paintwork, and blackleading the grate. She washed all four of the shells from the Great war, then polished them with plenty of Brasso, and replaced them on the mantelpiece.

She brought down her bedside rug to put in front of the hearth. She took another bowl of hot water out to the shed and set to work on the pram. When she was satisfied there were no blood stains left, she sprinkled a shovelful of dust from the floor over it and tossed some bits of coke in the bottom. Nobody cleaned a pram they kept for collecting coke.

Elin was up and walking about, a grey-faced ghost of herself.

'Don't get dressed. You're going to bed upstairs when you've had breakfast.'

'I couldn't eat.' Elin couldn't stand still either. She was pacing the kitchen, wringing her hands.

Laura felt empty as well as sick. She made porridge and tea, and felt better when she'd eaten.

'Do you think Percy . . .?'

Laura had seen the question in Mam's eyes long before she voiced it. This was the part she was dreading.

'I'm going to see.'

'No!'

'I've got to. And I'll have to report him missing.' Elin was silent, agonising. 'It would look suspicious if I didn't.' Laura put on her mackintosh.

'There's blood on it,' Elin screamed. 'Don't wear that.'

Laura's eyes jerked down in horror. Not a big stain, and not immediately identifiable on dark gaberdine but blood all the same. She tore it off and reached for her coat.

'It'll wash out,' her mother was saying more calmly when they heard a ratatat on the front door.

A voice called, 'Are you all right, Elin?'

'Beattie Higgs!' Laura froze. 'Did she hear?'

Elin shook her head numbly. 'I don't know.'

Laura wanted to ask if she'd made much noise when she'd killed Percy, but choked on the words. Beattie wouldn't miss the stench of burning. Could she have missed their journeys across the yard? Their greatest danger came from Beattie knowing what had happened.

'Elin?' the voice came again.

'She knows nothing, Mam,' Laura said firmly. 'She'd have come straight round wanting to know every detail, offering to help.' She opened the door.

'Morning, Beattie.'

'Are you all right?'

'Da hasn't come home. I was just going to look for him.'

'He'll be safe and sound. The Devil looks after his own. What's that smell?'

'Awful, isn't it? The blast brought soot down the chimney. I think there was a bird's nest or something with it.' She stood with her back to the grate. 'I wish it would burn up and finish. Did you have a bad night?'

'Terrible. Hardly slept a wink. I've run out of tea, you couldn't let me have a few spoonfuls? I'll pay you back when I get my ration tomorrow.'

Laura's hand shook as she transferred tea to the packet Beattie handed her, the dried leaves rattling down on the draining board as they spilled.

'You've cleaned up early,' Beattie said from the kitchen.

'Yes,' Elin agreed. 'Laura cleaned up for me. Shaking the house covers the place with dust and bits of plaster. I don't know where it all comes from.'

'Waste of time,' Beattie said. 'They could be back tonight.'

'Heaven forbid.'

'Thanks for the tea, love.'

Their house shook again as Beattie's front door slammed. Laura closed her eyes and took a great shuddering breath.

'Beattie knows nothing. Go to bed, Mam, try and sleep.'

Laura closed the front door softly as she went out. Ten

hours since they'd dumped his body. She prayed it would be gone, removed to a mortuary by now.

She had to pretend she was looking for her father. It would seem strange if she didn't. It was after nine, and the raid had been very heavy. A normal family would be worried. She'd never been more worried in her life.

Across a river grey as molten lead she could still see a lick of orange flame here, a dull red glow there. A great pall of smoke drifted upwards. She could taste it on her tongue. Muted by distance came the scream of a fire engine.

Much closer, she could hear voices, and the strike of picks and spades on masonry, then the rumble of falling bricks. There was trouble on this side of the water too. She rounded a corner to find the end of a terrace of houses in ruins. There was nothing left of the first house, the roofs had gone from the next three, and doors and windows had been blown out halfway down the street on both sides. Their occupants were sorting through the fallen debris and the all too familiar piles of belongings were building up on the pavement. Neighbours huddled in groups, but they were making jokes and managing to smile. An ambulance waited, a WVS van dispensed cups of tea.

Laura slowed her step. She and Mam had come this way last night. If only they'd left Da right here, their troubles would be over. She watched an ARP warden helping an elderly man rehang his front door. His familiar navy uniform jerked at her mind.

Da should have been wearing his uniform! His shift started at seven, but he'd had on his grey suit. Why hadn't they thought of that? The warden tipped his tin hat to the back of his head. She froze, recognising his thick bristling eyebrows. He was one of Da's colleagues. Her heart raced, he was watching her.

'Where did your dad get to last night?' he called. 'Trust Percy to be missing if there's work to do.'

She forced herself to walk nearer. 'He hasn't come home this morning, Mr Black. Mam's a bit worried. I was wondering if you'd seen him.'

'No, we don't see as much of him as we should.' His face

was streaked with brick dust, it gave his brows a reddish look.

'I'll walk on to the ARP post and see if he's there.'

'He won't be. It took a belting last night.'

Laura had to stop herself breaking into a run. It couldn't be worse. They'd been home again when the bombs had fallen here, say around midnight. Mr Black was ready to tell everyone Da hadn't turned up for work, and when he was found wearing his grey suit, somebody was going to ask where he'd been, and with whom. The neighbours might have seen him come home. Could even have heard Mam belting him.

The church had lost its spire! She broke into a run. She had a stitch in her side when she turned the last corner to find fifty yards of street laid flat and the police cordoning off where a shelter had been. Several teams were digging and a fire engine was damping down. There was a bustle of homeless people, services, ambulances, trying to cope. Horrific for so many people, lucky for Mam.

The church had lost most of its roof too. The grave stones had been blown higgledy piggledy everywhere. The shop that had been the ARP post was down too. The sandbags hadn't saved it.

She heard the words land mine as she tried to pinpoint the exact spot where they'd tipped Da out. It was no longer possible. All the bearings had altered. In that moment her heart sang. Mam was in the clear.

She turned for home. It would be soon enough to report Da missing this evening. In the present emergency, a responsible warden would work on. Mam was in the clear, providing Da's body hadn't been found before the raid. It had been pitch dark, and he'd been there an hour at most. No, Mam must be in the clear. It was hard to believe, but their luck had changed.

When she got home, Elin was dozing. The good news didn't seem to relax her. She dozed off and on all day, but real sleep wouldn't come. Laura kept telling her their luck had changed. Her mother stared back at her with frightened eyes, unable to take it in.

Laura spent an hour walking in the park with Tom. It cleared her head. That evening she took Elin to the police station to report Percy missing.

'Let me do all the talking,' she warned. She needn't have worried, Elin could do no more than mop at her eyes. They were treated with sympathy in their bereavement, though Laura had to steel herself to identify his body. They showed her two; neither was Percy.

His death was attributed to the land mine dropped on Fulbright Place. He was not the only person missing without trace. The heavy raids on Merseyside during May had caused extensive damage to residential property and resulted in a high death toll among civilians. No awkward questions were asked. Condolences from neighbours were the most difficult thing they had to handle.

On Monday morning, Laura telephoned her mother's foreman from her office, telling him of their bereavement. It was agreed Elin should take a few days off work. But she couldn't stop crying.

Laura felt balanced on a knife edge. She wasn't sleeping well. Her mother was in a worse state; she was a nervous wreck.

Tom's leave finished and he returned to his ship. Laura saw nothing of him for the next year.

It was a difficult year. Mam didn't improve. She went back to work for a few days, but couldn't cope. Her doctor gave her something for her nerves, and she sat about the house all day, doing nothing.

Laura had to pull herself together. She did what she always had when troubled. She opened her books again, set herself increasing amounts to master, and thought of the pleasant things in her life.

From an early age she'd taken on some of the household chores, and tried to support Mam against Percy. Now she felt their roles had reversed; she was the parent and her mother the child. She took charge of Elin, looking after her completely.

She made a point of going to Talbot's shop regularly; Mrs

Talbot usually had news of Tom. One day she said he was coming on leave again. Laura felt a spurt of pleasure, and hoped there would be more outings to the pictures.

On Saturday, she ran down to the shop to see him. It was very busy, both his parents were serving, she was surprised not to see Tom helping. His mother looked grey with misery. She sent Laura through to the living room to find him. He had his back to her, staring out across the yard, his shoulders hunched in despair.

'Tom?' He turned from the window with tears in his eyes. Her smile faded, she felt cold with shock.

'Tom!' She rushed at him, throwing her arms round him. 'Whatever's the matter?' His head collapsed on her shoulder and the tears flowed. She'd never seen a man cry before, she found it harrowing.

'You know,' he said blowing his nose, trying to regain control. 'I told you.'

'Rosemary?' Guilt stabbed at her because she'd welcomed the news.

He nodded miserably. 'She wants a divorce. I've got to sort it out, and I don't know where to start.'

So it was compassionate leave. Laura ached with sympathy. She knew how to reassure, how to suggest ways and means to solve the problem. She'd done it for old Mr Burdon at work, she was doing it for Mam. She could comfort Tom too.

'It's not just Rosemary.' She had to wait while he blew his nose again. 'My nerve's gone. I was given another ship. The west coast of America again, but my bowels turn to water at the thought of seeing the enemy. I'm terrified I'll be torpedoed again. All that time on the life raft in the freezing sea. I couldn't face it again.'

Her hug tightened. 'Everybody's afraid, Tom. It would be very unusual if you weren't. I'm far more worried about air raids now. I shake every time I hear the warning. Honest. Mam's a nervous wreck too.'

Tom was soothed. He went to wash his face and change into his uniform. They would go to the Ritz to see Betty Grable and Alice Faye in *Tin Pan Alley*. Already he looked less down in the mouth. Laura was relieved, because there was no one she wanted to help more than Tom. She enjoyed the film, and Tom said it had taken him out of himself.

On the way home they stopped at the Crown for a drink. Tom was able to get a pink gin. Laura sipped her lemonade, suggesting the first steps he should take to get his divorce. She wrote them down for him, on a page torn from her notebook.

'You're good for me, Laura,' he said outside her front door. 'I don't know what I'd do without you.' She lifted her face to be kissed, feeling full of love for him, pleased he was turning to her at last.

Over the two weeks he was home, Laura spent as much time as she could with him. Tom was much better when the time came for him to return. His divorce proceedings were in hand.

She began to receive letters from him, not regularly at first. It was support and reassurance he needed, and she sent it in unstinting amounts. She thought of him often, and looked forward to his letters. They came with increasing frequency.

He'd been gone eighteen months when he wrote telling her he loved her and proposing marriage. They'd have to wait till his divorce was absolute, and the war over, but he had to know if she wanted it too. Laura wrote back telling him she'd loved him since she was thirteen, and had dreamed of being his wife ever since. She reread his letter many times. It was wonderful to know Tom loved her.

Elin was doubtful. 'If it's what you want, Laura,' she said carefully. 'If you're sure. You'll not have him home much. He'll still have to go to sea.'

'I'll have my own work, Mam, to keep me busy.'

Everybody began to talk about the end of the war. It was coming closer. The Allied armies were freeing Europe from Hitler's grip.

Church bells were signalling victory. How long since they'd heard church bells? Peel after peel rang from St Catherine's, just down the road. They carried on the breeze from more distant churches, St Werbergh's in one direction, St Peter's in another. Carillons could be heard on the wireless, the joyous sound everywhere. Victory had come in Europe at last.

For so long they had waited and hoped. Neighbours were rushing into the street. Shrieks of joy. Tears of relief. Beattie Higgs crushed Laura to her bosom, her curlers out at last, her grey hair crimped into tight curls.

Front doors stood wide open all down Jubilee Street and from inside the houses, wirelesses blared out music and roaring cheers from the crowds in Piccadilly Circus. Tables and chairs were being carried out, and food hoarded for this celebration shared. Cups of tea and bottles of beer were being passed round. Many were good-temperedly drunk. Laura wished Tom were home to share in the party.

Today, Mam's apathy had gone. It seemed years since Laura had seen her fully alive and laughing like this, her gold slanting eyes shining with happiness, her red dress lighting up her hair to gold again.

'We can put it all behind us, Mam, it's over and done with,' Laura rejoiced. It wasn't the war she was talking about. Da's death had left scars which she hoped would fade now.

All around, there was talk of a better future. Better housing, better wages, a health service and a good education for everybody. All Laura asked of the future was to share it with Tom. Britain still needed food, so the convoys were continuing, but his letters told her she wouldn't have to wait much longer. Soon they could set the date.

'With his pay, you could afford a home of your own,' Elin said, twisting her apron between finger and thumb. Laura could see clouds of fear gathering, diminishing her fragile golden sheen. Tom had already suggested she look for a house in Prenton or Bebington.

'Tom will be going back to sea.' She wanted Tom home with her all the time but that couldn't be. For her, marriage wouldn't be perfect. 'I'll still be going in to Liverpool every day.'

She wrote back to Tom, 'Tranmere is more convenient

than anywhere you mention. We can think about a house of our own later.'

'You'll continue to live here?' Mam asked, a flicker of hope in her voice. 'Will Tom want to?'

'Of course, where else would we go?' Laura slid her arm round her mouther's shoulders. 'With all the bombing, there aren't enough houses to go round.'

Elin's face brightened. 'We could change bedrooms. You and Tom can have mine. I can't walk through your room . . . I mean . . .'

'Lovely,' Laura said. 'If you don't mind, that is.' What she felt for Tom was pure adoration. She thought of it as a romantic love, rather than physical. Somehow Tom wasn't the sort to show physical love, but perhaps that would change. 'I was thinking of moving my wardrobe to the head of the stairs,' she went on. 'Back it up against the rail where it would screen the bed. We could do that for you.'

'Good idea, and we'll redecorate. Needs it. Hasn't been done for years.'

'There was no point while the war was on. The whole lot could have come down in another raid. When was it last done?'

Elin tried to think. 'We've only done it once. About nine years ago I suppose.'

'Let's try your wardrobe there now,' Laura said, wanting to strike while her mother's energy levels were high.

They tossed most of her clothes out on the bed – old-fashioned hats and long forgotten low-waisted dresses, shoes worn almost through. Even then the wardrobe was heavy to move.

'There's something behind it.'

'What?' Elin's head pressed close to the wall to look. 'Oh yes, pictures.'

'What pictures?' Laura heaved out an enormous package tied up in an old curtain.

'Percy – he brought them from Oxley's attic.' The colour had gone from Elin's face. Using nail scissors, Laura cut the string that tied them.

'He said . . . Laurence Oxley said we could choose a few

things from his attic. To furnish this house. I don't think he meant Percy to have these. I saw him hide them in the curtains and bedding.'

'They're beautiful!' Laura was studying the heavy gilt frames and the two oil paintings which dated from the early part of the last century. One showed a family of father and mother with three small children by a stream. The other seemed to be of the same family, on the steps of a large country house, but there were five children and two dogs as well.

'Too big for here. Percy did hang one, but it nearly filled the wall. Overpowering it was, you couldn't look at anything else.'

'I love them. They're charming. Absolutely right in line and colour. Oxley ancestors, do you think?'

'I don't know.' Elin peered closer. 'Are they like them?'

'Could be. They're signed.' Laura tilted the picture to catch the light. 'Henry Denton Hope.'

'Never heard of him, have you?'

'No,' Laura frowned. 'I wish I knew more about art. More about these. I think they're very beautiful.'

'They'll be good pictures, Percy had an eye for things like this. He wouldn't have brought them otherwise.'

'We'll keep them. One day, I'll buy a big house and we'll hang them. What colour paint shall we get?'

CHAPTER SIXTEEN

Laura felt deeply engrossed in the fortunes of Burdon's Biscuits, and was happiest when poring over their accounts. The only office help she had now came from Mr Burdon's secretary, also nearing retirement, and a fourteen-year-old office girl. On the factory floor, Burdon's was continuing to lose workers.

Laura had problems at home. Mam didn't improve much, she had her good days and her bad. She pottered about the house, doing most of the chores, but she hadn't been able to go back to her work at Ledsham. She'd tried to, but after two or three weeks she'd gone off sick.

'I'll get a small cleaning job,' she'd said. 'Then, when I'm better, I could get another to go with it. Like I did before.'

'No, you do the shopping and cooking. We'll manage on what I earn.'

Laura grew accustomed to looking after other people; everybody seemed tired and ill after the long years of effort. Young Mr Burdon, their General Manager, was now a total invalid and hadn't been to the office for the last two years.

'Got to keep the place ticking over for Anthony,' old Mr Burdon said when his other grandson James, a pilot, had been killed. 'He's the last of the Burdons, but one day he'll want to run the family firm.'

Old Mr Burdon wasn't coming in so much either, only two or three days a week. She'd hear his silver-headed cane tapping along the passage before he reached her door. He'd come in, his white hair flattened by the old-fashioned homburg he'd just taken off. He wore his grey moustache twirled at the ends, in the style of a Victorian villain, though Laura found him a benign old man.

She'd show him any important letters that had come, and would bring him up to date with what was happening. Over coffee, they'd discuss what action needed to be taken. Usually Laura was left to take it. She would dictate the letters, and old Mr Burdon would sign them next time he came in. In April, he had to go into hospital for an operation. He said before going: 'You know what's needed, Laura, see to things for me.'

The hospital was close to the factory, and Laura popped in every day. It was more difficult when he went home, but she kept in touch by telephone. He didn't come to the office for two months. In that time, she realised she was managing the company. Then he started coming in for half a day, but she still dealt with everything. He came to talk about policy now.

'We won the war, but only just in time,' he joked. 'I'm seventy-six, and I want a bit of time to enjoy myself.'

'You've enjoyed yourself here,' Laura smiled. 'Don't tell me you haven't.'

'Over the first years. It was good to be needed.'

'It was marvellous. The war forced you back to fill a gap, and you made a success of it.'

'Yes, we've kept the flag flying over Burdon's between us, but I've had enough, and I've left too much to you.'

'You know I've enjoyed it too. I'm getting quite a power complex.'

'It's time you moved on, Laura.' Her eyes met his. She saw affection there. He knew she'd left school at fourteen, and the effort it had taken to carry on studying.

'I couldn't have done without you. It's your energy that's kept Burdon's going. But you'd be wasted helping the returning heroes settle into the top jobs again. Without qualifications, you'll be elbowed aside when I go.'

'I know, Mr Burdon.'

'You know John Hadlow? He's audited our books for the last twenty-seven years. I've spoken to him about you, and he'll be glad to article you.'

'Hadlow and Smith?'

'You won't do better in Liverpool.'

'I know. I'm thrilled they'll have me but . . .'

'You've had plenty of dealings with John Hadlow over the years, he knows you're running Burdon's now. He doesn't usually pay his articled clerks anything. In fact, they usually pay him a fee for the privilege.'

'I know, and—'

'I've explained your circumstances, he'll be glad to pay a stipend in your case.'

'Really?' Laura was blinking hard. She'd been unable to see how she could manage two years without pay. 'You're very kind, fixing it up for me.'

'You deserve all the help I can give, Laura. I'm grateful for what you've done. Anthony will be back next month. You could move to Hadlow's then.'

'It's what I've always wanted.' Laura clasped her hands, her green eyes shone with satisfaction.

'The least I can do is see you get a chance.'

'I can't believe it.' There were stars in Laura's eyes. 'I can't thank you enough.' The problem of how to proceed had been bothering her for months.

'If, after you're qualified, you want to come back, I'm sure there'll be a place for you.'

Laura tried to smile, tears were clouding her eyes. Mr Burdon knew exactly how much she appreciated this opportunity.

'Before we both go, I want you to get the place tidied up a bit. Get it looking better for Anthony.'

Laura pulled herself down to earth. The office had not been touched for years. After an air raid, it had been a question of getting the lines working again with as little fuss as possible. When she'd started at Burdon's, her desk had been beside a glass partition overlooking the factory floor. It had shattered in a raid early in 1941 and had never been replaced. It was easier to move staff when their number was contracting. Everywhere was in desperate need of a coat of paint.

'What colour do you want?'

He sighed. 'You know more about colour schemes than I do. See what you can get. Just a clean-up, Laura, nothing extravagant. Anthony will probably want to modernise as he expands.'

Laura put their maintenance staff to work. The only paint available was cream or pale grey. She chose grey emulsion, and had them start in the boardroom. Mr Burdon had his desk in there now, as well as the big mahogany table.

With the parquet floor repolished, and the red turkish carpet and curtains cleaned, it looked lighter and fresher.

Mr Burdon was pleased. 'Just as it used to be. I'll get the picture out of safe storage. Anthony will be glad to see it back.'

The following day, he came again with two men carrying a large package. When Laura went in to the boardroom, they had hung the picture over the marble fireplace. It portrayed a middle-aged man in eighteenth-century costume, standing on the steps of a building. It niggled at the back of Laura's mind, reminding her of something, but she couldn't think what.

'Joshua Burdon, 1764 to 1842. Our founder.'

Fascinated, Laura moved closer. 'Is that the factory?'

'Yes. It's grown a bit over the years, hasn't it? Lovely to see the picture back, and none the worse for being in a vault for five years.'

'Best place for it, with the air raids.' Laura went closer. Sizzling with sudden excitement she stood on tiptoe to read the signature.

'Is Henry Denton Hope famous?' She almost choked out the question.

'Sir Henry. Yes indeed, a founder of the National Gallery. One of our foremost portrait painters.'

Laura tried to stamp down her shivers of excitement. 'Is it very valuable, Mr Burdon?'

He sighed. 'It's the only picture we have of Joshua Burdon, who started all this, so it's irreplaceable as far as I'm concerned.'

'But on the open market?'

'Who's to know what it's worth till the market settles down. Everything is bringing sky-high prices these days. So much was lost in the war.'

'I think we have two Denton Hopes at home.' Her voice shook, but she had to talk about them. Get information while she could. Nobody else she could talk to knew anything about art.

'Really? He painted a prodigious number of pictures, I believe. Highly regarded. But are you sure yours aren't prints?'

Laura took two deep breaths. No, she wasn't sure. 'Were prints made of his pictures?'

'Yes. Before the First World War we commissioned thousands of prints to give away with our biscuits. It was the custom in those days. Art helping commerce. They framed them nicely. Ours were in maple. I remember a firm of art publishers coming to look at Joshua here, but they decided he wouldn't have enough popular appeal. They were making cheap prints to give away with lemonade or soap, anything. We had Joshua's picture put on our three-pound presentation tins one Christmas.'

Laura decided she must look at her mother's pictures again. Would the Oxleys keep prints given away with biscuits? They'd not valued them greatly to consign them to the attic. Nor apparently missed them when Da removed them. Her hopes were sinking. They'd probably be valueless prints.

'How big are they? Your pictures?'

She tried to think. It was a long time since she'd seen them. 'Enormous.'

'We had these cheap prints reduced to quarter size. To fit the smaller rooms of artisans.' Laura felt hope surge upwards again. 'But of course good prints are always done the actual size of the picture.'

'They have ornate gilt frames.'

'I don't know, Laura. Go across to the Williamson Art Gallery if you're interested. They used to have several there.'

The paint card fluttered from her fingers. 'Good enough for the Williamson Art Gallery?'

'Could still be packed away in some vault for safe keeping, but the Curator could tell you more.'

'I'll go this lunch time.' Laura smiled, anticipation was

prickling her finger tips. 'If ours are real, Mr Burdon, and we wanted to sell them, how should we go about it?'

He sighed, curling the ends of his moustache round. 'The best advice I could give would be to keep them. Values will soar.'

'But if—?'

'Christie's have a place in Chester, they have fine art sales every few months. I'd take them there. They'd give you an estimate of what they might fetch at auction.'

'Thank you.' Laura decided she'd unwrap the old curtains tonight and take another look. She had to make sure they weren't prints. She considered what she might do after that, and decided nothing for the time being. Keep them had been Mr Burdon's best advice. The time might come when they'd want the money. Mam's Denton Hopes were safe enough where they'd always been, behind her wardrobe.

Laura started at Hadlow and Smith. She found she had to concentrate, the work was very different. She had to find time to study again too, but she was enjoying it. It gave her immense satisfaction to know she'd be able to achieve all she'd planned. It had seemed pie in the sky for so long.

Her wedding day was drawing closer. Her plan for her studies had been worked out in her head. The urge to marry Tom came entirely from her heart. She thought about him every spare minute she had.

She wrote to him every day, telling him how much she wanted him with her. He wrote back frequently, telling her how much he needed her. She could feel anticipation building up inside her. Every day found her at a new level. She wanted marriage to Tom more than anything else. Three days before the wedding, he telephoned her at the office when his ship tied up. She rushed to meet him at Central Station, feeling as though she was treading on air.

He was standing by the newsstand with his back to her. He seemed thinner, his shoulders hunched inside his smartly pressed, gold-braided uniform. Tall as a bean pole, his red hair made more carroty by the strong sun. He turned so she saw his tanned face, but there was a dejected droop to his mouth, and a nervous twitch in his cheek. She knew immediately he wasn't living in the fever heat of excitement she was. He seemed at that moment an unresponsive stranger.

Laura hurled herself at him. She had so much love to give him, she'd soon change all that.

Elin felt a lump in her throat as she climbed the steps to the Registry Office. She'd not been inside since she'd come here with Percy. She remembered taking a dislike to the light oak panelling. She'd wanted a proper wedding in chapel, and he'd cheated her out of it.

She'd not wanted Laura to be married here, it seemed a bad omen. But Tom was divorced, there was no alternative, and Laura didn't seem to mind.

Elin looked round the wedding party gathering in the hall. Another marriage was taking place in the Registry Office, they were having to wait. Mostly they looked ill at ease, uncertain of what to expect. She felt so proud of Laura moving among them, looking radiant and full of hope, and yet a little overcome, as though her happiness was too much to bear. She was almost twenty, but looked younger, more vulnerable, though she was a good bit older, Elin reflected, than she herself had been when she'd come here with Percy.

She hardly recognised Beattie Higgs, her crimped grey curls showed under a red hat and she wore a new coat in red and grey checks. Elin had never seen her before without holes in her stockings and down-at-heel shoes.

Laura had asked old Mr Burdon to give her away. He looked every inch a gentleman, with his silvery hair and pale grey suit. He kissed Laura on her cheek and wished her well for the future. She was introducing him, though Elin guessed immediately who he was. His handshake was firm, his grey eyes kindly; he stood beside her for a few moments, making polite conversation before Laura led him off to meet Tom. Last Thursday, he'd sent her a three-pound box of Burdon's biscuits and a cheque for £25. Laura said if she'd known, she'd have definitely bought new carpet for her bedroom.

Tom looked as though he should be in bed, grey and

sweating, and almost old enough to be her father. Elin saw him as he had been all those years ago, pushing his old pram round to Jubilee Street for Laura to use. She'd slept in his cot and sat in his high chair too. Strange to think of that. He'd been a callow youth, but he hadn't fulfilled the promise she'd seen in him. She would have liked to see Laurie marry a man of her own age. Somebody without a failed marriage behind him. She wanted so much for Laura.

Elin told herself firmly that Tom wasn't Percy, he could hold down a job. He was a ship's officer, and he had his Master's ticket. Beattie had said he was quite a catch, and one day he'd inherit the shop. His parents must have saved a bob or two.

Tom had hired cars to take them all to the reception at the Kingsland Café. He was paying for everything. They were to have chicken salad followed by trifle, and of course wedding cake. There was to be a glass of sherry first, and a glass of wine with the salad – not what Percy would have called style, but at least Tom could pay for it.

Mrs Talbot nodded at Elin from under a big-brimmed hat, and her husband came shuffling up on his bad feet to shake hands. They had always treated her well, though Beattie said Mrs Talbot was a bit snobby. She hadn't expected them to approve of Laura because her mother had been their cleaning woman, but in fact they'd said they thought Laura was a cut above the other girls in the neighbourhood.

Laura looked ethereal today, her pale green dress drawing out the colour of her eyes in the dim light of the hall, the wide skirt swinging over high-heeled shoes. A froth of green net covered her cap.

'Isn't it a bit too plain to get married in?' Elin had asked when she'd seen the Peter Pan collar and short sleeves.

'Nobody can afford a special wedding dress these days, Mam,' Laura had smiled. 'The coupons won't stretch to it. I can wear this to the office afterwards, and it isn't going to be a big wedding.'

'No . . .' Elin liked the soft, expensive material, but she could have made her something more dressy.

She wondered why she'd once thought Laura plain. She

had been disappointed Laura hadn't inherited her golden hair and slanting golden eyes. The Oxley looks had always showed. Not as dramatic as hers had once been, but Laura had always been a pretty child. Now in maturity, her high cheek bones and delicate features were striking. Her honey-blonde hair curled gently round her face, equally beautiful. Mostly Elin could see Leonard's tranquillity in her soft green eyes and relaxed manner. Today it was lost in the excitement of the occasion. She had Elin's slim neat figure, and Laurence's stamp was obvious in her firm chin and penetrating gaze.

An usher came to the door to tell them the Registrar was ready. They crowded out, filling the wide staircase, moving slowly upwards. Laura looked pensive as though she was seeing heaven. Elin felt a terrible urge to put her arms round her. She hoped she was doing the right thing. She took comfort from the fact Laura was surrounded by friends and neighbours; her own had been a lonely wedding.

Laura had always felt absolutely certain. Ever since she'd been thirteen years old, she'd wanted Tom. Three days ago when she'd met him off his ship she'd felt the first niggle of doubt. She'd put it down to pre-wedding nerves. All brides had them.

Now, as the wedding breakfast came to an end, she couldn't take her eyes from Tom's fingers. They were twisting and tearing the artificial flowers decorating the table. Loops of wire and crushed coloured paper covered the cloth in front of him. He looked flushed. She'd felt him moving restlessly in his chair for the last hour.

Her father-in-law nudged the table as he stood up to make a speech, spreading the torn petals across the cloth. He kept it short and then there was polite clapping along the table as, mopping his face, he finished and sat down again.

All eyes turned to Tom. Laura knew he'd been practising his speech. He'd written out what he was going to say. He had the crumpled page of an exercise book in his hand now. He seemed agitated as he scraped his chair back loudly, almost standing, and then collapsing back on his seat, kicking her ankle. Slowly he got up again, swaying on his feet in the sudden silence. Laura waited, and knew everyone else waited with her. He cleared his throat; she thought his brown eyes had a glazed look. He lifted his wine glass to his lips but it was empty. A waitress hastily topped it up.

'Come on, lad,' his father urged. It sent a flutter of laughter along the table. Beattie Higgs, feathers nodding on her scarlet hat, smiled at her. Laura felt cold with embarrassment.

'Thank you,' Tom choked out. 'Thank you, everybody.' He flopped back onto his chair with a gasp. After another moment's silence, the clapping started. Tom gulped at his wine, his face scarlet. Laura wanted the reception over, so they could be alone. They'd both had enough of ceremony.

At last it was. Mam went with her up to the cloakroom to get her coat. Mrs Talbot was there too, insisting Laura remove her hat, recomb her hair, and put on fresh lipstick.

'You want to look your best for him now,' she fussed.

'Be happy, love,' Mam whispered as she hugged her goodbye. Laura could see the tears glistening in her eyes. Her own cheeks felt fiery.

Laura had had to make her own honeymoon arrangements. At Tom's suggestion she'd booked them into the Metropole Hotel in Llandudno for a week. Tom's father was lending them his Austin Eight. She felt awash with emotion as they were waved off, happy to be married, privileged to ride in a car, relief it was over finally overcoming embarrassment.

Half a mile along the road, Tom pulled in to remove the old boots somebody had tied to the bumper. He used his handkerchief to remove the Just Married message chalked below the back window.

'Lovely to be alone at last,' she said. Tom dropped silently back in the driving seat. She felt sleepy after the wine, and supposed Tom did too since he didn't want to talk.

They were heading out past Queensferry when she noticed the car weaving a little. His attention might not be on her, but it wasn't on the road either.

'Are you all right, Tom?'

'What?' He turned to look at her, and swerved again.

'Careful!' Laura's hand covered her mouth in horror, but the oncoming car slid past with an inch to spare.

'Sorrv. I'm out of practice. Spend too much time on board ship.'

Her heart thudding, Laura closed her eyes wanting the journey over. Tom was nervous. She understood that, she'd been nervous herself during the ceremony, but he seemed to be getting worse. Surely he should be more relaxed now it was over?

At the hotel, they were directed round the back to the garage. Then a porter led them up carpeted stairs to their bedroom, which had printed cretonne curtains and a matching bedcover on the double bed. She was filled with sudden shyness; it was all so different from Jubilee Street. She started unpacking her case, not daring to look at Tom who'd thrown himself onto the bed without taking off his shoes. Restlessly, he sat up.

'Let's get out of here.'

Surprised, she said, 'Do you want to go for a walk?' As she combed her hair, she watched him take a full bottle of gin from his case, together with a bottle of bitters, mix a stiff drink in one of the thick tumblers from the shelf over the washbowl, and swallow it back. His eyes met hers in the mirror.

'Do you want one?'

'No. No, thank you.

He threw off his jacket and pulled a blue pullover from his case.

'Come on, let's go.' He took her arm and they went downstairs and out into a side street. A sharp wind gusted off the sea. Laura turned her face into it, enjoying the clean salt taste. After the formality of the day, it felt wonderful to have the wind blowing through her hair. Tom hunched beside her, his head down. She wanted to run to keep warm but Tom wouldn't be hurried. On the promenade she paused to look at the sea, ink-black as night came, with white horses racing to thunder on the empty beach.

'I hate the sea when it's angry,' Tom shivered. 'On a ship—'

'You're safe on dry land now.'

'Even so, storms can be terrible.' He shivered again, pulling her away. She was pleased to feel his more purposeful stride, but two minutes later she realised he was heading for a pub.

'You know Llandudno, Tom?'

'Had a holiday here. Several really. Mum likes it.'

Gusts of warm air and laughter greeted them as he opened the door. A lively group round the bar were exchanging jokes. Glass and brass sparkled under the lights. Tom ordered pink gin, Laura accepted an orange squash, and they carried them to a quiet corner. The atmosphere of animated jollity seemed to make Tom more morose. He drank swiftly and ordered another.

'Do you want something to eat?'

Laura's stomach was telling her it had had enough orange squash, but since the wedding breakfast had been taken in mid-afternoon, she was not hungry. Tom tried to order sherry for her when he wanted another pinkers, but was refused. In 1946 alcohol was not available in unlimited amounts, and publicans still spread their supply round their customers.

'Let's go back then,' she said. 'I'm tired.'

'I can't go back to that room.' She was taken aback by the desperation in his voice.

'Why not? It's very comfortable.' Laura compared it to her bedroom at home.

He shook his head miserably.

'Where else can we go now?' Laura stifled the thought of what the room was costing. 'What's the matter?'

'Nothing,' he said standing up. 'Let's go then.'

Once back in the room, he went straight to the tooth glass and gin bottle. Laura shivered. Da had drunk like this.

'Why do you drink so much, Tom?'

'I'm celebrating. We're just married, aren't we?' Laura put his jacket on a hanger.

'You don't look as though you're enjoying it.' She took

out her nightdress and the new dressing gown Mam had made for her. She'd already decided she'd feel less embarrassed if she undressed in the bathroom along the corridor.

'I suppose I need a little courage,' he choked.

'Courage, Tom? You need courage? I thought you liked me.' She shivered again. 'Loved me.'

'I do, Laurie. I do. It's all been a bit much, that's all. The excitement. Coming home and everything.'

Laura threw her arms round him. 'Silly,' she said. 'It's the bride who has the crisis of nerves. We'll be all right together, Tom. Just take it easy, try to relax.'

She was glad to escape to the bathroom. A bath was the ultimate luxury when she had no bathroom at home. She lingered a long time, running in more hot water as it cooled. Her fingers grew wrinkled and white. The doorknob turned several times and footsteps retreated. She had to soak her nervousness away. She hadn't expected Tom to be like this.

A crisis of nerves! Poor Tom, it must be the war. Of course he had been marooned on a life raft in mid-Atlantic, enough to make anyone's nerves raw, but it had happened in 1940, six years ago. He should be over it by now.

When she returned to the room, he was still sitting in the chair by the window. She wondered how many more pink gins he'd had. The bottle had taken a beating. She climbed into the double bed.

Tom started to undress then. Seeing a man take his clothes off for the first time ought to have excited her. All the novels she'd read conveyed that. It took him a long time, he was having trouble taking the pins and cardboard out of his new pyjamas. At last the bed sank under his weight as he got in beside her. She switched off the light.

He came lurching across to run a cold hand up her back under her night dress. It made her shiver with anticipation, and cling to him urgently. For the first time since their wedding he was kissing her. She was undoing his pyjama jacket when he threw himself across her, his weight pinning her to the mattress. She didn't really understand the fumbling, or the stress he seemed to feel. He was quite agitated. 'Sorry,' he muttered. 'Laura, sorry. I can't!' He collapsed away from her, throwing himself to the edge of the bed.

Laura felt overwhelmed. His rejection seemed a solid wall. 'Tom?'

'I'm sorry. It's no good.'

'I'm no good? What's the matter?'

He grunted. She didn't understand, she only knew it wasn't what she'd expected.

She was tired, but with his disturbing presence beside her, she couldn't settle. He tossed restlessly, making the mattress bounce and pulling the blankets off her. Outside, she could hear the surf pounding on the beach and the wind growing wilder. She heard a sniff. A moment later it came again. Could he be crying?

'Tom?' She moved closer. Gently touched his cheek. It was wet with tears. 'Oh Tom!' She put her arms round him and hugged him, pulling his body close to her own. 'What's the matter? You must tell me.' She knew now something was terribly wrong.

'It's my nerves,' he sobbed, and buried his face against her shoulder, releasing emotions that had been building all day. The bed shook with his sobs. She found his tears moving, and tried to dry his eyes on the sheet. She remembered him crying once before in the room behind the shop. His tears ran down her neck and wet her nightdress.

He must be ill. She felt frightened for him. Why had she not realised he was a wreck of a man? She tightened her arms round him. Tried to make him feel the love she had flowing out to him. He was oblivious of it. Wrapped in his own torment.

After what seemed hours, he dozed off in her arms. She slid away hoping to find sleep herself, though her mind churned with disappointment. She'd seen marriage to Tom as a fulfilment. She lay awake worrying about him; it was an age before she felt herself slipping into sleep.

Something jerked her back to wakefulness. Laura sat up her heart pounding. It came again, a scream so shrill she didn't think it could have come from Tom.

'No, Rosie,' he screamed. 'No, I can't.'

She switched on the lamp. 'Tom, wake up. You're having a nightmare.'

He blinked at her. 'Mum?'

'Laurie,' she said, her mouth dry with fear. 'What can't you do?'

Tom stared at her. 'Put the light out,' he said.

Laura did. 'You've got to tell me what's bothering you. I want to help, Tom. I can't unless I know.'

She heard him sniff, and she wondered if he was crying again. 'I can't do it with girls.' His voice sounded strangled. He withdrew further to the edge of the bed.

'What girls?' Laura felt at a loss. 'Do what?'

'You know. What you expected. Tonight.'

'I thought you loved me.'

'Yes,' he said. 'That.'

She tried to think. 'But you must know what's to be done. You were married to Rosemary.'

He was silent.

'You must have done it with Rosemary?'

'I thought I could. I really fancied her.'

'But you couldn't?'

'Sometimes I could. But Rosemary didn't like it.'

Laura wished she knew what they were talking about. She felt ignorant. She hadn't known such difficulties existed. 'Didn't like what?'

'Rosemary didn't like me having men.'

Laura heaved herself up the bed with a jerk. She was sweating. Tom wasn't thinking about her at all. He didn't like women, was that what he was telling her? He had nothing to give her, had never loved her.

'You find it easier to love men?'

'I suppose so. Yes.' To hear him say it was like having a bucket of cold water thrown over her.

'Then why marry me? Surely you'd rather be with someone . . .' Laura was aware her own voice sounded strangled. Tears were prickling her eyes. 'Someone you can love.'

'It's against the law. For men to . . . you know, do it together. Mum thought a wife would help.'

Anger was bitter in her throat. She wanted to lash out at him. Scream at him. Hurt him as he'd hurt her. Had he never given a moment's thought to her feelings? His misery made her anger burst like a bubble. She couldn't help but pity him.

'But Rosemary didn't help?'

'She wouldn't stay.'

'But if she had?'

'Perhaps . . .'

'What made you think I could?' She heard Tom turn his face into his pillow. Tears were stinging her own eyes, she was weeping for lost dreams. She'd wanted a shoulder to lean on. Someone to love her.

Laura sat huddled against the pillows long into the night. What had she done? Tom seemed unaware that he'd promised to love her. He hardly knew she was with him now. He was snuffling quietly, a troubling presence in her bed. The future she'd seen for them was entirely in her own mind. How could she have been so blind?

He slept at last. His travel clock told her it was three o'clock. She felt bone weary, dispirited. She'd so looked forward to Tom's love.

Daylight came. At seven o'clock Laura got up. Her eyes were heavy, she'd hardly slept, but she couldn't lie next to Tom's restless body any longer.

She let herself out of the room to walk, trudging for miles along the promenade, going as far as she could from the Great Orme to the Little Orme and back. The sand was wet and empty, the sky overcast. Seagulls wheeled overhead calling mournfully. She shivered as the wind tore at the coat she'd chosen for smartness rather than warmth.

The awful thought she couldn't drive out of her mind was that Tom didn't love her. He never had. He'd wanted her as a front, a facade to cover his inadequacy. She had to decide what she should do now. She ought to hate Tom for this, but he hardly knew what he was doing. She was sorry for him.

It started to drizzle. She turned into town to tramp the streets. The shops opened, there were other people about. By mid-morning it was raining heavily.

She was passing a back-street café when the scent of frying bacon reminded her she hadn't eaten. She went inside and sat at a linoleum-covered table, eating a bacon sandwich and drinking cups of tea. The urn hissed soothingly, sending out clouds of steam. It misted the window.

She tried to piece together what was happening. Tom was in some sort of crisis. She was sure the stress of getting married had driven him towards it. His distress was only too obvious. His misery made her feel worse.

He was homosexual and trying to hide it. No one dared admit such a thing. To have a wife almost proved him normal. Tom had never asked himself about the price his wife would pay.

She went back to the hotel and found Tom still lying in bed.

'If only you'd told me before . . .' She perched on the bed. 'I'd have helped you. You know how I feel about you, Tom.'

He turned his face away, couldn't even look at her.

'Come on, get up,' she said more tartly, losing patience. 'It'll do you no good to lie there all day.'

She made him dress and took him downstairs to lunch, but he wouldn't eat, and she couldn't, having breakfasted so late. Together they went out into the rain-swept streets, to walk. They spent a lot of time in Woolworth's; the lights were full on, it was crowded. Laura couldn't remember a more miserable day.

By evening, she could walk no further, and insisted on going to the pictures. The hotel room depressed Tom, and the only alternative he could think of was a pub. The cinema was no help. While her mind was swirling with her own problems, she couldn't concentrate on a fictitious romance. Tom was a distraction, going to the foyer to get chocolate, then again for cigarettes. Finally he dozed off. Laura was so tired herself she could barely keep her eyes open. They bought fish and chips on the way back to the hotel and ate them as they walked along.

There were still a few ounces of gin in the bottle. It hadn't gone down when she came back from having another bath, and Tom was already in bed. Once she'd put the light out, he moved closer to her to fumble with her nightdress.

'No, Tom,' she said, stilling his groping hands but holding him close. 'We neither of us want it. Talk to me. I don't understand what you feel for other men.'

He was snuffling again, but slowly he got it out.

'It's love, Laurie. You know what love feels like. It's no different.'

'Just that it's man to man?'

'Yes.' He started to tell her about Martin who had been Fourth Mate on the *Aureol*. The pretence, the jealousy if he looked at another man, the downright obsession they'd not been able to hide. The passion. The whole ship knew, and they had had to take care to hide the fact if they ever came ashore. Eventually, Martin had taken up with a stoker. There had been other affairs, more transient. Laura tried again to understand, and knew she failed.

'I really tried with Rosemary,' he whispered. 'I thought perhaps I was bisexual, I hoped so. Some people are.' Laura hardly dared move in case she distracted him from his confidences. 'But Rosemary had no patience with me. She thought my liking men was repulsive. Do you think it's repulsive, Laurie?'

She managed to squeak out, 'No.'

'She complained of all sorts of things. I didn't give her enough attention. I wasn't home much. I couldn't always do what she wanted. I should have tried harder . . .' His voice trailed away. Laura felt sleep creeping over her. She fought it when she heard his voice again.

'Then I joined the *Dawn Star* and there was this midshipman, Kevin, and it all started again. Kevin and I really loved each other. When I got leave, Rosemary seemed to sense it, and told me she wanted no more to do with me.'

'How long,' Laura whispered, 'had you been married?'

'Less than a year. It really upset me. I pretended to everyone we were still together, though I stopped her allotment from my salary. It was awful. Mam was mad at me. Rosemary told her, you see . . . It was having Kevin that kept me going, nothing else.' She felt him reaching for a handkerchief, heard him blow his nose. Then slowly he went on. 'Then we got torpedoed. I had six days on a life raft and Kevin was killed. That did for me, Laurie. I had this breakdown.'

'Breakdown?'

'A nervous breakdown. The shipwreck seemed to catapult me into it.'

'I didn't know . . .' Laura swallowed hard. There was too much she hadn't known about Tom.

'It took me years to get over that—'

'But you got another ship. You were still at sea.'

'I was in a psychiatric hospital for nine months, Laurie. Mam told everyone I'd got another ship. That I was on Atlantic convoys helping to fight the war like everybody else.'

'You did get another ship?'

'Eventually. Eighteen months after. But I went off sick after two months. Mum didn't want the customers to know.'

'Poor Tom,' she groaned.

'I went back into hospital and met Mervyn there. I was better after that. Even went back to sea for a couple of years. It's been off and on, Laurie.'

'You should have told me.'

'Yes,' he sighed. 'Mam thought it better not.'

'Did she?' Laura couldn't stop the surge of anger.

'She was afraid it would put you off.'

'But Tom, what made you choose me?'

'Mam said you were the obvious choice. You liked me and showed it. Always have.' Laura felt the bile rise in her throat. She'd been a sitting duck.

'You won't leave me, will you, Laurie? I couldn't stand it. I'll kill myself if you do.'

Laura heaved herself furiously up the bed. 'Now you listen to me, Tom. That's blackmail. I'm not standing for it. You married me on false pretences.'

She argued it out till she could stay awake no longer. Tom disturbed her twice in the night. Once he humped over and took all the bedclothes with him. Once he was talking in his sleep.

At daybreak she got up to tramp the promenade again. She couldn't think properly with Tom lying beside her. She wanted freedom and fresh air. Now she had a clearer picture, she had to decide what to do.

Tom needed medical help again, she was sure of that, and the sooner the better. She couldn't face five more days like yesterday, and the sky was overcast again. She wanted to go home.

But she couldn't drive, and Tom was in no fit state to do so. He'd frightened her on the journey out, and he was more agitated now. He'd made no effort to get into the car since they'd arrived. She'd put the keys in her handbag and he seemed to have forgotten the car was there.

She felt torn between leading Tom to the driving seat and hoping all would be well, and telephoning his father to ask him to come out on the train and drive them back. Church bells were ringing. It reminded her it was Sunday, and the shop would close when the Sunday papers were sold. She stopped at the next telephone kiosk and spoke to Tom's father.

'We want to come home. Tom's in no condition to drive,' she told him. 'If you don't want him to crash your car, you'd better come for us.'

CHAPTER SEVENTEEN

'I couldn't help it,' Tom moaned, as they took him home from Llandudno, slumped across the back seat. 'I couldn't help it, could I, Laurie?'

'No,' she soothed. His father ignored him, driving with rigid concentration, his trilby touching the car roof. She watched what he was doing. If she could save enough money, she'd like to take driving lessons.

'I couldn't help it, Laurie,' Tom said again.

'We've got to discuss it.' Her anger was welling up. His father hadn't asked why they were cutting their honeymoon short, nor why Tom couldn't drive. He'd cut across her explanation. He knew already.

'Wait till we get home,' he said now. 'His mother . . .'

She had to be content with that, though her anger smouldered. He doesn't want to discuss it, she thought, and I can't say what I feel with Tom listening to every word. It'll make him worse.

They pulled up outside the shop a couple of hours later. Mr Talbot rang the house bell and Tom's mother opened the door.

'I'll take Tom with me to put the car away,' he said. 'I've got a lock-up garage in Victoria Street.'

'You won't be long?' Mrs Talbot asked anxiously from the doorway.

Laura straightened her lips. Mrs Talbot didn't want to face her alone, not even for the length of time it would take her husband to walk back two streets. She followed her mother-in-law into the living room behind the shop. Mrs Talbot was plucking fussily at the tablecloth, repositioning the salt and pepper, straightening a fork.

Laura took a deep breath. 'Mrs Talbot, I have—'

'You ought to call me mother now.' She turned to poke the fire.

Laura only just stopped herself screaming with impatience. 'Mother-in-law, you should have told me about Tom. He's ill.'

'He was all right on Wednesday.'

Laura felt her hackles rise. 'Don't keep putting me off. He has a long history of mental illness. You should have told me. To let me marry him without knowing wasn't fair.'

'That's behind him.' Her rigidly waved head swung from side to side, denying it. 'Finished with. He's recovered, been working for the last two years.'

'I don't think it's finished. I'm worried about him.'

'He was quite all right before the wedding.'

'He found it very stressful.' Laura clenched her fists till her nails bit into her palms. Mrs Talbot had been her employer, Mam's employer, it was hard to stand up to her. She took another deep breath.

'You knew he was homosexual.' She saw Mrs Talbot flinch at the word. 'Rosemary told you. Yet you wanted him married to me. Just to save face.'

'You wanted it too.'

'Of course I did. I loved Tom. I thought he loved me. I had a right to know he couldn't.'

'You've made him worse,' Mrs Talbot accused, her grey eyes defensive, her face purple. 'In two days you've made him worse. He was over all that.'

'It was a very cruel thing to do,' Laura said with as much dignity as she could muster. 'For him as well as me.'

'We had to keep trying. We want him to settle down. Have a life of his own.'

Tears were stinging Laura's eyes, but she wasn't going to let his mother see how upset she was. 'I can't give him what he wants, neither can he give me what I want. I can't make him happy. No woman can. To persuade him to marry again was wrong. That's what's made him worse.'

Mrs Talbot was staring at her in silence. Laura could see self-pity in her crumpling face.

'I've brought him back because it can't be a normal marriage. I think you should take him to the doctor in the morning.'

Mrs Talbot pulled herself up. 'You can't leave him here.'

'What?'

'He can't come back here. I'm at the end of my tether with him. You said he could live with you and your mother.'

'Before I knew about this.'

'He's your job now, Laura. You handle him better than anyone else. His dad was saying so only last night.'

'I don't know what to do for him. At times he doesn't know who I am. He called me Rosie.'

'A lot of this is her fault. I blame her, myself. He'd only had a bit of depression till she walked out on him. She didn't even try. Not even when they were first married.'

'Then he had these . . .' Laura forced the words out . . . 'fits of depression even before he met Rosemary?'

'He was moody as a boy. He was in his teens when he first had one.'

Laura felt as though she'd been kicked. She couldn't get her breath. 'You mean, even before the war?'

'I blame the ships, too. Life's so different once they leave home. All those men together. Too much drink. There's nothing else for them on board.'

Laura hardly heard her. For the first time she realised the magnitude of Tom's problem. Rosemary hadn't been flighty, she'd had to face the same problem. She'd dealt with it the only way she could. By divorcing him.

She saw the back gate open and Tom and his father coming up the yard.

'I shall go and see a solicitor. You let me marry him knowing nothing of his problems. You wanted someone else to look after him. I'm not going to be put upon. I want a divorce.'

'Now then, sorted everything out?' Mr Talbot hobbled in with false bonhomie, rubbing his hands.

'It's going to take a lot longer than this.' Laura felt the blood rush to her cheeks. 'I think you both acted despicably. I'm going home.'

'I dropped your cases off.' Mr Talbot hung his trilby behind the door to the shop. He'd given up trying to spread a few long hairs over the dome of his head. It shone bald and pink. 'Your mother said if you didn't mind sharing a pair of kippers, she'd do tea for you.'

'I want Tom to stay with you.' Laura hadn't wanted to say this in front of him. She understood rejection only too well.

Mrs Talbot lifted her rigid perm, a mannerism she had when dealing with those she considered social inferiors. 'You married him. You've got to take him.' Poor Tom, Laura wondered how much of this he was taking in. He stood against the door, red head sinking between hunched shoulders. 'You want to go with Laura, don't you, Tom?'

'Yes.' His pathetic brown eyes implored her to take him.

'You're better off here with your mum.' Laura was trying to be gentle.

'I can't be doing with him any longer. Not with the shop as well.' Tears were rolling down Mrs Talbot's face.

'Help me, Laurie,' Tom pleaded. 'You said you would.'

She swallowed hard; he was right, she had. She turned scathingly on Mrs Talbot. 'You've got a nerve asking me to call you mother. You don't even want to mother Tom.' She took his arm. 'Come on, Tom. I'll help you.'

Elin felt thoroughly churned up. It had come as a shock to see Mr Talbot on the doorstep with the suitcases. It left her knees feeling weak.

'What's happened?' An even greater shock to see Tom's grey face in the back window of the car. Staring at her with no recognition.

'Tom isn't very well. They've come home early.'

'Laurie? She's . . .'

'She's with his mum. She's fine. They'll be round in a few minutes.'

It shattered the peace of Sunday evening for her. She'd been reading the *News of the World* and drinking her way through a full tea pot. She couldn't sit down to wait. It gave her something to do to clear her dishes off the table and reset it for two.

She carried their cases up to the front bedroom. The new wallpaper with yellow roses looked lovely, it still smelled of new paint. A good job she'd already made the bed up with new sheets and a new yellow bedspread for them. She looked through the bedroom window. No sign yet of them coming up the road.

She refilled the kettle, washed and put away the dishes she'd used. It must be something awful to bring them back off honeymoon after only two days. Tom had looked terrible.

She was at the parlour window when she saw them turn into the street, Laura half holding him up. Closer to, her face was white with tension. Elin felt a trickle of fear as she went out to meet them.

She was jumpy as she hustled them into the kitchen. Tom slumped down at the table, his head in his hands, saying nothing, looking morose. The plates rattled almost before she touched them. Laurie gave her a look that said she was a bundle of nerves, but Laura herself was like a caged lion. Tom pushed his kipper round the plate eating very little.

'Come on, try, Tom.' Laura yanked the backbone away from the flesh, and pushed the plate back in front of him. 'You hardly ate anything at the hotel.' She was treating him like a child.

'What's the matter?' Elin had to ask. It had happened so fast. 'Such a shock to see you like this, Tom. Rotten luck on your honeymoon.'

Laura's green eyes pleaded for silence. Her finger went to her lips. 'We'll look after you, Tom. Don't worry.' She was patting his shoulder. 'A good night's sleep will help. Would you like to go to bed now?'

Tom looked up but gave no other sign he heard. Elin glanced at the clock, it was only eight o'clock, but Laura had him on his feet and was heading for the stairs. It wasn't easy to get him up, the stairs were narrow and twisting. Laura pulled from above, Elin pushed from behind. His limbs seemed to have no strength. Laura stopped in the back room.

'The front room,' Elin almost smiled at having to remind her. 'It's all ready for you.'

'Tom will sleep in my old bed,' Laura said firmly.

'But . . .'

'He'll be better on his own.' Laura pulled the covers back. Elin just had time to grab her flannelette nightdress before he sat on it.

'Collect your things together, Mam. You and I are sleeping in the front.' Laura was already dragging Tom's things from his suitcase.

'But I've got it all nice for you . . .'

'Come on, Tom, get your clothes off.'

'Shouldn't we change the sheets?' Elin pushed her hair off her forehead. 'I slept here last night.'

'Tom won't notice,' Laura said wearily.

'Oh God!' She realised then things were worse than she'd supposed. Much worse. She waited till they were back downstairs with the door at the bottom carefully closed.

Laura's green eyes met hers. They were opaque with suffering, her face stark white. 'He's ill. Mentally ill, Mam.'

'Laurie, love.' Elin wished she could do more than hold her tight. Laura's head went down on her shoulder. She couldn't believe it was only two days since Laura had been a radiantly happy bride.

'He's hardly slept in two nights.' She could feel Laura's body shaking with misery. 'He moaned in his sleep, and he'd start shouting and screaming, waking me up and half the hotel too. He needs help.'

Elin's arms tightened round her. 'We'll get him to the doctor in the morning.' She thought of Percy; she dreaded Laurie being pulled down as she had been.

'He's had mental breakdowns before.'

Elin had never seen Laurie so tense, her heart went out to her. She was going to have that hulk round her neck for the rest of her life.

'His mother should have told you,' she said angrily. 'He should have told you.'

Laura sighed. 'They kept it hidden. All brushed under the carpet. He had a bad do when he was shipwrecked, but it wasn't the first. His mother told everyone he was away at sea when he was having treatment in mental hospitals.' Resentment thickened her voice.

It was only when they were curled up together in the front room bed that Elin heard the worst. She'd heard men could be queer, but she'd never known one. She felt sick with foreboding.

'If only I'd known before I married him,' Laura sighed, and the tears came at last. 'Oh Mam, I feel so angry, so hurt, so full of disappointment.' Elin put her arms round her again, pulling her close. 'I'm torn in two, between loving him and hating him.'

Elin stroked her honey-coloured hair, trying to comfort, but appalled at what Laurie was facing.

'They should have told you.' She felt bitter. 'It was taking advantage.' She'd wanted a good marriage for Laurie above everything else.

'But he's ill, Mam, frightened. Just a walk along the prom with waves splashing up terrified him. He was back on the life raft adrift in a storm, seeing U-boats everywhere.'

'You've done what you can,' Elin tried to comfort.

'He hardly knew I was there. At times he didn't know who I was.'

'He'll get better, love. It's you I'm worried about. If only we'd known.'

'I'll go to a solicitor,' Laura said. 'I'll file for divorce.'

'Annulment,' Elin whispered. 'You can get an annulment. It's never been . . . It'll cost though.'

'I've still got the twenty-five pounds Mr Burdon gave me.'

'I've got fifteen you can have. Isn't there going to be a free legal service soon?'

'Can't wait for that,' Laura said sleepily. 'I'm going to see about it tomorrow.'

'It'll take ages. These things do.'

Tom was admitted to hospital the next afternoon. He recovered more quickly than Laura expected.

She was glad when her fortnight's holiday was over and she could go back to Hadlows. She could cope with the problems there, and felt better once she was back on familiar ground. Also she could more easily visit Tom in hospital in Liverpool. She was told within a month he was ready for discharge.

'We don't have to have him back,' Elin said belligerently. 'Much better not.'

Laura could see no alternative, though her solicitor had told her it would simplify the annulment if he didn't live in the same house.

'Let him go home.' Elin's gold eyes blazed.

'I wish he could.'

'I don't want him round the house getting under my feet all day. I'm going down to see Mrs Talbot,' Elin said.

'You won't get anywhere,' Laura told her wearily. 'They don't want him. Too much trouble.'

'That's no reason why we should.'

'He's got to have somewhere to go. Just till he gets on his feet.'

'He'll hang on for years. He'll suck you dry,' Elin prophesied. 'Just like Percy.'

Elin admitted she was wrong when after a month's convalescence he went back to sea. Having him about the house wasn't as bad as she'd expected. He pottered, lighting fires, cooking the odd meal for them, going to the shops. He even paid for some things, though she told Laura he wasn't paying enough. Tom had tears of gratitude in his eyes when he said goodbye.

It took Laura eighteen months to get her marriage annulled. Whenever Tom had shore leave he came to stay and she moved into the front room to sleep with Elin. It dawned on her slowly that to be legally free of Tom was one thing, to refuse to give him a home was another. Unless he found someone else, she was never going to be free.

She didn't talk about her marriage, except occasionally to her mother. As far the neighbours in Jubilee Street knew, Tom was still her husband. At Hadlows, she never mentioned Tom and continued to be known as Miss Peck.

CHAPTER EIGHTEEN

'Congratulations, Laura.' Mr Hadlow hauled his bulk from behind his desk when she went in to see him. Thirty years of accountancy had given him a gut that bulged over his trousers. He emphasised it with a gold watch chain. 'We knew you'd do it, of course.' He was shaking her hand heartily.

Laura was bubbly with satisfaction. She'd achieved what she set out to do. She could call herself a member of the Institute of Chartered Accountants at last. It had taken two years of hard work, but she'd enjoyed it. It had opened windows in her mind. She understood things only half seen before.

'You've always wanted it,' Elin had exulted last night. 'Ever since you had to leave school. Your way of proving yourself.'

Laura knew what had spurred her on, and it wasn't that. Accountancy was a tool to help her run a business. She'd wanted to know what all those figures meant. How they were manipulated. To understand what was profit, and where it was being earned.

'I'd like you to join us,' Mr Hadlow went on. 'It's not often I offer a partnership on qualification, but I can to you, Laura, with every confidence.'

She hadn't expected this. She wasn't sure she wanted to be an auditor, though she'd been thinking about what she should do next.

'It's a great honour,' she managed. This could be the best thing going and, if so, she didn't want to miss out. 'I never expected . . . I'm very grateful.'

'Think it over. Take your time, it's a big decision.' He took out his gold hunter and polished it on his bulging waistcoat. 'In the meantime, here's something you can do. Burdon's Biscuits is due for audit, they want a valuation for sale as well.'

Laura's stomach muscles contracted with a jerk. One of the things she'd thought she might do was approach Burdon's. Hadn't old Mr Burdon told her there'd be a slot for her when she qualified?

'For sale? Why?' Mr Burdon would be horribly disappointed. She was disappointed. She'd worked on the last audit, she knew Burdon's wasn't making much profit then, but it was still ticking over. She'd talked to Mr Anthony at length, pointing out where better profits might be made.

'Anthony never got going. The war unsettled him. The family business must seem tame after routing Germans out of Africa,' Mr Hadlow said.

Laura was so gripped by the idea, she could hardly breathe. She stood holding onto the edge of Mr Hadlow's desk. She thought of the pictures hidden behind her wardrobe and her heart gave another lurch. Suddenly she knew exactly what she wanted to do.

To walk through the front door of Burdon's was like going home. Laura peeped into the offices as she went down the passage. Nothing had changed during the two years she'd been at Hadlows. The building was practically empty.

There was a new receptionist with ruby fingernails sitting at the front desk. She buzzed the boardroom, to announce Laura's arrival.

Anthony Burdon had a shrapnel wound down the side of his face. Drooping over his grandfather's splendid mahogany desk, he looked world-weary. The Denton Hope was still hanging over the marble fireplace.

'I don't think making biscuits is for me,' he said. 'I loathed working here before the war. I was persuaded to come back and try again because my family have been doing it for the past two hundred years. Grandfather was keen for me to carry on.'

'How is he?' Laura asked. 'Your grandfather?'

'Enjoying life, now he doesn't have to come here.'

'Good. He's still playing golf?'

'Yes, and going fishing. Even he can see it's much harder to make a profit now. The machinery and equipment is all pre-war. It's always breaking down. We need to invest new capital to become competitive.' As he spoke, Laura could feel a ball of excitement growing in her gut.

'The business is dominated by big companies now. They've got cash, always looking for new opportunities. Jacob's are planning to expand. I think they might buy us out.'

'They already have a factory in Liverpool,' Laura said. 'Surely a business can be run more economically if all the plant is on one site?'

'Well, I'm hoping they will. I've approached an agent to value the buildings and handle the sale.'

Laura tapped her pencil gainst her notebook as she tried to think. 'Of course, book value is one thing, market value could be very different.'

'I'm hoping so.'

Laura turned to look at Joshua Burdon's portrait. 'What will you do if you sell?'

'When I sell, not if. My mind's made up. My wife's Australian. She wants to go home. Her family have a sheep station. I reckon that's more my line. Outside work in the sun.'

Laura couldn't wait to get at the accounts. She was bursting to see how much profit Anthony had made last year, and the exact value put on the site and buildings, though of course it would be marked up to meet current market prices. Apart from that, she'd have to buy the plant and machinery, fixtures and fittings, the vehicles and good will.

Hours passed as she sat working out what it would cost to buy Burdon's. It seemed a prodigious amount. But a lot of the machinery was ready for the scrap yard, and the business hadn't made much profit over recent years. It was the right moment to buy.

Laura was tingling with excitement, she would need to ask Mam if she could get the pictures valued. Would she mind if they were sold? So much depended on how much one would cost and the other bring. She knew she wanted

Burdon's more than anything else. If anyone could turn it round to make a profit, she could. She'd put new life into it.

She noticed suddenly everyone was getting ready to go home; it seemed only moments since she'd opened the books.

Laura strap-hung on the underground train to Birkenhead Central, then caught the bus to Tranmere as she did every night. Her mind was buzzing with tremendous plans. She couldn't keep the inane grin from her face as she hurried down Jubilee Street. She bounded across the parlour.

'You're late tonight, Laura,' Elin called from the scullery. 'I'm ready to dish up.' Laura strode in as she turned from the stove. 'What's happened?'

'Wonderful news. Marvellous.' She could hardly speak. 'Burdon's is for sale. Mam, can we sell those pictures?'

Elin stared, her golden eyes blank. Then she picked up the pan of potatoes and started to drain them down the sink.

'Hang on.' Laura grabbed the pan from her and slammed it back on the stove. 'This is my big chance, Mam. Let's have another look at them.' She raced upstairs. She'd pulled them from their hiding place and laid them on the bed by the time Elin came to the door. The colour had drained from her face, leaving her hair looking too brassy to be natural. She was terrified of the whole idea.

'This is what I want to do, Mam.'

'Buy Burdon's? A factory?' Elin was overwhelmed. 'But whatever for?'

'To make money. We could be rich. Can't you see? I can run that factory. I did it in the war.'

'The war's over Laura. Things have changed.'

'I've changed too. I've worked my apprenticeship, Mam. First under old Mr Burdon, and now at Hadlows. I'm better qualified to do it than Anthony.' She was ripping the old curtains off the pictures. 'Help me,' she said. Together they lifted one and set it against the chest of drawers. Now they could see both.

'They're beautiful. It all depends, Mam, on whether you'll let me sell them. And what they'll bring.'

'How much,' Elin's voice croaked, 'do you need?'

'About seventy-five thousand.' She watched her mother's

jaw sag open. 'That will buy Burdon's and give me a bit extra to modernise.'

Elin's jaw sagged further, horror showed in her gold eyes. 'That's a fortune! We could live on that and never lift a finger again. Never need to.'

Laura's honey-blonde hair swung as she shook her head. 'I could build up Burdon's so we could afford to buy anything we wanted. I could do it. I know I could. If you'll let me sell these pictures.'

There was a hammering on the front door.

'Who can that be? Laurie, you've no idea what these are worth.' Elin's nerve had snapped, Laura could see solid disbelief on her face. 'Do you think I'd have kept them if they were worth much?' There was another hammering of the knocker. Elin went to the window and looked down.

'Let me try,' Laura pleaded.

'They won't be worth a lot.'

'I could borrow more from the bank if I have to, but I have to have capital. No good just walking in to ask if I can borrow seventy-five thousand.'

'Goodness, it's Tom!'

'Tom?' Laura peered over her shoulder. 'Can't be, he's not due home for another month.'

'It's Tom all right,' Elin said.

Laura was already running downstairs. Tom's face was grey as he stumbled over the step. He seemed to have a lot of baggage.

'You're back, Tom? We didn't expect you. For how long?'

'For good,' he mumbled, pushing past her. 'Got a bit of a problem. I've been paid off. Sacked.'

Elin dished up liver and bacon, trying to make what she'd meant for two look enough for three. The cabbage was overcooked, the potatoes soggy. Not that she felt like eating any more.

She felt sick with worry. If it wasn't enough Laura having such big ideas, Tom had to land on their doorstep when they least expected him. She'd known he'd be nothing but trouble since they'd come back from honeymoon.

'Surely, Tom, they can't sack you at a moment's notice?'

His brown eyes met Elin's uneasily. He looked ill. 'I told them what to do with their precious job. There was a terrible row this morning in head office.'

'What? You told them you didn't want the job?' Elin was aghast, the man was a fool. Ship's officer too, he ought to have more sense.

'It doesn't matter,' Laura was saying gently. 'You'll get another job, Tom.'

That infuriated Elin. He'd lost his job and it didn't matter! 'Africa is where you're supposed to be, man.' She pushed a plate of food roughly across the kitchen table to him. He was sitting in her place.

'I don't understand.' Laura prodded at her liver. 'Where's your ship now?'

Elin had to get up to get another knife and fork for herself. Sent home with no warning. He must have been caught doing something he shouldn't.

'She went aground in the mouth of the Forcados River. Sandbanks, moving all the time. Notorious place for it.'

'But you knew,' Elin said. 'I've heard you talk about sandbanks before. You knew to take care.'

'I was asleep at the time, they can't blame me. Can't blame the First either, not really. Sandbanks are notorious for shifting.'

Elin stared at him. 'You weren't drunk?'

'No. Had a bit of a hangover perhaps. Not well. I told the First to wait for high tide.'

'And she didn't float off then?' Laura asked.

'Didn't budge. So I had to tell them to jettison some of the cargo. To lighten the vessel. That solved the problem.'

'How much?' Laura asked, her green eyes appalled.

'A few thousand gallons. Had to do it. Couldn't stay there for ever. Hell of a row about pollution.'

'What about the petrol you lost?' Elin bristled. 'Do they expect you to pay for it?' Here was Laura, full of sympathy, welcoming him home as though he'd every right. Tom would be living on Laura as Percy had lived on her.

'It was fuel oil,' he sighed. 'And miles from civilisation.'

'Good job we don't rely on you to pay the rent.'

'Mam!' Laura said. 'Tom'll get another job.'

Elin chewed on the liver. It had gone hard with too much cooking. Another mouth to feed. He'd hardly put his hand in his pocket. She'd tried to tell Laura he should be sending something from his salary every month, but Laura didn't want it in case it affected her annulment. They had trouble making ends meet on what she got from Hadlows.

'It's meant to be an honorarium, Mam. Just to cover my expenses, and usually they pay nothing to articled clerks. It's free training I'm getting, you see.'

Elin had done what she could; she'd found herself a cleaning job three mornings a week. She'd had to.

'I'll walk down to the shop,' Tom was saying. 'See Mum and Dad and see if they have an *Echo* left. There's always jobs in the *Echo*.'

Laura got up to put the kettle on for tea. Elin put down her knife and fork, her stomach churning. How could she have been such a fool to let Laura marry him? But if she were honest, the thought of selling those pictures bothered her more. It frightened her. How could she sell valuable pictures through Christie's and give her address as 50 Jubilee Street, Birkenhead? Everyone would think they were stolen.

Elin gulped down the tea and tried to think. As she saw it, Laura had a right to the pictures. She had Oxley blood in her veins, must have, to want her own business.

Would Laurence Oxley even know the pictures were his? For all she knew, they could have been up in that attic all his life. He might never have seen them, and they'd been behind her wardrobe for the past twenty-two years. She was a fool to be frightened. They had to be sold, there was no other way Laura could have her biscuit factory.

Laurence Oxley hadn't charged her with stealing money from his desk, because he'd been afraid of the publicity. He had a reputation to protect. Surely the same applied now?

But fifty pounds was nothing to him. This was different. Laura thought the pictures worth thousands. Even to Laurence Oxley that was money.

Elin made up her mind. If Laurence Oxley claimed the

paintings when they went on sale, she'd open her mouth so wide, he'd be sorry. Oh yes, she'd make him pay. She would say he'd given them to Peck. Given them with three hundred pounds and some other bits of furniture to set up a home for his illegitimate child.

Laura felt drained, her head ached. This morning she'd been pleased because at last she'd qualified. Then when she realised she might be able to buy Burdon's, she'd felt such a surge of elation. She'd been brought down with a bump when Tom came home saying he'd got the sack.

He was out of work and unhappy. She knew he felt a failure, and she'd been full of her own success. She was afraid he might be tipped into another depression, and another long stay in hospital.

Mam was on edge, and making matters worse. To Mam, having no job and therefore no money was the worst thing that could happen to anyone. It was important to her that he paid his share of household expenses, and now he wouldn't be able to.

Poor Mam felt perennially short of money, and was often humped over her tea cup in silent misery now. Laura felt torn between the two of them. She couldn't refuse Tom bed and board when he needed it. She roused herself.

'Mr Hadlow offered me a partnership this morning.'

Two pairs of eyes turned to stare at her. 'He's asked me to join them as an auditor.'

'It's a marvellous opportunity for you.' Tom's brown eyes came to life. 'Take it.'

'Did he mention salary?' Elin wanted to know.

'Yes,' Laura said, and told them.

'Well, that's the answer.' Elin straightened up with relief. 'You know the job, you like it. Could you start right away?'

'Yes.' Too late Laura wished she'd kept it to herself. Mam saw it as the safe option. It would provide enough money to live in comfort. It would even support Tom too, if she wanted that.

'You'll enjoy it,' Tom said.

She might, but it didn't make her tingle as the idea of owning Burdon's did.

'Give up that wild idea of buying Burdon's,' Elin urged.

Perhaps it was wild. 'It could be my big chance,' she sighed. 'I've got to get Burdon's if I can.' She saw the glow fade from her mother's face. She was unusually quiet all evening.

'You think Peck stole those pictures,' Laura said when they were getting into bed. 'Is that what's bothering you?'

'Worried, I am, and it should worry you.' Mam pushed her golden hair off her forehead with a weary gesture.

'It does, but we can hardly give them back now and what good are they to anyone behind the wardrobe?'

The next day, Laura telephoned Christie's in Chester to make enquiries, and agreed when they suggested she take them in.

Even that was a problem. How did she get two pictures, six feet long and weighing so much she could hardly lift them, to Chester? On the very few occasions she'd been there, she'd gone on the bus. Tom solved it for her.

'I'll ask Dad if I can borrow his car,' he said. 'He's got a roof rack, and there's plenty of cardboard at the shop to put round them in case it rains.'

Tom continued to visit his parents. They were pleased to see him, as long as they didn't have to admit he was abnormal in any way.

'That would be a great help.' Laura was pleased, and arranged to take an afternoon off work to go to Chester. 'Come with us, Mam,' she invited.

When she saw how taut her mother's face was growing during the journey, and how she was twisting the handles of her handbag, she wished she hadn't. Elin's anxiety made her feel worse. She was stiff with tension as they went into the sale room. So much depended on the outcome.

She helped Tom carry them in one at a time and prop them side by side against a wall. They peeled off the cardboard and the old curtains.

Christie's representative was younger than Laura expected. He gazed at them silently from a distance.

Examined them closely with a magnifying glass. Stepped back again and rubbed his chin thoughtfully. The suspense made Laura damp with perspiration.

'Can you tell me something of their history?' He was looking at Elin. Laura closed her eyes and hoped. She'd primed her mother to meet questions like this. He was very polite. 'How long you've had them, and how did they come into your possession?'

'Twenty-two years.' Laura heard the nervous creak in Elin's voice. 'They were given to my husband at the time of our marriage. That's how I know exactly when.'

'A wedding present?'

'Yes, from a relative of my husband's. I lost him in the war, my husband I mean, and I've not kept in touch with his family.'

He stroked his chin again. 'Do you have any documents that would prove them genuine? The bill of sale, for instance.'

'I don't know if we ever had a bill of sale. No, it was all so long ago.'

Laura began to breathe again. It sounded plausible.

'You don't know anything about the family portrayed here? Their name?' Elin shook her head regretfully.

'Never mind, they're charming pictures. Need cleaning, of course. Can we arrange that for you? They'll bring more if they're cleaned up first.'

Laura saw her mother freeze as she always did at the mention of any expense. She answered for her.

'We'd be glad if you would.' Then she put the question that was foremost in her mind. 'How much are they likely to fetch?'

'If they are genuine Denton Hopes, then quite a lot.' He went forward with his magnifying glass again. 'I'm expecting a colleague up next week. Our expert in fine art. I'd like to have his opinion before I commit myself. Could you leave them with us?'

'Yes,' Laura said firmly.

It was two weeks before she had any news. Then Christie's assessor telephoned her at Hadlows to say they had no reason to doubt they were genuine.

'I'd put a value on them of about thirty-five thousand pounds each, and I'd suggest a reserve of thirty-three thousand.'

Laura could hardly speak.

'We think they might do rather better in our London saleroom. Would you agree to them being sent down there?'

That suited her very well. In a London sale, they'd be less likely to come to Laurence Oxley's notice. She would have liked to have seen them sold, but it was out of the question now. Laura's hand shook as she put the phone down. Seventy thousand pounds!

When she had recovered, she went down the corridor to Mr Hadlow's office.

'Thank you for your offer of a partnership. I'm very grateful, but no.' She told him of her plans. Then she walked round to Burdon's and told Anthony Burdon she intended to buy, if they could agree a price.

The prospect of owning Burdon's kept Laura's adrenaline racing. She couldn't rest, and was sleeping less. Ideas came fast, one after the other, about factory layout, new recipes, sales techniques. She'd never felt so alive, but she was on edge too. She had to have Burdon's, it had become an obsession.

Old Mr Burdon came to meet her at the factory. He said she was better qualified to breathe new life in to the factory than anyone else he knew. And if a Burdon no longer owned it, he was pleased it would be her.

It took over three nerve-racking months, but eventually the pictures were cleaned and put in a sale. Together they made eighty-three thousand. Laura couldn't believe it.

'You could buy a house too,' Tom said. He was still with them, not having managed to get another job. He was trying to grow a beard, ginger hairs spiked his jawline. He rattled his newspaper at her, his thin fingers prodding at a photo. 'Four bedrooms and a garden in Bebington, for the odd three thousand.'

'No,' Laura said.

'Don't you like it?'

'Yes, it would be a big improvement on this, but . . .'

'Well then, how about this one in Heswall?'

'Not yet. We're happy enough here. I've got to concentrate on the business first.'

A photograph on the front page of the paper caught her eye. She turned it up.

'You used to draw my attention to anything about the Oxleys,' she began and stopped, feeling cold numbing fingers clutching her stomach.

'What about the Oxleys?' Her mother was trying to take the page from her. Laura spread it out on the table so they could all read it.

'It's Jane. She's had an accident.'

Laura read on. Jane had been riding her own horse along the beach at Caldy when for some reason she'd lost her seat. The horse had gone home, dragging her behind with one foot caught in the stirrup. She'd been taken to the Cottage Hospital at Hoylake only just alive, and later transferred to Walton Hospital in Liverpool.

'How horrible,' Laura said, thinking of the fierce rivalry between them at school, how each had struggled to score over the other. Mostly, she thought ruefully, Jane had succeeded.

'Laurence Oxley, he'll be feeling this,' Elin said slowly.

'I'm feeling it,' Laura said quietly.

'I thought you didn't like her,' Tom said.

'She is Laura's half-sister,' Elin's voice was choked with emotion. Slowly, she began telling Tom the whole story.

'And to think we hated each other,' Laura whispered. 'I wonder if it would have made any difference if we'd known.'

Over the next weeks, Jane hovered only just alive, while newspapermen waited for every snippet of information. Her story made the national dailies, and the BBC News. There were headlines about the poor little rich girl who would never walk again, family pictures of private grief made very public. It was said to be a blessing when she died. Every detail of the funeral was emblazoned in the papers.

Laura found the whole episode upsetting. The Oxley name was on everybody's lips. It made her think about them more. She knew it brought back bad memories for her mother.

'Jane was not one of the winners after all,' she said.

The following week, Tom got a job as First Officer on the Irish boats. He'd be sailing out of Liverpool. A short trip, there and back in twenty hours.

'Almost office hours,' Laura smiled. 'I'm happy for you.' She was still torn in two by Tom, half hating, half loving him. Sometimes, when he was going away, he would kiss her cheek.

'You're a good friend to me, Laurie,' he'd say. His beard was thickening and curling, it had darkened to auburn. She thought he looked the epitome of a ship's officer. A very masculine man. It was hard to believe he wasn't.

'You're far too good to him,' her mother told her. 'You'll never get rid of him this way.'

But Mam seemed to be quite fond of him too. He'd got into the habit of lighting the fire for her every morning, bringing in a scuttle of coal when it was needed. He could put washers on taps, and mend fuses. He'd repainted the kitchen. He did things for them they couldn't do for themselves.

'He'll not be away much,' Elin said suspiciously, 'but I'm pleased.' Laura knew she meant relieved. He'd be earning his own money again.

From the day she'd heard Burdon's was for sale, Laura thought continually about biscuits. She knew what Burdon's made now were not as good as they had been. Over the years, expensive ingredients had been replaced with cheaper ones, scarce ingredients with something easier to come by. She knew she still had a lot to learn.

She started by buying a selection of biscuits, trying to work through every brand on the market. Most carried no identification. She noted those with the best taste, and those most attractive to look at.

'You're wasting your time,' Elin told her. 'I can tell you all you need to know about biscuits. Brands don't matter, they all have a wartime taste. It's a question of whether you want to spend your ration points on biscuits or whether you want to keep them for something else.'

'It won't always be like this,' Laura said. 'Do you know,

Mam, Burdon's are still selling their biscuits loose? They go into the shops in twenty-pound tins and get weighed out into paper bags as they're bought.'

'Of course,' Elin retorted. 'I buy them.'

'How can you be sure the last half-pound sold is as crisp as the first?'

'I keep telling you, they're all sold the same day. People queue for them. It's like this, Laurie. A big tin of chocolate biscuits is opened on the counter, sometimes the shopkeeper puts a notice in the window, but mostly he doesn't need to. The people in the shop buy, and those passing think how lucky they are. Everybody is allowed half a pound, and no more. The queue starts and soon it's out on the pavement and halfway down the street.

'Passing shoppers ask the end of the queue what they're waiting for and if they want chocolate biscuits they join it. It's only when they reach the counter, or if the queue ahead suddenly eddies away, that they find the chocolate tin is finished and there's only digestives left.'

'Things are improving, Mam. You know they are. You don't have to queue for ordinary biscuits.'

'Perhaps not,' Elin sniffed. 'But there's no question of them getting stale in the shop. People want them even if they don't taste all that good. We all have to fill our bellies.'

'The war's over,' Laura said. 'I'll need new recipes. There's a new machine that wraps and weighs biscuits into half-pound packets. I'd have attractive wrappings. Customers would know they'd keep fresh till they were opened. They'd buy more.'

'They can't buy more, they're on points.'

'They won't be for ever. And they'd buy more of mine. People will get more selective.'

'Who's going to pay extra for a fancy wrapper? You can't eat that.'

'Everybody will, in another year or so.'

'But that's way in the future.'

'It's coming,' Laura said. 'I've got to be ready.'

She thought more about it, delved a little deeper. She found the wartime system of allocating scarce commodities to food manufacturers was still in force, but easing. More was becoming available, but the search for sweeteners to replace sugar, edible oils to replace butter, raising agents to replace eggs, was perennial. Only baking powder was obtainable in adequate amounts.

She made Mam and Tom taste all the biscuits she could get, and tell her which they liked best. She handed what was left round the office at Hadlows in the tea break, and got their opinion too. They couldn't believe she was giving them away. Gradually she built up a picture of what would be most popular. She started experimenting at home with new recipes. Then she examined the cost and availability of the ingredients she would need. Elin complained about the expense, and that all their ration points went on biscuits or ingredients to make more biscuits. But Laura wanted her biscuits to be at the top of the market, to deserve to be known as Burdon's Best. She was determined to provide a quality product at a value-for-money price.

She wrote to companies selling biscuit-making machines, and studied their brochures. One company took her to see their machines installed and working in Crawford's factory. She discussed the finer points with their production staff, and then ordered what suited her best.

'I've decided,' Laura told Tom, 'on a two-tier system.' Since the war, less than half the production lines at Burdon's had been in use. 'I'll start modernising the idle ones. Those working will continue making what they are now. It will occupy the work force and bring income. I'll make cream crackers and water biscuits on the new lines.'

'Why?' Elin asked. 'There's plenty of those in the shops already.'

'They've all got the wartime taste, even though no scarce ingredients are needed. I'll use a pre-war recipe and put them in packets. I'll have high bake and light bake. Mine will be luxury crackers.'

'But they'll still need marge or cheese to go with them,' Elin objected. 'No good on their own.'

'Soon,' Laura said, 'there'll be plenty of everything in the shops. I have to be ready to change with the market.

I'd love to start making all-butter shortbread, but it would be a nightmare trying to get supplies of butter.'

At last the day came when her solicitor telephoned to say she could complete the sale. The documents were ready for her to sign. Nothing in her life had ever given her such a thrill as walking through the office to the factory knowing she owned it all.

'Let me come in with you,' Elin said. 'I've heard so much about Burdon's, but I've never been inside.'

The fragrant scent of baking came from ovens which were almost new. Laura counted herself lucky Anthony had replaced the old ones when he'd first taken over. The bakers were mixing the next batch of dough in huge vats. Further down the line it was being rolled out and stamped into circles by a machine that had been in use since 1904. In the packing department, an earlier baking, spread on trays, clanked along on ancient rollers to be packed by hand into twenty-pound tins. Behind Laura, Elin trod carefully on the greasy floor, her hands clasping her golden hair against her ears to shut out the noise. Untidy mounds of tins took up a huge area of space. They had to be collected from the shops and re-used. Men scurried about, moving trolleys piled with more tins. Laura led her mother away to the quiet of the boardroom.

The first thing she noticed was Joshua Burdon staring down at her from his place over the marble mantelpiece. The sight of him almost floored her.

'You've got a replacement Denton Hope.' Elin's gold eyes marvelled. 'We seem to pick them up easily.'

'Not this one.' Laura had paid for the fixtures and fittings but the price had not included another Sir Henry Denton Hope.

She counted herself lucky to have found some Victorian furniture in a secondhand shop. New office furniture was not being made yet, and domestic furniture was on coupons. Elin flopped into an armchair which Laura thought would be elegant when she'd had it re-upholstered.

Laura swivelled in her chair behind the vast mahogany desk, staring up at the picture, appalled at Anthony's lack of financial acumen. He'd taken his Chippendale desk as expected, but left Joshua Burdon.

She lifted the phone and asked the operator to connect her with old Mr Burdon.

'I'm bringing your picture straight over,' she said. 'I'm getting a taxi.'

Mr Burdon, now a fragile, silvery-haired old man, had a large house in Noctorum.

'Joshua Burdon will look very well in your hall,' Elin told him. He insisted they have a glass of Madeira while his gardener was brought in to hang the painting.

Laura had the taxi drop her at Hamilton Square Station, before taking her mother home. She took the underground back to the factory, eager to get down to work.

Laura knew she had a firm hand on costs. Thrift had been second nature to her since she was a child. She would aim for a good turnover and keep expenses low. She didn't find it difficult to spend nine or ten hours a day working. For her it was an all-absorbing task to get every detail slotted into the right place.

When biscuits were de-rationed, she knew she couldn't have chosen a better time. The British public had been starved of luxury biscuits since the beginning of the war. Demand was huge. The market bottomless. The packets disappeared off shop shelves as fast as they could be put out. Within six months the profits had tripled, and Laura knew she was on a winner.

'Good,' Elin said. 'You can spend more time at home now and relax.'

But Laura didn't want to relax. She was happier at work than at home, her ambition was not yet satisfied.

She had an extension built on the factory, and laid down several more production lines. She started making her butter shortbread, and it was an immediate success. She improved the recipes for her ginger nuts and digestives and switched them to the new lines. Three months later she added a new almond biscuit. These too hit the market at the right moment.

A piece of land adjoining her factory came up for sale. She bought it as a yard for her fleet of delivery vans, and had a better loading bay constructed. It would make her business more efficient.

She gave a lot of thought to her growing work force. When she took over the business, she had known most of the people working there. She knew those she should keep, and those she wanted out. She knew she had a unique advantage in that they remembered her as a fellow employee. She encouraged them to tell her their problems.

As she prospered, she improved wage rates, paying a little more than other factories. She installed a system for relaying music to the production floor, and improved the canteen and cloakrooms. She wanted Burdon's to be a good place to work. She had no staff disputes and no strikes.

After arriving home very late one night because there had been an accident on the underground, she flopped into Percy's old chair and said: 'I'd like a car, Tom, I can afford it now.'

'You'll have to put your name on a waiting list for a new one,' he told her, but within a few weeks he'd found a pre-war Alvis for sale, and recommended she buy it to learn on. 'I'll teach you to drive.'

'Lovely.' But after the first attempt she arranged for professional lessons too. 'It's harder than I thought,' she said grimly.

Tom laughed. 'Only average aptitude for driving, Laurie? At last something you aren't going to master in half the time everyone else takes.'

'I'm going to do it, though,' she said.

'Of course you'll do it.'

'It's this old car.'

'It's a bit heavy. If you can drive this, you'll drive anything.'

Whenever it was possible, she drove to work with Tom beside her. He would then run down to the docks for the Irish ferry. If Tom were not back in time, then a foreman in the packing department who lived close by was more than happy to have the lift home. She passed her test, bought herself one of the new Morris Minors and gave the old Alvis to Tom. She found it saved time to travel to work by car.

At the end of the second year, she appointed a personnel manager and delegated responsibility for the staff to him. By the end of the third year, she felt she'd developed Burdon's to its full capacity. She appointed Gerald Kimber as General Manager, and a good team to help him run it. It was producing more profit than she'd ever dared hope. She said as much as they were finishing tea one evening.

'You mean we can live in comfort on Burdon's for the rest of our lives?' Elin said, her voice thick with satisfaction.

'You're not living in comfort,' Tom said. 'You're earning all this money, Laurie, and you're still in Jubilee Street, living exactly as you always have.'

Laura looked down at her plate with the herring bones laid out along the rim, and knew he was right.

'I've got the car,' she said defensively.

'And we've got television,' Elin supported. She'd been proud to be the first in the street to have it.

'But Elin still makes your clothes.'

'I like sewing for Laurie. You know I do.'

Laurie smoothed down her blue wool dress. It was very like the dress she'd been married in five years ago. Mam had used that as a pattern when it grew shabby, but she'd cut the skirt longer to give it the new look. Her dressmaking was improving, and Laura told her it saved her the bother of shopping for clothes.

'You're right, Tom,' she admitted. 'I've been thinking about it. I've decided to buy this house.'

'You want to stay here?' Tom asked in amazement. His parents had sold their newsagent's business and moved out to Bebington. He thought Laura should do the same.

'For a little longer. You see, my talent lies in interpreting a company's balance sheet and getting every detail right to maximise profits. I'm feeling a real itch to do it all over again. I'll need my capital.'

Tom's brown eyes stared into hers. 'Your ambition isn't slaked at all?'

'No.'

'But you've got more money than you know what to do with,' Elin said. 'Why start all over again?'

'It's not work to me, more an indulgence. I'll be spending my time doing what I want.' Her mother's golden eyes looked into hers, not understanding. 'I thought we could do something with the scullery,' Laura went on. 'Get rid of the corrugated iron roof. Have a proper extension with a bathroom above.'

'A real bathroom here?' Elin asked.

'Yes.'

'You'd have to knock through from the back bedroom,' Tom frowned, running his fingers through his hair so it stood up in a red halo round his thin face.

'But we wouldn't have to go across the yard when it's raining.'

'You'd still be sharing a bed with Elin.'

'I don't mind that. We'd be walking backwards and forwards past yours.'

'You already do. Makes me feel one of the family,' he laughed with her.

'And I thought a new grate. One that would heat the water.'

'You can run a few radiators from the modern ones. Make the place really cosy.'

'Could you find a builder to do it, Tom?'

'Yes, I'll look around.'

'How much are you paying for this house?' Elin wanted to know.

'Seven hundred and fifty pounds.'

'Good Lord! Percy could have bought it for two hundred and ten.'

'He couldn't now.'

'And we'd have paid no rent! Think of the rent all these years.'

'Money is easier to come by now, Mam.'

'Easier to get rid of, too.'

'There'll be less upheaval this way,' Laura said. 'And I'll be able to think of other things. Thank you, Tom.'

She got up to clear the table, thinking of Tom. He was like one of the family, yet he made her uneasy. He clung too closely, achieving little for himself. Mam said she did too much for him, but he did a lot for her too. She thought of him with warmth, a close friend.

She began looking for another business in earnest. She considered a company making dog biscuits and dog meal, and then decided against it. The vendors had squeezed most of the potential from it already. She couldn't see how to develop it much further.

Then she heard Quick's Cakes was for sale. Quick's had built up its reputation on seed cake in the thirties, but seed cake was no longer popular. The company was plodding along making cup cakes and swiss rolls. It needed new recipes, new machinery and new packaging. There was room for expansion on the same site and it was only half a mile from Burdon's. Better still, the products were sold through the same outlets. Laura started to study the cakes on sale in Liverpool's grocery shops. The shops themselves were growing bigger, and some specialised in the top end of the trade. Burdon's products were already in them.

For the first time she would have to borrow money. That made her think again about waiting. She could almost pay the asking price, but she'd need to invest large sums to modernise and expand. She did her sums carefully, and then signed up for a loan, knowing she could finance Quick's on the profit from Burdon's.

She sent the office boy out to buy cakes, and every evening she brought home a different brand to taste.

'Mam, what do you think of this?'

'Dry, too much baking soda.'

'Tastes sharp and artificial,' Tom said.

'Cakes should be made with real eggs and butter.'

'I don't know about butter.' Laura munched thoughtfully. Some foods were still in short supply.

'You can't make quality cakes without it,' Elin told her.

'I'll have to use edible oils and margarines, but perhaps one day . . .'

After a lot of thought, Laura decided to keep on the cup cakes and swiss rolls, because the lines were functioning efficiently. She increased the fat and egg content of all the cakes, and cut down on raising agents. She increased the amount of chocolate and butter cream in the decorations. She added more jam to the swiss rolls and made them bigger. She started a sell-by date system, and designed new airtight packaging to keep them fresh. She made all-butter luxury Christmas cakes.

Within two years, Quick's was making excellent profits and the money she'd borrowed had been paid back. She'd modernised the plant, hired extra staff and it was running without day-to-day supervision from her. She hadn't done all she wanted to with Quick's. She was considering several new expensive cakes, but she needed more floor space to put in the lines.

She knew her factories were in the right place. Flour was milled in Birkenhead, sugar and cocoa refined in Liverpool. Edible oils, cocoa and peanuts were imported direct from Africa. Food was what everybody wanted in abundance, and Laura aimed to provide it at its best. She was in the right trade.

She heard of another business down on its luck and went to see it. Morton's Meats cooked, sliced and packaged ham and luncheon meat. The thought of expanding into savoury products excited her. The price asked was cheap. The buildings were old, and had not been designed for their present purpose. The packing room had once been a chapel. The factory fronted onto Keel Street; only this morning she'd heard it was to be widened and upgraded to link in with the proposed new motorway system. Road and rail links with the rest of the country were excellent, but the site was already cramped, and she'd lose another fifteen feet when the road was widened. She knew the big drawback would be lack of space to expand.

At Quick's Cakes she'd thought she had plenty of space until she'd started. It had limited her possibilities. At Morton's Meats the problem was more acute. Apart from that she liked what she saw. She was tingling at the thought of a new challenge, but the need for more space was paramount.

As she went slowly down the worn front steps into Keel Street, Laura wondered if she could buy adjoining land.

Morton's Meats was on a corner, a side street prevented expansion in that direction. On the other was a shabby public house, with dark brown tiles to first-floor height and windows still boarded up. She put her head round the door; it smelled of sour beer. Comfortless and dark, there was only one customer. The place would have to come down for road widening. It didn't look worth redeveloping. Perhaps she could tempt the owner to sell.

Beyond it was a bomb site only partly cleared. She walked over the hard-packed earth with broken bricks and rubbish sticking up. The end wall of a terrace of houses still stood, showing peeling wallpaper and an iron grate at bedroom level. Pink blooms of rosebay willow herb flourished in the downstairs rooms. There were patches of nettles and docks, a pile of twisting rusty metal and a rotting mattress.

Behind Morton's Meats and all this was another business for sale. She'd seen it advertised by the firm of commercial estate agents she used. It occupied a huge site and manufactured brake linings for the motor trade. Unfortunately it was not her line of business and too expensive to alter to her purpose. She couldn't expand in that direction.

Laura paced out the space, dust and grit pushing through her open-toed sandals. There were the crumbling remains of what had been a cinema, beyond that a garage, more houses, a row of shops. About eight hundred yards in this direction.

She stopped to consider, the July sun warm on her face. This was a crumbling inner city area. A fair market price would not be all that expensive. It was derelict waste land. Eight years since the end of the war, and its owners had done nothing with it. It was not providing income. Surely they'd want to sell? She should be able to get all the space she could use.

Laura retraced her steps to her car. She didn't think anybody else was interested in Morton's Meats. She would put in an offer dependent on getting the freehold of enough land to expand.

When she spoke to her solicitor about it, he thought tracking down the freeholders might be a bigger problem than persuading them to sell.

Laura knew she was in luck when it was discovered the two streets of houses and some of the shops belonged to one landlord. He'd died during the war, and they'd passed to his wife, an old lady now in her eighties who had no plans to redevelop the site. Laura offered her the price her estate agent had put on it, and she was glad to accept and be rid of the encumbrance.

Laura also managed to buy the freehold of the pub and the cinema site. The owners of the garage, however, had decided to rebuild now that the road was to be upgraded. It would be busier and bring more trade. It took a large bite out of the road frontage, but she'd still have more than enough space for her purpose.

Laura went to her solicitor to sign for Morton's Meats feeling pleased with her bargain. She liked the idea of making savoury products as well as sweet. She wanted to make scotch eggs, and possibly products needing pastry, meat pies and quiches. She would apply the same principles she'd used at Burdon's and Quick's. It ought to be easier, now she'd done it twice already.

Everything began to fall in place. Laura kept Morton's Meats going, trimming the overheads, while she designed an entirely new factory to be built behind the existing buildings. She had two years' grace before the road widening, and then of course there would be compensation for the loss of her fifteen feet.

In January, old Mr Burdon died. He was eighty-four. Laura took Elin to his funeral, and tried not to be saddened at his death. He'd had a good life and a long one. She owed him a great deal and would always be grateful. She found he had left her the picture of Joshua Burdon in his will. Laura hung it where it had hung before, over the marble fireplace in the boardroom at Burdon's.

Tom left his job on the Irish boats, and found another on the Wallasey ferries. He didn't care much for it, and after a few months threw that over too. Laura suggested he help Gerald Kimber in the biscuit factory.

The day he started, Laura decided the time had come to

buy another house. She didn't talk about the capital she'd built up, or her income, but she always knew exactly what she was worth. She knew she could afford a superb house, and she had the time and energy to look for it now.

By the early fifties, Liverpool had recovered from the war years and was growing prosperous. Elegant homes were being built in the smarter suburbs. The smartest suburb on the Wirral was Caldy, but the Oxleys lived there and she didn't want to be near them.

Tom went round the local estate agents for her and brought back details of any houses he thought might suit. Then in the evenings or at the weekend they would inspect the ones Laura thought most hopeful. Sometimes they all went, sometimes just she and Elin.

After months of searching, she had still failed to find a house that pleased her. The most common fault was that they were too close to their neighbours. Always, Laura felt disappointed. What she was looking for didn't seem to be on the market.

They had spent the best part of Saturday afternoon inspecting two houses in Heswall, both of which Laura had decided against. On the way to Hoylake, she directed Tom down a lane leading to Thurstaston shore. She'd picked up details of a farm for sale down there.

'I could sell off some of the land,' she said, 'if the house is right.' She was beginning to feel depressed by her lack of success.

'Humph,' Elin snorted. 'I liked the last one we saw in Heswall. The sitting room—'

'I want a bigger garden,' Laura said. 'Big enough to provide privacy. I'd like a swimming pool, or space to build one.'

'Who's going to take care of all that?' Elin demanded.

'We'll have a gardener. We can afford it now.'

'Gracious!'

Tom was slowing down. 'We should be able to see the farm . . . There it is, two hundred acres of good farm land.'

Laura's eyes followed his pointing finger. She sighed with disappointment at the white stucco house built just before the war. 'It's too modern, too brash. Not even worth looking inside.'

'It might be,' Tom said. 'The position is right.'

'I like the fields all round,' Laura conceded. 'There'll be a view of the river. Plenty of privacy, and more than enough land.'

'Mostly a big garden means a big house,' Tom said, 'but here . . .'

'I thought you wanted a big house,' Elin said.

'Not something with ten bedrooms and attics above that. Not just for the two of us.'

The moment the words were out of her mouth, Laura was aware of their effect on Tom. The estate agent's particulars fluttered to the car floor. He was motionless, staring out across the river.

She wanted to kick herself. She'd meant to talk it over with him. Point out his need to stand on his own feet, be independent. After all, their marriage had been annulled for five years, and he was still living with them.

'Tom, I'd like you to have the Jubilee Street house when we move out. It would give you your own base.'

There was an awkward pause. 'I'll rent it from you,' he choked.

Laura pushed her honey-blonde hair back from her brow. What a fool she'd been to blurt it out like that. What a thoughtless, clumsy fool.

Even Mam looked aghast. 'You'll come to dinner often. We've got used to each other. You're almost like family.'

'I thought I was family,' Tom said unhappily.

Laura sighed. Tom could still sting her. If only he'd been like other men. Even now she wasn't over him. She couldn't help asking, 'Do you want to come with us? I meant to talk it over.'

He didn't answer.

'Think about it,' she said.

CHAPTER NINETEEN

Laura felt the silence crushing down on her. It was broken by a squeak as Elin wound down the back window of the car.

'If you want your dream house, you'll have to build it.' Tom ruffled his red hair, he looked fraught. She knew he was struggling for self-control.

'I have thought of it. Building plots are hard to get and they're usually measured in feet. I saw one of an acre a couple of months ago, but it was narrow, so the house would end up close to its neighbours.' She was talking to give Tom time to recover.

'Over there,' he pointed, scooping the particulars up from the floor. 'There's the original farmhouse. It says it burned down in nineteen thirty-six.'

Laura got out for a closer look. 'The facade's old sandstone.'

'The shell is intact.' Tom was towering over her. 'Lovely old walls round it, even the gateposts, and all sandstone.'

'Remnants of the drive, and planning permission too.' The new house had been built closer to the road, and didn't obstruct the river view.

'A modest-sized house,' Laura pondered, 'but with big rooms. A sitting room, dining room and kitchen. We'll each have our own bathroom, Mam, and I want my own little sitting room or office.'

'A suite,' Tom said, 'with a dressing room.'

'Yes, and the same for Mam.'

'Who's going to look after it all? Keep it clean?'

'We'll get a housekeeper, perhaps a couple to live in. And we'll need good guest accommodation, of course.'

'It might be possible,' Tom nodded. 'Come on, the owners are expecting us.'

Laura felt a surge of excitement the moment she stood within the ruined walls. This was what she'd been looking for. She was laughing, only the nettles stopped her pacing out where the kitchen would go. She could see the ground floor in her mind's eye, all reconstructed, just as she wanted it. She described it to them, feeling uplifted, euphoric. Elin laughed with her, and even Tom seemed to catch her mood and cheer up.

The modern four-bedroomed farmhouse was not to her liking, but it was roomy by Jubilee Street standards, and would allow them to move there as soon as it was legally hers.

Laura was fascinated by the farm, it was after all another business, and she would make it pay its way. Since her mother had been brought up in the Welsh countryside, farming ought to be in her blood and Laura hoped it would interest her too. She ordered books on farming, read them herself and recommended them to Elin. She talked cows and milk yields to her, and tried to involve her in buying and building up the herd of Hereford milkers. Laura bought a flock of Suffolk Down sheep, and ordered some hens, since her mother had spoken of looking after them when she was young.

But once the summer weather slid into autumn rain, Elin didn't want to go near a field or milking parlour. It was Laura who arranged for the milk to be sold to the Birkenhead dairies; the monthly cheque alone was sufficient to support life at a comfortable level. She found a farm manager. He and his family would be able to move into the farmhouse eventually.

She tried to involve her mother with the architects and builders when rebuilding the old house got under way, but Elin had no interest in moving again. She said why bother to build anything bigger? The farmhouse was more than big enough. She was lost in so much space, especially as Tom hadn't come with them. Laura worried because she was listless. She tried to interest her in furnishing and redecorating the farmhouse, hoping that having something definite to do would be good for her. They chose paint and paper and got decorators in. Together they visited the shops and sale rooms. She tried to push her mother to make the choices, but it wasn't easy. Elin spoke of missing Tom's company, of being lonely without the Jubilee Street neighbours to pass the time of day.

Slowly, over many months, the roof went on the old sandstone shell. The interior was taking shape, but Elin was sliding downhill. She wouldn't even spend money. She began buying remnants again in Birkenhead market and running up dresses for Laura and herself on her ancient sewing machine. Laura had to take her to the shops, make her try on clothes and then convince her they were easily affordable.

Laura was sitting at her Victorian mahogany desk in Burdon's, worrying about this, when the phone rang.

'John Taylor here.'

Laura recognised the deep voice of her solicitor.

'We've received an offer from Dufton and Jones acting on behalf of Oxley's. They've bought a factory making brake linings situated behind Morton's. It fronts onto Foxton Street, but that's narrow and there's to be a one-way traffic system. They want access to Keel Street too. They're offering double the price you paid for a corridor of about thirty feet.'

Laura felt nervous excitement fork through her. She'd always been conscious of Oxley Enterprises operating businesses around her, but this was the first time they'd contacted her. Her fountain pen trembled slightly in her fingers.

'No,' she said coldly. What had Laurence Oxley ever done for her?

'Since you failed to get the garage,' John Taylor went on, 'the cinema site beyond is of less use to you.'

'Tell them I'm not interested,' Laura said. It made her feel good to have something Laurence Oxley wanted. Her refusal was instantaneous, a decision made from the heart without consideration. She didn't normally function like this. 'I haven't decided what to do with it yet, but I don't want to sell.' Usually she was very careful to think everything through. She knew that had it been anyone but Oxley's she would have considered taking the capital appreciation.

Two days later, John Taylor rang again to say Oxley's had offered treble the price she'd paid for the land.

'No deal,' she said again. She didn't want to give Laurence Oxley what he wanted. When she and Mam were desperate for help, he hadn't lifted a finger.

A week after they moved into the new house, Elin seemed really ill, complaining of a sore throat. Laura called in their new general practitioner, a doctor used to dealing with affluent patients.

When Laura was showing him out he said: 'Your mother has 'flu. She'll be poorly for a few days, keep her warm in bed. Aspirin, there's not much else.' He paused. 'I'm more worried about her state of mind, her underlying depression. I really feel you should persuade her to have treatment.'

'There's no problem about persuading her,' Laura said. 'It's finding something to help. Nothing does her much good, she's tried almost everything.'

'But not psychotherapy. I'm sure that's the answer.'

Laura froze.

'She could talk her problems out to a trained therapist. Over several sessions he would identify and help her face them.'

Laura felt cold shivers run down her spine. Mam didn't need professional help to identify her problem. If Percy had really been killed by a bomb, Mam would be a different person today. She couldn't get over killing him. She certainly couldn't talk about it to anyone else.

'She seems to think there's a stigma attached to mental illness,' the doctor said. 'She's refused psychotherapy, but it might help.'

Laura swallowed. 'I wouldn't want to force her against her wishes.'

'There's no question of forcing. She would have to co-operate. Talk openly. It would be a waste of time otherwise.'

Laura opened the front door for him, wanting him gone.

'Mental illness is illness, as much as 'flu,' he went on earnestly. 'It responds to treatment in the same way.'

'Yes,' Laura said. After living close to Tom, she knew all that. 'But it's my mother's decision.'

'I wish you'd try and persuade her. There really is no stigma these days.'

Laura leaned against the door when she got it closed behind him, taking deep breaths to steady herself. Better let him think they were both too stupid to admit Mam's problems were in her mind.

She went slowly back to the bedroom. Mam's eyes were closed, her hair spread out like a halo across her pillows. Once it had been much brighter, real sun-gold, now it was fading. Laura could see silver threading through it. The lines were deepening on her forehead, she looked ill. Her slanting gold eyes flickered open nervously. Once she must have been very beautiful.

'Did I do right?'

'Yes.' Laura sat on the bed and felt for her hand. That was workworn, too.

'This psycho thing . . .'

'Psychotherapy.'

'It terrifies me. I can't admit . . . Not after all this time.'

'You don't have to, Mam.' It wouldn't do her any good, to confess she'd committed murder, even if doctors were like priests and unable to tell. 'We'll work it out between us. Do you want to talk about it?'

Elin turned her face into the pillow. 'What is there to talk about? I want to forget.'

Laura squeezed her hand, unable to put into words what she felt for her.

'I'm useless,' Elin said, her voice muffled by the pillow.

'That's not true.'

'What have I ever done? Look at you.'

'I couldn't have managed it without you. Without your help and support.' She saw her mother's head shake hopelessly. 'I find it hard to believe you were only seventeen when you had me.'

Elin stared up at the ceiling.

'It must have been very hard for you. I always felt you loved and wanted me. Valued me. You gave me a core of security.' She could see Mam's eyes clouding with tears.

'Security? Living with Percy? We were on a knife edge the whole time.'

'Inner security. You gave me that.' She changed the subject.

'Do you like living here?'

'It's a lovely house,' Elin said. But she'd been better in Jubilee Street. She'd even managed to live with the shell cases on the mantelpiece and Percy's leather armchair.

Laura felt her conscience prick. She'd brought her mother to live in a house that fulfilled her own ambitions. She'd given no thought to Mam's needs, believing them to be the same as her own. She'd taken her for granted over the last five years, believing time alone would heal.

'I wish I could make things easier for you. Is there nothing that would help?'

'Nothing.' Elin was staring at her helplessly. Laura squeezed her hand again, it was the only comfort she could offer.

Although she counted herself a success in business, on a personal level her life was a mess. She'd neglected her mother. She was finding her relationship with Tom more and more difficult. Living close to him set up all sorts of frustrations; living apart was not the answer either. She saw him during the day at Burdon's. He wasn't settling down, or showing much interest in the job. She was failing both of them.

She must let her business interests ride for a while. Devote more time to her mother. Mam was locked away from all professional help by the manner of Percy's death. Any help would have to come from her. She would have to think of something.

The traffic snarl-up in the Mersey tunnel had made Laura fifteen minutes late. Knowing her mother was filled with needless anxieties, she always phoned her if she expected to be late. That she hadn't today would cause a thousand disasters to crowd Elin's mind.

Laura could see her home now. A beautiful building of eighteenth-century sandstone nestling against a gentle hill. In front, open fields swept down to the Dee estuary. She drove faster, wanting to put Elin out of her torment.

She swung the car through the wrought-iron gates and pulled up outside the front door. Through the sitting room windows, she could see her mother pacing, her shoulders tight with tension. She hadn't heard the car.

Laura's feet tapped across the parquet floor of the hall.

'Mam?' Laura hugged her, feeling the thin bony shoulders. Elin's gold eyes poured out relief.

'Thank God! What would I do if anything happened to you?' When Elin was flustered, her Welsh accent was stronger.

'Nothing's going to happen,' Laura comforted with another hug. 'Happy Birthday, Mam.'

'Thank you.' A nerve twitched in her cheek.

'The new outfit looks good.' Last week, Laura had taken her to George Henry Lee's to choose it. The long skirt in softest maroon wool was slim and elegant. The jacket had a black grosgrain collar. 'The colour suits you.'

Another thought hammered inside Laura's head. Only forty-five, and already Liverpool's beauty salons could do nothing about her mother's deep worry lines. She looked much oider than her age. Laura had to gulp down her sadness.

'I'll go and change. Five minutes.'

She ran up the wide sweeping staircase. The house never failed to give her a surge of pleasure. She had commissioned a foremost Liverpool architect to design it, but the ideas were largely her own. It was built on two floors; she had her own suite upstairs. She went through the bedroom, which she'd furnished in soft greys and pinks, to her dressing room which had wardrobes all round, and took out a grey silk Chanel suit she'd bought specially for this occasion. Off the dressing room was her bathroom in grey marble, with gold taps. She'd installed every luxury she could think of. She also had a sitting room which doubled as an office. It was cosy in winter, with stunning views over the estuary and out to the Irish Sea.

She washed and changed. She'd grown her hair till it was a thick honey mane swinging round her shoulders. She redressed it into the French pleat she usually wore when working, and hurried down again. On the ground floor were the entertaining rooms they both used, dining room, sitting room and library. Elin had her own suite there too.

'Ready?'

Elin jerked round from the window, upsetting a cup of coffee she hadn't drunk. The house was too big for her to manage. She'd been worried about keeping it clean even before they moved in. Laura had employed an Irish couple to look after them. Now she rang for Oona to come and clean up the mess.

Laura had taken the afternoon off to give her mother a birthday treat, booking seats for a matinée at the Royal Court Theatre. James Stewart in his new play *Harvey* was touring the provinces before opening in the West End. Afterwards, she planned to take Elin to the Adelphi, the best hotel in Liverpool, for champagne and dinner.

She'd invited Tom to come with them. She was getting worried about him, she hadn't seen him for ten days. He'd thrown over his job at Burdon's without any explanation. Gerald Kimber told her he was drinking more than was good for him. It seemed he couldn't settle to anything.

'Has Tom not arrived?'

'No. Does he expect us to pick him up on the way?'

'The arrangement was he'd come here.' Laura felt a surge of dismay. Tom was no longer reliable. She hoped he wasn't heading for another depression. 'Let's go,' she said, 'we don't want to miss the beginning.' She took mother's arm and led her out to the car.

In the darkness of the theatre, she heard Elin's chuckle. So her birthday treat hadn't been spoiled. Laura tried to relax, but she was concerned about Tom. He'd seemed pleased when she'd invited him. She'd left his ticket at the box office, but was afraid he wouldn't come now. She wished she knew what he got up to all day by himself.

Thinking about Tom brought on a gnawing ache. She had thought that once their marriage was annulled he'd go, and she could forget him. But he was clinging to her, her fate and his seemed bound up together. He had nobody else to lean on, and the years had proved beyond doubt Tom needed friends.

He said he didn't like living alone in Jubilee Street, that he felt cast off, excluded. She felt she was losing patience with him. She wanted him to cope on his own, settle into a job and be independent, but with Elin the way she was, she'd made up her mind to invite him to live with them again. Laura sighed, wishing she was better at handling people, but this wasn't the moment to worry about Tom. She made herself concentrate on James Stewart.

It was a fine evening, already dark, when the show ended and the audience spilled out into Williamson Square.

'Shall we walk to stretch our legs?' Laura had parked her car near the Adelphi. It wasn't far.

'Perhaps a taxi?' Elin hung back.

'Of course, it's your day.' Laura wondered if a spa would help Mam. She needed building up, a good diet, more exercise, and most of all a break from her. They all needed to be more independent.

Moments later they were getting out and the front door of the Adelphi was being opened by the doorman. Laura, leading the way into the lounge, was thinking how comfortable it looked. She jerked to a sudden stop.

'Tom!'

'Kept a table for you.' Sheepishly he rose to his full height. With flaming hair and bushy beard to match, he drew every eye. His presence dominated the room. 'I've ordered champagne.' An unopened bottle was cooling in a silver bucket. 'Happy birthday, Elin.' He produced a gift-wrapped package. 'Chocolates, not terribly original I'm afraid.'

'Thank you.' Elin sank into a chair. 'You know I love them.'

'I'd given you up,' Laura said.

'Sorry I missed the play.' He was wearing the grey pin-striped suit she'd persuaded him to buy. He pushed away the glass that had held pink gin and signalled the barman to open the champagne.

'Was it good?'

'Excellent,' Laura said sharply, but she mustn't make a fuss, not now. It would only upset Mam, and ruin the whole evening. The champagne bubbled into the glasses. 'We enjoyed it. To you, Mam.'

'To Elin.' Tom raised his glass and drank. 'We're all agreed on that, but I want you to drink to me too.'

Laura crashed her glass down onto the table. Drink to Tom? He should be apologising. 'Any special reason?'

His smile was tight.

'Let me guess. You got here. Remembered Mam's birthday. Congratulations.'

'For God's sake, Laura! Stop needling me.'

She gulped at her champagne, afraid she'd gone too far.

'I've got a job,' Tom said quietly. 'Let's drink to that.'

'A job?' She felt her interest quicken. She hadn't had a chance to talk to him about walking out of Burdon's. He'd telephoned her at work, said he'd had enough of biscuits and put the phone down. When she'd tried to ring him back, he hadn't answered. She'd have lost her temper with him if he had.

'It's what you keep telling me I need. So I've done it.'

'Good. A shore job?'

The auburn beard went slowly from side to side.

'Seagoing then?'

'Sort of. I'll be based in Lagos.'

'Lagos? How often will we see you?'

'It's an eighteen-month tour. Then I'll have three months at home.'

'Eighteen months?' Laura had a sinking feeling in her stomach. He'd find it hard, so far away on his own. Why did she always feel responsible for him? If he could do it, it would be marvellous.

'Will you come with me? There's a house provided.'

She was so shocked, she could hardly get the words out.

'I couldn't, Tom! What about my business? The farm? I have to be here.'

'I know, but you could take a few weeks off. You're a sort of anchor to me, Laurie. I'm getting cold feet, I don't know whether I can cut myself off from you.'

'Of course you can,' she said, sounding full of certainty. But that was to bolster Tom.

'Once you'd have given anything to see Lagos. Remember?'

'When I was a child.'

'Remember that essay?' Tom knew how to harness her nostalgia.

'I expect they'll pay well, if you go there.' Elin twirled her glass on its stem.

'Yes,' Tom said.

'About as much as I paid you to manage the biscuit factory,' Laura retorted.

'I hated going there every day. And I didn't manage it. You and your Gerald Kimber were looking over my shoulder the whole time.'

'I wanted you to learn. Gerald has had twenty years' experience, you—'

'I know, but I can't work up any enthusiasm for biscuits.'

Laura swallowed, wishing she'd been able to help Tom more. Perhaps she hadn't tried enough. She certainly couldn't say she'd succeeded. It was more than eight years since they'd been married, he was draining her of hope.

'You'd have made a good sales manager. You do know about selling. After all you used to help your father.'

'That isn't my sort of a job, Laurie, and you know it. I have to feel the rise and fall of a ship beneath my feet.'

Laura drained her glass. The trouble was Tom was not flexible enough to change. To keep a job, if he could, might bring back self-respect.

'Another bottle of champagne?' he suggested.

'Let's have dinner.' Laura got up hastily. 'We'll have another bottle with it. You've accepted?'

'I've signed a contract for three years. Come with me, Laura. I need help to make a fresh start.'

'I'll have to think.'

'Just say you'll come. Damn it, you never take a holiday. It would do you good.'

The dining room was half empty because they were early. That didn't matter; preventing Tom drinking too much did, stopping the bickering did. It wasn't turning out much of a treat for Mam.

Laura was forking roast beef into her mouth without enjoyment when she noticed the couple at a nearby table. She felt her stomach muscles contract with a burst of anxiety.

'Who is that?' Elin had been watching too, the lamb cutlet growing cold on her plate.

'Mary Oxley,' Laura mouthed. 'With her cousin.'

Yes, it was her, though Laura had had to look twice. Time had soured her. Deep lines of discontent had carved furrows from nose to mouth, and her lips had a peevish twist. Her hair was still ash-blonde and fluffy, but much shorter. The new style looked untidy, it didn't suit her.

Laura had recognised Robert Oxley immediately. Once she'd thought him a slip of a boy in comparison with Tom. In maturity, his shoulders had broadened, his colouring seemed darker, his face deeply tanned. He was a wonderfully handsome man. The years fell away. The last time Laura had seen them together, Mary had been throwing her arms round his neck, a laughing, loving teenager.

A quarrelsome haze seemed to hang over their table. Mary was asking, even pleading, for something. Robert implacably ate roast beef and refused her. Their voices were low, but the tone unmistakable. A silver-headed cane lay across an empty chair. Mary fingered it, as though she'd love to belay it across his shoulders. Her mouth was twisting with frustration. Once Laura had thought Mary beautiful, but not any longer.

She couldn't help but see Mam's dinner was forgotten, and her hand shaking.

'Take no notice,' she advised. 'They won't recognise us. Mary is engrossed in her own problems.' But Laura found it equally impossible to drag her eyes away. She wondered what they were fighting about.

She'd searched the press for information about the Oxleys, but what she'd found all related to their businesses. Their private lives had been kept very private indeed since Jane's accident. She felt again the numbness in the pit of her stomach she'd had when she'd read about it in the *Birkenhead News*. Time didn't alter that.

Laura sighed, the birthday treat was turning sour.

Laura dropped Tom in Birkenhead, where he'd left his car. He'd gone down to London by train for the interview, and come straight into Liverpool afterwards.

'It brings it all back, to see Mary,' Elin said quietly.

'But Mary was a child of four. Now she's a grown woman. How can she remind you?'

'She belongs to him. She's close to him.'

'Put it out of your mind. It was all so long ago.'

'I've tried. Believe me, I've tried, but I can't get the Oxleys out of my mind. They haunt me.'

Laura was silent.

'Laurence has had his bad times too. First Jane, and now Mary. She's obviously unhappy, things can't be going her way. He won't enjoy seeing her like that.'

Laura was surprised Mam could think of Laurence's lot with sympathy. She'd never been able to talk openly about him. If only she would, it might help.

'Did you love him?' Laura asked. A silly question; of course she had once, and it had left her like a piece of flotsam.

They were leaving the streets of Birkenhead and heading for the country lanes.

'Tell me about him, Mam. It might help.' Laura felt for her mother's hand and squeezed it.

'I don't think I can. Help or not,' she choked. When she spoke again, her tone had changed. 'Tom does remind me of Percy.'

'What?' The car jerked involuntarily to the right. Laura took a firmer grip on the wheel. 'No, Mam, surely not.'

'Yes, I'm serious.'

'In what way?'

'He leans on you, as Percy leaned on me.'
'This job will wean him off. It's too far away.'
'Do you think he'll keep it?'
'I hope so. It's almost his last chance. He's got to get going now if he's ever going to.'
Laura put her car in the garage and went with Elin to the kitchen to put the kettle on. It was a comfortable room where they could cook for themselves if they felt like it. There was a rocking chair and a settle near the Aga, a bookcase full of cookery books, and a little desk. Laura had given Oona the evening off.
'You're changing, Laurie.' Elin's gold eyes were searching her face.
'I'm getting older.' Laura was not sure she wanted to change.
'It's not that, you don't look twenty-eight. You look the success you are. You've gained in confidence, and it shows in your face.'
Laura half smiled. She hadn't expected to grow personally with her business, but she felt she was.
'You're looking more like your father. Sometimes I see power in your green eyes. With that hair style . . .'
'The French pleat? Makes me look more the business woman. More the boss.'
'And more like Laurence Oxley.' Elin kissed her good night, and thanked her before taking the tea to her own room.
Laura took her tea upstairs. She took off the grey silk suit, put it on a hanger, and snuggled into a soft wool dressing gown. With her hair swinging loose on her shoulders, she felt more comfortable. Her eyes stared back at her from the mirror. She could find no sign of power in them.
She sat in her window seat to drink her tea. The tide was in, and the full moon was turning the estuary waters to molten silver. She found it achingly beautiful. Some of her best moments were spent in this room, working at her Hepplewhite desk, giving her attention to the details of her business, making phone calls, solving business problems.

Sometimes she worked through the night, loving the house most when it was quiet.

She was not pleased to see the headlights of a car turn into the drive; she felt ready for bed. It looked like Tom's car, and she wondered why he was coming at this time of night. It took a long time for the bell to ring. Reluctantly she went downstairs, not wanting to face him again. The moment she saw his height curling against the porch, she was filled with foreboding.

'Tom! Come in.'

'I'm a fool . . .' She had to help him over the door step. 'I'm sorry about Burdon's. Throwing it over.'

'It doesn't matter if you've got another job.' She took his arm. 'Let's go upstairs. What's happened?' His limbs seemed locked with tension, she was almost pulling him upstairs.

'I had to come.'

'Of course.' She could smell gin on his breath. It was a bad sign. He always drank too much when he was worried. He collapsed onto a little Victorian chair by her hearth, overflowing the seat.

'You're good to me, Laurie. Always have been. I shouldn't keep pestering you like this.' His voice was agonised. 'I'm getting cold feet. Lagos seems so far.'

'It's right for you to do your own thing,' she tried to reassure.

'I want you to come with me. I can't manage without you.'

'I can't come on board ship with you when you're working. That's the hard part. You'll manage perfectly well at your new home. Look how well you're doing in Jubilee Street.' She turned to the window, and the tranquil silver water.

'I had to tell them I was married.' He took out his handkerchief and blew his nose.

'What?'

'Well, I didn't have to exactly, but they asked. They want married men. A settling influence, they said. Married accommodation is available.'

'We aren't married, Tom. We had it annulled.'

'Sometimes I wish we hadn't. Help me this one last time. Come with me, please.' It shocked her to see tears clouding his eyes. He looked such a big manly man, but she knew he wasn't. She hadn't seen him cry for years. It brought home to her just how stressed he was.

'All right, I'll come, Tom.'

He shambled towards her. 'I'm scared, Laurie, I'm no good at anything. If I don't make it this time I'll be finished.' She saw a tear roll down his cheek, and took out his handkerchief to wipe it away.

'I'll come with you. I've had time to think. You're right. We've never had a holiday. It might help Mam to get away, see something different. But only for six weeks or so, till you settle.'

'Thank you, Laurie, thank you.' His head went down on her shoulder, his tears flowed.

'Hey,' she said, lifting his head away. 'I thought that would cheer you.'

'It does.' He tried to smile. 'Have you got any gin?'

'Come on, Tom, the bed in the guest room is made up. You're in no fit state to drive home.' He swayed a little. Laura took his arm to steady him, and led him across the landing.

His cheeks were flushed. 'I want to work, but I can't let you make jobs for me, and I hate being kept.'

'I know, Tom.'

'In Jubilee Street, people think we've just split up.'

'We managed to keep quiet about the annulment.' She threw open the casement; the shimmering silver reflection from the estuary filled the room with peace. It didn't reach Tom.

'Beattie told me not to be downhearted, you'd be generous. She said I'd made my fortune marrying you, but I hated being left. It made me feel rejected.'

Guilt-stricken, Laura put out an arm to comfort him. 'You know why . . . You know how I feel,' she said. She felt his arms fold round her and stiffened against his touch. 'You've only to pull me close against you like this to start me off.' She couldn't help herself, she was almost sobbing. She wanted to kiss him, to run her fingers through his hair. 'Damn it, Tom, I've never got over you.' She was shaking. 'I can't live close to you without feeling teased.' She felt the tears prickling. 'That's why I want you to have a place of your own. It's not rejection, far from it, I've missed your company. Mam's missed you.'

'You'll come with me?'

'Yes, I've said so, haven't I?'

'I've got to do something on my own, haven't I?'

Laura nodded. 'I should be grateful for your friendship, it's better than nothing. See how readily I admit everything to you.'

'You've never let me down, though what I did to you was terrible. I owe you.'

'Tom, you've done a lot for me too. Despite everything we've been good for each other.'

'But I can't give you what you want.' He paced restlessly to the window. 'Poor Laurie.' His voice changed. 'You need a husband to love you properly. Someone equally successful. A man you can respect.'

Laura sighed. She knew there was a void in her life. 'Where do I find him, Tom?'

He shook his head.

Book Four – 1954
CHAPTER TWENTY

Laurence Oxley found it soothing to stand at his office window in the Liver Building, watching the shipping going about its business. Beneath him, the Birkenhead ferry boat disgorged passengers. They came streaming up from the floating landing stage to join the bustling crowds on the Pier Head.

It was high tide and the stiff breeze was making the brown waters of the Mersey choppy. A tug fussed past towing three lighters, and out against the Birkenhead bank a tanker throbbed upriver to Ellesmere Port.

Three throaty blasts of a ship's siren penetrated the quiet of his office, warning river traffic that Elder Dempster's mail boat, the MV *Accra*, was nosing out of Princes Dock into the river. He craned his head to watch her swing round and head down stream. She was going out on the tide, bound for Lagos. Easy to pick out because of her tropical white livery. Vessels trading in cold waters were painted predominantly black.

He'd been meaning to make another trip to Lagos for weeks. David Mountford had proved he could handle the Lagos end of the business very nicely, and Laurence had got into the habit of leaving it to him. As he was Mary's husband, he felt he could trust him, but neither he nor Mary were there now.

Everything had changed so quickly. He'd felt a vague disquiet for months, yet he kept putting the visit off. He'd go next month before the rainy season set in. He ought to go to see what Jake Lode was making of the job.

He turned away, impatient with himself for wasting time.

If he wanted access to Keel Street for the new brake linings factory, he'd have to do something more about it. He'd left the handling of that to Dufton and Jones. It had seemed at first a routine matter. For the tenth time, he wondered why they'd failed. Usually they were effective. He wouldn't have used them all these years if they weren't. It was only when his second offer was refused that he'd given it much thought.

'Who owns the land?' he'd demanded.

'A woman called Laura Peck bought it quite recently.'

Laura Peck. The name hammered home. Laura Peck. He couldn't get it out of his mind. If it was the same girl, if she knew he was her father, if she was out for revenge, then it would explain it.

He went back to his desk and picked up the document to read yet again. He'd had a dossier put together on Laura Peck. It was something he did from time to time when he was buying into a new business. Sometimes he needed to know the background of the managers or owners to decide whether or not to retain their services.

She was the right age, a chartered accountant, but there was nothing to explain how she'd managed it. Surely she couldn't own Burdon's Biscuits! Not to mention Quick's Cakes as well as Morton's Mighty Meats and that piece of land he wanted so much. Laura Peck. She might just be his daughter. He felt a burning curiosity to find out.

He remembered her at thirteen, the day he'd handed her that essay prize. A too-skinny girl with a hole in her stocking and a shiny seat to her gymslip. He remembered the feelings of guilt she'd aroused. His daughter, yet the deprived background she came from only too noticeable.

It didn't seem possible. She couldn't have left school at fourteen to become a shop assistant and emerge now running a successful business. Not just running, owning. The more he thought about it, the more convinced he became that it couldn't be her. Laura Peck. She was deflecting his mind from more important matters, and probably the name was no more than a coincidence.

He badly wanted access for his new factory. The access he had via Foxton Street meant a half-mile detour through narrow streets before returning to Keel Street and the outlet to the proposed motorway. It was the name Laura Peck that had kept him vacillating. He couldn't get her out of his mind.

He strode to his desk, his mind made up. Picking up the phone he asked his secretary to get Miss Peck at Burdon's Biscuits on the line. It was a disappointment to find she was out.

'I'd like her to spare me ten minutes,' he told her secretary. 'As soon as she comes in. If that isn't convenient, I can come over any time. Can you let me know?' He'd had to put it like that. He wanted to commit himself so he wouldn't be able to put it off again.

Laura Peck. He waited for his call to be returned, more on edge now, watching the seagulls swoop and turn and call as they followed a fishing boat. The Isle of Man boat cast off. If it was her, then he was more than curious. He might as well admit it, he was intrigued. But it wouldn't be. He was churning himself up for nothing, and he really needed that access road.

It had occurred to Laura some time ago that it might help to take her mother to work with her. She would have less time to mope alone, and would meet more people.

Elin said she enjoyed the first few days. Laura began giving her little jobs to fill her time and make her feel useful. But Laura found it harder to concentrate on her own work because half her attention was on her mother.

This morning she'd tried to send her out to buy meat pies. She wanted to sample what was already on the market before settling on the recipe for Morton's to make in the new factory.

'What sort of meat pies?' Elin hovered at the door.

'Go to Cooper's and see what they stock. Buy the most expensive.'

Her mother's golden eyes stared back blankly.

'Wall's make pies, and Bowyer's and Dunmow's.'

'But how many?'

'One of each. You remember what I did with biscuits? We want to see what's available throughout the country. Not what the local baker makes.'

'Yes.' Still she hesitated. 'Couldn't you come with me?'

Laura would have preferred to spend an hour working out the costings on her own, but she'd decided rehabilitating Mam was more important, so she went with her.

It was hot in town and Laura made the mistake of taking her own car instead of ringing for a taxi. She'd not been able to park near Renshaw Street and now they were juggling with paper bags containing sixteen meat pies and having to walk back to the car.

'Why don't we have lunch in town?' Laura suggested, hoping to divert her mother.

'When are we going to eat all these pies?' It was ingrained into Elin that eating out was an extravagance only to be indulged in now and again, when they had something to celebrate.

'We'd better taste them on an empty stomach,' Laura agreed, trying to sound more cheerful than she felt. 'We could underestimate the opposition otherwise.'

'I don't feel very hungry,' Elin said as they went back into the cool of Burdon's office and headed towards the cloakroom to freshen up. 'I feel so hot and sticky.'

As Laura went in, her secretary Miss Foster said: 'A Mr Oxley telephoned, asking if you could spare him a few moments.'

Laura jerked with surprise, dropping a paper bag onto the typewriter, scattering pies on the desk.

'He wants to come round straight away.'

'Mr Laurence Oxley?'

'That's right.' Miss Foster was peering up at her through hornrimmed spectacles, her face plain and square. 'He said if it isn't convenient now, I was to let him know when you had ten minutes free, and he'd come then.'

'Oh!' Laura took a deep breath. She'd been going to say she didn't want to see him. Why hadn't she foreseen this? He'd given up hoping his solicitors could get what he wanted. He was handling the problem personally now. He must want access badly.

'Tell him to come now then.' She snatched up her pies, rushed to the boardroom, and dumped them on the table. Suddenly she felt she was teetering on the edge of an abyss. All her newfound confidence was gone.

She'd felt excited when she'd first known Laurence Oxley was her father. He was a public figure, someone seen from afar. She'd imagined herself saving him from some dire consequence. A fire in his office perhaps, or an accident in his car. When he found out she was his lost daughter, he would tell her he'd spent years searching for her and Mam. He would throw his arms round them, saying he loved them and would never leave them again.

Laura had been old enough to recognise this as fantasising. But knowing he was her father seemed to bestow some of the good fortune Jane and Mary Oxley had enjoyed at school. In reality, she never expected to see him close to, nor to acknowledge the relationship.

Hearing now that he was coming to her office set her nerves jangling. She felt stunned. She decided she would treat him simply as a fellow businessman. She wasn't going to claim relationship, not when he'd denied it all these years.

She had to do something to fill the time before he walked in. She went to the kitchen for plates and knives and paper napkins. She picked up a knife meaning to slice a pie in half. Panic fluttered at her fingers, the knife slipped. She felt the sharp sting and saw blood spurt from the cut on her finger.

What a fool she was to let herself get worked up like this. She went to the cloakroom to run cold water over the cut. Elin was still there. She'd washed her face and was smoothing cream onto her cheeks.

'Laurence Oxley's coming here,' Laura said.

Elin froze. 'When?' Shocked golden eyes stared into the mirror and met hers.

'Said he'll be here in fifteen minutes.'

'I'll leave.' Elin suddenly galvanised into action, pushing creams and comb into her handbag.

'No, I need you here, Mam. You know him . . .'

'What's he coming for? No, I can't possibly.' Her slanting eyes glittered with panic. 'No.'

Laura held on to her arm. 'Why not? He won't eat you.'

'I've got to go.'

'Nonsense.'

'You don't understand . . . Last time I saw him,' her voice choked with dread. 'Well, I stole from him. Fifty pounds.'

Laura knew her mouth had dropped open. Mam set great store on being honest. Not just honest, conspicuously honest. She'd felt she had to be, working among other people's possessions. Mam had told her she worried about throwing out wilting flowers, slivers of soap and day-old newspapers, lest her employers thought she took them for her own use. Yet if she left them, some thought she hadn't done her work properly.

'I had to get money from somewhere. You'd have gone behind the counter at the Maypole otherwise. I knew you had it in you to do better than that. It paid for your course at Skerry's.'

Laura felt cold. She remembered now the amazement she'd felt when her mother found the money to send her there. Remembered asking where it had come from.

'You never told me.' Her voice was no more than a whisper.

'I went to see him.' Mam bent over the washbowl, her eyes wild. 'In his grand office in the Liver Building.'

Laura swallowed, she knew the effort that must have cost her mother.

'I asked for money for you. He refused, but I could see a pile of notes on his desk in front of me. A small fortune. He was pacing up and down. You know, like a caged tiger. When he turned his back I snatched them up and pushed them in my pocket. I had to have money. I didn't want you to know. Didn't want you to think I was a thief.'

'Mam!' No wonder she was a wreck! Laura ached for her, tears prickled her own eyes. She pulled Elin towards her, hugging her tight. 'You kept that to yourself for fifteen years! Oh Mam! You did that for me!'

'I can't stay, you see.' Elin's anguished face looked into hers.

'Yes, you must. This will be on your mind till you face him.'

'I couldn't, Laura.'

'He'll not bring it up even if he remembers, I promise you. He wants a favour from me. He won't want to upset you.'

'I'm scared.' Elin searched for her handkerchief and blew her nose.

'No need to be,' Laura said firmly, ignoring her own churning stomach. A better idea was forming in her mind. Mam wouldn't have to think of herself as a thief any longer, and it would embarrass Laurence Oxley at the same time. Perhaps even make him feel guilty for not doing more.

'I want you to do your hair, and put on some lipstick. Come out and show him we've managed very well without his help. Promise you will.'

Elin stared back at her silently.

'Mam?'

'All right,' she sighed.

Laura's cut was still bleeding, she needed a plaster to cover it. On the way to the first aid post, she stopped at Miss Foster's desk, scribbled out a cheque and asked her to go down to the bank and get cash. She was crossing the reception hall on the way back to her office when she saw Laurence Oxley come in.

The strength ebbed from her knees. Intense blue eyes looked into hers. Bristling brows met above them. Crinkling pepper and salt hair framed his face. She'd studied photographs of him, but had never stood close to him like this, knowing who he was. He had high cheekbones like hers and a strong chin. Plain to see he was accustomed to privilege, that he'd always got exactly what he wanted. Once it had been a powerhouse of a face. He was older than she'd expected.

'Hello,' she said. 'You must be Mr Oxley. I'm Laura Peck.' She stepped forward to shake the hand he offered. She'd thought of him as strong and powerful, a man who had done Mam down. But he didn't look strong, he looked an old man. She ought to hate him. Kick him down.

He followed her down the corridor, and she ushered him

into the boardroom. He was impressed, as she'd meant him to be. She'd made her office at Burdon's her main one, doing much of the work for Quick's and Morton's here, because she liked its gracious air.

'I'm sure you know why I've come, Miss Peck.'

'Yes. Can I offer you a cup of coffee?'

'No, thank you. His hands were clenched on the arms of his chair. He crossed his legs and uncrossed them again. Laura didn't miss the signs of tension. Did he realise he was looking at his daughter for the first time in twenty-eight years? No, that wasn't true, he'd handed her that essay prize at school. How she'd envied Jane a father important enough to present prizes. Probably he hadn't known then and he didn't know now.

She leaned back in her chair. 'Access to your site,' she prompted. She wasn't going to help him argue his case, though she'd made up her mind to sell him the land he wanted. It would offset some of her costs, and his business wasn't in competition.

'Yes. As you know, I've acquired Perkins Brake Linings, and you've bought up every inch of land round it.'

'I need space to develop. The land I bought is also round Morton's Meats.'

'You've plenty of land without the old Coliseum site. Surely you don't have plans to develop that?' His searching blue eyes met hers and fell away.

'Actually I have.' Laura wasn't going to be intimidated.

'Oh?'

Her plans were none of his business. She didn't have to tell him anything. She saw his lips straighten. He was getting the message. He'd not ask directly again.

'I understood it was a disappointment. That you didn't get the garage. The Coliseum is now cut off from the rest of your site. You'll have had to change your plans.'

Laura half smiled. He'd done his homework, or more likely had it done for him.

'True. We all have to cut our coat according to our cloth, Mr Oxley.'

'Look, I want access to Keel Street. I'll pay you three

times what you paid for the freehold of the old Coliseum. I'm prepared to pay a premium.'

'I want it for much the same reason you do,' Laura said slowly. She had him on the run now. 'I m planning a one-way route through Morton's. The vans will come in through the present entrance and out behind the garage through the cinema site. Reduces congestion, less risk of minor accidents, and I'm thinking of a staff shop at the back. Sell off company products without the retail mark up.'

'All right, four times what you paid for it.'

Laura deliberately let the silence lengthen. 'We might compromise,' she said at last. 'I'll sell you the freehold on condition you build the road and allow traffic from my site to use it as an exit.'

'It would be both exit and entrance for my factory. How wide is it exactly?'

'Fifty-five feet. My vans will enter from the left, and turn left into your road.'

'What about staff cars?'

'Those too. There'll be a small car park.'

'You're driving a hard bargain.'

She'd meant to. It had nothing to do with access to either site. She wanted to show this man she couldn't be pushed about in the way Mam had. Circumstances had given her a chance to get the upper hand. She meant to exercise her advantage.

He'd started to say something about construction and maintenance costs when Laura heard a nervous tap and the door creaked open a few inches.

'Come in, Mam,' she called.

Laurence Oxley leapt to his feet as though stung by a scorpion.

'This is my mother,' she told him. His face was suddenly crimson, and he was gasping for breath. He knew now who they were all right.

Mam had done her best to pull herself together. She looked well groomed. Her fair hair had been combed and redressed into its bun, her plain grey dress looked and was, expensive, but her golden eyes were panic-stricken.

'Hello, Elin,' he said awkwardly. 'It is Elin Jones?'

He was offering his hand. Laura saw the tremor in his fingers.

'Elin Peck, sir. You haven't forgotten I got married?'

'No, no. How are you?'

'Fine,' she said. His eyes were raking her up and down.

'How's Peck getting on?'

'Peck?' Elin sounded befuddled. Laura knew it was guilt that made her like this. 'He was killed in the blitz, didn't you know?' It was a lie she'd practised; that bit rolled off her tongue all right.

'I'm sorry, no. I'm sorry . . .'

Laura swallowed, nobody was sorry.

'Your home, was it bombed?'

'No, he was out. An air raid warden. Nineteen forty-one, it was. We were all right.'

'Poor old Peck.'

'Yes,' Elin agreed.

'The truth is,' Laura said coldly, 'he was difficult to live with.' No point in shielding Laurence Oxley from what he'd done. 'He was a parasite living on what Mam could earn, and he always took the lion's share, leaving us short. His death came as a relief. No need to waste your sympathy.'

It took her a moment to realise Laurence Oxley didn't know what to say. His face had crumbled, he had difficulty choking anything out. 'I'm sorry, I didn't realise . . .'

'It doesn't matter now,' Laura said. 'Without him dragging us down, we managed.'

'I was in a difficult position,' he was blustering. 'Very difficult when Sybil was alive.'

'Alive? Is she . . .? What happened?' Elin's hand covered her mouth.

'She died of cancer five years ago.'

'How awful for you!'

Laura could feel anger bristling inside her. He was trying to excuse his lack of care. The presence of his wife had made it difficult!

'You could have done something for us. A few pounds would have meant a lot. We were hungry. Do you know what it is to have no money for food?' She saw him wince.

Laura pulled up a chair so her mother could sit on her side of the desk. Us against him. But Elin was moving to the table where she usually sat.

'So you're Laura.' His deep blue eyes were raking her face again.

'Yes.' She knew now he hadn't been sure, not till he saw Mam. 'Not so easy to recognise a daughter, if you don't see her till she's twenty-eight.' She was choosing her words to hurt. He winced again as she'd meant him to. She saw her mother's eyebrows arch in horror.

'I recognise some of the Oxley traits now,' he half smiled.

'Only the better ones, I hope,' she snapped.

'Laura always knew what she wanted,' put in Elin hurriedly. 'And worked very hard to get it.'

'You've done very well.' He forgot himself sufficiently to get out of the chair and pace up and down as though in his own office. 'To build up a business like you have. Who helped you do it?'

'Mr Burdon taught me all about biscuits, and a lot more besides.'

'I meant with capital. Somebody must have provided the initial . . .' The light glinted on his pepper and salt hair.

'Nobody,' she said coldly. She wasn't going to admit she'd raised money by selling his pictures. He had provided the capital, though he didn't know it. 'I had to manage on my own, except . . .' An idea was coming to her. 'You did help a little with the loan.'

'What loan?'

'Mam came to your office years ago, and asked you to help. Do you remember, Mr Oxley?'

'You'd better call me . . . er . . . Laurence,' he said gruffly.

'I had to take the money,' Elin gasped.

Laura was conscious of her mother's agonised face, her thin body rigid in her chair; of her father, stilled in his pacing.

'We are in a position to repay the loan now.' Laura rang for her secretary. Miss Foster brought in fifty pound notes.

'They are for Mr Oxley,' she said, and Miss Foster put them in his hand.

'I didn't expect . . . It isn't necessary.'

'We would prefer to repay you.'

'I really don't want to take it,' he blustered. 'I mean . . . It was a long time ago.'

'Mam always considered it a loan. She'll feel better now it's repaid.'

'I'd forgotten,' he said, and couldn't look at her. Good, that was what she wanted. It wouldn't have hurt him to help Mam. He could have afforded it so easily.

Ever since she'd known, she'd wanted him to recognise her as his daughter. Show them both some care and affection. But he never had.

'I'm grateful for the loan,' she said. 'It made all the difference. Without it, I wouldn't have got where I am today.'

'Fifty pounds? Could it make much difference, one way or the other?'

'It paid my fees at Skerry's Commercial College.'

'Shorthand and typing? What good did that do you?'

'What good does it do to learn anything? I also had lessons in grammar, and I had my first lessons in bookkeeping which proved invaluable.'

'It got her a job in the accounts department at Burdon's,' Elin said. 'Made everything else possible.'

'Bookkeeping?'

Laura could see he didn't believe it. 'It's true,' she said. 'As an accounts clerk I got a practical grounding. I learned how the system works from the bottom up. A boon when I started auditing. No accountant can hide anything from me.'

'I'm so proud of Laura,' Elin said. 'She's had to work so hard.'

'But we managed, didn't we, Mam? And now we're comfortable and enjoying life. And you, Laurence? Have the years been kind to you?' She knew they had not. His wife dead from cancer. Jane killed in that terrible accident, and now clearly Mary had problems.

'Not entirely,' he said. 'Look, I'm not a young man any more. Everything's changed for me. Could I offer you both lunch? Take you to—?'

'Oh no, thank you, we have this.' Elin waved her hand across the sixteen meat pies, some of which were melting in the heat and looking less than appetising. Laura tried to explain her reasons for tasting them. He was no longer listening. He stood up.

'I must go.' She'd given him what he'd come for, but he looked defeated. 'The freehold of the cinema – I'll get Dufton and Jones to contact your solicitor.'

Laura led him to the front door, conscious of his footfall, and of Mam's heels clicking in the rear.

'I'm glad we've met, Laura. I see a lot of myself in you.'

Well, that was it, he had acknowledged his paternity. She noticed he cupped Mam's hand in both of his, and that he had a Rolls-Royce with a driver waiting for him outside.

Laura turned back to her office feeling victorious, elated. She'd driven a hard bargain. She'd made him feel a heel. She'd let him know how low he was in their estimation. The fifty pounds was still on her desk. Surreptitiously she slid it into a drawer.

'What did you do that for?' Elin slumped back in her chair. 'You should have told me you were going to try and pay him back. You gave me such a shock. I'm still shaking.'

'It cleared the air,' Laura said firmly. 'I wanted to do that. Make it quite clear it was a loan. Make you more at ease.'

'We were none of us that,' Elin retorted.

'He didn't get the better of me.'

'No.' Elin's blonde head sank lower. 'I always knew you'd be a match for him.'

'It's what you wanted, isn't it? We showed him we didn't need him.'

'He's had his troubles, Laurie. Lost his wife and one daughter. At least we always had each other.'

Laura felt her bubble of elation burst.

'It was strange seeing you together. I never realised just how much alike you are.'

'He's still very interested in you,' Laura said,

remembering how his gaze had been riveted on her mother.

Suddenly Laura knew what she must do. She had been searching for some way to help Elin over her depression, make her forget what she'd done to Percy. Laurence could do it; after all he had swept Mam off her feet once.

'No, Laura, it's you he's interested in. So he should be. Finding his daughter after all these years.' Elin's slanting eyes were aflame.

Laura felt chastened. She'd gone at him with both feet kicking, showing gut reaction, like a child wanting to avenge herself. She'd played it all wrong. Mam was no longer dwelling on her own problems. She was thinking of Laurence.

'I wonder when he shaved off his moustache? Thin pencil moustache, it was. Suited him.'

Laura hadn't stopped to think, as she usually did, of what she wanted to achieve. It had all happened too quickly. She had wanted to help Mam, and what had she done? She'd choked him off. She'd let a chance slip through her fingers. She'd been too wrapped up in her own feelings. Too slow.

She hadn't expected Mam to be interested in him after all these years. Not like this. She'd felt Mam's emotion. She'd loved Laurence once. Perhaps she still did. He'd not been unfriendly, he'd made the first move at reconciliation by inviting them to lunch. Why hadn't she accepted, or at least said some other time? She'd turned him away, at their first meeting in twenty-eight years. It could be another twenty-eight before fate brought them together again.

Laura shivered. She could no longer think straight. Meeting her father had been an emotional onslaught. She felt she'd been jousting with him. It left her mind racing and her body drained. What burned most was the faraway look in Mam's golden eyes as she wondered when he'd shaved off some moustache or other.

But at last Laura knew how to help her.

Laura could hear excitement vibrating in Tom's voice as it came over the wire.

'Got my ticket this morning. My passage is booked on the mail boat. The MV *Aureol*, sailing a week tomorrow.

I've enquired, there are double cabins still available. Shall I book for you and Elin?'

'Tom! I can't possibly leave next week. I'm starting scotch eggs at Morton's, and Gerald Kimber's on holiday. I didn't expect . . . You said about a month.'

There was a shocked silence. 'You promised you'd come, Laura.' Tom's voice was stiff and accusing now.

'I want to come. I'm looking forward to it. Haven't I always fancied seeing Africa? It's just—'

'You said you could manage six weeks.'

'Let me think . . . We'll fly out, Mam and me. The day you arrive. That will give me two more weeks here. You'll enjoy the sea trip, Tom. Make a change to be a passenger. You don't need me for that.'

'I want you with me, you understand me,' he said, still upset, but she knew she'd gone some way to appease him. She needed to devote time to him. If he could keep this job they'd all feel more settled.

'I'll be able to spend more time in Lagos this way,' she persuaded.

'I wish you were coming on the boat. Just thinking of the new job . . . You know how it is with me. Tension starts screwing me up.'

'You'll be able to get your bearings when you arrive, Tom. You won't start work straight away. They'll give you time to settle into your new home.'

'All the same, Laura—'

'I'd love to be coming on the boat, Tom. We all need a holiday, but I've got to make arrangements for the businesses to run without me.'

All the time she'd been speaking, Laura had been conscious of her mother's disapproving back as she sat at the table, conscious she was listening instead of writing. When she put the phone down, Elin said: 'Wouldn't it be better if we just had a couple of weeks in the south of France? I'm not sure I want to go to Lagos. Snakes and mosquitoes, a very unhealthy place.'

'We're going, Mam. Tom needs us. It will do us all good.'

Laura longed to see West Africa. It had held a certain

ever since she'd written that essay. It had another attraction now. It was the centre of the Oxley empire and they might see something of Laurence Oxley there. Surely he still went from time to time to keep an eye on his business?

Even with three weeks to get ready, Laura felt rushed. She had fewer distractions at work because her mother was occupied putting together her holiday wardrobe and came to the office less often, but even so, she had to stay late every night during the last week. It had come at a busy time for her, she was still in the midst of reorganising Morton's.

Elin went along the rack of dresses, picking out those she liked. Once, she'd thought it would give her immense pleasure to buy any dress she fancied.

The most expensive shops in Liverpool were in Bold Street, but she didn't feel at ease in them. The atmosphere was too rarefied, the shoppers too few. Elin felt she couldn't step through the door without being set upon by a superior shop assistant in a smart black dress. They all seemed to look down their noses as if they knew she'd only recently moved from Jubilee Street, Birkenhead. Their prices were wildly expensive too. Even if Laura had plenty of money, it seemed silly to throw it away. She could buy clothes that looked equally good at half the price.

She preferred the big department stores in Church Street, though they were expensive enough. An assistant was in attendance now, looping the dresses she picked out over her arm.

Laura had told her to get swimsuits, sun tops and shorts. Elin had never owned anything like that, couldn't imagine herself in a bathing suit, but she'd have to try. Laura said she'd need them and would lose patience with her if she didn't get herself kitted out for the trip. She picked out three swimsuits before the assistant led her off to the changing room.

Alone at last, thank goodness. She couldn't make up her mind about anything with the assistant fussing round her. All the swimsuits were very revealing, but she had to have one. She chose the red and white stripes, though she'd need to be very daring to wear it in public.

Dresses were easier. She was pushing her arms into a grey crepe de Chine cocktail dress when the shop assistant tapped discreetly on the door. She helped her zip it up, smoothing the fit across her shoulders.

'It suits you, madam.'

'Oh God!' Suddenly Elin couldn't get her breath. The years went spiralling away, she could see Sybil Oxley again in a tube of material exactly like this.

'No! No, I must have cotton. What was I thinking of? The tropics, you know.' Elin swallowed hard. Laura had said more than once she had a phobia about Laurence Oxley. Well, perhaps she had.

'Come with me to Wales,' he'd suggested all those years ago, and she'd refused. Would things have turned out any different if she'd gone?

Ever since chance had brought her face to face with him again, she'd felt inflamed, on edge, unable to keep her mind off him. Laura had been quite rude to him.

He'd clasped both her hands in his. Her flesh had burned to his touch. She'd felt the tingle long after he'd gone out to his car. Seeing him brought back the past with frightening clarity. His looks haunted her. He still had a good head of hair, growing low on the back of his neck. It would feel thick and crinkly against her fingers. Once it had sparkled pale bronze, now it was pepper and salt. She tried to work out how old he'd be. Surely not sixty? He looked years younger than that.

She could feel her heart pounding as it used to when he came to her room all those years ago. But she was older and wiser now. She wouldn't let him amuse himself with her again, lift her up, make her hungry for his kisses only to drop her when he lost interest. She knew Laurence Oxley's ways too well to expect he would do otherwise, even supposing he was in the least bit interested in her after all these years. Laura seemed to think he was, but then Laura was a romantic at heart; God knows she'd had little enough in her own life.

CHAPTER TWENTY-ONE

Laura flew with her mother from Harwarden to Heathrow in an old Dakota that had survived the war. It vibrated and rattled and the unpressurised cabin made all her teeth ache.

Elin was complaining too, gripping the seat in front of her, convinced she could see daylight through cracks in the ceiling. At Heathrow, they took the bus to the overseas terminal.

'It might have been better to go by sea,' Elin said nervously as they walked away from the check-in desk.

'Mam, I couldn't afford the time.'

'It's claustrophobic up there, and such a long way. I don't know whether . . .' Her cheeks were flushed.

'This will be different. A bigger and more comfortable plane. You'll enjoy it. Let's get some magazines to read while we wait.' Laura led Elin along the newsagent's rack and between them they picked out half a dozen.

'And some books. Must take plenty to read.'

Elin chose two paperbacks and stuffed them in her BOAC cabin bag.

'We'll go through Immigration, then we can relax,' Laura said. Elin's heels tapped behind as she led the way through to the departure lounge. At one end was a bar, with people drinking on high stools, their cabin bags at their feet.

There was something familiar about one man. He had a glass of beer on the bar, but he paced off to the window and stood surveying the planes outside. He was light on his feet, generating energy, like an animal ready to pounce. He turned and swung back to his drink.

'Oh God!' Laura heard her mother struggling to get her breath. It was Laurence Oxley.

Laura felt a rush of adrenaline. It seemed a second chance. She hadn't expected to get it so soon.

'A cup of coffee, Mam?' As she edged her towards the bar his eyes met hers then quickly slid to her mother.

'Elin?' He laughed with amazement. 'We meet again so soon?'

'Hello, Laurence,' Laura answered. 'Are you going to Lagos?'

'Yes, Mary ought to be there seeing to things, but she isn't well.'

'Oh dear, nothing serious I hope?'

'I don't know.' He ruffled his hair till it stood up round his face, a bronze aura. 'Her knee, she fell and hurt it. It doesn't seem to get better. She's been home for a long time. Has a new baby too.'

'So you're a grandfather? Congratulations.'

'Yes, well . . .' He didn't look as though that gave him pleasure.

'That makes me a half-aunt.' Laura wanted to remind him of their relationship. Wanted to get closer to him. It seemed the best way to help Mam.

'You've been that for some time. Carlotta's ten now. Then there was . . . Anyway, I need to keep an eye on things out there. Shall we sit down?' He took his drink from the bar and led them to a small table surrounded by arm chairs.

'Ten?' Laura couldn't believe Mary had a daughter as old as that. Laurence seemed just as edgy as he had in her office, but she felt a little better. She had to use this opportunity.

'I take it you're off on holiday?'

'Yes.' Laura took a deep breath, fighting for confidence. This wasn't the place she would have chosen to talk about personal matters, but she had to do it. 'Laurence, I hoped I'd see you again. I want to apologise. Mam said I was rude to you the other day, and she's right, I was.'

'I've got over it,' he said. 'You drove a pretty hard bargain, too.'

'You must forgive me. I could see you wanted access, and I went out of my way to make you pay through the nose.' His blue eyes searched into hers.

'I've felt prickly about you for years. It's hard to talk about feelings, but . . .' Laura knew she had to if he was to understand. 'When you came to my office, I deliberately gave you a hard time. I meant to hurt you if I could. I'm sorry. Put it down to misplaced pride. We had a bad time, didn't we, Mam? We could have done with a little help. I was full of resentment that you didn't give it. Mam doesn't feel like that though.'

Around them the collective sound of other people's conversation rose and fell. Cups and glasses clinked, a burst of laughter came from the far corner.

'You make me feel ashamed,' he said uneasily. Their coffee came and he insisted on paying for it. 'Your mother told you about me?'

Laura took another deep breath. 'Percy Peck let it drop like a bombshell – when I called him father, in a family row. I was seventeen at the time.'

Laurence's intense blue eyes clouded with pain.

'You needn't concern yourself about that. It didn't upset me. I was glad. I hated Percy.'

'He didn't ill treat you? Knock you about?'

Laura shook her head. 'It was Mam he went for. She was black and blue some mornings. I couldn't cope with it.'

'Elin?' His mouth was open, disgust and disbelief fought in his face.

'I told you the day I came to your office,' she whispered. 'You didn't believe me.'

'Once I knew you were my natural father, I thought our problems would be over.' Laura sat back and surveyed him. 'I saw you as a knight in shining armour. I dreamed of you coming to take care of us, giving us money for food.'

Laurence sat frowning into his beer. 'Elin, when you came to my office, I told you to get in touch again if Laura needed help. You knew how.'

Elin's golden eyes stared into his. They all knew why she hadn't. The theft of fifty pounds had made that impossible.

'I'm the one owing an apology,' he said. 'I'm sorry, Elin. I should have done more for you. Made sure you were all right. I should have kept in touch.'

Laura half closed her eyes, letting his words soak into her soul. She couldn't bring herself to be completely honest and tell him about raising capital on his pictures. That might make him feel better, and deep down she still wanted him to squirm. She'd managed it, she'd apologised, made him understand why she'd been so prickly. Made a friendly overture. Her mother sat silently drinking her coffee. The tannoy blared again.

'There's the second call for my flight, I'd better go.' He put his half-finished beer on the table and felt for his hand luggage.

'Ours too,' Laura said, getting up.

'You're going to Lagos?' There was no mistaking the surprise in his voice. 'What for?'

'A holiday.'

'A holiday?' He looked shocked. 'Where are you going to stay?'

'With a friend.'

'You must let me show you round. Not that there's much to amuse you in Lagos.'

'Thank you,' Elin murmured.

'Your friend?'

'He sailed on the *Aureol*. Should be arriving today.' Laura felt she had to volunteer some information, but explaining exactly who Tom was, was too long and personal a story. She couldn't talk freely about him to anyone but Mam.

'Ah, a boy friend? A good-looking girl like you, I'm not surprised. That explains a lot. What's he doing there?'

'He's a marine officer.' They joined the line filing past the hostess checking boarding passes.

'Really? On contract to Ports Authority?' Laurence's vivid blue eyes searched her face. She could see he was trying to equate her position, running a successful business on Merseyside, with a boy friend contracted to spend several years in Lagos. It wouldn't make sense to him.

'Yes.'

'Where does he live?'

She had to explain that as he was going out for the first time, not returning from home leave, they didn't know. His questions were an inquisition, and her replies inadequate. She knew he thought them foolhardy to go chasing half across the world knowing so little about where they were to stay.

'You should have waited a week or so. Let him settle in. You'd have found conditions more comfortable.'

Laura offered up their boarding passes and discovered when she reached the first-class cabin they were seated two rows behind him, on the opposite side of the Britannia.

'He's really very nice, isn't he?' Mam's golden head nodded in Laurence Oxley's direction as she slid into the window seat.

As the plane taxied to the end of the runway, Laura could see her mother's alarm building up. She was gripping the arms of her seat.

The engines roared, they went hurtling down the runway and then the fields were spinning away beneath them. A ball of fear exploded on Elin's face. She was craning as far from the window as she could get, burying her face against Laura's shoulder. As soon as the notice flashed up that they need no longer stay in their seats, Laura changed places with her.

A hostess served champagne cocktails. Laura could see her mother pulling herself together. Another cork popped, and champagne bubbled onto the brandy. Elin clutched her drink like a lifeline. Laura heard Laurence Oxley's laugh. She could see her mother's golden eyes fixed on the back of his head as she gulped at her drink.

'He's worn that ring for years.' Elin tugged at her, encouraging her to peer round the seat in front. His arm lay along the arm rest, his hand wrapped round a tumbler. He wore a heavy signet ring on his third finger. Laurence Oxley was drawing Elin's attention like a magnet.

There were more drinks, canapés, and then a meal. Elin picked at her food. Laura felt mesmerised by the throb of the engines and the vista of sunshine on fluffy white clouds. Suddenly, Laurence was standing in the aisle at her elbow, a drink in his hand.

'Will your friend be meeting you?'

'I expect so . . . I don't know.' Already he was attaching himself to them. Advising what they should do. Guiding them, seeming to care. It was what she had hoped for.

'What will you do if he doesn't?'

'We'll be staying overnight in Claridges Hotel. We're going to help him move into his quarters tomorrow.'

'Claridges? You can't stay there.'

'Why not?'

'It's nothing like Claridges in London. You'll be very uncomfortable. It's right in the middle of town. Very noisy and hot.'

'Which is the best hotel then?'

'There are plans to rebuild the Bristol. It'll be Lagos's first luxury hotel. Jo Harold's at the airport is as good as any. Or the Rest House in Ikoyi.'

'But in Lagos itself?'

Laurence shrugged. 'Most people put their friends up. It's no trouble, plenty of domestic help. I could take you home with me. Plenty of space.'

Laura felt a little jerk of pleasure. She wouldn't have to make opportunities to see him. She was tempted to accept, but she had come to help Tom too, and he wouldn't like a change of plan now.

'We have to meet our friend. We can put up with Claridges for one night.'

'You're sure? I'd like to help. I'd like us to be friends.'

'You're very kind,' Elin murmured. Laura wished all this had happened years ago.

'Did your friend take a car on the boat?' Laurence asked.

'No, he'll have to get one in Lagos. Is that possible?'

'Oh yes, we can help you there, and you'll need transport for the first day or so. At least allow me to provide that.'

'Thank you.'

'Walk down to our office. It's not far from Claridges. I'll be there tomorrow, but if I'm not about, ask for Jake Lode. He's my Lagos manager. I'll mention it to him.'

The Britannia droned on over stark rocky desert which gradually changed to scrub. The scrub greened to parkland which in turn thickened to tropical rainforest. As the last daylight left the sky, Laura felt the plane start its descent to Lagos. Elin closed her eyes and clutched Laura's arm when the time came for landing, as though her endurance had been stretched to its limit. The landing was smooth and over in minutes.

As they went down the steps to the tarmac, the night wrapped itself round them like a hot wet blanket. Tomtoms thumped in the distance, then answered louder in the forest nearby. Laura could see people meeting the plane, waiting on the other side of a hedge. She tried to pick out Tom. Usually his height and red hair made him easy to see, but the light was in her eyes.

'I hope he's here.' Elin's voice was thick with anxiety. They followed the other passengers towards Immigration and Customs. The standing around seemed interminable. Laurence was in attendance, making desultory conversation. At last they were free to leave. He helped them through the door with their suitcases.

Laura could hardly breathe in the cloying heat, the alien atmosphere made her senses reel. Relief came flooding through when she saw Tom leaning against the building, shoulders hunched, visibly wilting in the heat, his beard darkened by perspiration to deep auburn.

'Tom!' Her lethargy gone, she bounded towards him, hauling Elin along by the arm. He rocked upright for a moment and then curled down to give each of them a chaste kiss on the cheek. Laurence Oxley was still behind them, Laura had to introduce him.

Tom towered over him, his shirt unbuttoned at the neck, his tie loose, the knot at mid-chest level. Dark circles of sweat showed under the sleeves of his shirt. The only concession Laurence made to the heat was to carry the jacket of his suit over his arm. Laura saw his eyes go questioningly to her mother. She could see he didn't take to Tom.

A native porter seized their bags and was leading them towards the taxi rank when a smartly dressed driver intercepted them. He wore the Oxley Enterprise logo on his uniform.

'Mr Oxley, sir. I bring car, sir.'

'Hello, Sylvester.'

'Mr Lode away. Trouble in Ibadan, sir. Can't meet you, but he be home tonight.' He was stowing Laurence's suitcases in the boot of a highly polished Humber.

'Elin, can I offer you a lift to Claridges?'

'I've got a taxi waiting,' Tom mumbled. 'It brought me up.'

'It's kind of you, Laurence,' Laura said. 'But we'd better stick to the arrangements Tom's made. I'd like to take up your offer of a car tomorrow though. You'll be in your office first thing?'

'Yes, I'm an early bird out here. Come and see me. Anybody can direct you to Oxley's.'

'See you tomorrow then.'

The taxi was an old Standard Vanguard. The nearside door was a different colour, the offside wing had deep rusting indentations, and the boot lid had to be tied down with string. The black driver wore a torn T-shirt.

Elin's face was crimson with heat and exhaustion. Laura ushered her onto the back seat and got in beside her. She couldn't remember ever feeling so hot, though she'd taken off her stockings and suspender belt in the plane. The windows were wound down to their full extent.

It seemed a wild ride through a black velvet night, lit only by stars. Laura could see the road rushing past through holes rusted in the floor. The vehicle rattled and rolled, yet still seemed capable of ferocious speed.

They flashed between half-seen cyclists and little stalls selling native produce, each lit with a tiny oil lamp flickering in the night. A hot, fierce breeze tore at her hair, pulling it free from its French pleat. Heavy strands whipped against her face.

Tom leaned over from the front seat. 'Different from Birkenhead. I wish it wasn't so damn hot.' Tom at least had known what to expect. He'd been here before.

The driver was holding the crown of the road, hurtling towards oncoming headlights. Just when Laura was bracing herself for the inevitable crash, the driver jerked to the left and they slid past a lorry, with only inches to spare. Elin lay back on the seat with her eyes closed.

Ramshackle shanties appeared on both sides of the road, which suddenly teemed with life. Pedestrians jostled between families eating, washing and sleeping on the verges. The noise was prodigious. Everybody shouted to be heard and shrieked with laughter. Horns honked, cycle bells rang continually, hi-life music blared from almost every corner. Toddlers danced only inches from heavy traffic. Dogs, goats and chickens did their best to stay out of harm's way. They had reached the outskirts of Lagos.

Laura was relieved to get out of the taxi alive. She better understood now the comfort of a safe vehicle. A Claridges bellboy wearing a uniform that was not as clean as it could have been carried their suitcases inside. Tom had reserved a room for them.

'Doesn't compare with the mail boat,' he whispered. 'Still, it's only for one night.' Laura looked round with distaste. Everything was worn and shabby, and none too clean. Up in the room, the paintwork peeled, and the mosquito net had holes which a previous occupant had blocked with twists of toilet paper.

Laura closed the window the boy had just opened for them, wanting to shut out the crescendo of noise from the street below. After two minutes she had to throw the casements wide again. Better to suffer the blaring horns than suffocate in the airless heat. There was no air conditioner.

Elin collapsed on a chair, mopping her face. Laura inspected the adjoining bathroom, it smelled of damp and decay. There was no shower. She started running cold water into the chipped bath. Two woodlice and a spider had to be evicted first.

'You'll feel better after a bath, Mam. We'll have an early dinner and go to bed.'

'I couldn't eat. Not in this heat. Besides, there was so much food on the plane. I've got a headache. Just bath and bed.'

'What about a cup of tea?' Laura opened the cases in search of washbags and nightdresses. Laurence had been right when he said they'd be uncomfortable here.

Elin took her tea under the mosquito net, complaining it cut out even the slightest movement of air.

Laura ran another bath. The thin cotton dress she'd travelled in was sticking to her back in sodden discomfort. The cool bath refreshed her. She changed every garment she'd been wearing. Her mother seemed to be dozing. Laura put out the light and went in search of Tom.

They shared a bottle of wine, sitting at tables in a central courtyard. Trees rustled overhead, lizards flicked across the concrete and sand. Laura picked at dinner, she had no appetite either. They sat on till the dew glistened in a film on every surface. It was blessedly cooler at last.

The lights were on again in the bedroom when she went up.

'What's the matter, Mam? Can't you sleep?'

'No. Just seeing him brings it all back,' she sighed. 'Can't get him out of my mind.'

Laura started to undress. 'Why? Tell me, Mam. I want to know.'

'Well, you do know.'

'Not everything. You'll feel better if you talk about it.' Mam had bottled up her feelings for thirty years, Laura blamed that for her present nerve-racked state.

Elin took a deep steadying breath. 'I can't, I don't know where to start.'

'At the beginning. When you first saw Laurence Oxley. When your troubles began.' She crawled under the mosquito net and tucked it in behind her. The street noises were augmented by the soundtrack of a film showing at an open-air cinema nearby. She was fighting sleep as she lay down. Her mother's voice, still with its Welsh lilt, whispered in the dark.

'It's just that it unnerves me to come face to face with him.'

'Even after all this time?'

'He's changed, and I'm searching in my memory trying to remember exactly how.'

'We all change, Mam.'

'He's lost his power. It's as though he's blowing in the wind.'

'Nonsense, he heads a huge business.'

'He's not as strong as I remember him, hasn't the drive he had.'

'He's still running it very successfully.'

'He has some quality that disturbs me. I can't sit in the same room as him and not be aware . . . There seems to be some sensory device in me that makes me conscious of every move he makes.'

'He feels the same way about you.'

'What do you mean?'

'He's talking to me, but he can't keep his eyes away from you.'

'Nonsense, you're imagining it.'

'I'm not. Why else would he invite us to stay at his house? Offer us a car? I tell you, Mam, he's still got a soft spot for you.'

'It's you he likes. You he wants. A daughter to be proud of. It worries me a bit. I have nightmares he'll lure you away. That I'll be left on my own.'

'Never, Mam. I wouldn't do that.'

'He's your sort, Laurie.'

'He won't come between us. Honest.'

'It's different for you, Laura. You're never afraid.'

'You aren't afraid of Laurence?'

'Of course I am.'

'He'd never raise a hand to you. Just because Percy did—'

'I know that. He wouldn't resort to physical violence.'

'Then what are you afraid of?'

Elin's voice was suddenly louder. 'I'm afraid . . . He can reduce me to a state of wanting. He's only to touch me and I'm totally inflamed. You don't understand, Laura, you aren't laced about with your own needs. You handled Tom, continue to handle Tom in just the right way.'

Laura felt herself stiffen. Betty Grable's voice filled the pause. 'Not true, Mam. I have ached for Tom. It took me years to accept he felt so much less.' A car screeched round the corner on two wheels. A nearby amplifier started to blare out another discordant hi-life record.

'You're telling me you want Laurence. Well, I can't see

what you're worried about. He's making all the running.'

'What I'm saying is, he knows how to make me want him. If we start seeing something of him, then I will.'

The noise from the soundtrack was coming to a crescendo. Laura couldn't see her mother's problem.

'I can't face another rejection,' Elin said in agonised tones.

'What makes you think he'll reject you? He's going out of his way to be friendly.'

'He was more than friendly last time. He played on my feelings. I was a good-looking girl then, and he dropped me. Now, well, I'm older. My looks have gone. Why wouldn't he dump me again when he's had his fun?'

'He's older too. His looks aren't what they were.'

'Laura! He's a handsome man.'

'He's got nobody else now, Mam.'

'He's got Mary. That's another thing. How would she take it? Hardly likely to welcome me to the family. Or you.'

'Forget Mary. She has her own problems.'

'I think he's had a lot of women. Probably still has. So why me again?'

'That seems to be what he wants. The way you want it too.'

'No, I'd rather he went his way, and I went mine. Safer all round.'

'You have to take a risk sometimes. Don't be afraid, Mam.'

Elin talked until nearly three in the morning. Laura knew most of what she was telling her, she'd lived through most of those years too. What she hadn't expected was the raw emotion it generated. All that her mother had suffered came over like water bursting through a dam. Laura was left aching, emotionally drained.

She'd been unable to sleep then, knowing she was the reason her mother had made the choices she had. Mam had felt forced to marry Percy Peck because of her. She'd even killed for her.

It was easy to say all killing was wrong, but Peck had

provoked and tormented her mother for years. Some might say she had got off scot-free, no publicity, no charges brought, as though God had decided she'd suffered enough. But she hadn't got off scot-free. What she'd done had played on her mind and tormented her almost as much as Percy himself had done.

It saddened Laura, tying even more tightly the strings that bound her to her mother. She could remember only too well the everlasting scrimping to put food on their plates, the small helpings Mam took, so that she might have more. No sacrifice had been too great.

'You've had a terrible life till now. Nothing but abuse and poverty.'

'No,' whispered Elin in the dark. 'I had you.'

'I was another responsibility, another mouth to feed.'

'I wanted to give you a better life.'

'But I brought you more drudgery.'

'I had no other reason for living, Laura. You were my reward.'

Laura choked. 'I'll make it up to you.'

'You already have.'

Laura woke early. The day was already brilliant as the sun climbed in a cobalt sky. The noise from the street was muted, she could hear birds singing. Elin slept on, her hair, with greyish streaks amongst the gold now, spread across her pillow.

Laura slid out from under the net, feeling sticky with perspiration and needing another cold bath before she dressed. When she went along to Tom's room, he was already up.

Downstairs, the courtyard had been hosed down and was still wet. It was pleasantly cool under the trees.

While they were waiting for breakfast, Laura said: 'I think we should try and buy a car. We passed a garage when we came, just round the corner. We'll be stuck without transport, and it'll take a day or two to get anything on the road.' A waiter brought them slices of pawpaw with lime, boiled eggs and toast. She ordered the same to be taken up to Elin on a tray. Then they sauntered round to the garage she'd noticed last night.

'Owned by Oxley's, of course,' she laughed. It was open for business though it was only eight o'clock. The choice immediately available was a new Morris Minor or a secondhand, low mileage Austin Healey.

'What's it to be, Tom?'

'Cheapest version of the Minor, I suppose. Better value for money.' But he was gazing longingly at the ivory-white Austin Healey sports soft-top.

She asked if they might take it out for a test drive. Tom had trouble fitting his bulk into the seat, but was soon nosing it out into the street.

'This would be more fun.' She closed her eyes against the glare, already the dusty breeze blowing in her face was hot. 'Have this.'

'Not very safe to leave on the dock. A knife could rip . . . Nice, though.' She hadn't meant to make the decision for him, but it seemed she had. She felt then she had to pay for it.

'You don't have to,' Tom said awkwardly. 'I can get a government loan.'

'I'm going to use it while I'm here. My parting present, Tom.' They arranged to pick it up the next day.

'You're a softie, Laurie, as far as I'm concerned.'

'Don't I know it.'

'It'll be fast,' Tom said with satisfaction. 'I'm going to love it.'

They walked back to Claridges together. Tom wanted to hold her arm, it was his way of showing he was grateful. Already she felt clammy in the morning sun, and his touch made her more uncomfortable.

A car and driver were waiting to take Tom to his flat. Laura copied the address from Tom's letter of tenancy.

'You take Mam and get the unpacking started,' she told Tom. 'I'm going to get the car Laurence promised us yesterday. We'll have to buy food, and probably half a dozen other things. See you soon.'

She looked at her watch, it was just on nine o'clock. She'd

walk round now to the Oxley office. She stood for a moment to get her bearings. Claridges Hotel was in a side street, only yards from the harbour. She went in that direction.

There were no pavements, and the dirty sand at the edge of the road was gritty against her toes. The open drains released pungent odours. On the marina, the palms hung lifelessly over the water. There wasn't a breath of air. Traffic swept past dangerously close, cars hooted, and bicycles weaved in and out of pedestrians. She felt assaulted by the squalor and the vitality, and the noise.

The offices that housed Oxley headquarters were above their main department store. The doors were just opening. Laura climbed four flights of stairs and pushed open a door to find herself in a roof garden. A boy, dressed only in khaki shorts, was snaking a hosepipe to water shrubs growing in tubs and boxes. A pergola provided welcome shade even at this hour. The scent of blossom and wet leaves was refreshing. Laura picked her way over the wet tiles to the front door which stood wide open. Inside, the reception desk was deserted. She went on. Typewriters clicked, dark heads were bent over desks. A uniformed messenger came towards her carrying a used coffee cup.

'Is Mr Oxley here? Can you show me to his office?'

'Mr Oxley no here. Mr Oxley in England, Miss.'

'He's in Lagos,' she told him, but clearly he hadn't come to the office. 'Mr Jake Lode then? I'm Laura Peck. Ask him if he could spare me a few moments, would you?'

'Mr Lode not on seat.' A wide smile flashed across his black face. 'Here somewhere. Had coffee.' He went out to the roof garden and peered over the wall. Laura followed. Below was a half-empty car park.

'Still here, that his car.' He pointed, and at that moment it began to reverse slowly and swing round.

'He's going,' Laura said dismayed.

The messenger leapt to an outside staircase and hurtled down the almost vertical flights. Laura followed more carefully. She could see the stairs ended where the car would have to nose out into the street. The messenger almost threw himself in front of it.

'Mees Peck asking to see you, sir.' She could see the top of Jake Lode's dark head. He was sitting behind the driver, speaking through the open window.

'Who?' She shivered as she recognised the note of frustrated irritation in his voice. How many times had she felt exactly that when someone delayed her?

'Mees Peck, sir.'

'Hell!' There was a pause. 'Hell!'

Laura felt her toes curling in embarrassment as she watched him get reluctantly out of the car.

Only then did he see her standing on the bottom step. There was no mistaking his discomfort. He put his hand across his eyes in a gesture of apology.

Laura felt a certain repugnance about asking Laurence or anyone else for favours, and would have preferred to hire a taxi for a few hours, even one like she'd ridden in last night. The real reason she'd come into Oxley's was to cement the relationship with her father.

'Hello.' Jake Lode was coming towards her, moving like an athlete, a man of medium height and build.

'I'm Laura Peck,' she said. 'I'm delaying you, I'm sorry.'

'It's of no consequence.' Suddenly it seemed it wasn't. His impatience had evaporated, his smile was friendly.

'Laurence suggested I call in this morning. He said he'd be here, but I don't think he is.'

'He's not well, and we have a bit of a problem. He's got some documents to read, easier at home, no interruptions. He'll probably be in later.' She judged him to be in his late thirties.

'He offered to lend me a car.'

'Yes, he told me.' His dark hawk-like eyes surprised her. They were examining her minutely. His hair was dark too and wavy, with a sprinkling of silver over the temples. His manner was friendly. Very friendly. 'I'll see to it. Would you like some coffee while you wait?'

'Love some.' It was only a short time since she'd left the breakfast table, but unaccountably she wanted to spend time with this man. A cup of coffee would give her an excuse to stay. She had the feeling he offered it for the same reason.

She followed him into his air-conditioned office, feeling as though she were back on familiar ground. He had a wide modern desk. She sank into the comfortable leather armchair provided for visitors. He used the internal telephone. Spoke to somebody else about providing a car.

'Not all the expatriate staff are in yet. They drive themselves home and have the use of the vehicle after office hours. During the day, the cars go into the pool for business use.'

Laura studied his face as he spoke. It was deeply tanned with fans of white creases at the corners of his eyes.

'Is there anything else we can do to help? Laurence said I was to be sure to ask.'

'Yes. How do I get domestic help here?'

'Word of mouth.' He smiled, and the fans of creases closed up. The same messenger brought in a tray with two cups of coffee and placed one on the desk in front of her. 'What sort of help? A cook or a steward?'

Laura knew Tom's finances were limited. 'One person to do both. Is that usual?'

'Yes, Yemi will help. Miss Peck needs a good cook steward. Do you know of one?'

'Yes, sir,' Yemi nodded. His uniform had the Oxley logo on the breast pocket. 'My brother need job. He downstairs now, waiting to see cafeteria boss.'

'Does he want a job in a private house?'

'Yes, sir. Any job.'

'A flat,' Laura said. 'Will I be taking your applicant?'

'No, we've always plenty of those. Too many. Not enough jobs to go round. Experienced, is he, Yemi?'

'Yes, very good cook steward. Got references.'

'Send him up, we'll talk to him,' Lode said, and when he'd gone, he went on, 'Yemi's good. Can't vouch for his brother. Might not be his brother at all. Could be a distant relative or just someone from the same village.'

'I have to start somewhere. What's the going rate?'

'If he looks all right, offer him ten pounds a month, and a month's trial. Here he is. I'll leave you to talk to him.'

Laura looked at his black face and wide smile, deciding

he was worth a trial. He wore clean khaki trousers, and had several fulsome references. Pleased she had someone to help, she asked him to wait in the roof garden until she was ready to leave. Jake Lode returned to drink his coffee.

'Are you a family connection? An Oxley?'

'Did Laurence tell you that?' She was pleased, hoping he had. It would mean he was accepting them, could talk about them.

'No.' The dark hawk-like eyes didn't leave her face. 'But you've got the Oxley colouring. The same jawline as Mary.'

'I come from the wrong side of the blanket.' She laughed self-consciously. She'd never spoken about it before. 'I'm not sure whether Laurence wants people to know.'

'Laurence? He's your father? Good God! I've never heard the slightest whisper . . .' His mouth sagged open. Amazement filled his eyes.

Aghast, Laura pulled herself up in her chair. 'What am I saying?' Suddenly she realised that to spread her story could queer her position with Laurence for ever, the opposite of what she wanted. She couldn't understand the effect Jake Lode was having on her. She usually kept a tight control on her tongue. The last thing she wanted was to embarrass Laurence.

Her voice was urgent. 'Please don't say anything to him. It's very awkward, not knowing . . . well, whether he wants to recognise me or not.' His dark eyes were hunting hers again. 'I mean, he hasn't up to now, but we've just met. I suppose this sounds very strange . . .'

He laughed out loud. 'Don't worry, I won't accost him with his past. Mary's never hinted—'

'I don't think Mary knows anything about me or my mother. He kept it to himself. That's what makes it . . .'

He laughed again, throwing back his head till she could see the muscles in his throat vibrating with amusement.

'I'd never have thought it of Laurence.'

'Don't mention it to anyone. Please. It might upset him.'

'It'll be our secret,' he said and his eyes laughed into hers. He wore a tie with his white shirt. The sleeves were rolled up showing tanned arms with golden hairs growing down to his wrists.

Laura took a deep breath. He was the sort of man she'd be glad to have working for her. She knew instinctively he'd be very able. That was the sort of judgement she made regularly, and she'd learned to trust. On a personal level, she was never as sure. He was sending strong sexual signals towards her. It had happened often enough for her to think she was right about that too. They'd get on well, and she'd enjoy his company. She hoped she'd see more of him as well as Laurence.

A driver knocked on the door to take her down to the allocated car. Jake Lode walked with her down the corridor. For the first time she noticed a door with the name Mrs M. Lode on it.

She stopped, taken aback, wanting to ask but not knowing how. She'd thought him unmarried. His whole manner said he was interested in her in. How could she have misread the signals to this extent?

'That's Mary's office.'

'Your wife?' She couldn't keep the note of stunned amazement out of her voice, and despised herself for it.

'Yes.'

Suddenly it dawned on her. 'Not Mary Oxley? You're not married to her?'

'Yes,' he said slowly. 'Didn't Laurence tell you?'

Laura made herself smile. It wasn't easy. His hawk eyes wouldn't leave her face. 'No.'

CHAPTER TWENTY-TWO

Jade Lode lashed out at the ball and missed it. He was lathered with sweat. The sound of balls bouncing off concrete reverberated in his head, and his reactions were those of a tortoise. He knew he was playing the worst game of squash in his life.

He was in the habit of coming to the club in the early evening for a game of squash, a few lengths up and down the pool, and a drink. It kept him fit and helped him relax.

He liked the Apapa Club because David Mountford, Mary's ex-husband, had never been a member. The tennis and squash courts were good, and cinema shows were held twice weekly. It was somewhere to spend his leisure time and find a bit of company while Mary was in England. Tonight nothing could make him relax.

Mary had been in a foul temper when she'd put through a call by radio telephone. A few weeks ago, she'd told him to send the accounts home to her. She'd expected him to do exactly that, and was not pleased he'd chosen to interfere.

'I did all the work at home two years ago. In fact I've done it several times.' Her voice had been sharp with irritation.

'You should have taken the books home with you. Or asked me to bring them when I came.'

'I was ill. I couldn't think of work.'

'What if they got lost in the post? It would cause a fiasco.'

'Why should they get lost? For God's sake!'

'It's easier and cheaper to get the work done here, Mary,' he said and caused her to explode.

'The accounts have nothing to do with you. I wish you'd do your job and let me do mine.'

That had riled him and made him bark back: 'If I'm Lagos manager everything is my business, including the accounts. If they're late—'

'If you'd sent them to me when I asked, they wouldn't be late. I see to the accounts, I always have.' The phone had crashed in his ear, and he'd let out a string of expletives. Being Mary's husband was not the sinecure everybody thought.

It was no good saying the accounts were not his problem. He'd been worried she wouldn't finish, she didn't seem to take the job seriously. If she gave up altogether, he could employ a permanent accountant and life would be a whole lot easier. He'd even thought she might.

He'd booked another person-to-person call to Mary. He was told the line to England would be closing in ten minutes and they wouldn't be able to place his call until tomorrow.

What was happening to them? Mary had hung up on such a bitter note. He could hardly believe their marriage had disintegrated to this after only ten months. Damn it, he hadn't seen her for nine of that ten, except for the week he'd flown home when the baby was born, and the odd weekend when there had been a directors' meeting. It wasn't really marriage at all. Had he been naive to expect Mary to live with him?

Laura was another reason he couldn't relax. Her green eyes disturbed him. There was something very attractive about the way her honey-coloured hair swung about her face. She drew his attention, made him feel alert. It would be too easy to establish bonds; already they were kindling into life. It would bring complications he couldn't afford.

He hadn't the energy to swim tonight. It was getting dark anyway, and the mosquitoes would soon be out in force. He showered quickly and decided to have a drink.

He'd been dropped into the ex-husband's job and, after twelve months, felt he'd found his feet and was enjoying it. He just wished he could say the same for his marriage.

He'd had a lot to learn about the job. He'd talked to the Oxley managers about it. They'd all had plenty to say about David Mountford too. He had been both popular and efficient. Jake had inherited his secretary and his files; they told the same story. He was a hard act to follow. Jake could stomach that. What he resented was the way David Mountford infiltrated his private life.

Mountford had designed and built the house he lived in. He'd had to tell the steward to clear out Mountford's shorts and T-shirts from the wardrobes before he could unpack his own cases. David's books were around the house in large numbers. Jake read them because there was nothing else. He played his records. Jake had found reels of amateur movie film stacked in a cupboard one Sunday in the wet season. He'd set up the projector hoping to learn more about Mary.

It had brought a lump to his throat to see her as a slim young bride in white, smiling up at her groom in morning dress. She'd been seven months' pregnant when he'd taken her to the Registry Office, and the few photographs they had showed only their heads and shoulders.

He couldn't stop running the reels, though each was painful. Mary looked younger and prettier in them, smiling into the camera, looking happier than he was able to make her. He felt he knew more about Mary's ex-husband than he knew about Mary herself. He even wondered if he could be jealous of him, but that was ridiculous. Mary had proposed to him.

Jake hadn't been able to leave David's old home movies alone. When he was feeling lonely because Mary wouldn't join him, he'd dig out yet another box of reels and wallow in misery. He wanted to know what Mary's life had been like before he knew her. There were pictures of his stepdaughter Carlotta as a baby, toddler and young child playing and laughing, on the beach, and at the pool. He'd met her during her half-term holiday, a hostile ten-year-old, not accepting him in her home, very unhappy to find him in her daddy's place. He'd had no time to get to know her.

He had found a reel labelled Dinah that showed another, younger, child with Carlotta and her nanny. She seemed to be in Mary's home. Both were like her, with the Oxley blonde colouring. It seemed inconceivable that she'd had two children and only ever spoken of one.

But when Lucinda was born and was found not to be normal, Laurence had told him that there had been another baby with the same problems. He'd asked Mary about her.

'Oh yes, Dinah.' As far as her mother was concerned, she might never have lived. It worried Jake that Mary had never mentioned her existence till now.

'What happened to her?'

'She's dead.'

'But when . . .?'

'She was six.'

'An accident?' He knew he probed too hard. He could feel her reluctance.

'Not exactly. She was never right. Better that way, really.'

When it was first suggested Lucinda had problems, he hadn't taken the matter too seriously; she'd seemed perfectly normal to him. Laurence spoke to him.

'They call it slow development, but really the poor babe doesn't develop at all.' He seemed devastated. 'A tragedy for Mary, to have it happen twice. With different fathers, too.' That brought home to him the magnitude of the problem. He wished Mary would come back, so he could show her he loved her.

Jake had first come to Nigeria because he'd wanted to see something of the world, and Standard Oil had been advertising for a construction engineer. He stayed with them long enough to learn the business, take an external degree in petrochemicals, and discover fortunes were not earned by those who worked for others. He could see business opportunities all round him, but which to choose and how to start were problems he couldn't overcome.

He'd been twenty-eight when a Nigerian acquaintance, Akim Owere, who owned a plant making colas, a tarmacadam surface for roads, asked for his technical expertise. Jake had driven out to the plant the following Saturday to discover the work force was made up of Owere's relatives from his tribal village community. The company was desperate for capital as well as technical know-how.

He advised Owere to sack the six most senior of his staff and hire one expatriate manager with relevant experience.

Owere didn't take his advice. Six months later he was on the verge of bankruptcy and appealed to him again.

Jake thought very hard. Expatriates were no longer allowed to set up a business in Nigeria without at least one Nigerian partner. He decided to throw up his own job to run the colas plant. He put in his savings, borrowed heavily from the bank, and went in as Owere's partner. Three months later Owere died in a car accident, and Jake found his partner was Owere's wife, Comfort.

Cash flow continued to give him major problems for the first year. He'd thought the business was going under more than once, and the whole thing a disaster. Then a government modernisation programme demanded Nigeria's laterite roads be tarmacadamed. He obtained public works contracts and they brought him prosperity. He paid off his loans, and Mrs Owere, keeping her only as a figurehead.

More public works contracts were forthcoming, and on the strength of them he started another plant in Ibadan and a third in Kano.

By the time he was thirty-five, Jake knew he was growing dissatisfied. His colas plants were a success. He had all the money he wanted, but his tastes were not extravagant. He'd had enough of working in the Nigerian bush and living in rest houses. He wanted theatres, restaurants and civilisation. He wanted to get married, have a family and a settled home. He'd known various women, but he didn't think he'd find what he wanted in the bush.

When Laurence Oxley put feelers out about acquiring his business, Jake decided to sell, if he could get the price he wanted. When Oxley came to look over his plant he brought his daughter Mary and her husband David Mountford with him. Jake thought David astute and a likeable fellow. He took the trio with him to Ibadan, and Kano.

Then the haggling started. Oxley had a reputation for never paying over the odds for anything. Jake wasn't going to settle for a penny less than his business was worth. Oxley offered him the job of building a new oil storage terminal in Lagos. He turned it down flat. The weeks dragged on.

Jake stalled, and longed for civilisation and all he'd do when he got there.

Suddenly all Lagos was agog with the news that mild-tempered David Mountford had floored Robert Oxley in a fight at the club, had packed his bags and flown home. Rumour had it he'd abandoned both his job and his wife.

A day later Laurence Oxley told him he'd meet his price for his colas plants, provided he took some of the value in Oxley shares. At the same time, he offered him David Mountford's job as manager of Oxley Enterprises in Lagos. He hoped he'd be able to oversee the building of the oil storage terminal too.

Jake almost refused. The fleshpots of Lagos were not what he had in mind when he'd dreamed of civilisation. For the sake of a smooth parting from Oxley, he agreed to think it over while he took leave in England. As he was waiting for take-off, he recognised Mary Mountford smiling at him across Lagos's airport lounge. He asked if he might sit at her table.

Mary had intrigued him when she'd delved into his colas accounts, and he liked what he saw now. Her intelligent face was framed in a cloud of fly-away blonde hair. She was sophisticated and self-confident, and her opinions were worth listening to. He thought at first she was a little older than he was. Her fine fair skin was developing lines. But there was a fizz about Mary, she laughed a lot. And if what the gossips said was true, Laurence Oxley's daughter might be in need of a new man.

'I'm being divorced,' she confirmed, and for a moment seemed serious. Then her wide smile came again. 'And I need a bit of a fling, to lift me out of it.'

Jake laughed with her and thought he was falling in love.

'I'm going to do all the things I enjoy. Live it up. Have some fun. See my daughter.'

'Don't you see her?'

She shook her head. 'She's ten now and away at boarding school.'

Jake thought of all the years he'd wasted, and couldn't believe she had a child of ten. He told her so.

The plane was grounded at Rome with engine trouble, and after sitting around the airport for hours they were ferried to a hotel. They were each given a room for the night; they used only one.

Mary came into his life like a shaft of light. She knew all the best places to go in Liverpool and Manchester. She had a wild energy, organising trips here, a dinner there, dancing somewhere else. Jake couldn't believe his luck. He'd meant to spend some time with his parents in Southport, but Mary persuaded him to stay in Caldy with her.

'Is this your house, Mary?' he'd asked in amazement when she took him there. 'It's very grand.'

'Well, I chose it, and I live here, but Dad bought it for me. He owns it really. He says he's willed it to me and provided I behave myself, it'll be mine. Do you like it?'

He'd been thinking it was a mansion, and worth a fortune. He hardly liked to put that in words.

He had three months' leave, and was more than happy to spend them with her. They were inseparable, and he'd never had so much champagne.

Jake loved her, and he'd been so sure she loved him. Why else would she ask him to marry her? He'd been almost too surprised to speak, but he remembered elation surging through him and over-flowing like a fountain.

'Queen Victoria had to propose to Prince Albert, did you know?' she'd laughed. 'She was afraid he'd never get round to it. I was afraid you'd never get round to asking me.'

Till then he hadn't thought of it but he'd jumped at the chance. He'd seen it as a whirlwind courtship. Mary wanted to marry as soon as possible; he'd been filled with love for her and ached to please.

The wedding was already arranged when she told him she was pregnant. She'd been in floods of tears, and he'd held her close and whispered comfort. He loved Mary so much, he didn't see it as a problem. It was months before he wondered if she might have planned things that way.

Jake returned to Lagos alone to take over the vacancy Mary's first husband had left. Laurence Oxley was suddenly more generous, talking of a directorship and grooming him to take over eventually as Managing Director. Jake tried to tell him he wanted no special favours, he loved Mary and needed no inducement to marry her.

But they couldn't marry till Mary received her decree absolute, and she'd been seven months pregnant by that time. He'd gone home for the wedding and brought her back with him, but only three weeks later she'd fallen and injured her knee and had to go back to Liverpool. He'd gone home to see the baby when she was born, but the news about her was depressing. It hadn't been much of a marriage so far.

Jake walked across to the bar. It filled one end of the big club room where on Saturday nights there was dancing to records and a late supper. It was not smart, its wooden armchairs had khaki drill cushions to cover their slats. Condensation from cold beer bottles had long since ruined the tables.

He was gulping down his beer when Robert Oxley came and perched on the next stool. Jake inched away. The less he had to do with Robert the better he liked it. He knew Mary and her father had been at loggerheads over him for years, and that she was fond of her cousin.

'Hello, what will you have?'

Exactly what Robert had done to offend Laurence had never been spelled out to him, though he'd asked.

'I'm all right.' Ungraciously Jake indicated the two inches of beer left in his glass. It was a family quarrel he didn't want to be drawn into.

An attractive dark-skinned girl hovered in the doorway, luminous brown eyes scanning the customers in the bar. To Jake's surprise, Robert signalled to her. Her face broke into a brilliant smile as she came towards them.

'Do you know Giselle Ayella?' Robert drew her closer, fondling her arm. 'My new secretary,' he explained, but his blue eyes smiled down at her possessively.

Jake shook her hand warmly, glad to have proof the gossips were wrong when they said Robert was in love with Mary. This girl was far too young for Robert, but she was clinging to him, had eyes for nobody else. 'You've just come out?'

'No, I've been in Nigeria nine months.'
'You're not English?' He couldn't place her accent and she had an exotic air.
'My father was half English and half Spanish. I'm a bit of a hotch-potch,' she laughed. 'I grew up in Algiers, my mother was half French, half Algerian.'
'I poached her,' Robert said, 'from the British and French Bank in Port Harcourt. How's Mary?'
'Upset about the baby. There are problems.'
'Yes, I'm sorry.' A nerve jerked in Robert's cheek. 'She told me. I saw her when I was in Liverpool recently.'
'I suppose you know Mary had a child some years ago, affected in the same way?'
'Yes, Dinah.' The finality of Robert's tone told Jake he didn't want to talk about her.
'Mary's taking it very hard.'
'Yes, it's the Oxley affliction.'
'Do you have any children?' Jake asked. There was an odd sort of pause.
'No,' Robert replied. 'Just as well, perhaps.'
Jake gulped his beer and mused that marriage and family were not bringing him the pleasure he'd expected.
'How's Mary's knee?' Robert asked.
'Improving. She'll be back soon.'
'Will Carlotta come with her?'
Jake resented the interest Robert took in his stepdaughter, though he knew Mary encouraged him to visit her school and take her out when he was in England. Carlotta seemed to adore Robert, in marked contrast to her hostility towards Jake. He'd not liked that.
'She'll not come before the summer holidays.'
'She'll stay for all of them?'
'Possibly, I don't know.'
'Carlotta wants to come. I think she should. She needs to get to know you. She rather resented being packed off on one of those children's adventure holidays at Easter.'
'It's up to Mary,' Jake said stiffly. It was an unpleasant experience to find Robert advising on his stepdaughter's needs.

* * *

Laura looked at Ignatius's hair growing in tight tiny curls against his black neck. He sat in front with the driver, enjoying the novelty of a car ride, as they headed towards Apapa. At ten in the morning it was uncomfortably hot in the Morris Oxford that Oxley's provided for expatriate managers. Laura knew she should be watching the route they were taking so she could find the way by herself next time, but she couldn't concentrate on anything. The current that had sparked between her and Jake Lode left her feeling breathless.

For years, Laura had felt an empty space in her life. It was so obvious, even Tom talked about it. She knew the factory girls at Burdon's envied her money and success but pitied her because she had no man. Apart from Tom, Laura had never met a man who attracted her. At twenty-eight she was beginning to think she never would. She had prided herself on being in control of her feelings, cool and objective in her decisions. Now Jake Lode had shattered all that in one short meeting.

The sun blazed down, she was sticking to the plastic seat. The traffic was heavy, every vehicle they passed blew clouds of dust into the car. It made her skin feel gritty. Impossible to close the windows, it was like an oven with them open. She relived the moment when Jake's hawk-like eyes laughed into hers. If only he wasn't Mary Oxley's husband. She couldn't get over that he was.

'The Apapa Club, miss,' the driver told her as they were entering a road shaded by tall casuarina trees. A little further along he pulled into a compound surrounding a block of six government flats. Laura got out.

The block was three stories high and built of concrete blocks coloured green. Tom had been allotted a middle-floor flat. The compound had sparse tufts of rough grass in hard-packed earth. A lone bed of dusty canna lilies grew under one window.

A pick-up came in behind them. It took Laura a moment to realise it was bringing Tom's heavy baggage and the crates of household effects she'd asked Oona to pack for him.

The cement stairs were dusty, the front door opened into the living room. There were two bedrooms with a bathroom between, a pleasant balcony, and a slit of a kitchen leading to some back stairs. There was no telephone. Tom led her from room to room, telling her it wasn't too bad.

'Better than Jubilee Street,' she agreed. It was a far cry from the comfort and elegance of her new house.

He was delighted to see Ignatius, and gave him the key to the servant's quarters over the garage block. Ignatius humped their baggage up the stairs, a permanent grin slashing his black face. There was no air conditioner and the mosquito nets had holes.

Tom seemed lost, hardly knowing what to do next. Laura had to direct him towards the crates which were being hauled up to the balcony. He began to lever them open. Laura wished she knew which one held the brooms and mops; she unpacked three before she came across them.

The slightest exertion in the heat and high humidity made the sweat run off her. She remembered reading somewhere that on the human face, eyebrows were provided to stop sweat running into the eyes. She hadn't believed it till now. But her meeting with Jake had given her a tremendous surge of energy, and she threw herself into making up beds, stowing crockery and cutlery, turning the flat into a home.

Elin, dripping with perspiration, was hanging the crimson curtains they'd used in the farmhouse. They barely reached the living room sills, and were still stiffly holding the creases of the iron. Laura decided it would be less exhausting for her to go shopping and sent her off to wash her face and change her dress.

'The driver says Oxley's have a store here in Apapa, so there's no need to go back to Lagos. Take him inside to carry the stuff; we need absolutely everything. Be sure to bring some polish for this furniture.'

Laura was pleased to see her mother go off alone without asking for a shopping list. She seemed better.

Ignatius swept the parquet floor, first dripping water on it to lay the dust, and Tom helped him lay out the carpet square. It wouldn't lie flat because it had been folded in the crate, but the room was beginning to looked more settled. Laura had to direct Tom towards filling his bookcase and Ignatius towards cleaning out the fridge and kitchen shelves.

By the time Elin returned with the food, Laura's hair was wet with sweat, and her clothes sodden and sticking to her. She pushed two armchairs onto the little balcony, and she and Elin collapsed there drinking tea and nibbling halfheartedly at the sandwiches Ignatius made to go with it. Tom took the car to report for duty.

It was too hot to do any more, none of them had any energy left.

It was almost three o'clock when Tom returned with the car. His new colleagues had taken him to the club for a drink; his membership had been proposed and seconded, and their temporary membership arranged. He didn't want the sandwiches Laura had kept for him. He went to lie down on his bed.

Ignatius asked if he might take their bucket and brooms to clean his quarter. Laura gave him Tom's lunch as well. Then she closed her eyes and tried to think. She had to return the car to Oxley's, and they hadn't seen Laurence yet.

'I don't want to see him,' Elin said. 'What's the point?'

'We have to thank him, Mam, and he'll be able to tell us where we can get an air conditioner. Probably sells them himself.' Elin had been loud in her praise of the air conditioning in Oxley's store. Laura decided she'd have to get one for the flat if they were to survive.

She ran a deep bath of tepid water to refresh herself, and put on a white cotton dress printed with sunflowers. Laurence should be in the office by now. She hoped she'd see Jake too. All the time she'd been hanging pictures and putting out ornaments, he'd been on her mind.

As their borrowed car turned into Oxley's car park they came bumper to bumper to Jake's car going out. He had to back up to let them in.

'I don't seem to time my visits very well,' Laura laughed. She felt no embarrassment this time. 'I'm delaying you again.'

His eyes wouldn't leave hers. 'Any time is fine. You know that.'

'Is Laurence in now?' she asked.

'No, he isn't coming today. Not feeling well.' She noticed his frown as though he were perplexed by this. 'I told him you'd been in, he seemed pleased. Told me to look after you.'

'I need more help. Can you tell me where I can buy an air conditioner? We're melting in this heat.'

'You've come to the right place,' Jake laughed. 'We import them, and sell them through an agency.'

He took charge, leading them back into his office, advising on the size needed, checking there was one in stock, and arranging for it to be fixed in their bedroom window first thing in the morning.

'I'm very grateful.' Laura was getting to her feet to leave.

'How about a trip round the harbour?' It seemed a spur of the moment invitation. 'Laurence asked me to show you round. The only cool place is out on the water.'

'That would be imposing on you.'

'No, I want to take you.' His dark eyes smiled from her to Elin. 'I don't spend enough time in my boat. It's fun.'

'In that case we'd love to.'

'The boat's at Apapa, I keep it on the site we're developing. There's a small creek there. I'll ring now and ask them to put it in the water.'

'A new venture here?' Laura asked, as they went down to the car park.

'Yes, an oil storage depot.' He was leading them towards an Austin Healey, the same model she had just arranged to buy, except that it was scarlet.

'You've got a car like the one Tom and I have just bought,' Laura laughed. His face jerked towards her, his hawk-like gaze catching hers. She knew it was because she'd mentioned Tom. He didn't ask who he was. She didn't explain.

'It's Mary's. It's been standing idle for weeks. I thought I'd make sure it was all right before she came back.' He didn't seem to want to talk about Mary. 'When Laurence is here, I have to leave the Humber standing by for him.'

Laura climbed quickly into the rear seat, leaving Elin to sit beside Jake. The top was down, the hot moist air tumbled her hair. She couldn't lift her eyes from tanned arms and the golden hairs growing down to his wrists.

He turned off towards the harbour. 'This is the little creek.'

'Attractive,' Elin murmured. It was an inlet from the harbour, palm trees leaned out over it. A small jetty was under construction at its head. Large and shabby, a once ostentatious day boat was moored there.

'Rather a vulgar boat, I'm afraid,' he smiled at Laura. 'American-built. For the Florida Keys.' The scarlet fibreglass had faded and showed a large patch on the stern. It had been too lavishly trimmed with chromium which was now spotted with rust. 'Once it was Akim Owere's pride and joy. My Nigerian partner's. When he died, his widow wanted to be rid of it.'

Laura stood back to read the name painted on the hull – *Hoof Hearted*. 'Your idea?' She was laughing.

'I'm afraid so. Totally vulgar, but it suits the craft. It's great fun, though.'

He held it steady while they climbed in. It had a cuddy on the front, with a padded bench along each side, Aft, a striped awning provided shade. Elin lowered herself awkwardly on to the seat and Laura followed. It rocked gently as Jake slid behind the steering wheel.

'What was it called before?'

'Owere hadn't got round to naming it.' The powerful outboard fired, and they were moving out into the harbour. She asked about Owere, and was fascinated to hear about his colas plants.

Laura had never been in a small boat before. They gathered speed. She loved the exhilaration of racing across water that was like blue glass, loved the way the breeze fluttered her hair, and the sun made their wake sparkle.

Jake headed down the length of the wharf. She looked up the steep smooth sides of the ocean-going cargo boats towering over them. Ships from all over the world were tied up at the quay. She caught the scent of tar and rope and diesel on the breeze.

'This is wonderful,' Elin said happily, trying to restrain the tendrils of hair flapping round her face.

Jake turned across the harbour, making the little boat roar past the landing stage where the ferry boat was waiting. Even that seemed enormous as they looked up its side.

They were passing the gracious white buildings of Lagos crowding the waterfront. A fat negro woman walked like a queen along the promenade, a load of wood balanced on her head. A native fished from a canoe near the bank, circling the net in the air above his head before throwing it.

Jake flung out his arm. 'There's Oxley Stores.' Laura saw the evening sun sparkling against white stucco, the Union Jack on top, hanging limp in the heat.

'Can I have a go?'

'Of course. Easier than driving a car.'

Laura slid behind the wheel. She was very conscious that he remained behind her seat, half leaning over her. She sent the boat on, level with the marina, just about keeping up with a taxi heading out to the suburbs. He pointed out the General Hospital, and Government House where the High Commissioner lived. At the Yacht Club, members were sitting under bright umbrellas on lawns stretching down to the water's edge. Flags fluttered from a line of flagstaffs, and a fleet of small sailing boats rocked on the water nearby.

Laura felt exhilarated, fully alive for the first time for years. The world was opening up for her. She found herself laughing aloud with sheer joy. Beside her, Jake was laughing too, flinging his arms wide in an exuberant gesture. She expected them to close round her in a bear hug, and felt a sting of disappointment when they didn't.

Jake smiled self-consciously at Elin. Laura pulled herself together with a jerk. For God's sake! He was Mary Oxley's husband. What was she thinking of?

CHAPTER TWENTY-THREE

The next morning they got up early only because workmen were coming to fit the air conditioner into their bedroom window. Laura meant it to be a lazy day.

Tom was picked up after breakfast by a colleague and taken to work. They pottered about the flat, Elin rearranging furniture to its best advantage, Laura listing things they still needed.

By mid-morning they were walking down to the club at the end of the road. Tom had explained they could phone for a taxi there if there wasn't one waiting. A family with towels and swimming rings was paying one off as they arrived.

They went to pick up the white Austin Healey from the garage. Laura tried it round Lagos and then drove out to Ikoyi, the main residential area, trying to get her bearings.

They went to see the beach, a long stretch of almost deserted golden sand. A few Europeans were sunbathing or splashing in the shallows. The ocean crashed in mountainous waves to race up the beach. Tom had told them the undercurrents could suck the strongest swimmer out to sea, and sometimes the triangular fin of a basking shark could be seen beyond the line of breakers.

Bare-footed, they walked in the shade of the palm trees fringing the beach, but their feet sank into the hot fine sand and they found it hard-going.

Laura was pleased to have her own transport, but it meant she had less reason to contact Oxley's. It bothered her that they hadn't seen Laurence since their arrival. Jake had said they must go over to his place for drinks, but no definite time had been arranged. Laura hoped he'd make contact again.

Ignatius served their afternoon tea on the balcony; it was a pleasant place to sit once the sun left it. Laura felt a frisson of anticipation as she watched the Morris Oxford they had used yesterday nose into the compound. It pulled up beneath them, and the door slammed. Moments later there was a knock on the flat's front door. Ignatius reached it before she could. The driver in his Oxley uniform was handing in a letter. It was addressed to Elin.

'Open it, Mam. What does he want?'

'It's from Laurence.'

'Yes.' Laura tried not to sound impatient.

'He's inviting us to lunch on Saturday. Tom too.'

'We'll look forward to that, won't we?' Laura said, feeling pleased; this was what she'd wanted.

'Will Laurence be well enough? I, mean, if he's sick . . .'

'Mam, it's three days off.'

While the driver waited, Laura found a sheet of paper and insisted Elin wrote a note of acceptance.

'Go with the idea of enjoying it. You'll be meeting on equal terms. You're his invited guest, not his housemaid now. Doesn't that help? You've reached his social standing.'

'No,' her mother groaned.

'Of course it does. What will you wear? Your navy and white cotton?'

'Yes. Oh, what does it matter?'

'Mam, he's my father. You are my mother. I'd like you to get on.'

'We were never like other parents.'

'He's my father, my flesh and blood, and I know next to nothing about him. I want to.'

Elin's golden eyes showed resistance.

'He loved you once.'

She opened her mouth to protest.

'Must have,' Laura insisted. 'I think he still does. What have you got to lose?'

'I shall be at sea,' Tom said when she told him.

'I thought you said you'd be back on Saturday morning?'

'Due back, but you never know. It would be a rush to be ready by lunch time. Anyway, I don't want to go. I can't imagine eating with the Oxleys. Do they eat from gold plates? They're people I read about in newspapers when they open a new factory.'

'Don't be an oaf.' But Laura, too, felt she might be getting out of her depth. Jake was tearing at her nerves. She must be careful not to betray her feelings.

Jake found having Laurence in the house an uncomfortable experience. He tended to treat the establishment as his own, ordering special menus, wanting normal meal times altered. Jake had to be careful not to countermand his instructions. Having Laurence as both boss and father-in-law did not make for an easy relationship.

He was glad to escape to the club for his usual game of squash when he finished work. He knew he was prolonging his stay, spending longer in the pool, and longer in the shower. As he walked across to the bar, he was surprised to hear rowdy singing.

The bar was less full than he'd supposed from the noise, but a group was getting in some solid drinking in one corner and a strong baritone was leading it in song. Jake had not seen him before, and he knew almost everyone at the club. He guessed he was Laura's friend, and felt such a surge of curiosity he couldn't drag his eyes away.

His naval shirt was splashed with pink gin and hung outside his crumpled shorts, drying stiffly. Sweat had darkened his red hair and matching beard, and shone across his crimson cheeks. Jake found it hard to see what a girl like Laura would have in common with him. He hoped he'd got it wrong; perhaps he was Elin's friend. He must be nearer Elin's age. He turned away, repelled.

As always, Iolo Cathcart was sitting on a bar stool by himself, a gin and tonic in front of him. His shirt was tucked like a dress shirt, and his white trousers had knife-like creases. He was engrossed in the singer.

Other people saw Iolo as a bit of a joke. There were too many gold chains round his beautifully tanned throat. His long, carefully disordered hair was both bleached and permed and drew the eye, advertising his trade as a hairdresser. Mary used to have her hair done at the salon where he worked.

Iolo turned and smiled at him.

'Hello,' Jake acknowledged. He supposed Iolo must be lonely. He didn't seem interested in sport, or seem ever to have a companion.

'Got a good voice, hasn't he?' Iolo stabbed his cigarette in its six-inch holder towards the singer. He was older than his slight figure suggested, probably over thirty.

Jake felt in no mood to talk to Iolo Cathcart. He made his escape by moving up to where the barman was serving and ordering a bottle of Star Beer.

He had drunk most of it when he sensed the door swing open behind him and immediately recognised the white dress with sun flowers on it. Laura walked past without seeing him, her honey-blonde hair swinging. She joined the group at the bar.

The singer recognised her too, and 'Paddy M'Ginty's Goat' petered out in mid-chorus. The man beating time with his tankard stopped.

'I think you ought to come home, Tom, dinner's ready.' Jake heard her voice clearly in the sudden silence.

Tom staggered as he tried to drag up a chair for her. His companions gave him a round of applause.

'It's only eight o'clock,' Iolo Cathcart protested, pulling another chair next to Tom's. There was a burst of laughter and somebody else started singing.

'Tom has to get up at three to catch the tide.'

'Barman, give her a drink.' Tom's speech was slurred. 'Just one for the road, then we'll go.'

Laura stopped the barman serving her and persuaded Tom to his feet.

'She knows how to handle him,' someone sniggered into his beer.

Jake was amazed Tom didn't seem to resent Laura coming to take him away. It made him think Tom must love her. He'd seen other wives do this and be censored.

Tom was staggering, he was a big man and she was slight. She could hardly keep him upright. He wanted to help her, but couldn't make his legs move. He stood clutching his beer, his eyes glued to her face, despising himself. Iolo Cathcart went to support Tom on the other side.

He wasn't ready to meet Laura's green eyes when they found his, but there was no mistaking she was embarrassed too. She steadied herself against the bar for a moment, but was quickly in command again. She smiled and nodded, acknowledging their acquaintance.

'Come on, Tom.' She gripped his arm, her voice steady.

'Can I give you a hand?' Jake managed, but she didn't hear.

Nobody spoke while they led Tom to the door. As it swung shut, there was an explosion of laughter. Jake was in time to see Laura's chin lift and knew she'd heard it too.

Laura, jarred out of a deep sleep by the alarm clock, groped for the light switch. She got out of bed and went to Tom's room.

'Tom, it's five past three, time to get up.' She saw him twist his face into his pillow in the sudden glare. 'Tom!'

'All right,' he gasped, but made no further move.

'Come on, I'll run a bath for you.' Tom had been given a ship and orders to take it down the coast. She pulled the mosquito net away roughly from his side of the bed, and made him sit up.

'Oh God, Laurie, I feel awful. I need a drink of water.'

'It's self-inflicted,' she said grimly. He'd gone to bed without eating last night. She watched him stagger to the dressing table and feel for the vacuum flask of iced water. She could almost see the first mouthfuls clearing the fuddling effects of sleep and alcohol.

He lit a cigarette and squinted at his swollen eyelids in the mirror. 'I feel as though I'm getting prickly heat rash in my beard.' His fingers were parting the wiry red curls.

'Shave it off then,' she said shortly. 'What do you expect in this climate?'

'You aren't being kind.' Tom headed towards the bathroom.

'Are you surprised? You're drinking too much. You won't keep this job unless you cut down.'

She was going back to her own room to get the clothes she'd worn last night when she heard the door of the medicine cabinet creak open, heard the neck of the gin bottle he kept there clatter against the tumbler. Heard him get into the bath. There was a great swishing of water.

In order not to disturb Elin too much, Laura brought her clothes into the passage. She was dressed when she heard Tom call: 'Laura?'

'What do you want?' She went to the door he'd left half open, careful not to look at the mound of his body rising through the soap suds. As he reached for the tumbler standing in the soap dish, Laura saw the tremor in his fingers.

'Another measure,' he grunted, nodding towards the gin bottle on the window sill.

'I'll make you some black coffee. It'll do you more good.'

'Oh, for God's sake! It clears my head and settles my stomach. The hair of the dog. How many times do I have to tell you?'

'No, Tom. You listen to me. Your seamanship is competent. You've had sound training and years of experience. Your problem is your own mind, and gin doesn't help. It causes more problems.'

She flounced off to the kitchen, busied herself making coffee, wondering why she tried so hard. She ought to let him get on with it.

When he came padding into the kitchen in his white drill uniform of shorts and knee-length stockings, he was holding his shoulders back. His damp hair was sleeked, his beard combed, and he'd lost the grey tinge from his cheeks.

'Where are my shoes?' He pulled the cup of coffee across the table towards him.

'Here as usual.' Ignatius always picked up Tom's shoes from where ever he kicked them off and put them in the kitchen after cleaning them. He took pride in putting a shine on them. Tom went back to the living room and took a full bottle of gin from the sideboard.

'What did you do with my bitters?' He was rattling the bottles about in the cupboard.

'Please don't take them. Don't take drink on board. Damn it, Tom! Don't you ever learn?'

He straightened up. Then, after a moment, put the bottles back.

'Drink your coffee.'

He gulped it down. Laura started to refill his cup.

'I've had all I want. Come on, let's go.'

She sat beside him in the Austin Healey and tried not to notice the way he drove. Tom never liked being driven. She told herself there was no other traffic about at this time of the morning, nothing to cause an accident. They went through the dock gates, past the sleepy policeman on the barrier, and onto the brightly lit quay.

'Goodbye, Laurie,' he said, patting her on the shoulder. 'Forgive me for being such a pig. I'm a bit scared of this. It's been a long time.'

'You'll be all right, Tom. Just relax.'

'I'll be back on Saturday.' He reached for his grip. 'Thanks for everything.'

She watched him bound athletically up the gangway of his ship, musing on how wrong an impression it gave, before driving home and going back to bed.

Even after a broken night, Laura didn't find it difficult to get up. It was pleasantly cool first thing in the morning, and the thought of seeing Jake again brought a lift to her spirits.

Laura dressed carefully in a slim dress of peach-coloured cotton, and added strappy high-heeled sandals. She wanted to look her best for the lunch, and then told herself she was being a fool. She shouldn't dress up for Jake Lode. He had the effect of heightening all her senses.

Ikoyi was a leafy suburb with large opulent houses set well apart. Mostly they were modern with wide shady verandahs. The Oxley house was painted white. Laura ran her car behind the two already parked in the compound. Wide steps led up to a shady verandah, running the length of the house.

French windows stood wide open. Laura could see two ceiling fans spinning in an empty sitting room.

The front door was closed. As she rang the bell, she was shocked to hear voices raised in anger. Her mother's stricken golden gaze met hers.

A steward in starched white uniform opened it immediately, ushering them in across a mosaic-tiled hall to the sitting room they'd already seen. There was a faint smell of new paint in the air as the ceiling fans spun it round. The carpet was large and thick, the armchairs deep and comfortable. Everything was smart, fresh, immaculate, a show house.

'I wasn't born yesterday. I know when the books are being fiddled.' Laurence's irate voice was very audible. 'You won't get away with it, I'll have the Fraud Squad out.'

'Don't rush into something you'll regret. I can't make sense of the figures either, but neither of us are accountants. It's probably a simple bookkeeping error. Something to be sorted out.' Jake's voice was defensive. She heard the steward's lower tones. Then Laurence's rapid footfall coming to the door.

'Hello.' His face was tight with anger barely suppressed. Behind him, Jake stood with clenched fists, his hawk-like eyes flashing.

'How very nice to see you, Elin.' Laurence's voice had come down an octave, but he looked anything but pleased. 'Let's go to the back patio. Pleasanter in this heat.' He was damping down his anger, trying to play host. They sat on the floral cushions of the fashionable garden furniture. Stress hung over them like a pall.

'Drinks, yes. What'll you have, Elin? We have all the usual things. Or perhaps Dubonnet or Pimms?'

The steward hovered.

'Two Pimms and a beer for me, Abel,' Laurence ordered.

'Beer for me too,' Jake said as the steward passed him.

The silence grew uncomfortably long. Laurence paced.

'Sorry to hear you've been unwell,' Laura tried.

His pepper and salt head turned towards her. 'I'm all right.'

'Palpitations,' Jake said. 'Raging headache. I called the doctor out.'

'I'm all right, I said,' Laurence snapped at Jake. The silence was growing uncomfortable again.

'I enjoyed the boat trip the other night,' Laura said. 'Much the pleasantest way to see Lagos.'

'Yes, I'm going to use it more often,' Jake said.

'If you stay,' Laurence spat.

'Why shouldn't I stay?'

'It depends on what the Fraud Squad find.' His face had flushed crimson again.

'I've told you, it's not me.'

'Who is it then?'

Jake got to his feet abruptly, his dark gimlet eyes raked them all. 'I'd better go, or your lunch will be a disaster.'

'No,' Laura protested. 'Please don't.' But he was off, almost bumping into the steward carrying out the tray of drinks. Laurence's face contorted with rage.

'We've come at a bad moment.' Laura looked at her mother over the top of her Pimms. She looked frightened. 'Would you rather we came some other time?'

'No, of course not.' His steel-blue gaze met hers. 'Not necessary.'

The awkward silence returned.

'Then what's the matter?'

'We've got a problem.'

Laura stifled a smile, that was obvious. 'Can I help?' He stopped pacing to stare at her. 'I'd like to if I can.'

'Perhaps.' He rushed indoors and reappeared moments later with a sheaf of papers, some ledgers and files.

'You're an accountant, aren't you? What do these figures suggest to you?'

'Well I can't just—'

'Of course not, let me explain.' He shuffled through the paper, jabbing his finger on a page, his irritation bubbling over. 'The Farmer's Bank of Nigeria at Akifpo. We have a plantation at Akifpo, but we've never used a bank there. Akifpo's a small place. We've never had any dealings with the Farmer's Bank, anywhere.'

'Come and sit down, Laurence.' Laura pulled his chair nearer her own. She was thinking of the palpitations and headaches he'd had. He threw himself on it.

'Huge sums have been transferred there without explanation. Not directly, but in and out of other accounts to confuse the picture. Nowhere in the records are there any statements for the account, or any explanation of what it's for, nor has it been put to any use. Worse, it's never paid interest.' He stood up abruptly. 'Come inside. You can look through all this and think there. I'd like your opinion. Please excuse us, Elin.'

Laura found the cool study calming. It didn't calm Laurence, the words came out in a torrent.

'Here in Nigeria we have seven different companies, all of which run their own bank accounts and keep their own books. There's the palm oil mills up country, three factories manufacturing beer, soap and fruit squashes. Retail stores and garages in most of the larger towns. Oxley Enterprises is a holding company, so the accounts are amalgamated into one balance sheet.'

'Yes, I understand.' Laura had always read all she could about Oxley's. She knew exactly how the company was structured. Laurence was going back to Elin, his face grey. He looked ill.

Laura knew Oxley's financial year had ended four months earlier. At a cursory glance, the accounts for the year 1953/1954 seemed meticulously kept and ready for audit. She was beginning to believe Jake Lode was right, the problem was a minor bookkeeping error, not the major fraud Laurence's frayed nerves indicated.

After fifteen minutes concentration, she changed her mind. Laurence had pinpointed the problem for her. As she trawled backwards and forwards, the extent of the shortfall became apparent. She couldn't believe she was right, but it seemed two million pounds had disappeared.

There was a proliferation of investment, contingency, and capital accounts, as each company had its own. Some were held in different banks, in different towns. Statements of the amounts being held in each, on the last day of the financial year, were not all to hand.

Laura felt tension twisting her muscles. Surely not? She emptied her mind, and started examining the figures again.

Embezzlement was the only reason she could think of for transferring unexplained sums totalling almost two million to an account with the Farmer's Bank.

Since Mary Oxley was the accountant, it had to be her work. For someone in her position, taking the money was easy enough, but she must know that however well she covered her tracks through the books, the loss would be discovered sooner or later. She had not covered her tracks well, and could hardly expect the accounts as she'd drawn them up to survive an audit.

Laura stretched back in the chair and thought of the difficulties all embezzlers face: making a safe getaway with the money, ensuring they'll never be caught when the law started looking for them. Laurence had said Mary was in England. Laura thought it time she was heading for South America.

Then another thought hit her like a hammer blow. Why should Mary Oxley fraudulently remove two million pounds from the company accounts? It didn't make sense. A huge proportion of the shares were still in her father's name. For all she knew, Mary could have a fortune in her own right. One day she certainly would. So why steal now? And what on earth could she spend it on? Mary must have everything she could conceivably want.

That brought her back to Jake Lode. Laura took deep breaths, and tried to think. Was he being deserted? His dark flashing eyes, his whole body language spoke of his interest in her. Perhaps the marriage had broken down. Perhaps Mary had another man and wanted enough money to keep them in comfort for the rest of their lives. Laura wanted it to be something like that. Jake seemed honest and open. She wanted to think he had no part in this.

She went slowly back to the patio. Elin was silently sipping her drink, looking ill at ease. Beside her, Laurence seemed suddenly bent and defeated. He turned when he heard her step.

'Well? What do the figures suggest to you?'

'You're right. They suggest Oxley's has been defrauded of about two million.'

'I knew it!' His face went crimson. 'Jake kept insisting it was nothing of the sort. After all I've done for him! Welcomed him into the family and the business, and all the time he's been cheating me.'

'Not necessarily. More likely to be Mary,' Laura said calmly. 'She couldn't work on the books and not be aware of what was going on.' There was a painful silence.

'Mary hasn't worked on the books for months. She wouldn't defraud the company. Why should she? She's got all the money she can use. If she wanted more, she's only to ask. What could she possibly spend two million on?'

'Another business?' Laura suggested.

'We're considering new ventures all the time. If Mary wanted to be involved in something new, there would be no problem. Not if it was viable. No, you've got it wrong.'

Laura felt sick. If it wasn't Mary, it had to be Jake. 'If Jake has taken the money, why is he still here?'

'I'll get the Fraud Squad out,' Laurence fulminated.

'Find out what's in the account with the Farmer's Bank at Akifpo first. Who opened it. Who withdrew the money, if it has gone. The proof is there. A clever embezzler could cover his tracks better than this.'

Laurence's intense blue eyes stared into the middle distance. Then he got to his feet. 'I'll put a call through to Mary now. She can come back and sort this out. It's either her or Jake.' Coiled tight with tension he began to pace. 'On Monday I'll postpone the audit, and telephone the bank.'

'They won't tell you what you want to know over the phone,' Laura pointed out. 'It would have to be a letter or a personal visit.'

'Have to fly to Enugu and get a car there. It's the back of beyond,' he sighed. 'I don't feel up to a long journey.'

'A letter then. Statements are needed from some of the other banks too.'

'It'll take a week at least. Probably longer.'

'A week won't matter. More discreet that way.'

'Mary will have to come out. I'm not putting up with this.'

Afterwards, Laura could not have said what she'd eaten for lunch. Nothing was said that didn't have a bearing on the missing money. Laurence was locked in worry about it.

He'd thanked her, and said he appreciated her support. But she wanted to support him as a daughter, not as an accountant. She'd given him professional advice. And the lunch hadn't furthered his relationship with Mam one iota.

The fear that Jake might be implicated bothered her more than anything else. She could still see the burning hurt in his eyes as he made that hasty exit.

'Where will Jake have gone?'

'I've no idea,' Laurence spat. 'Probably the office. He's that sort.'

Laura and Elin left as soon as they reasonably could.

'We'll call at his office,' Laura said as they drove out of Ikoyi. But the street door was locked, and so were the gates to the car park. There was no sign of his car in the vicinity.

'He might be anywhere,' Elin said. 'A bar?'

'The club's the only place we know.'

There was no sign of him there either. After she'd dropped Elin back at the flat, Laura decided to go down to the new oil storage site. She drove along roads almost deserted in the afternoon heat, hoping she wasn't going to make a fool of herself over Jake Lode. She was acting like a schoolgirl meeting her first personable man. She'd always prided herself on her ability to think things through, to keep a cool head and be objective. Yes, she'd loved Tom, but she was able to do what was best for both of them. Now came this passion for Jake. Already it raged out of control. She could no longer think of the long-term consequences.

The sun sparkled on the waters of the creek. It looked serene and beautiful with palm trees leaning out over it. The red fibreglass boat was not to be seen; she wondered if he'd gone out in it.

She drove slowly on, looking across nineteen acres of semi-scrub sloping down to the harbour. New tarmacadam roads had been laid through it, and footings put in for new buildings.

She came to one of the site's original buildings. Through the open double door of a garage she could see the red fibreglass boat winched on its trailer. A boy was cleaning it.

She drove on round the building to the section which Jake had told her was being used as an office, until he could build something better. A huge roof of corrugated iron which had once been painted red overhung three small rooms and the garage, and formed a covered walkway. Laura felt a jerk of satisfaction when she saw the red Austin Healey parked in front. By the time she was getting out, Jake's dark eyes were watching from the walkway.

'Hello, Laurence said you'd be working.'

'I had to get away. Work helps, takes my mind off other things.'

'A true Oxley trait.'

'I'm only an in-law.' Jake had a wry smile. 'And he's talking of throwing me out on my ear.'

'You didn't do it, Jake?'

'Do you have to ask?' The dark gimlet eyes challenged hers. She looked away.

'It was Mary then?'

Jake sighed through his teeth. 'Hell, I don't know. But I haven't taken Laurence's money.' The fans of white creases at the corner of his eyes closed in anguish.

Laura began to relax, she believed him. 'Laurence is writing to the Farmer's Bank at Akifpo. Everything will be clearer when he gets a reply. You know that will prove your innocence, or why come to work now?'

'There's a lot to do . . .'

'On Saturday afternoon? Isn't it supposed to be a half day?'

'Yes, we finish at twelve on a Saturday, like everybody else.'

'Well then?'

'Mary should have set up an accounting system for this site. The work's contracted out, but we're supplying the materials. Piping, plant and machinery is coming in by the ship load,' Jake sighed. 'There's an avalanche of bills coming in too. I'm just stuffing them in a cabinet. I've got an accounts clerk starting next week, but I have to organise some system and show him what to do. I'll bring some ledgers on Monday.'

'But Mary's coming back.'

'She won't want to do this. She'll think it's beneath her.'

'Isn't she interested in the business?'

He ran his fingers through his dark hair. 'Not since I've known her, and Laurence is determined to make her sort out last year's accounts. She'll be overwhelmed.'

Laura tried to equate her recollections of Mary with his picture. Once, nothing would have overwhelmed her.

'Laurence is going to advertise for an accountant for this terminal, but it'll take time, and I have to build him a house first. I just want to set the books up, so the clerk can maintain order.'

'I could help.' As soon as the words were out, Laura knew she'd told Jake she was interested in him.

'Willing to give up holiday time?' His eyes were probing hers. She felt the flush run up her cheeks.

'It wouldn't take us long.' She wanted him here too. It would defeat her object if she was left to do the job on her own.

'We could do it on Monday. Can you come then?'

She nodded, pleased.

'Thank you, all this paperwork gets me down.'

'Among other things,' she smiled.

'No point in working Saturday afternoon if you're coming to help.' He went inside the office. From the door, Laura watched him stuffing bundles of bills in the filing cabinet. 'About the other things getting me down,' he said.

'The missing money?'

'Yes, but Tom too.'

'Tom? Don't worry about Tom.'

'Laurence refers to him as your boy friend.'

'Yes,' she said. Something else was needed. 'Not in the accepted sense.'

'What sense then? Aren't you going to tell me?'

'It's a long story,' she sighed. A story that could still make her ache. Jake was upset, belligerent even, not in a mood to listen.

'Come and have a cup of tea at the flat. You'll probably meet him, and when you see him—'

'I have seen him. At the club the other night.' His voice told her he'd disliked him on sight.

'Jake, you're prickly. Just come and talk to him.' He allowed himself to be drawn outside to where the two Austin Healeys were parked side by side. Laura drove ahead.

As soon as she turned into the compound, she knew Tom had company, because Iolo's maroon Morris Minor was parked as close to the main entrance as he could get it.

She led the way upstairs; sand and dust gritted under their shoes. She saw the place through Jake's eyes. It would seem cramped after his house. As she put her key into the door there was the sound of laughter.

Tom and Iolo had been sitting together on the sofa. They moved apart as she went in.

'I've brought Jake for a cup of tea.' She introduced them. Jake seemed surprised to see Iolo and Tom seemed embarrassed. 'Where's Mam?'

'She went to lie down.' Tom's beard nodded in the direction of the bedroom.

'You'll need to make fresh tea.' Iolo got to his feet and stacked the cups and plates he and Tom had used on a tray. The living room was untidy. She'd given Ignatius some time off because they'd been going out to lunch. He wouldn't return till it was time to start cooking dinner.

Jake stood in the kitchen doorway watching as she boiled the kettle and washed out the teapot. Tom was on his best behaviour, making stilted conversation about his new job. He was thrilled because he'd been given command of a ship.

She couldn't find so much as a biscuit or a piece of cake to offer with the tea. Iola was restless, he was sitting on the sofa fingering the gold chains round his neck. Eventually, Tom noticed and suggested they go down to the club. Relieved, Laura carried the tea into the living room.

'Iolo's a strange lad.' Jake sank down beside her on the sofa.

'You know him?'

'Not really. I've spoken to him in the bar. Never seemed to have a friend till now.'

'I'm hoping they'll be good for each other,' Laura smiled.

Haltingly, she started to tell him about helping Tom carry a coffee table home. About how she'd loved him since she was thirteen, and how she'd believed he loved her.

'Over the years we've grown close. Despite everything, we've been good for each other.'

Jake relaxed and sat back, drinking his tea. Laura waited for his explanation of Mary. It didn't come. A marriage couldn't be explained away. He didn't mention estrangement, separation or divorce.

She got up to take Elin a cup of tea, telling herself she was a fool. Her revelations about Tom had only served to bring Jake closer. If she had any sense at all, she'd choke him off.

CHAPTER TWENTY-FOUR

'I'm going to help Jake on Monday,' Laura said. 'At his new site.'

'You're going to work?' Elin's voice was filled with amazement.

Laura felt a tinge of guilt. Mam was much better, but she shouldn't be left too long on her own.

'It won't take more than a couple of mornings.' Laura paused. 'What will you do?'

'Walk down to the club and have a swim. I enjoy that.' Elin's eyes followed her.

'We should see more of Lagos while we're here.'

'We've looked round the cathedral and been to the beach,' Elin said. 'What else is there?'

Laura tried to think. They'd also seen hawkers with wares piled high on their heads. Beggars with untreated fractures. Blind men being pulled along by a relative, begging bowl in hand. Dust and noise, and appalling odours.

Yet it attracted Europeans. Colonial officers maintained law and order, running essential services. Foreign commercial entrepreneurs like the Oxleys saw the means of acquiring wealth. Missionaries wanted to promote alien Gods. Lesser mortals were attracted by higher salaries.

'We'll have lunch out tomorrow,' Laura said. 'And then have another look round. When you've had your swim, come to the site. Get a taxi. If there isn't one outside the club, ask the barman to phone for one.'

'I'd like that,' Elin said. 'Good.'

On Monday morning Laura set out early, excitement making her grip the wheel tightly as she nosed into the road leading to the site.

Already the mangrove swamp had disappeared, and gullies and hillocks had been made a uniform height. Chains of lorries had come full of sand and shale, and an army of African workmen, bare from the waist up, were spreading it with shovels. More lorries were arriving with concrete blocks.

The office was open, she could see a steward raising a cloud of dust with a broom made of twigs, but she knew Jake hadn't arrived because there was no car outside. She walked on behind the building. The ground fell away a few feet to the harbour, a sheet of pale green glass.

In the distance, several big ocean-going freighters were tied up at the Port of Apapa, cranes were beginning to swing over the holds. A ferry boat travelling between Lagos and Apapa came so close she felt she could almost reach out and touch it.

A few hundred yards to her right a tanker was tying up to discharge its cargo to a space-age terminal. Snaking pipework, rows of mammoth silver tanks and spheres glinted in the morning sun. There were new buildings, offices, filling sheds, tanker bays, all served by new roads and a rail link. She could see the flurry of figures working, road tankers and cars moving.

Jake seemed to be building something similar on his twenty acres of wilderness. Laura was surprised Oxley's had allowed someone else to get in first.

Jake pulled his car out to overtake a cyclist with a mattress on his shoulders. The early morning traffic crawled through the streets of Lagos, holding him up. He was in a hurry, he wanted to get to the site office before Laura.

He groaned as a handcart piled high with green oranges blocked his way. For the past week, every time he closed his eyes he'd see her face before him. Green eyes with heavy lashes smiling at him. A dusting of freckles spreading across her cheeks. She'd taken him over, robbed him of the ability to concentrate on anything.

He'd been trying to analyse what he felt for her. He hardly dared call it love, but what he craved above everything else was to make love to her. He could feel her flesh beneath his fingers now, yielding. Mary had never burned her way into his mind like this.

The next question he asked himself was what did he intend doing about it? He just didn't know. What could he do, when the trauma of Lucinda's birth was still fresh in his mind and the whole affair with Mary so recent?

It made matters worse that Laura was an Oxley too, and Mary's half-sister. He was glad she'd told him that before he'd done something stupid, like telling her he loved her. He'd do nothing. In his position, Laura was dynamite.

Her car was outside the office when he arrived, but she wasn't inside. He went round the back and saw her coming towards him, the thin cotton pleating of her skirt swinging with her body.

'Good morning.' There was bounce in her step. Her green eyes sparkled with life. She was everything Mary was not, and yet he could see the Oxley likeness.

He led her into his office, dumping the pile of ledgers he'd brought with him on his desk, trying to still the jerking of his heart.

He would have asked for coffee, but she set about the task immediately. Her air of efficiency surprised him. She was asking questions, shelling out of him all the information he'd meant to give. His own thoughts weren't in order. Having her close like this set him on fire, body and mind.

She worked fast, telling him now exactly what was needed.

'Let's get the new clerk in. Until we set him to work, we're providing all the push and not making progress.'

Jake fetched the stout Nigerian from the next office. He was middle-aged, wore steel-rimmed spectacles and an executive-style shirt and tie.

Jake watched fascinated while she explained his duties with greater clarity than he could have done. The clerk's black face screwed up in concentration. She seemed to know instinctively when he hadn't grasped a point, going over it again from a different angle. Jake knew he was superfluous to this, but he had no intention of leaving her to it. She was a joy to watch.

He helped to carry all the documents back to the clerk's

office, and arranged a filing cabinet to store them in. Laura was writing out labels for the drawers. She seemed happy to have work to do. He smiled to himself.

'What's the joke?' She didn't miss much either.

'I was just thinking how like Laurence you are. Enjoying work.'

'You enjoy work too,' she said. 'Am I more like Laurence than Mary is?'

That made him straighten up in his chair. 'In some ways.'

'You must forgive me, I feel a little jealous of Mary.' That brought him to the edge of his seat. She was doodling on the blotter. A complicated flower bloomed as he watched.

'She's known him all her life.' The green eyes were smiling into his. He wondered if she felt greater jealousy because Mary was his wife.

'You've got his drive, his business acumen, his love of work.'

'And Mary?'

He couldn't talk about Mary. Even to think of her choked him with feelings of guilt and failure. Total desperation, too, because he'd let this happen.

'Here I am related, yet I hardly know them. Laurence isn't exactly broadcasting I'm his daughter.' Her voice was soft. The flower sprouted two leaves.

'He's thrilled he's found you.' His heart ached for her. 'He wants to see more of you, but he doesn't feel well. I organised a drinks party, business contacts, but he went up to bed after an hour. He's not socialising with anybody but you.'

'What are they like? You know them better than I do.'

'Everybody knows the Oxleys. Out for themselves. Use people.'

In the silence, a series of buds began to emerge from the original flower.

'Do they use you?' Suddenly her green eyes were searching into his. Seen close to, they had gold flecks in them.

'Laurence expects me to put myself out on his behalf. I work for him, so I do.'

He knew she'd meant Mary, but he wasn't ready to discuss her. Not yet. The silence lengthened. He jerked to his feet.

'It's time you went home. Shouldn't still be working. It's lunch time.'

'You want me gone?' For the first time, she seemed vulnerable. She began closing the books, putting them away.

'Never that.' His voice shook with emotion. It brought her eyes jerking to his again. She was reading what his body was telling her.

He felt hot, his heart was pounding. Suddenly he was reaching for her, pulling her close, finding her mouth with his. Doing what he'd been wanting to do since the day she'd walked into his office.

He felt her cling to him and knew a moment of utter bliss. He'd been right about her. She felt the same electricity sparking between them. Suddenly she was pushing against him. Loosening his hold.

'You're Mary's husband!' She threw herself back against the filing cabinets. There was no mistaking her agitation now. 'Just think of the awful complications.'

'I already have,' he said, reaching for her again, kissing her again. She smelled wholesome, of toilet soap. Her honey hair was freshly washed. It took longer for her to break free. The blood was coursing through him. 'There's Tom as well,' he said as steadily as he could.

'Forget Tom.' She was pulling her handbag from under the desk. 'It's Mary I'm bothered about.'

'She'll be here tomorrow, but not because she wants to be with me.'

'She's just had your baby.' He heard the accusation in her voice, the hurt.

He had to get away from her searing green eyes. He would have gone tearing out into the afternoon sun if the phone hadn't rung. Somehow it brought him down to earth. He lifted it; a woman was asking for Laura. He passed the handset over.

'Hello. Is that you, Mam?'

'No, I'm Giselle Ayella, I work for Apapa Oil Terminals. The next site to yours.'

'Yes?'

'Your mother's here with us. Her taxi driver misunderstood where she wanted to go and she'd paid him off before she realised.'

'Oh dear! Tell her not to worry. I'll be over to get her right away. Do I have to come round by the main road?'

'No, there's a track, just laterite, but not too rough, branching off to your left. It's not far to walk.'

'Is it all right for a car? Mam won't want to walk back.'

'Yes, if you don't mind the bumps.'

'I'm on my way. Thanks for letting me know.'

As she drove over, Laura saw a car going up to the main road. She couldn't see much of the site, it was behind an eight-foot wall. She came to huge double gates. Above them a sign read Apapa Oil Terminals, but an attendant waved her further down the road to the office, where a house flag fluttered in the breeze. An African clerk directed her into the building and indicated a door. She knocked and went in.

Elin was flustered. 'So silly of me, Laura.'

'It's understandable.' Mam was not alone.

'This is Mr Oxley, dear. Mr Robert Oxley.' Her voice was heavy with all she wanted to imply. 'He's been very kind.'

'I'm flattered taxi drivers here know only one oil terminal.'

Laura found herself staring in disbelief. Robert Oxley, her half-cousin, here too! He was taller and broader and heavier than Laurence. Darker, too, with handsome good looks. It took an effort to pull herself together. It wasn't a conscious decision not to make herself known to him. She was taken unawares. It was easier not to.

'Is this what Oxley's are building next door?'

'Something very similar.'

'You're functioning already?' Laura tried to digest the news.

'Yes, started two months ago.'

A model was laid out on a table. She went over to study it. 'Oxley's are having pressure spheres as well as tanks.'

'It won't be a better site than this.' She saw the pride in his blue Oxley eyes. He started to point out the roads and filling sheds.

'What are filling sheds for?'

'There are no pipelines in a country like Nigeria, and

distances are vast. Our wharf is here. Petrol comes in by tanker and we store it in our tank farm here. Before we can ship it up country, we have to put it in forty-five-gallon drums. You're working for Oxley Enterprises?'

'Yes,' Laura said. How else would she explain it?

'A secretary?'

She shook her head. 'Just temporary, to do a small accounting job.' She paused as another thought came to her. 'Who owns Apapa Oil Terminals? Some big oil company?'

His eyes jerked to her face. It took him a moment to answer. His tone was offhand. 'No, a local company.'

Elin was edging towards the door. 'Thank you for being so kind.'

'Yes, thank you,' Laura added. 'Come on, Mam, let's get some lunch.'

In the car, Elin said, 'Mr Robert was such a skinny child. Now look at him. Hard to believe. I don't think he recognised me.'

'No, Mam. He doesn't know who we are. I can't believe it, but he's upstaged Laurence Oxley! Got in first.'

Jake sat in the back of the Humber being driven to the airport. It wasn't so long since he'd wanted Mary to come back. Now he was filled with apprehension.

He'd watched Laurence rampaging about the office, his face crimson and sweating. Afraid he was going to have a heart attack after those palpitations.

Mary wasn't coming because she wanted to be with him but because she dared not refuse Laurence. He'd ordered her to get on the next plane. Jake had heard her making excuses on the other end of the wire.

'If you don't, I'll cut off your allowance,' Laurence had threatened. He knew how to force her to his will. He held the purse strings, that was his power.

Laurence indulged her, he was generous. Mary had everything money could buy. He lavished gifts on her and provided a high income, but he held onto all the capital. She spent every penny he gave her, why shouldn't she? There was always plenty more as long as she behaved herself. Jake sighed, he had more real wealth himself than Mary.

He could understand why Mary had taken the money. To her, capital would represent independence, freedom from her father's purse strings. She wouldn't have to jump to his bidding.

He'd expected her to defy Laurence. Two million would give her the income she needed. Mary was astute, she knew how to invest it properly. And she knew her father well enough to know he'd never call the Fraud Squad in if she admitted it. He wouldn't risk a scandal like that hitting the tabloids. He was terrified of personal and family publicity. Mary knew all that.

Jake couldn't understand why she was coming back now. He only knew she didn't come to be with him.

After such a white-hot, whirlwind courtship, he couldn't believe the fire had gone out with equal speed. It had been blighted from the start, by her unexpected and immediate pregnancy. He blamed himself for not being more careful.

The car came to a halt and his driver leapt out to hold the passenger door open. The night was hot and dark as Jake walked across the car park. The plane was already in; not long to wait.

He'd known all along his relationship with Mary was being weakened by the long periods they were spending apart. Worse than anything else, the baby was not normal. That added a bitter strain to their separation. But through it all he'd loved her and believed she loved him. He couldn't believe they'd both changed so much.

Passengers were coming through, he was watching uneasily, wishing the first awkward moments were over. She was coming now, elegant in a straight-skirted dress, her hair sparkling white-gold under the lights. But her shoulders drooped, making her look woebegone, and she was still limping. Behind her bounced a younger woman with a swinging pony tail, weighed down with a carrycot and two bags.

Close to, Mary's face was tightly controlled, with deep sour lines round her mouth. Her eyes were dull and wouldn't meet his. He took her hand; it was stiff with tension. He kissed her cheek. She took it as homage due. There was no response.

The baby was screaming. He peered in the carrycot, Lucinda's podgy face was shining with perspiration. He felt the ache of responsibility. He had to do his best for the poor mite he'd fathered. His best for Mary, who was taking it so badly. Their daughter continued to rage. There were rolls of fat on her arms and legs. How could he and Mary, who were both lean, have produced an infant like this?

They had almost reached the Humber, Sylvester was opening the boot, when he sensed Mary turning from him. She was watching a broad-shouldered figure lifting bags from the boot of an American limousine parked nearby. It was Robert Oxley. Jake's spirits sank. An encounter with Robert was unlikely to cheer Mary.

'Did you have a good flight?' he asked to draw her attention, but it was too late.

'Robert?'

He looked up, his expression telling everybody he was not pleased to see her. But she went towards him, coming to an abrupt halt when she noticed Giselle Ayella was with him. Jake heard her swift intake of breath.

'Hello, Mary, how's the knee?' His affability seemed forced. 'Can't stop to talk. I'm already late for my flight.'

'Robert, I want a word. It won't take a minute.' She turned and her eyes met Jake's. The desperation in them shocked him.

'Don't hang about, Giselle, you've seen plenty of planes take off. Go straight home. I'll see you Friday night.' Mary froze at Robert's personal tone and stared, white-faced, as Giselle smiled at Robert and then got in the back of the Cadillac. The native driver over-revved the engine and Robert moved off, swinging his case.

'Robert . . . I have to . . .' Mary couldn't quite catch up with his hurrying stride; she limped awkwardly two steps behind, talking urgently. Jake could no longer hear what she said, and it seemed Robert didn't want to.

The cases were in the boot. The nanny was in the front with the baby. Jake got in the back, and Sylvester hovered holding the door open, waiting for Mary. She came at last, hobbling on her cane, her blue eyes wild with fury.

'Saturday,' she said. 'Saturday.'

'What about Saturday?' She seemed to be disintegrating before his eyes.

'He'll not be in the office again till Saturday morning.'

'Is that important?' Jake asked gently. Robert seemed to have shattered her carefully nurtured self-control.

Laurence was trying to stifle his impatience with long slow sips of beer, regretting his decision not to meet Mary at the airport. He wouldn't settle till this was straightened out, but he didn't want her complaining he was bulldozing into her. He'd thought it wiser to let Jake go alone, especially as room in the car was limited with the nanny coming too.

At last the waiting was over. As Jake's car slid into the forecourt, he caught a glimpse of Mary's anxious face. He went out through the french window to meet her. Abel, the steward, in starched white suit and bare feet, was there before him lifting suitcases from the boot. Mary got out slowly, leaning on her cane.

He bent to kiss her cheek. 'How are you?' Her face looked drawn.

'Exhausted,' she answered tartly. 'The journey seemed endless. I couldn't move my knee in the cramped space.'

'Isn't your knee better yet?'

'If it was better, I'd have come back before now, wouldn't I?' Her limp seemed worse than it had at home. Her ash-blonde hair looked wispy. For years she'd worn it loose halfway down her back, and had her hairdressers fluff it into a cloud round her face. Her fine hair had suited that style. When she'd decided she needed something more sophisticated, she'd had it cut short. Now her fine hair couldn't hold the shape and looked untidy, giving her a wildness that matched her mood.

'I must have a cup of tea.' She slid stiffly into an armchair. Jake followed behind with her cabin bag.

'I'll ask Abel to make you one.' He went towards the kitchen.

'I'm sorry I had to bring you back,' Laurence said. 'I'm worried I can't give the accounts to the auditors as they are. They show fraud, Mary, and Jake swears he's innocent.'

'Exactly what is the matter?' Mary lit a cigarette, and Laurence noticed that her hand shook. She was barely in control of her nerves, and obviously under great strain. He felt a growing certainty that she was responsible.

'You took the two million out of the business, didn't you?'

Her cigarette jerked. She laughed, it sounded forced. 'Pounds?'

'Of course pounds.'

'Why would I do that?'

'You tell me.'

Her powder-blue eyes stared into his with what seemed open innocence. As a child she'd used that guile when caught doing mischief. His suspicions multiplied.

'Damn you, Mary, doing this to me.'

'I'm not, Dad.' Her innocent eyes looked into his again. 'You're very generous. I can't think of anything to spend two million on.'

Jake had brought him another bottle of beer from the fridge. Laurence splashed it into his tankard, his irritation welling up. 'It should have been on ninety-day call at Barclay's. Just think of the interest we're losing. I tell you, when I find it, somebody's going to pay me interest. If you're cheating me, Mary, after all I've done for you—'

'I'm not, I'm not. How many times do I have to tell you?'

'Somebody is. If it's you, you might as well tell me now. Own up.' He went tearing into the study, snatched up the pile of ledgers and files, and brought them back. He opened the first and held it under her nose.

'Look, the fourteenth of May, three hundred thousand pounds was transferred from—'

'Leave it, Dad. I've just completed a three-thousand-mile journey. Can't it wait till tomorrow?'

'I'm tired of waiting. There's the audit coming up.'

'Jake said it had been postponed for a couple of months.'

Damn Jake. He'd known it would reduce the urgency. Hadn't meant her to know.

'I had to delay it. No point in making our problems public knowledge. I want it sorted.'

'I'm too tired to start now.' There was no mistaking Mary was on edge, but she was fighting back.

Abel came in with a tea tray, and set it beside her. 'About time,' she told him.

'I beg your pardon, ma'am?' He was waiting.

'Nothing, thank you.' She waved him away impatiently.

'I don't see why we can't discuss it now,' Laurence said through clenched teeth. 'What's so tiring about talking?'

'I can't think what you're on about, Dad. I'll have to look at the books. What's so urgent?'

'There are questions to be answered.'

Mary struggled to her feet. 'I need an early night. I don't want any dinner.'

'You have to eat now you're feeding the baby, Mary,' Jake said mildly. 'You're too thin.'

'I've put her on the bottle.' There was an irritable note in her voice. 'She's been much better since, and Sally can see to her. Anyway, I'll have something on a tray.'

'No, you won't.' Laurence felt his hackles rise. 'You'll have a bath and come back down and talk about this.'

She jerked away and went limping off without another word. She seemed at the end of her tether. The sight of her worried Laurence and tightened the band of tension round his head. Why should she do such a thing knowing it would hurt him, and hurt the business which would one day be largely hers?

He couldn't fathom Mary out. Never had been able to. Little Jane had been sweeter natured, easier to understand, but she'd been snatched from him.

'Mary's very uptight,' Jake said.

'So am I,' he retorted. 'What is she up to?'

'You're really belting into her.' Jake rang for Abel to bring more beer. 'Lay off her for tonight. Give her a chance.'

'As a father, I'm a failure,' he sighed, watching Abel tidy away the tea tray and put out little bowls of olives and peanuts. He was getting too old for the tropics. The searing heat and dust. What was the point if he had nobody to leave it to? If Mary was bleeding him, as he suspected, he'd leave it to the dog's home rather than let her have it.

When Jake went up to bed, he was surprised to find the room in darkness. Mary was a dark mound in her bed, already breathing deeply. He left the landing door ajar and started to undress in the half-light.

Mary grunted, and turned over. He stopped, afraid he was disturbing her. She tossed back, and he knew then she hadn't been asleep at all. He slid into his own bed; it creaked softly.

'I do think you might have more consideration,' she grumbled, flashing on her bedside light. 'Waking me up like this. Good God! It's midnight.'

'Let's get to sleep, Mary. Why don't you put the light out?'

'It's all right for you.' Mary flounced to the adjoining bathroom, switching on more lights as she went. 'You know I can never get back to sleep once I'm woken, and I'm right out of my routine. God, what a day!' She banged the toilet seat. The plumbing sounded like Niagara. She came noisily back and flung herself into bed.

Mary's breasts bounced as she moved, her nipples showed through her black lace nothing of a nightdress. Jake no longer felt tired, a wave of sexual desire washed over him leaving him breathless. He felt himself hardening.

Mary grunted as she flipped off the light and settled herself to sleep. Jake turned over. He'd felt shattered as he'd come upstairs fifteen minutes after her, now sleep evaded him. He punched his pillow. He had too much on his mind. No, he was fooling himself, there was only one thing on his mind.

Really it was Laura who'd excited him not Mary; raised him to a degree of sexual awareness he could barely control. Mary was his wife, and he'd not seen her for months. He'd been celibate all that time. No wonder a pretty girl had only to pass within a hundred yards. He needed to feel the comfort of Mary's arms about him; she could blot out this unbidden picture of Laura. It would calm him, and bring Mary closer.

He switched on the light and moved across to her bed. Mary lifted her face from the pillow, full of reproach. He pulled the sheet round them both and kissed her lips. She lay rigid in his arms for a moment, her lips cold and unyielding. Then her whole being seemed to retreat from him. She was pushing against him.

Jake drew back sharply. 'I'm sorry.' Quickly he reached up and extinguished the light.

'There's no need to go, if you don't want to.' Mary's hand caught halfheartedly at his arm. He shook it off and went back to his own bed.

Five minutes went by; he was more wide awake than ever. Sleep would never come while every nerve in his body craved sex. He had to still his wanting. He crashed back to her bed and, ignoring Mary's grunt of displeasure, took her. It brought little relief and no pleasure.

From two doors down the passage came Lucinda's wailing screech. He felt Mary stiffen in his arms. The nanny's voice crooned softly in the night, and the crying stopped. If Laurence felt a failure as a father, so did he. He was a failure as a husband too.

'I know you took the money, Mary,' he said quietly. 'It has to be you or me, and I know I'm in the clear. I know why you took it too.' He could feel her holding her breath, stiff with tension.

'Why did you come back? Why didn't you tell him to go to hell? He wouldn't have the Oxley name dragged through the mud. You'd have been quite safe.'

'You don't know anything,' she snarled.

He went back to his own cool bed. He couldn't get over the difference in her. She'd changed so much from the fun-seeking woman who'd seduced him only thirteen months ago.

He must be to blame. He'd fathered this poor child, and it had knocked the life out of her. He didn't understand why it should, or how he could be so fickle as to want to abandon them both. He only knew he did.

He also knew he wouldn't. He wasn't that much of a cad. He couldn't turn his back on her and Lucinda when they really needed his support. He sensed Mary was in a state of crisis, that she was being pushed closer and closer to the edge. She would surely crack if he deserted her in her hour of need.

CHAPTER TWENTY-FIVE

Laurence could hardly contain his impatience. He was taking Mary into the office every morning, and making her stay there, but he was certain she was stalling.

The figures she was supposed to work on were always spread out on her desk. Whenever he enquired about progress, she pleaded for more time, kept assuring him she'd sort it out. Yet he could see her falling apart before his eyes.

This morning, he'd gone in to find her staring blankly at Jake's overseas *Daily Telegraph*. The dark circles under her eyes so worried him he began to regret putting pressure on her.

'Mary, you can't go on like this.' He was almost pleading. 'Just tell me what you've done.'

'It'll soon be sorted. Just be patient.' But her eyes were agitated, and he could see her shaking.

'When? My patience is exhausted. When?'

'Saturday.'

He could only grunt with exasperation and return to the office he was using.

In his eagerness to get the reply from the Farmer's Bank at Akifpo, he was sending the messenger to empty their post box at the Post Office half a dozen times a day. Jake complained Yemi was never around to make coffee when he wanted it.

Now, on his desk, another three envelopes waited for inspection. On one, Laurence recognised the postmark immediately. Akifpo.

He hadn't expected a wave of fear to knife through him like this. It took him a moment to get his breathing under control. At least now he would know where he stood.

He ripped out the letter and the bundle of photocopied notes that supported it. Mary's signature was on every one. He was almost choking as he found the statement and twitched it out. He'd expected to see one single transaction, but there was a whole series. Money had gone into the account and out again, sometimes in large amounts and sometimes in small, on several occasions to an account with the British and French Bank at Mogadu. He couldn't get to the bottom of this without a statement from them. But he was right about one thing, there was no money worth mentioning left in the account.

He could feel the cold sweat on his forehead. Why? The whole exercise seemed pointless. He turned to the letter, feeling sick.

The account had been opened five years ago by David Mountford. Laurence had forgotten, but it was all coming back now. It was a scheme he'd thought up to subsidise the sinking of wells in outlying villages, a philanthropic gesture that hadn't cost too much. Not that there was any shortage of water in the east. The oil palms needed a rainfall of a hundred inches a year to thrive, but the people were drinking polluted water from creeks and rivers. Oxley's had provided a source of clean drinking water. The money had been paid through this account.

Laurence felt another surge of anger boiling up. He went back to Mary's office and sent the letter and all its attachments skidding across her desk, taking other papers with it.

'I knew it was you. Explain this. Come on, explain this.'

Mary's white face was turning grey. She pulled herself out of her chair and retreated to the window.

'You took that money, didn't you?' His face was twisting savagely. 'Didn't you?'

'Yes,' she admitted in a choking whisper.

'What? You did?'

'Yes, yes, yes.' She was cowering back as though she expected him to attack her.

'Well, come on,' he spat. 'Where did it go? You can't

have forgotten what you did with two million. Two million of my money.'

'Leave me alone,' she screamed. She looked terrified.

'I'll leave you alone,' he felt an explosion of fury that she could do this to him, 'when you tell me what you're playing at.' He knew he was shouting at the top of his voice. 'I've worked all my life to build this business up and you're going to ruin me. You're going to ruin us all.'

He didn't realise Jake was behind him until he heard the door close with a firm click. Mary started, trembling.

'Listen,' Jake said quietly. 'Silence. Every typewriter in the building has stopped. Every member of staff is enjoying your row, trying to figure out what it's about.'

Mary dissolved in tears. Laurence felt he would choke with rage. Jake's air of calm was the last straw.

'Give me another day or two.' Mary's face was mottled with tears. 'I'll straighten it out.'

'I'll get the Fraud Squad out,' Laurence was snarling at her when another thought slashed home. He couldn't call out the Fraud Squad if Mary was responsible. The story would be emblazoned on the front pages of the British tabloids. It wasn't hard to imagine what they'd say. Rich girl caught with hand in father's till. Any hint of fraud or dishonesty would send the shares plummeting.

He brought his fists thumping down on her desk in a gesture of frustrated despair. Mary had robbed him of two million, knowing he could do nothing about it. This had to be kept quiet.

'Come on.' Jake was leading him away. 'I've got to break this up. How about a cup of tea?'

'What good will tea do?' He felt sick. He knew at that moment what Mary wanted the money for. She'd broken free of him. She'd never ever do anything he wanted again. After all he'd done for her!

He closed his eyes and tried to take deep calming breaths. He'd never trusted Mary, that was the truth. Perhaps he'd been too tough, keeping her on a short financial rein. Once, he'd intended giving her capital on her twenty-fifth birthday, when she'd learned sense. But somehow Mary never had learned sense. Instead, he'd indulged her tastes. Her allowance was generous but he paid it monthly. The cars she used were registered in the company's name. The houses he gave her were bought in his name. He'd believed she hadn't the guts to cut herself off from wealth.

David Mountford had had capital. Nothing like his, of course, but enough to be independent. Mary could have thrown in her lot with him and been comfortable. Jake Lode had been well paid for his asphalt plants. He could afford to be independent too. What was Mary doing? There were times when he wondered if Mary knew what she was doing herself.

Tom was on edge. Laura had listened to a long account of his difficulties and could think of no suggestions she could make to resolve them; it would take Tom time to settle.

She and Elin were finding the flat hot and cramped, it was throwing them together, making them share his life style. They had less patience with each other.

'At least now you're getting something out of this for yourself,' Tom said as they sat alone on the balcony one night.

'What do you mean?' Laura frowned.

'Jake Lode. He's right for you.'

'He's not!' She almost spat the words out, and couldn't say anything else. Every nerve in her body was raw.

'Come on, Laurie. We've always been able to talk to each other.'

Tom's brown eyes were gentle, waiting to hear her reasons, offer advice. She couldn't. To speak of what she felt for Jake was impossible. She'd pushed him away when he'd kissed her in the office, but his touch had been electrifying. Something else was holding Jake in rein. He must have his reservations too. Married to Mary so recently. A baby of four months. Why hadn't fate led her to Jake last year before that happened?

Laura couldn't get him out of her mind. If she gave him encouragement, he might well leave Mary, but she had to think of Mam too. If Jake left Mary, it might be difficult to stay on good terms with Laurence. It could prevent Mam resolving her difficulties. Laurence was her father, she wanted to be on friendly terms. Surely he'd see any liaison with Jake as stealing Mary's husband?

They hadn't made as close a relationship with him as she'd hoped, but they knew him well enough to invite him to dinner at home. They didn't have to stay in Lagos for that. There was so much she wanted to discuss with him. Whether he thought it feasible for her to open a chain of retail or coffee shops. After all, she made cakes, biscuits and savoury snacks. Whether she should look for a bakery and make bread too. Laurence had the experience to help her think her ideas through. She felt he'd enjoy it. She'd never had anyone to use as a sounding board, and the prospect was inviting.

She needed to accept that her business would be her whole life. It was what she was good at, what she enjoyed. She had to put Jake Lode out of her mind. She ought to find the strength to go home now. It would be easier in the long run.

She turned to Tom. 'Do you want me to go? We're getting on each other's nerves. It might be better.'

'No, Laurie. Not yet. I need you.' The very suggestion upset him. He hadn't found his feet yet. 'You promised to stay six weeks and help me fix this flat up.'

Laura sighed. Was it only three weeks since they'd arrived? 'Tom, you aren't showing much interest in cushion covers.'

'I am,' he argued. 'Let's go shopping tomorrow morning and get the cloth.'

'Really?'

'You and Elin know more about furnishings than I do.'

Laura shuddered, recognising his ploy to keep her with him. Recognising, too, she'd accept any excuse to stay near Jake.

Tom drove the Austin Healey into Lagos, and since the Oxley Stores had the best selection of everything, they went there, climbing to the third floor, which was given over to home furnishings.

Laura threaded her way through the rolls of carpet, past

the traditional carpet squares, popular because they could be moved easily when another quarter was allocated, and on to the rugs. They had brought only two out with them, which meant the floor in Tom's room was still bare.

The scent of new carpet was strong, dust motes danced in the air. They were all somnolent in the heat. Tom ambled along behind her, forcing an interest in rugs he didn't feel. Elin was interested though, flipping back the top rugs to see those stacked below, drawing Tom's attention to a creamy rug patterned with pink roses.

His red beard twitched. 'Not my style. More for a lady's boudoir.'

'Too pale,' Laura agreed. 'Remember Ignatius has no Hoover to keep them clean. How about this, Tom?' She indicated a thick, deep, crimson rug.

'Great, go with the curtains.'

It didn't particularly, but Laura was relieved to be making progress. 'We'll have two of those. Material next for cushion covers,' she said. 'Brighten the whole flat up.' Fabric was displayed within a few yards of the carpets. Elin was already fingering a grey cotton rep.

'You've got a patterned carpet square in the living room,' she said, 'so plain material for cushions.'

Tom's brown eyes were surveying the selection blankly.

'Why not a mixture of plain colours?' Elin was enthusiastic. 'Look, I've brought a few threads to match. The carpet is mostly red, but there's grey in it and yellow. See, this rep is exactly the same red, and they have yellow and grey in the same material.'

Laura smiled; Mam had a better eye for such things than she had. 'Tom?'

'Sounds great.'

'But will it wash?' Elin was demanding of the salesman, who didn't know. 'Colours might run, Tom. You'll have to be careful.'

Laura had already worked out the total yardage they needed, now she was dividing it by three. Seeing her mother straighten up from the material and the sudden tension on her face made her turn round.

Laurence was threading his way through the rugs and carpets towards them. He was all smiles, clasping Elin's hand in both of his. She positively sparkled in response. It was only then that Laura saw Mary, who had been following in her father's footsteps. She was scowling at his show of affection for Elin.

'You haven't met Elin Peck, have you, Mary? And Laura, her daughter?'

The Lower Fourth had been in awe of Sixth-formers, and Mary had stood above the rest. She had always reflected her father's prominence. For the first time, Laura thought she looked vulnerable. The fragile skin of her forehead was showing ridges of tension. Laura felt a rush of sympathy.

'You may remember me, Mary, from school.' She offered her hand, wanting to be friendly.

'Laura Peck? Of course I remember you. Home haircuts and holes in your stockings. Always down-at-heel.' Her eyes sparkled blue ice, full of dislike.

Suddenly Laura was transported back over the years. She felt again a thirteen-year-old, the butt of Mary's scorn. A peasant if ever there was one. How many times had Mary said that to her? She had to say something before Mary said it again.

'Most of the girls had home haircuts,' she managed.

'Mary,' her father said, 'I'd like us to get to know Laura and her mother.'

'Didn't you get a job as a shop assistant when you were thirteen, and get withdrawn from school?' Mary's eyes fastened on Laura's flat sandals disdainfully.

'Don't be so bloody condescending,' Tom blurted out, suddenly coming to life. He towered over Mary, his red hair curling in damp tendrils against his forehead. 'Why does having a rich father make you feel so superior?'

'It doesn't,' Mary retaliated. 'It's more a matter of breeding.'

'The breeding's the same.' Tom threw back his head and chortled. 'Exactly the same.'

Mary was clasping a box file to her chest, her shoulders

hunched round it. Her china blue eyes stared up at Tom without comprehension.

'Let me put it more simply,' Tom went on, smiling. 'Laura is your long lost half-sister.'

Mary paled to the colour of whitewash. 'Sister! Don't be obscene. That's slanderous. Dad, don't let him get away with saying such things.'

'It's the truth,' Tom laughed. 'But Laura's a sister you can be proud of.'

Laura knew she ought to stop him, but Mary deserved some flak. She resented her aggression after all these years.

'Dad?' Even Mary was aware now that Laurence was not refuting the claim.

'For Christ's sake,' he said. 'Let's go to the office. We can talk about it there.'

Mary rounded on Laura again. 'You won't get away with this. Hoping to make your fortune, are you? Claiming to be related to us brings big advantages.'

'Laura doesn't need her father's fortune,' Tom said haughtily. 'Laura's built up a business that rivals Oxley's. Have you heard of Burdon's Biscuits, and Quick's Cakes? She's done it all by herself. No help from big Daddy.'

'Dad, stop him,' Mary screamed, dropping the box file to press both hands against her ears.

'Just proves she's a chip off the old block.'

'She can't be.' Mary's voice had risen three octaves. Other shoppers were turning to watch the commotion. 'It isn't true, is it, Dad?' Her fluffy blonde hair stood out in wild disorder.

'Let's get out of here.' Laurence tried to take her arm, but she shook him off.

'Mother will turn in her grave. A half-sister I've never heard of, at my time of life?' Mary's teeth rested on her lip in a snarl.

Laura tried to think on her feet and knew she was failing. There was no way to soften this.

'You must be crazy!' Mary's eyes rested on Elin, who cringed. 'She's your mistress? Her? It's been going on all these years?'

'It wasn't like that, Mary,' Elin protested.

'It's all long since over, we lost touch. Now your mother's dead, I'm lonely. I'd like us to know each other. What's the harm in that?' Laurence was brusque.

'I don't want to get to know them,' she shrieked. 'I don't like them. Peasants, that's what they are. From the slums of Birkenhead.'

'Oh, for God's sake.' He turned and went striding off down the shop.

Mary screamed as though she'd been stabbed, tears streamed down her face. Shoppers and staff no longer went about their business. They stared at Mary transfixed.

Laura took charge at last. 'Mam, buy that material, then you and Tom wait for me in the car.'

Mary continued to wail loudly as Laura led her upstairs to the office, pulling at her arm. Mary's thin body was stiff and resistant to her touch.

Damn Laurence marching off like that and leaving them to it. Laura hoped Jake would be in the office. She couldn't cope with Mary having hysterics. She'd read somewhere a slap across the face could cure it, but she couldn't bring herself to slap Mary, who continued to scream.

Jake was sitting at his desk, making out the additional purchasing orders he wanted to put in today's overseas post. The quiet was suddenly broken by someone screaming on the stairs. He rushed to the door and found Laura urging Mary upwards.

'What's the matter, Mary?' He ran down to help.

'Tom told her,' Laura gasped. 'That I'm her half-sister.'

'It's not true!' Mary shouted wildly. 'Dad would never do such a thing. He's very strict about right and wrong.'

'It's true,' Jake said as gently as he could. Mary took a long shuddering breath. Her eyes, mad with hate, rested on Laura.

'I'll leave you to it.' Laura looked stricken. He heard her light step skipping downstairs.

He had the feeling Mary was being pushed over the brink. She slumped in the chair, looking totally deflated, her fair skin blotchy, her hair an untidy mass of wispy ends. She was shaking.

'I'll take you home,' he said, but she made no sign she heard. He took her arm and she rose to her feet like a zombie.

By the time he'd got her down to his car, Sylvester was holding open the door. Jake eased Mary onto the back seat and got in beside her.

'It's all ancient history,' he tried to comfort.

'Not to me. She's the same age as Jane. Dad . . . I can't believe he'd do it. His reputation . . . He goes to church. Everybody knows he's above this sort of scandal. Oh God, what's happening to us?'

Jake leant his head against the car window for a moment. Her desperation was obvious.

'Why did you take the money?' For once he didn't care what the driver heard. 'Why don't you tell your father? It's got to come out, Mary. It would get it over and done with.'

'I'll get the money back.' He saw stark determination round her mouth. 'I'll get it back first.'

As the car turned into their drive, Jake could see the nanny pacing back and forth in the shade thrown by a date palm, trying to soothe the baby on her shoulder. He could hear Lucinda's screams before Sylvester cut the engine. Mary leapt out and snatched the howling baby, hugging her tight, seeming to seek rather than give comfort.

After a moment's peace, Lucinda started to shriek again, no amount of patting her back and rocking soothed her.

'She's not an easy baby to handle,' Jake said as Mary became more agitated because she couldn't quieten her. 'Poor Mary.'

'Poor Lucinda, you mean,' she spat. Mary's tears mingled with those of her child.

'Poor little mite,' Jake said.

'It's not her fault,' Mary gulped. 'It's mine. Mine and Robert's.'

'Robert's? Is he interested in babies?'

'He's very fond of Carlotta. You know that.'

He didn't understand the connection. Didn't understand

why Mary had taken the money in the first place, but they'd sort it out. It was only money. The problem of Lucinda was harder to accept, and there would be no end to it.

He took the child from her arms, but he was no better at quietening her. He turned her over, her face scarlet and sweating with rage, her fists and feet pummelling the air. She was saturated at the other end too.

He felt a wave of guilt that he couldn't love his child, and resentment too, that this tragedy had happened to him and Mary. Lucinda was a responsibility he didn't want. He felt caged by it, and that made him feel even more guilt.

'Sally,' he called. 'Sally.' The nanny came and whisked the child away. It was a relief to have the screams grow more distant.

'You're getting mixed up, Mary. You were wrong to take Oxley money, but there's no reason to blame yourself for Lucinda. Her problems are outside your control.'

'You don't understand.' Tears were streaming down Mary's face, she no longer tried to stem the flood. 'It's all my fault. Mine and Robert's.'

'Mary, your father's angry now, but he'll come round. You've got to talk to him about it, and we'll work something out.'

'Don't interfere, Jake. You don't understand.'

She was right, he didn't. He went to the kitchen to get himself a bottle of beer. The first long, eager pull was ice-cold. It revived him. Guinea fowl and salad were being prepared for lunch, but he didn't feel hungry. As an afterthought, he went to the sitting room and poured Mary a stiff brandy. He had to calm her down.

She was in their bedroom, staring at her ravaged face in her looking glass. The air conditioner had been turned off, the sun was streaming through the open windows and the curtains were moving in the breeze. He put the drinks down.

'Come and lie down, Mary, till you feel better.' He meant to lead her towards the bed, but seconds later she was clinging to him. He didn't want to feel her body against his now.

'Don't leave me, David,' she moaned. That brought another stab of anxiety.

'He already has, I'm Jake.' It wasn't easy to keep his manner relaxed. 'Come on, lie down. You aren't bothered about David going.' He took her sandals off. Pulled up a chair for himself.

'No, I don't love David, never have.' She gave a wild laugh.

'You must have once, to marry him.' He wondered if she'd switched off for David in the way she had for him.

'I didn't.' Suddenly she was snarling. 'It was Robert. Always Robert. That's why this hurts.'

All right, so she'd had an affair with Robert. He'd heard that before. 'How long did it last?'

'All my life.'

Jake sighed. 'But you were married for ten years.'

'David was just a front. To fob Dad off.'

Something cold clutched at Jake's entrails. 'Nobody could do that. Not for ten years.'

'We did. I trusted Robert. All this is his fault, but I'll make him pay it back.'

Jake swept the hair from his forehead and tried to think.

'You gave the money to Robert?'

'Why can't you understand?' Tears were streaming down her face again, she made no effort to wipe them away.

'Try me,' he said. 'Why did you want Robert to have two million pounds?' His shirt felt damp with her tears, there was a malodorous patch where Lucinda had rested. He felt in his wardrobe for a clean one.

'He wanted it. To build his oil terminal.'

Jake froze with one arm in his clean shirt. He felt as though she'd kicked him in the stomach. No wonder she couldn't bring herself to tell Laurence. He took a deep breath, slowly inserted his other arm into the sleeve and buttoned it up.

'You must have known you were giving Robert a huge advantage. Letting him start up first.' He kept his voice as calm as he could.

'You think I'm a fool, don't you?' She took a mouthful of brandy. 'I trusted Robert. I wanted to help him.'

'But why?'

'I loved him, I tell you,' she shouted. 'Why can't you understand?'

'I do.' His beer was finished, he wanted more.

'Take what you want and pay for it.' She took a wild gulp at her brandy. 'I took what I wanted, I was prepared to pay, but I'm paying twice over. First Dinah, now Lucinda.'

'What on earth are you talking about?'

'It was my fault, mine and Robert's.'

Jake felt another wave of irritability. She couldn't get away from Robert. 'What can Robert possibly have to do with Lucinda?'

'He's her father.'

He went cold and then hot. 'Lucinda's father?' He saw Mary's parchment face through a wavering haze.

'And Carlotta's and Dinah's, I keep telling you. It was always Robert.'

He couldn't take his eyes off her face; she was unbalanced, she didn't realise what she was saying. 'David was your husband for ten years, Carlotta and Dinah are his children.'

'Why do you think he left in such a hurry?'

Anger, horror, reproach crowded his mind. 'Then Lucinda really isn't . . .?' Waves of nausea were rising in his throat.

'I was pregnant when I met you. It was a mistake, we didn't intend—'

'Then why marry me?' Jake felt numb.

She was staring up at him. Incredible that she'd done such a thing. Even more incredible to think Robert had wanted to.

'As you say, I married David, and it worked for ten years. I suppose I thought it would work again. Isn't that what we all do? Bring out the same answers?'

'I loved you, Mary. I was crazy about you. We loved each other.'

She wouldn't look at him and was slow to answer. 'Would you call that love?'

He was choking. Love was what he'd felt.

'I wanted a husband. You were ripe for the taking. I wanted you to stand between me and Dad.'

Jake went rushing for the bathroom, slamming the door before being violently sick, retching and retching on the beer. What a fool he'd been! What a trusting innocent fool. He'd never doubted Lucinda was his daughter.

He drank a glass of tepid water from the tap. It cleaned his mouth, cleared his head, while a searing sense of release flooded through him. A sense of freedom. He could turn his back on Mary now. He owed her nothing. Robert had fathered Lucinda.

When Jake went back to the bedroom, Mary was flat on her back, her face blotched and sweating.

'You could have said the baby was David's.' He hardly recognised the voice as his own.

'David left after a very public row. Everybody would have counted on their fingers and known it couldn't be. Dad's first guess would have been Robert. No, I had to have an alternative.'

'That's what I was to you, an alternative?'

'No, I was fond of you, Jake. We had some good times.'

'You should have married Robert, and told your father to go to hell.'

There was a sob in her voice. 'Do you think I don't know that now? He's got another woman. He doesn't want me.'

'Yes, the Algerian girl.' Jake stared out of the window, his gut still churning. 'I want a divorce, that goes without saying.'

'You're in love with her, aren't you?' Her eyes burned into his. 'The woman who claims she's my half-sister. God, what a can of worms!'

'Laura, yes.' What was the point of denying it?

'Seeing you together, I knew.' Mary was up on her elbows again, spitting fury. 'You made it obvious she's your mistress. You couldn't take your eyes off her.'

'She isn't, not yet. Give me time.'

'The scheming bitch!' Mary flashed at him. 'Prefers you to that boy friend she's living with?'

'I want a divorce, Mary.'

'Well, I don't. Why should I let you marry her?'

Jake took a deep breath. 'What's the point in going on like this for the rest of our lives? We're neither of us happy.'

'Happy? Who's talking about being happy?' Suddenly her face contorted and she began to cry again. 'Jake, I'll try and make it up to you.' The words came out in a rush. 'Don't leave me now. I have no one else.'

'You're evil, Mary. I'm not staying for more.'

'You've had compensations,' she said abruptly. 'You've got your directorship in Oxley's.'

'I've worked hard. Oxley's has had its pound of flesh from me.'

'You only got the directorship because you were my husband. You're ambitious, Jake, you were glad to accept.'

Fury was rising in his throat, he could hardly speak. The urge to hit out at her was so strong, he had to push his hands deep in his trouser pockets. 'It's over, finished. You didn't buy me in the first place, I loved you, remember? You can't buy me now.'

Mary was silent.

'I want the legal position sorted out. I'll draft a letter this afternoon, asking Willie Lamb to suggest someone for me. Naturally, you'll want him to act for you?'

'No.' Her face twisted. 'No, I don't want a divorce.'

'Mary, it's over.' He had to keep his temper tightly controlled. 'Nothing could make me live with you now.' He slammed the bedroom door behind him and went hurtling downstairs. He had to get away.

He drove like a mad thing out to Apapa, intending to take his boat out. Getting out on the water always soothed him. He needed fresh air. At the last moment, he decided he needed Laura more. Instead of turning down to the harbour, he drove on to the flat where she was staying.

CHAPTER TWENTY-SIX

Laura felt hungry. The table was set for three. From the kitchen came the sound of butter and oil sizzling in the pan. A delicious scent eddied forth, bringing saliva to her mouth. Lunch was almost ready.

After the row in the shop, they'd all been on edge. Elin had bickered with Tom, ticking him off for telling Mary so bluntly. It had sobered them all.

'She asked for it,' Tom justified himself. 'Did you hear what she said to Laurie?'

Laura felt out of sorts. Mary's disintegration was too fresh in her mind. To see Jake running down to Mary, full of sympathy, acting as a husband should, left her feeling bereft.

They'd been back at the flat by late morning. Elin called them in to Tom's room to admire the new rug she'd spread on his floor. Then she was eagerly unwrapping parcels of cloth, unfurling lengths over sofa and chairs so there was nowhere to sit. Tom, his face exasperated and hot, said: 'Let's go to the club for a drink.'

Laura felt less than keen. Elin hardly looked up.

'Could ask the barman about getting somebody to make cushion covers,' he added.

Elin's interest quickened. 'If only I had a machine, I could do them.'

'Let's have a swim,' Laura suggested. 'It'll cool us down.'

She had thrashed up and down the pool till she was exhausted, sometimes passing Elin, sometimes seeing her hanging on the handrail, getting her breath back. It restored her equilibrium, made her feel better. Tom stayed in the bar, but he had only one bottle of beer. Now they were all eager for lunch.

They heard the screaming tyres as a car pulled up violently below the balcony. She knew it was Jake before she leaned over and saw the red Austin Healey. He was coming upstairs at the double. The first glimpse of his face shocked her. His frenzied dark eyes raked them.

'Laura, come with me.' His speech was barely coherent. 'The boat. I want you to come out. Please.'

Elin was taken aback. 'Stay and have a bite to eat first,' she invited. But in his agitation he couldn't even stand still.

'You don't mind if we leave you, Mam?'

'I'll keep Elin company,' Tom said. 'You go.'

Laura was already in the kitchen. Keeping her eyes averted from the browning omelette, she pushed food into a basket. Cheese, a crusty loaf and some tomatoes from the fridge. The change in Jake worried her, but she had to have something to eat. She asked Ignatius to fill a flask with coffee.

'Won't be a minute.' She passed Jake on the way to her bedroom. She'd just changed out of the swimsuit she liked best. It was hanging on the line, dripping moisture. She found a yellow bikini with black daisies and pulled it on, wondering if it showed too much white midriff. Hurriedly, she replaced her shirt and trousers, snatched a towel from the bathroom, and pushed it into the bag she'd taken to the club earlier.

Elin was showing Jake the lengths of cloth while Tom waited patiently for his omelette. Ignatius was keeping it warm.

'What happened?' she asked, as soon as they were in his car.

'It's Mary.' The knuckles of his hands showed white as they gripped the wheel. 'She admits it. Everything. Gave the money to Robert. It built Apapa Oil Terminals.' He kept turning to look at her. 'She won't tell Laurence. Daren't. He won't stomach Robert having it. She couldn't have done anything worse with the money, letting Robert build next door to our site.' He was too excited to put it clearly. 'Letting him into the market first.'

'I half guessed.' Laura pushed the hair back from her forehead and tried to think. 'It's not our problem, Jake.' His eyes switched to hers, still frenzied.

'Oh, there's worse to come. Much worse. She told me . . .' His mind was rioting in anger. The story came out in a jumble of words. Laura understood at last. The child wasn't his. Mary had lured him into marriage when she found she was pregnant.

Laura stared out over the water knowing now what had held Jake back. She need not have felt jealous of Mary.

'It alters everything,' Jake said fiercely. 'My loyalty was misplaced, I could have lost you. Lucinda isn't my responsibility. I'm free.'

They had to get the boat from the building, run the trailer down the bank and launch it. The task seemed to calm Jake.

'I've told her I want a divorce.'

Laura held on to the painter while he pulled the trailer above the waterline.

'Is she willing?'

'No, but I don't care. I'll get it. I've told her it's finished.' His fury was boiling up again. 'I'm not staying with her. I must have been out of my mind, falling for Mary's play-acting. She was pretending the whole time, I can't get over that.' His hawk eyes looked into hers, anguished.

'Put it down to being out in the bush, starved of female company for years,' Laura smiled.

The boat rocked as she got in. The engine roared into life and they swept out into the harbour. It soothed Jake to have the wind in his hair and open water round him.

'It'll be embarrassing, suing for divorce. Double trouble when my father-in-law is my boss too,' Jake sighed. 'I'll offer to resign. Laurence will be bowled over.'

They were speeding alongside the marina, the engine flat out sending up spray and leaving a wake of glistening foam. They passed the Yacht Club, went along the mole. He slowed down.

'Feel better after that burst?' Laura asked.

He nodded. His anger had cooled. 'Want to eat?'

'Yes, I'm starving.'

He made a wide turn, careful not to go close to the harbour mouth where the ocean swell heaved and foamed and headed back inland. On this side of the harbour, thick dark vegetation grew right down to the water's edge, and they were well away from the deepwater channel and big ships.

The boat chugged on. 'I've heard,' Laura said, 'these creeks lead into a network of inland waterways stretching for hundreds of miles up the coast.'

'Yes,' Jake said. They came to a small inlet, overhung by tall palms, and he turned the boat into it. Ripples from their prow washed against the banks. Soon the tropical bush gave way to grey-green mangrove scrub, where hundreds of bare roots went down into the muddy water like railings. The sun didn't penetrate here. It was cool but evil-smelling, and the mud was alive with midges, sand flies and crabs.

'Ugh.' He turned the boat as soon as there was space, and went back to the harbour. As soon as they were far enough out to catch the breeze, he threw out the anchor and started to rig the awning for shade.

Laura was hot. She took off her shirt and trousers, very conscious of Jake's gaze. He smiled for the first time that afternoon.

'Haven't your men friends told you you're worth a second look?'

'The only man friend I have is Tom. He never looks at me like that.'

'There must have been others.'

'Not really.' Kenneth Quick had taken her out to dinner a few times, but something had made her choke him off. Meredith Drew had made a pass at her. She'd even taken him home to meet Mam, but somehow his interest had faded. Nobody seemed to turn her on as Tom had. She'd given up expecting to fall in love again. Jake had come as a surprise. She couldn't trust herself to look at him.

She took out her suntan lotion and started to rub some into her midriff. He took the bottle from her, and the next moment his hand was sliding sensuously in the oil across her abdomen. She closed her eyes, suddenly intoxicated, unable to breathe.

She felt his fingers glide across her shoulders, round again and down her back. She sensed, almost felt the wave of excitement run through him, and knew their relationship had entered a new phase. His lips were slightly parted, there was passion in his eyes.

'That should stop you burning.' He offered the bottle to her. 'Put some on my shoulders.' Taking off his shirt, he turned his back. Laura took a shuddering breath; it was more than she could bear.

'Can't reach.' She forced herself to sound normal. 'You're too tall.'

He sat on one of the padded benches in the cuddy and she shook oil onto his skin. He radiated warmth, his muscles moved to her touch. Her fingers were caressing his back, though she'd meant to be businesslike. The scent from the oil was heady, his skin supple. She couldn't go on letting her hands glide over his flesh like this. She wouldn't have believed touching him could ignite such fire within her.

Suddenly he snatched the bottle, snapped the lid on and flung it down. She felt his arms tighten round her. His lips came down on hers. She could taste sun oil, it was everywhere, making his body slide against hers.

She fell back against the bench. It wasn't enough to feel his touch, now she was reaching for him, pulling him closer.

'I've been aching to do this since I first saw you.' She saw love in his eyes, in his whole manner. 'I love you, Laurie.'

Elin felt Iolo's fingers against her scalp, the soothing twitch of his comb as he arranged her set. She watched him in the glass, standing back now to get a more distant view of the style he'd created. Lifting it with a little backcombing here, smoothing it lower there. As a hairdresser, he was a perfectionist.

'There, Mrs Peck.' He flashed the hand mirror behind her head, but she was mesmerised by his thin wiry frame moving like a dancer's round her chair.

She had looked in her mirror this morning and decided her hair must be cut. It was not a decision to be taken lightly. Since her father had hacked it off, her one thought had been to grow it. She'd screwed it into a knot when she'd gone out cleaning. Recently her hairdresser had shown her how to dress it into a bun on top of her head. It made her look older than her forty-five years. She was past wearing it hanging down her back, it would be too hot anyway. She'd wanted a more up-to-date style.

'Very nice,' she said, and it was. He'd suggested a gold rinse to cover her grey hairs. It seemed to lift the gold in her eyes too. Surely she was looking years younger?

She felt the hair spray come across in choking scented clouds. It made her feel good to have money to spend on her appearance. She liked the navy and white dress she'd made just before coming out. She felt she was looking her best.

'Nobody else does it quite so well.'

'Thank you.' His voice was high-pitched, almost feminine.

Elin looked into his thin whippet-like face. She couldn't believe Tom could like him. Not that way. Not in preference to Laura.

She opened the salon door, and the hot air hit her in the face with much the same force as opening the oven door in Jubilee Street had done, except here she had to walk out into it. She clattered down the stairs into the street, blinking in the harsh sunlight.

She'd go into Oxley's before taking a taxi back. She only had one swimsuit, and though they'd be going home soon, she could do with another. She'd never been swimming before and hadn't believed she'd want to do it often, but walking down to the club pool had become her favourite way of spending the morning.

Laura said they needed exercise, and in this temperature the only comfortable exercise was swimming. Elin had practised her laborious head-bobbing breast stroke till she could do the length of the pool. She had to hang onto the handrail at the deep end taking great gulps of air afterwards, but she could do it. Not bad at forty-five, learning to swim in a couple of weeks. Tom said she'd taken to the water like a duck.

She enjoyed dozing in the shade too. She hadn't set out to get a tan. She couldn't sit in the full sun, it was too hot, but she'd lost the pasty look she'd had in England. She looked better and she felt better. She hadn't had freckles like this since she was a girl. They gave her face a golden sheen.

'Elin?' She turned to see Laurence Oxley beside her. He was sweating in the heat, and looked exhausted. 'Nice to see you. Have you come shopping?'

'I came to have my hair done.'

'I should have known. Very nice, it suits you.' His blue eyes had lost their piercing intensity, they were filled with stress.

'I must apologise. Terrible scene with Mary. In my own shop, in front of everybody.' He sounded anguished, and couldn't look at her. 'Totally embarrassing, and then I went off and left you to cope.'

'Laura coped.'

'Yes, well, it should have been me. It was unforgivable. Mary—'

'Tom stirred it up,' Elin said quietly. 'Rushing to defend Laura, of course. He thinks a lot of her.'

'We can't talk here, Elin.' He took her arm. 'Come and have a cup of coffee with me? Such trouble and strife. I'm getting too old for it.' A nerve twitched in his cheek.

'Thank you, that would be very nice.' Laura would want her to go, even if she kept her waiting for lunch.

'I was dreading telling Mary. I knew she wouldn't like it, but that was worse than anything I imagined. Such a public place.'

'Where are we going?' As far as she knew, the cafeteria in Oxley's stores was the only place to get coffee in Lagos, and they'd passed the main entrance.

'We'll go up to my office,' he said. 'Better coffee and greater privacy.' He held the door open and Elin felt the welcome cool of air conditioning again. She could think better out of the infernal heat.

'It was worrying me. I wanted to tell Mary quietly on her own, then have you to lunch at home where she could meet you in private.' Elin thought he looked ill. An old man, pacing to the window. 'Will you and Laura come to lunch on Saturday? Last week it was a fiasco. I really ought to apologise for that too.'

Elin paused. Laura wouldn't want a repeat performance of last week. He'd done nothing but rail against Mary and bemoan the loss of his money. If anything, he was more worked up about it now than he had been then.

'Why don't you come to our flat? Let us return some of your hospitality.' It wasn't much of a place to entertain. Laura could book a table at the club if she preferred.

'No, Mary is going to apologise to you on Saturday. I can't have her dictating what I do, or the company I keep. She's upset me.' Elin could see his fingers trembling. It was harrowing to see him agonising over his problems.

'I am sorry,' she said for what seemed the tenth time.

'Everything's going wrong. I wish I'd never come.'

Elin sipped the coffee she didn't want; the hairdressers served coffee to their clients while they were under the driers. It gave her a sense of power to talk about Mary like this. Laurence seemed on an emotional skid.

When it was time to go, she reached up and planted a kiss on his cheek. He caught both her hands in his, as though she offered a lifeline.

'Elin, we suited each other once. Let's try again. Lunch on Saturday. You and Laura, we'll make peace with Mary.'

Mary stuffed her feet into slippers and shuffled downstairs, tightening the sash on her pink dressing gown. Saturday had come at last.

She had a blinding headache, but she had to get herself together and get the money back. She could hear the clatter of dishes from the dining room, and the scent of frying bacon was everywhere.

'Morning, Mary.' They were all down before her, eating breakfast. Even after a string of broken nights, the fresh bloom of youth was on Sally's round face. She was tucking into egg and bacon as though it was the first food she'd eaten in a week. This was normality. Mary felt light years away from them.

Cold dread was a dead weight in her stomach. What if Robert couldn't or, worse, wouldn't return the money? She'd asked for it months ago, when he'd come to Liverpool. He'd promised then she'd have it in plenty of time for the audit. It was only when time was running out that she'd begun to grow anxious. She'd still believed he'd pay, till that dreadful moment in the airport car park. He'd seemed so bitter.

Mary sat at the table, smoothing the short wisps of hair closer to her head.

'Aren't you coming to the office?' Her father's aggressive eyes cut into hers.

'Yes, Dad, of course.'

'You aren't ready.'

'I won't be long.' She forced a note of calmness into her voice. Dad was like a jailer, escorting her to that dreary office, where time crawled. She felt she couldn't endure another hour trying to look as though she was working.

If she'd known Robert was going away for four days, she'd have stayed at home where Dad could only heckle by phone. She had managed to give him the slip on Wednesday and go round to Elders Travel Agency to book a return flight on tonight's plane. Whether she got the money or not, she was not putting up with any more of this. Not that there was anything to stop Dad following her. Probably would, but it was easier to evade him there where she didn't have to live with him. Jake poured out a cup of coffee for her.

'I thought you were asleep, I didn't want to wake you.' She'd heard him creeping about the room, but she couldn't face any more of his advice. At least Dad still didn't know the worst. If she could get the money back, he'd have less to gripe about.

'I had a bad night,' she said. 'I never sleep well here.'

Mary pushed her hair off her throbbing head. Damn Dad. Full of talk about how she was betraying him, not a word about how he'd betrayed her. Producing his inamorata and natural daughter. Laura Peck of all people. She'd always hated Laura Peck. A total insult. How could he be so high and mighty about her and Rob, when all the time he was carrying on with that slut?

'Good morning, madam.' Abel came in with more hot toast. 'Eggs and bacon for you?'

'No, just grapefruit this morning.' She looked up to find Jake's powerful dark eyes on her. Everyone was against her. She hadn't stopped crying since yesterday.

She couldn't take much more, it was only the return passage booked for tonight that had got her this far. Today was her last chance to get the money back. Anything was better than telling Dad that Rob had it and it had gone for good.

She would take the baby with her. Rob would want to see his child again. She wanted her fed, washed, and made pretty first, but it was hard to hurry Sally without letting Dad know she was planning something.

'Shouldn't you be seeing to Lucinda, Sally?'

'She was fast asleep when I came down.' The girl smiled, pouring herself more coffee.

It was all Mary could do not to snap, 'Get the baby ready.' But that would show everybody what a state she was in.

She played about with her grapefruit, willing them to leave. It helped when Sally went back to the nursery. Then the men too were pushing back their chairs.

'I'll be in later, Dad. An hour or so.' She made an effort to sound normal.

'Shall we take your car, Mary?' Jake was watching her again. She hated his dark penetrating gaze, he seemed to see too much. 'Leave you Sylvester and the Humber, so you don't have to drive?'

'I'm perfectly capable of driving.' She didn't want Sylvester to drive her to Robert's office. Dad would ask him where she'd been. If she could get the money, she'd think of something to tell him. 'I prefer to, thank you.'

It was too late for Jake's pretence of sympathy. He'd turned against her when he knew she was fighting Dad with her back to the wall. Asking for a divorce! That he wanted to marry Laura Peck made it twenty times worse. Tears prickled her eyes again. She'd never felt so totally bereft. Everything, absolutely everything in her life was going wrong.

Once the Humber was gone, she went upstairs. Robert was not going to get away with this.

'Feed Lucy,' she said round the nursery door. 'Get her ready quickly. I want to take her out for an hour.'

'Do you want me to come too?' Sally came to the door.

Mary was already at the other end of the passage.

'No,' she snapped. 'But don't go away. I won't be long.'

Mary threw off her dressing gown, put on her red and white striped shirtwaister, and pushed her feet into white high-heeled sandals.

She sat in front of her mirror, gazing at her reflection with dissatisfaction. She had to look half decent to see Robert. She could disguise her pallor with make-up, but there was no way of hiding the deep lines. She looked haggard and tense. She controlled her wispy hair with hair spray. She lifted it away from her face and gave it another blast to keep it that way.

She might have known Lucy wouldn't be ready. Sally was just lifting her out of the baby bath onto her knee.

'Won't be a minute,' she said, mopping her dry with expert hands. 'Will you take her in the carrycot?'

'Moses basket,' Mary said. 'Cooler for her. Bring her down as soon as she's ready. I'll get my car out.'

Mary felt the pressure bands tighten as she waited. At last Sally came running out with the Moses basket. Lucinda's silver-blonde hair had been combed into a damp roll along the crown of her head, her bright blue eyes stared silently up. She wore nothing but a terry napkin and a pink cotton smock. Getting the basket onto the occasional back seat of the Austin Healey wasn't easy.

'Carry cot would have been better,' Sally said cheerfully, pushing it down. 'This is wider. Still, it's safer if it's wedged tight.'

Laurence felt clamped to the uncomfortable chair. His head ached and the site office was claustrophobic. He should not have agreed to see the site this morning, but Jake had wanted to bring him up to date on progress.

He tried to concentrate on what Jake was telling him as he unfurled map after blueprint on the desk in front of him, prodding his finger to explain a point here, turning quickly to something else. It was too technical for Laurence to grasp easily. Really it was beyond him this morning. He'd been tossing and turning half the night. He suddenly realised Jake was at the door, waiting expectantly.

'What?'

'Let's go while it's still cool. See how they're getting on,' Jake repeated.

'Still cool?' Laurence couldn't help gasping as he stepped out of the air conditioning. It wasn't yet nine, but the heat was nailing. He felt ill. His palpitations had come back even though he was taking the pills. It was just one more turn of the screw.

The stress of the last few days was getting to them all. Jake was striding ahead like one pursued. Laurence put on a spurt to catch him up.

'You can see the whole site from here,' Jake explained. 'It has every natural advantage. Frontage to the harbour, and deep water for a wharf. There, overlooking the creeks, you can see the staff houses going up. One's got the roof on. There, where the creek runs into the harbour, is the new office. We'll have a closer look later.'

'How soon before it's ready?' Laurence said. Damn Mary, she'd admitted she was responsible. All week, she'd been play-acting, looking over the accounts, pretending she was going to produce the money like a rabbit out of a hat. He didn't believe it for one minute. He felt as though the Lagos end of the business was about to explode in his face.

He didn't hear Jake's reply to his question. He was gasping in the humid air and running with perspiration. He should not have let himself in for this. Jake paused, there was sympathy in his eagle eyes.

'It's a good feeling, building on ground that hasn't changed since primeval times. Performing a technological miracle.' Jake's enthusiasm was obvious, it wasn't just another job to him. 'Deciding what's needed, and fitting it together so it works. It's hardly off the drawing board yet, but it's going to be the best site I've ever built. I'm going to put the tank farm over in that corner,' he pointed to a clump of mangrove, 'and the filling shed here.'

Laurence followed his pointing finger. Work on the site was well on target. Already, buildings were going up and roads were in, but it was hard to imagine the finished terminal. He shaded his eyes from the sun and looked across at the adjoining site, where a space-age terminal was functioning.

'You said Robert Oxley has an interest in that place?'

'Owns it. And runs it.'

Serried ranks of silver tanks sparkled in the sun, spheres for liquid petroleum gas glistened. A small red car was racing down the road towards it.

'Isn't that Mary?' No mistaking it was a red Austin Healey.

'Yes,' Jake agreed, his voice thick with guilt.

'What's she going there for?' He watched her pull at the Moses basket in the back seat and tried to think. What did it mean?

Suddenly Laurence's feet were covering the rough ground to Robert's site at twice their previous speed. Where else could the money have gone?

'You knew about this, didn't you?' The tightening round Jake's mouth confirmed it. Why was he always the last one to find out what was going on? Jake was trying to hold his arm, slow him down. Laurence shook him off angrily.

Mary knew exactly where to go, though Robert's office had been only half built when she'd gone home. She found her way onto a small car park and recognised Robert's limousine parked in the only patch of shade. His uniformed chauffeur was asleep behind the wheel, his cap pulled forward to cover his face.

She had kept the hood up so Lucy would not have too much draught, but the heat was suffocating as soon as the car stopped; already there were beads of sweat across the child's nose. Mary tugged on the handles of the Moses basket, it wouldn't come out.

Her need for assistance went unnoticed. Annoyed, she stalked over to Robert's car and thumped her handbag on the bonnet. The driver sleepily moved his cap and stared blankly at her. Then with one bounding movement he shot out of the car.

'Morning, madam.' His teeth flashed in a smile of recognition.

'Sorry to wake you, but I need help.' His smile widened, her sarcasm lost on him.

'Lovely baby,' he beamed, taking the Moses basket out with ease. 'Is it boy?'

'Girl.'

'Sorry, madam.'

'Hell!' As if the sex mattered! A normal child was what she'd wanted. 'Take us to Mr Oxley's office.' She followed imperiously. The building still smelled of cement and paint.

'This room for his secretary, madam.' He tapped on the door and pushed it open. Mary looked round the small room; it was bare except for a desk and some metal filing cabinets.

'Thank you.' The baby drummed her heels as Mary took the Moses basket from him. She flung open the communicating door and went in.

The slim dark girl she'd seen with Robert at the airport was taking shorthand dictation on one side of a large executive desk. Robert's elegant bulk occupied a comfortable swivel chair on the other. He had inherited the Oxley nose and strong chin, but on him the proportions were better. He was taller and broader, and had less crinkle in his hair. He was the most handsome of the Oxley men, she could feel the pull of attraction now. But his blue eyes so like her own were regarding her as if she were a common intruder. For a moment she thought he was going to tell her to wait outside.

'Mary,' he said. 'What a surprise!' He was not smiling, and made no move of welcome. The secretary snapped shut her notebook, preparing to go.

'But not a pleasant one, I take it.' That brought him to his feet. He took the Moses basket from her.

'Of course it's a pleasant surprise.' There was no warmth in his voice. 'I'm always pleased to see you and Lucinda. Have a seat, Mary. Would you like some coffee?'

'It's not a social call.' She perched on the edge of the chair.

'Giselle, would you mind taking that letter down to the bank now? It's rather urgent. And perhaps you'd cash a cheque for me?' Mary couldn't look at the girl. Dusky-skinned, exotic and more than a decade younger than she was. She was saying something to her in an attractive accent, but Mary pretended not to hear. Instead, she watched Robert writing in his chequebook, taking comfort because he was sending the girl away. 'Could you organise some coffee for us before you go?'

'Acoustics bad here?' Mary asked when they were alone.

'No point in letting the whole world know our business.' He looked in the Moses basket. 'How's Lucinda? She's a bit overweight, isn't she?'

'She doesn't smile.'

'Are they – quite sure?'

'She doesn't focus either,' Mary said sadly. 'She doesn't see things move.' She lifted the infant out to show him. She was whimpering softly.

'But she's only four months old. There's plenty of time.'

'Not for those things. She's seventeen weeks, and making no attempt to hold her head up. Classic signs, they tell me. She'll be like Dinah.' Lucinda felt hot and moist against her bare arms.

'A pity.'

'Is that all you can say? A pity!' Her anger spurted up and spilled over. 'It's a bloody tragedy to have it happen all over again. It was bad enough the first time.'

'Well, we didn't intend . . .'

Mary took a firm grip on herself. 'I haven't come to talk about Lucinda. There's nothing new. I've got to have the money back, Robert. Right now.'

There was a tap on the door and a steward brought in

two cups of coffee. As the door creaked open, Mary had a view of the secretary's empty chair. Not a muscle moved in Robert's face till the door closed behind him.

'I can't possibly pay you back, not now.' His eyes looked straight into hers. Hope exploded and died.

'But you promised!' A knife seemed to slice through her gut. 'Before the audit, you said. You knew I had to replace it.'

'I've spent it building this terminal. You knew I intended to.'

'You said you'd take a mortgage. Raise it from somewhere.' She was clutching the desk for support.

'I've changed my mind.'

'But you can't! Dad's suspicious, he's asking questions.' She hadn't really believed he'd let her down. Not Robert! 'I can't tell him, he'll be furious.'

'Mary, your father cheated mine out of his inheritance. He persuaded him to leave the money in the business for me. Then he threw me out without a penny. Laurence will understand perfectly why I've done it.'

'He'll never forgive me.'

'He'll get over it. He's treated others this way. He'll say I'm a chip off the Oxley block.'

'But I did this for you, Rob. Because I loved you . . . To help you. You said you loved me.'

'A long time ago.'

'Don't you care enough not to drop me in this mess?'

'Laurence doesn't play fair. I have to use his methods if I'm to even the score.'

'But what about me?'

'You're an Oxley too. You wanted to have your cake and eat it. Marry David Mountford, yet spend time with me, have my children. Love can't thrive like that, Mary, not for any of us.'

'You bastard.' She couldn't help her tears. They'd barely been under control all week. 'You've got yourself another woman. That was her, you sent her off to the bank, to get her out of the way. You don't want her to know about this.'

'Yes, Mary, you could put it like that. We Oxleys understand each other. You've used Jake Lode.'

'You dirty bastard. I'll get even with you, you'll see.'

'Mary, please—'

'You can't mean it. You can't do this to me.' Once, she'd thought she was strong enough to manipulate Robert as well as Jake and her father.

'I want it to end,' he said.

She was brimming with hate. She wanted to hurt Robert, hurt him more than he was hurting her. She wanted to pummel his handsome face with her bare fists until he was black and blue. She wanted to scratch him with her nails till he bled. She knew if she tried Robert would hold her at arm's length and tell her to calm down.

'You want to get rid of me!'

'I can't stomach any more.'

'It was your idea as much as mine,' Mary said.

'You thought nobody would get hurt except David, and you didn't care about him. It was a disaster for Dinah and now Lucinda. It's changed me, and as for you, just look at what you've become. You've got to cool it, Mary.'

'Don't be so bloody condescending.' She felt hate for him welling up again.

'This isn't the time or place.' He looked pointedly at his watch. 'You should have telephoned first.'

'It's urgent. I have to have the money now, otherwise—'

'I know your father's in Lagos. I know you're due for audit. Explain it to him. I'm not giving the money back.'

'Rob! I have to have it. You could raise it.'

'I've recouped my loss. Taken back what your father took from me, that's all. It's what I meant to do.'

'You used me.' A tide of fury washed over her. 'You used me to get your own back on Dad!'

'For heaven's sake stop shouting,' he hissed. 'The whole office will hear. Perhaps I did use you, Mary. We Oxleys are good at that. You both used me in the past.'

'No, I loved you. I thought you loved me. I wanted us both to be happy.'

'But we're not. It didn't work out.'

The money she'd loaned him was meant to tie him closer. She hadn't known about Giselle then. She felt the tears coursing down her cheeks. 'Look at the mess you've got me into, quite apart from the money.' She knew she was screaming. 'Now you say you don't care.'

His face came closer. Distorted by her tears he seemed a stranger. 'You've never cared who got hurt. Well, now it's your turn.'

Even now she couldn't believe he'd do it to her. She felt rejected, beaten, her pride in shreds. The thought of her father's temper forced her to plead.

'Please, arrange for me to have the money, I must put it back.' She couldn't bear the revulsion in Robert's blue eyes, it was the end of everything.

CHAPTER TWENTY-SEVEN

Laurence's fury came to a slow rolling boil, driving him forward at a jog across the rough ground. Soon there was a band of iron round his chest and rasping breaths tore at his throat.

'Slow down. What's the hurry?' Jake kept catching at his arm. 'You'll kill yourself in this heat.'

What a stupid fool he'd been not to realise Robert had his money! His fists itched to lash out at him, he couldn't slow down. Waves of fury kept erupting through him.

The size of Robert's terminal came as a shock. House flags, great double gates, even a rail link, and he'd called it Apapa Oil Terminals, to make it sound more important than Oxley's.

The sun glinted on the windows of the new office. The hard wood door was smart. Laurence almost ran inside. A native clerk leapt out of his way as he crashed successive doors back on their hinges.

When he found them, Mary's horrified, harrowed face twisted to his. She screamed.

'Bloody hell, Mary!' He'd meant to roar, but there was no breath in his body. He was gasping, unable to get the words out. He had to lean against the desk. 'Robert, of all people!'

'You might knock before you burst in.' Robert scrambled to his feet indignantly. 'This is my office.'

'Not yours. Mine. All mine. My money paid for it.' He was choking with rage as he swung back to Mary. 'How could you do this? Robert, always Robert! Haven't you any sense?'

Mary looked like a cornered animal, tears were streaming

down her face. The Moses basket was balanced on a chair. It shook as the baby started to protest.

'You let him get in first, Mary! With our money!' He felt the blood racing up his cheeks again, throbbing in the veins, across his temples. He brought his fist crashing down on Robert's desk. Pens and files leapt in the air. Lucinda began to cry in earnest.

'Robert!' His fist hammered again and again. 'I should have known. The nerve, setting up here in competition! I'll break you.'

'Not possible now.' Robert's face had all the Oxley confidence. 'I've had a year's start on you.'

Laurence felt his last vestige of self-control snap. He charged, belting his fists into Robert's smug face.

'You womaniser. You tricked Mary. I'll get the money back.' He'd beaten Robert into submission in the past, he'd do it again.

'Hell!' Robert swore, letting his chair roll back on its castors, his hands clutched his chin. 'Hell.'

Jake was pushing Laurence to a chair. 'Let's talk about this calmly.'

'What made you bring the child?' Laurence turned on Mary. 'Can't you keep her quiet? She's getting on my nerves.'

Mary bent over the basket trying to soothe her baby.

'You owed me the money,' Robert growled. 'I asked for it and you refused. It was the only way I could get it. I took what's mine by right.'

'I'm sorry. I'm sorry, Dad,' Mary was sobbing. The baby was writhing with temper. The Moses basket looked as though it would slide to the floor. Jake pushed it to a more secure position. Put a hand on the child.

'Mary,' Laurence shouted, 'you've got a Princess Christian trained nanny! Why don't you use her? Who else do you expect to nursemaid that baby?'

With a furious heave, Mary dragg·d the Moses basket onto her lap and jogged it up and down. It didn't help.

Laurence was on his feet again, pointing at Robert. 'He accepted money he knew to be stolen. He put her up to it. Like he put her up to everything else.'

Jake pushed himself between them.

Laurence couldn't stop. 'It's shareholders' money, not mine. You understood that, Mary, you're an accountant.'

'Robert promised to pay it back,' she choked.

'How naive can you get? I'll get the Fraud Squad out.' He was reaching for the phone. 'Let them sort it out.'

'No.' Jake put his hand on it first. 'Let's calm down. Think this through before we do anything.'

'There's no alternative unless somebody pays the money back into the business,' Laurence blustered. He paced to the window.

'You can afford it,' Robert sneered.

Mary jumped to her feet, accidently sending the cup of coffee streaming across the desk. She jerked the door open and was gone.

They went out after her, in time to see her car scorch away, her tyres spraying sand three feet in the air.

'Wait for us, Mary,' Jake was shouting. She turned out of the car park without slowing and roared off up the road.

'Are you up to walking back?' Jake was asking Laurence when he heard another screech of tyres followed by the clash of tearing metal. In the shocked silence that followed, the strength seemed to ebb from his knees. He saw Robert's mouth open with horror before he went sprinting across the car park. Then Jake was gone too. Laurence followed as best he could.

His stomach turned over. Mary's car was almost under a petrol tanker that had been turning into the site. Already there were several panic-stricken Nigerians round it. Above the noise, he could hear Mary whimpering. There was no way they could reach the driving seat.

'I stop. Not my fault. She ram me. I stop, then she ram me.' The black tanker driver was in a frenzy.

Laurence felt sick. The road was newly constructed, it was wide enough for two tankers to pass. Mary hadn't had time to increase her speed, she'd only driven a few yards, but she hadn't straightened up after swinging out, she was on the wrong side of the road. The body of the Austin Healey was low. Most of it had gone under the tanker's front bumper. Only the boot was to be seen.

'Mary?' The moaning had stopped.

'Ambulance,' Robert gasped. 'Phone.'

Laurence couldn't move. 'No!' He wanted to deny it had happened. Put the clock back a few minutes. His mouth was dry, he felt he would drop.

'Crushed to death,' Jake breathed. It was only then they thought to look for the baby. She'd been thrown out of the car. A Nigerian boy in a dirty fez was tenderly holding what appeared to be a broken doll, wiping blood from her face. She was dead too.

Laurence straightened up, appalled. He could feel everything spinning.

Jake felt as though he were on a roller coaster, everything was coming at him at once. He was numb, drained of energy.

Time had stopped when he'd gone back to Robert's office to telephone for an ambulance. He'd still had enough of his wits about him then to speak to a European policeman, an acquaintance from the club who sometimes partnered him at squash.

The awful waiting seemed unending. Laurence had passed out. Jake had dreaded that he'd had a heart attack, but it was a simple faint.

After Mary and Lucinda had been taken to the police mortuary, Jake had taken Laurence home and sent for their doctor. Sally had come running out as soon as Sylvester pulled up at the house. She'd gone ashen when he'd told her about the accident. It had come as another shock to hear her stammering that Mary had booked seats for them to fly to London on tonight's plane.

They had to help Laurence upstairs to his room. Jake ran a cool bath for him, and turned on the air-conditioner. Then he looked through Mary's things and found the air tickets in her dressing-table drawer.

'You'd better use yours, Sally,' he told her. 'No reason to stay now.'

He would have liked to suggest to Laurence that he went

too. But he wasn't well, and a long flight on top of everything else might be too much for him. There wasn't time to think about it.

There were a thousand things he had to do, and he had no idea how to set about any of them. He was slumped on the patio overcome with lethargy when his friend telephoned to say the bodies had been examined by the police surgeon and would be released for immediate burial.

That made him fight off his torpor, go out to the Humber, be driven to the office. It had all happened too quickly to be believable. He felt he was dreaming and would shortly wake up and find it hadn't happened at all.

He went to Doug Hanley's office to tell him. Although he was young, he was a very able second-in-command. It came as a relief when he said: 'Leave it to me.' Jake remembered that one of their junior expatriates had electrocuted himself at the Yacht Club while using a faulty sanding machine on his boat. He'd been on leave with Mary at the time. Hanley had had to arrange his burial.

Jake stared out of his office window, trying to pull himself together. He felt strangely apart from what was going on, his perception of everything blunted.

Eventually, Doug Hanley came to tell him the burial would take place at half past six tonight. In this climate there could be no delay. There would be a memorial church service at three o'clock tomorrow.

He was going out to his car when he remembered about the nanny. He went back to Hanley, asked him to send a car to the house to take Sally to the funeral, and then straight on to catch her plane.

Then he collapsed in the back of the Humber to be taken home again. It was only when he saw Laura and Elin getting out of their car on his drive that he remembered they'd been invited to lunch. He told them what had happened.

'Would you rather we went?' Laura asked, her green eyes dark with horror. But just to see her helped throw off some of his inertia. He shook his head, leading the way to the patio at the back. Abel brought drinks. The cold beer revived him a little.

'How's Laurence taking it?' Elin asked.

'Knocked him for six. He's resting on his bed.' It was only then that he realised, with a spasm of guilt, that nobody had been near him for over two hours.

'I'd like to see him,' Elin said quietly.

She followed Jake upstairs. His dark eyes were dull, his step slow; he'd taken it hard. The house had a subdued air, the landing stretched ahead more like that of a hotel.

Jake opened a bedroom door, and she went in.

Laurence was lying on top of a double divan, his feet bare, but dressed in slacks and an open-necked shirt.

'Hello, Elin, good of you to come.' He was struggling to sit up. The room was small, luxuriously furnished, but lacking any personal touches. The door to the adjoining bathroom stood open.

She was shocked at how much he'd changed since yesterday. His face was grief-stricken, the picture of desolation. She pulled up a chair to his bed.

'Anything I can get you, Laurence?' Jake asked awkwardly from the door.

Laurence shook his head and Jake retreated, closing the door behind him.

Elin slid the drink she'd brought up with her onto the bedside table, and felt for his hand.

'Mary's gone.' He spoke in an agonised whisper. She hadn't expected to feel such throat-stopping sympathy.

'Yes, I know,' she said gently. He tossed about, creaking the mattress, in awful agitation. 'You need to relax, Laurence.'

'I'm upset. I can't get over what Mary did.'

'You must forgive her,' she tried to soothe.

'I pushed her, Elin. Pressurised her.' His eyes were full of horror. 'She'd never have come here if I hadn't bullied her.' A tear rolled down his face. 'It's my fault.'

'No.' Elin slid an arm round his shoulders and pulled him closer in the way she comforted Laura when she was upset. 'Mary was a grown woman, she went her own way.' He buried his face in her shoulder and wept. She found his tears harrowing, more so because he'd always seemed so strong.

She couldn't share his grief. Her sharpest memories of Mary were as a four-year-old screaming for cake at breakfast, yet able to read almost as well as she herself could.

Laurence pulled himself away at last. His eyes were anguished. 'You're right, Elin. Mary was always difficult. What she did was unforgivable. It took me years to build up this business. She didn't care. She's thrown it away. My own flesh and blood.'

Elin shook her head, feeling at a loss. She wasn't sure now whether his grief was for Mary or the loss of his money.

'I still can't believe it. Giving Robert such an advantage. He could have built his terminal anywhere, but she let him do it right next to ours. I'll have to sell shares on the open market. I dread to think what will happen.'

'You'll survive. Your company will survive. You must put all this out of your mind.'

'It hurts. I feel raw.'

For the first time Elin realised money wasn't everything. Too many years of poverty had conditioned her to thinking it was.

'You're damn lucky to have a daughter like Laura, a girl to be proud of.'

'It isn't a question of luck,' she said firmly. Laurence didn't realise he had to give love before he could get it. His eyes looked into hers, but she didn't see any dawning of understanding.

'None of them left. I've got nobody now.'

'Laura is your daughter too. And you've got me.'

Laurence leaned over and kissed her cheek. Elin felt the bonds between them tightening again.

Jake came to tell them lunch was ready. Laurence said he didn't want any, and wouldn't come down. Jake persuaded him to try some soup, and went to the kitchen to arrange for it to be sent up on a tray.

Elin was directed out to the patio where a table had been set up in the shade. A steward, in immaculate starched suit and bare feet, had spread a white cloth and was setting out silver and crystal. Laura watched, her green eyes pensive.

Jake returned to hover. He looked stunned, as though he'd had the stuffing knocked out of him.

'It was to be something of a party . . .' He opened a bottle of chablis, condensation glistened on its cold surface.

The steward reappeared with a large silver platter of shellfish, langoustines, prawns and crayfish. There were hot crusty rolls and three sorts of mayonnaise, plain, mustard and garlic. Elin thought it a feast, but Jake slumped against the table in distress.

They ate in silent misery till Elin's efforts to remove the shell from a prawn brought a fleeting smile to Jake's face. He showed her how to do it.

The sun blazed hot gold. Everything shimmered in the heat. They peeled off shell after shell. Jake pushed his dark hair back from his forehead and forgot his duties as host. Laura refilled their glasses. Abel brought strawberries and cream for pudding. Then coffee.

Time was standing still. The thought of the funeral was paralysing them all, conversation died.

'I'll go up to Laurence again,' Elin said, needing something to do. 'See how he is.'

Jake was trying to rouse himself. 'Would you sit with him this afternoon?'

She paused. Sitting with him this afternoon was what she'd intended.

'I mean,' Jake looked ill at ease, 'he shouldn't be alone, at a time like this. Would you keep an eye on him?'

'Of course.'

'I'm sorry, I can't just sit here waiting for half past six. I'll have to do something. Take my mind off . . .'

'We all ought to do something,' Elin said.

'I'd like to take Laura out in the boat for an hour.'

Elin nodded. 'The best thing for you.' Her eyes went to Laura. 'Best thing for both of you.'

Laurence was out of bed when she went back to his room, pacing from window to bed and back again. This was how she remembered him, more his normal self. He started to describe the blazing row he'd had with Mary, and was getting agitated again. Elin went up to him and put a finger across his lips.

'Don't. Forget what Mary did. This does you no good.'

The next moment his arms locked round her and his face buried against her shoulder. She knew from his uneven breathing that he was weeping again.

She tried to swallow her anguish, finding it traumatic to see Laurence cry. She meant to comfort when she put her arm round his waist and drew him back to the bed.

She felt the current run through him, the effect of her touch. He kissed her, his face damp with forgotten tears. Butterflies were struggling against the prawns in her stomach as she recognised what was happening. He wanted to make love. Her body was responding to his in a way she'd forgotten.

Suddenly he was standing over her, taking off his shirt. Elin was surprised by her own response. A stirring of excitement ran to meet and blend with his.

His body had aged more than hers, the once firm flesh now sagged. The muscular shoulders she remembered had gone. The blond hair on his chest had turned grey. He dropped his grey palm beach trousers. His manner of doing it took her back nearly thirty years. He was standing beside her bed at Birchgrove again.

She enjoyed his lovemaking as she never had before. No, that was not true. All those years ago Laurence had awakened something. But she'd been so utterly terrified of getting pregnant, she could think of nothing else. After all, she'd only been a child. Sixteen, and a very innocent sixteen at that.

Laurence collapsed beside her, his eyes closed, gulping for breath. 'There's never been anyone to match you, Elin.' He was silent for so long, she thought he was dozing. Then he said: 'I want you to stay with me. I love you.'

Elin tensed in his arms, unable to move.

'Say you will. We'll be married, that's what you want, isn't it?'

She lay back letting his words soak into her soul.

'Elin? Marry me. There's no reason why not now. I need

you. I love you.' She felt his finger trace the outline of her chin.

She roused herself. Once she'd longed to hear those words. He'd never told her he loved her till now.

'I was a fool to lose sight of you. I didn't realise I'd found love. You want to be married, don't you, Elin?'

She wasn't sure. She wasn't sure of anything any more. 'I need to think.'

'Of course. Take all the time you want.' He lay back and closed his eyes again.

Elin stared up at the ceiling. Once she'd have jumped at it. She'd have been grateful for anything Laurence offered. The best she'd ever hoped for was his company. A small house like the one in Jubilee Street. Enough money to buy food and coal. Not a fortune. She'd have valued his love beyond everything else, but he hadn't said the word until today. That's what she'd wanted all those years ago. His love.

And now? She had to ask herself if she wanted it now. He really needed her. She could give him pleasure and comfort, support him now as she could not have done thirty years ago. Now, she would fit more easily into his life.

But that was for Laurence. She wanted to help him, but she had to think about her own needs.

Didn't she want love in her life? After all those empty years, she knew she did. She needed Laurence as much as he needed her. She would draw comfort from his arms, pleasure and companionship, too. Yet something held her back.

She realised, now, she was not afraid of Laurence but of marriage itself. It had tied her too completely to Percy. For the first time in her life she had a choice. She needn't be pushed in any direction she didn't want to go. It made a difference.

He opened his eyes. 'Will you, Elin?'

'Perhaps. Perhaps not.' She didn't think he'd desert her again, but she couldn't trust him either. Not completely. Not yet. 'It's a big step. We've got all the time in the world.'

She could see it wasn't what he expected, and added: 'I'm not sure it's what I need.'

'But you love me?'

She waited a little too long to answer. 'Ye-es. There's no one else.'

'But we'll see each other when we get home? You'll let me take you out?'

'Yes.' She could agree to that. 'I need to start living a bit. Enjoying myself, in my way.' Marriage to Percy had locked her away from pleasure. Turned her in on herself. 'I've been wondering whether I should try my hand at designing and making clothes. I've always enjoyed that.'

'There's no need for you . . . I want to look after you, Elin.'

'This is for me,' she said.

Laura sat beside Jake as the boat shot out into the harbour, the speed making it bump on the calm water. To look across the open water shading from pale turquoise to dark green was soothing. The sun added sparkle, its golden brightness lifting her spirits.

Jake was brooding silently, the breeze fluttering at his dark hair. She knew that for him Mary's death was terrible. She felt for his hand, wanting to share his grief. Death demanded it. Mary was her half-sister.

'Are we playing truant? I feel we shouldn't be here,' he said.

'Mam can comfort him better than we can.'

It was guilt she felt, because she had no grief for Mary. She'd never liked her. Guilt because Mary's going made things easier for her. No need for an acrimonious divorce. Less to upset Laurence now.

They anchored again where they had yesterday, away from the shipping lanes. Made love again, too.

Afterwards they clung together, each wanting to feel the other close. She could feel his breath on her cheek, his arms about her, and that was how she wanted it.

Jake whispered: 'Mary's death changes everything for us, Laurie. You realise we can get married immediately?'

She smiled. 'Soon as you like.'

'Laurence might find it upsetting.'

'I won't be able to hide my happiness. So inappropriate just now.'

'Don't try. We're all entitled to happiness, as much as we can get. We'll talk to Laurence. Can't make plans till we do.'

They stayed rather longer than they intended. Laura wasn't sorry. It helped to be in a rush. They went back to the flat to pick up suitable clothes for herself and Elin. Then to Jake's house in time to bath and change for the funeral. It meant less time for Jake to brood.

By six thirty, the sun had set and dusk was gathering fast. Faje cemetery was made darker by the surrounding breadfruit trees. The fruit bats they harboured swooped above their heads as the coffin was lowered into the red laterite soil, huge flocks of black bats wheeling against the fading light, darkening the sky further. Laura watched the mourners lifting their faces to the sky, distracted. Except Laurence, whose face was locked in anguish.

The Oxley personnel had turned out in force, the men wearing grey palm beach suits and black ties, the women dressed in sober colours. Representatives from other businesses, too, had come to pay Mary their last respects.

Laura glanced surreptitiously at the surrounding graves. The bodies of the early traders and consuls lay here, many dying within weeks of arrival, few surviving more than a year. In the past, they had lacked the medical knowledge and modern drugs needed to survive.

Death traditionally came fast here. Poor Mary, what a place to spend eternity, miles from her homeland. The drab, rainswept streets of Birkenhead seemed suddenly like the promised land.

'I'm glad we're not staying much longer,' Elin shivered, clutching Laura's arm on the way back to the car. 'This place really is the white man's grave.'

Jake fell in step on the other side and put a hand under Laura's elbow.

'Don't go yet,' he whispered. 'Got to have you near.' So

Laura kept the Austin Healey in the long line of cars returning to the house in Ikoyi.

With the sitting room fans whirring overhead, standing in the crowd spilling out through the french windows, it didn't seem so bad. Jake pushed a gin and tonic into her hand. The conversation rose and fell round her, none of it about Mary. Stewards brought round trays of drinks and cocktail savouries.

'Just like any other drinks party,' Jake said, relief spilling out of his dark eyes. 'God, what a day!'

Only Laurence looked desolate, slumped in a chair in the corner. Elin was perched on the arm, trying to cheer him.

By eight o'clock people were going home for dinner. Jake wanted her to stay, but looked drained. Laura felt she couldn't face a full meal. She had to get away from Laurence's misery.

It came as a relief to feel the car respond to her touch. To speed away into the night.

'Such good news, Mam. Jake and I, well, I've something to tell you.' She laughed aloud.

'I think I know,' Elin laughed with her. 'You can't hide it. All evening you've had eyes like green stars.'

'I've been trying.' Laura felt euphoric. 'I never expected to feel like this about anyone.' Her laugh came again.

'You've had to wait a long time,' Elin told her.

CHAPTER TWENTY-EIGHT

There was just enough room for three armchairs on the flat's little balcony. Laura lay back in hers, looking at the glow of light thrown up in the sky by the club. A week had passed since Mary's funeral. Ignatius in a drill suit, bright white against his black skin, brought after-dinner coffee. Laura felt a yearning for the greater comfort of her own home.

Distantly on the breeze came the thump of tomtoms from the forest, and from an adjacent flat came the strains of 'Rock Around the Clock'.

'There's a film tonight at the club,' Tom said. 'Why don't we all walk down?'

'What is it?' Elin asked. 'Have we seen it?'

Tom shook his red head. 'You can have a drink if you don't fancy it.'

'We'll go.' Laura roused herself. 'Jake said he would bring Laurence.'

When Elin went to her bedroom to get ready, Laura asked: 'Have we overstayed our welcome, Tom?'

'No,' he said, but she sensed a holding back in his manner. 'Of course not.'

'You'll be glad to have the flat to yourself. You've wanted to bring Iolo here, but it's been difficult, mam and me watching every move you make.'

Tom gave her a friendly dig in the ribs. 'You always know, Laurie, how I feel. You've been marvellous.'

'So you've settled? Enjoying the job?'

'I'm still feeling my way, but yes.'

'It'll take time. You've had two years away from the sea.'

'I'm all right now.'

'That's what I want to hear. I'm looking forward to going home. Getting back to work.'

'You've done all you set out to do here.'

Laura sighed. She'd wanted to get closer to Laurence, be able to think of him as a father, but perhaps that would come later.

'You've sorted Elin out too.'

'I don't know. Lagos has done her good.'

'She's a different person,' Tom assured her. 'She'll be all right too. I'm going out on the midnight tide tonight. You'll be gone when I get back.'

'Shall I run you to the ship?'

'No, Iolo will do it.'

'It's goodbye then. I'll leave the car in the garage.'

'Don't know how to thank you, Laurie. Keep in touch?'

'Yes. When you get leave, you must spend it with us. Iolo too, if you want.'

His hand gripped her shoulder. 'You're the best. Always have been. Thanks.'

They walked down the road three abreast, linking arms, Tom in the middle, Elin with a torch to light the way. He found them a table, fetched drinks for them, and then went back to the bar.

'I don't know what he sees in Iolo.' Elin twisted to see what he was doing.

'I don't suppose we ever will.' Laura saw Iolo's welcoming smile as Tom climbed on the bar stool beside him. His carefully casual hair styling was meant to attract Tom, as were the gold chains round his tanned throat. 'But he sees something.'

Laurence felt in limbo, shut away in an artificial place, bright with alien sunshine but threatening unknown terrors.

'I can't leave you here to mope.' Jake's eyes were sympathetic as they surveyed him from across the sitting room.

'Apapa Club? Can't be bothered. I'll have an early night.'

'You're spending too much time alone. You'll get the creeps in this house.'

Laurence shuddered. He was right about the house. It increased his feeling of not belonging. There was nothing of his here.

'Come and have a drink. Talk to Elin.'

Laurence withdrew further into himself. He'd been so certain of Elin. Certain he was giving her what she wanted.

'I'll be all right once I get home.' He belonged in the Liverpool office. Except that he'd be taking problems with him this time.

'Wednesday,' Jake said. 'We're all going together.'

'Yes, of course.' There was the directors' meeting to think of too, on Friday.

'You've got to shake it off,' Jake said. 'Stop blaming yourself. Come on, I'm taking you to the club.'

He ought to feel grateful Jake cared. Mary had given him some nasty kicks too.

Sylvester drove them. Laurence felt better sitting in the back of the car, glimpsing the teeming life of the Lagos streets. Though why Jake bothered with the Apapa Club, when the Ikoyi Club was so much nearer and smarter, he didn't understand. He'd argued about it several times. He'd meet the right people in Ikoyi. Better for business.

As they walked across the car park, he asked: 'You're sure Elin will be here?'

He saw her sitting with Laura as soon as the door opened. The light glinted on her gold hair, she hardly seemed touched by the years.

Laura stood up, greeting him with unusual warmth, her fair hair drawn back in a French pleat. The copper colour of her dress suited her. Her green eyes were laughing up at Jake with an intimacy that surprised him.

He looked round for a barman, but Jake was already going in search of one. He turned to Elin, feeling suddenly old.

'Can't stand too much of Lagos at my time of life. I'll be glad to get home.'

'Not much longer now. We're all going on Wednesday night.'

He was aware that the barman had brought four glasses

and was making a hash of opening a bottle of champagne.

'What's this?' he asked, wanting whisky.

'We've got something to tell you,' Jake said quietly, waving the barman away and proceeding to take the wire off the cork.

Laura's green eyes were starry as they met his. Laurence went cold, guessing what was to come. They were acting with indecent haste, Mary was hardly in her grave. He looked at Elin, her face seemed touched with gold.

'They're young. This is how love should come.'

Champagne bubbled and raced up the glasses. One remained on the table for him. Jake sat down. Laurence watched him reaching out for Laura's hand.

They were all waiting for him. Expecting his congratulations, but this was just one more in the series of knocks the last few weeks had brought. One problem after another. He'd thought Mary's accident the worst and last disaster. He hadn't conceived there could be more.

'I hope you're not planning to walk out on me, as David Mountford did.' They were blinking as though he'd thrown a bucket of cold water on them.

'No,' Jake said uncertainly. 'I feel I ought to see the oil terminal finished. If that's what you want.'

'Thank you very much. Eight or nine months at the most you said for that!' He looked at the shocked faces round him. 'I've been very generous to you, Jake. I've made you a director. I was grooming you to take over.'

Jake sighed. 'Wouldn't you prefer someone else?'

'Why?'

'You offered all those things because I was Mary's husband. I thought she'd be working here with me. I had to accept.'

'Had to!'

'How could I refuse? You urgently needed somebody to take David Mountford's place.'

'You don't want the job?'

'I don't want to stay in Lagos. Not for ever. Not three thousand miles away from Laura.'

'You're doing a good job. I need you here as manager.

Damn it, I can't go on for ever.' He was barking in his old bellicose manner. 'You'll be running Oxley's in five years. Where will you get another opportunity like that? You can't turn your back on it.'

'I'm not prepared to stay more than nine months. And I'd need a few days in England each month.'

'I'll come here for a few days in between,' Laura said.

Laurence felt defeated. 'I'll have to start looking for a replacement. It won't be easy.'

'He doesn't have to be a relative.' Jake's hawk-like eyes wouldn't leave his face.

'It's getting the right man, the right experience.'

'Doug Hanley could cope.'

'He's only a lad.'

'He's nearly thirty. Seven years' experience in Lagos on the job. He's in charge when I'm away. He'd do a good job for you.'

'He's an administrator. Knows nothing about construction.'

'Won't need to if I see the terminal finished. We'll get an engineer to operate it. Anyway if I'm to take over your job, you'd have to get somebody else this end.'

'Damn it, Jake, I feel punchdrunk.'

'Feel pretty punchdrunk myself.'

Laurence couldn't stop his disdainful sniff. 'You're in a bed of roses. I've got a fight and a half on my hands. Probably drag on for years. You don't have to sue Robert.'

'You don't either.' Laura's serious face came close to his, he could see the sprinkling of freckles across her nose. 'You'd hate having the family scandals aired in public. It isn't worth it. Don't do it.'

He leant back in the chair and closed his eyes. If he didn't have to face that it would help, but it wouldn't get him out of the wood.

'I've still to sort out the accounts. Sell two million pounds worth of stock on the open market to put the money back. It'll make the share price slump.' He felt weak at the thought.

'I can help you,' Laura said gently. 'I've been thinking of buying in.'

'You?'

'Provided we can negotiate a price. It would be a private deal, needn't upset the market.'

'How much?'

'I'll have to think about it. Perhaps a quarter of what you want. Perhaps a bit more.'

He couldn't think straight. It would help, of course . . .

'And you could sell Mary's house,' Jake added.

That brought a rush of irritation. 'Don't point out the obvious.'

He felt Laura's arms go round him.

'Don't get tetchy, Dad. I can sort out the books for you. We'll raise the money discreetly, and get it back in the business. Keep it in the family, nobody else need know.'

He felt moved. He was struggling to hide the sudden tears. Couldn't believe she'd think of herself as family, want to give real help.

'It won't be all bad. I'm really looking forward to hearing what you think of Burdon's and Quick's.' She was smiling at him, her lips wide, her teeth perfectly symmetrical. An Oxley jaw if ever there was one. Like Mary.

No, not like Mary! He had to rid himself of this bitterness and grief. He had Laura now, a daughter to be proud of.

'You've done wonderfully well. Starting without capital, or help.'

She laughed. 'You helped. There's something I haven't told you.'

Elin was laughing too, and telling him some story about pictures Peck had taken from the Birchgrove attic. He hadn't known they existed, but it made him feel better.

He reached for his glass of champagne, raised it high. 'Laura and Jake. Be happy, both of you.'

He could see a hint of tears glistening behind the green eyes smiling into his. Behind the gold, too.